THE GARBAGE MAN

A KATE HOLLAND SUSPENSE: BOOK 1 IN THE HIDDEN VALOR MILITARY VETERANS SUSPENSE SERIES

CANDACE IRVING

BLIND EDGE

DEDICATION

To my husband David,
for everything.

ACKNOWLEDGMENTS

My eternal gratitude to CJ Chase for her late-night brainstorming, vigilant eye & razor pen.

My profound thanks to my editor, Sue Davison, for her outstanding editing.

I'd also like to thank Judi Shaw for her fantastic input, as well as my Beta readers/ARC team in the Goat Locker. I appreciate all the awesome support!

Finally, a huge thanks to Ivan Zanchetta for yet another gorgeous—and perfect—cover. And for all the amazing extras & support along the way.

You're all incredible!

"Here they lie, never to hope, never to pray, never to love, never to heal, never to laugh, never to cry."

— PRESIDENT RONALD REAGAN, MAY 5, 1985
BERGEN-BELSEN CONCENTRATION CAMP

1

SOFT. Cold. Wet.

Wrong.

Kate jerked away from the insistent jabbing at her neck and jackknifed to her feet, instinctively reaching for the 9mm strapped to her thigh twenty-four/seven as she clawed through the sleep still clogging her brain.

The SIG Sauer was missing.

Along with its holster.

Confusion seared in, her pounding pulse skyrocketing as she spun around to search the tan, battle-worn canvas of her Army cot. Bright blue sheets greeted her instead.

How—? Why—?

Where?

Kate shook her head, fighting the fog. The growing panic. A muted whine filtered through her scrambled thoughts. Reality joined in.

Ruger.

The German Shepherd was on the far side of the bed—her bed. Her house. Seven thousand miles from that sweltering hell.

Evidently not far enough.

She pulled the crisp, early-morning Arkansas air deep into her lungs. It didn't help. Her heart continued to slam against her ribs. Worse, the gray Braxton Police tee she'd donned the night before was plastered to her torso, saturated with that distinctive blend of salt and fear.

Night terror. She hadn't had one in weeks. Before that, almost a year.

So much for progress.

Kate sank onto the clammy sheets, automatically reaching for the dive watch strapped to her wrist. Max's watch. It was like having a piece of him, still with her. Sometimes—if she was lucky—it was enough. She turned the oversized band around and around, drawing strength from the familiar friction as she attempted to drag the ghostly impressions into the cold light of day. It was no use; they'd evaporated. She had no idea which of her many demons had taken fresh delight in plaguing her nights. But for once, she knew why they'd appeared.

Grant. The man couldn't leave well enough alone, could he?

As much as she was loath to admit it, it was probably time to end things. She'd miss Grant's company, yes. The occasional, no-strings-attached sex they shared filled a void too. But no one—old friend and fellow combat vet or not—was worth the suffocating sludge that had been churned up from her gut.

Even now, less than five minutes into her spanking new, God-Bless-America day, it threatened to swamp her.

As if he sensed her thoughts, Ruger padded around the bed, his questioning whimper filling the room—her—as he tucked his muzzle into her lap. Kate released the watch and wrapped her arms around the dog, burying her face in Ruger's fur as she pulled him closer. There she remained, clinging to the German Shepherd's solid, familiar warmth until, finally, the band on her chest began to loosen...and the sludge began to ebb.

She stared into those soulful brown eyes as she straightened. "No, buddy; I'm not leaving you."

How could she?

Canine or not, Ruger was the only one who understood. He was there for her—*had* been there for her—for three years now. Strong. Steady. Best of all, silent. He didn't ask questions, much less demand answers. He simply loved. In a strange way, saving Ruger's life had given her own meaning. Purpose. There were days—weeks, even—when focusing on his needs was the only thing that got her through.

Ruger whined on cue.

She ruffled his ears. "I know—time to go outside."

His tail thumped against her old oak dresser as he backed away from the bed to give her room to stand.

"Just let me turn on the shower, okay?"

The thumping increased as Kate followed Ruger out of the room where she'd spent her high school years. She passed the sealed door to her father's room, still unable to use his bath, let alone commandeer the master bed. Perhaps if she'd come home sooner—if she'd had a chance to say goodbye—it would've been easier to fill his proverbial shoes, in and out of the police station. Or not.

Kate paused in the hall bathroom to turn on the shower, then headed for the kitchen to unlatch the dog door. She still couldn't sleep without securing it at night. Fortunately, Ruger didn't seem to mind. She waited for him to push through the flap, then headed for the shower, taking care to avoid that damning reflection in the bathroom mirror.

Twenty minutes later, she felt almost human. The fresh Braxton PD tee helped. Her hair was still damp, but the sweat had been scrubbed away. If only she'd succeeded in rinsing the lingering muck down the drain as well.

Unfortunately, she could still feel it, simmering low, ready to slosh up at a moment's notice.

Damn Grant Parish and his relentless slicing. Though he'd chosen a psychological scalpel, she'd have thought the surgeon in him would've operated with more patience and finesse.

Kate retrieved her coffee tin and scooped a generous serving of grounds into the filter of her machine. As breakfast began to perk, she scraped her shoulder-length hair into a ponytail, then headed out to the rustic porch her father had added to the house years earlier. Though Ruger wasn't prone to wandering, she wasn't taking chances. Not with deer season in full swing.

Ruger must've been of like mind, because he didn't disappoint. One short whistle and the dog bounded out from the mixed pine and hardwood forest that enveloped her split-log home, the slight hitch to his otherwise easy gait compliments of the bastard who'd somehow managed to mistake an abandoned Shepherd pup for a mature buck three years ago—then left him for dead.

If the screwed-up, military-turned-civilian cop in her hadn't been obsessed with seeking the source of that report on her private property, Ruger would've bled out behind the spare cabin her father had built.

Kate bent down to scratch the dog's ears as he reached her side. A split second later, Ruger tensed.

Visitors?

It took some moments for the distant crunch of gravel to register with her human ears. Several more passed before visual confirmation arrived in the form of a midnight-blue SUV flitting in and out of the trees that sheltered her drive. As the vehicle drew nearer, she caught the telling silhouette of a dark blond, closely cropped head.

Ruger's low growl echoed in her gut as the Bronco pulled up to the side of the house.

She didn't bother hushing the dog. Ruger had taken the same instant dislike to Grant that her sometime lover had taken to him. Then again, the Shepherd was wary of most human males save her boss and the retired animal doc who'd carefully fished a round from Ruger's weaponized namesake out of his pelvis.

Déjà vu struck as Grant climbed out of the SUV. He waved awkwardly before lowering his hand to push the sleeves of a white fisherman's sweater up his forearms. As Grant started up the stone walk, Kate had the distinct impression that once again she was being forced to mark time as a doctor attempted to salvage something that appeared all but unsalvageable.

Three years ago, it had been her budding relationship with Ruger. Today, it was her tenuous one with Grant.

Even more telling, this time around the urgency and prayers were missing...in her.

Grant took note of Ruger's presence—and fresh growl—and stopped several feet shy of the porch.

"Morning, Kate."

She returned his nod, letting her silence and stubbornness serve in lieu of reciprocating verbal manners.

Grant's sigh should've warmed the nip in the air, but it didn't. "I came to apologize. I never should've pushed it. Hell, I never should've pushed you. But I was worried. You don't talk about it. Not ever. It would be healthier if you did."

Healthier?

What in God's name was healthy about slaughtering nine men and not really remembering it? Eleven if she counted the two bastards she did remember taking out that fateful day. Uncle Sam might've touted her actions across the entire radical Muslim world, but she knew better.

And so should this man.

Kate studied the tattoo on Grant's right forearm. The four-inch inking was mostly black and white, a variation on the standard physician's caduceus. Except that in Grant's insignia, the winged staff with its twin, winding serpents had been replaced with a snake-seducing sword, the blade of which was buried in the still-dripping meat of a blood-red heart.

The former US Army criminal investigator in her who'd survived six tours in hell understood that bastardized tattoo.

The POW who'd survived a mere eleven hours in captivity and taken down an equal number of terrorists to avoid staying longer, really understood it.

So why didn't the bearer of that tattoo understand?

Worse, why did she even care?

She and Grant had been screwing each other for six months and they'd yet to spend an entire night together.

What did that say about this? Them?

"Forgive me?"

Kate stared at Grant's extended hand. Part of her wanted to take it. The rest knew better.

"Please?"

She shook her head. "I don't—"

"But I do. Trust me. It will get better. I'll get better. You've obviously showered, so you and Ruger have finished your morning run. Call Lou. Tell him you'll be in late. Let me take you to breakfast—explain. Please."

He wasn't going to make this easy, was he?

It was clear Grant needed to talk. But was he willing to listen? It wasn't as though they'd gone into this with their eyes closed, let alone clinging to hidden hopes. He might be the older brother to one of her many dead friends, but companionship and sex was all this was supposed to be. For a pair of ex-soldiers condemned to the backwoods of the Deep South by fate and their respective monsters, it should've been enough.

It had been for her. If Grant needed more, it was time to pull the pin on their quasi-relationship. Today.

Kate clipped a nod as Grant's hand finally fell down to his side. "Just let me feed Ruger." She should grab a jacket too. It was chilly this morning, even for early November in Arkansas.

Grant's smile was characteristically crooked, and more than a little relieved.

Kate forced herself to ignore the latter.

"Great. I'll wait out here while you grab your keys and lock up."

Given Ruger's still unwelcoming stance, that was probably for the best.

Kate turned to let the dog through the door. Fortunately, Ruger obeyed. There were times—moods—when he wouldn't. Truth be told, Ruger was a bit like her.

Guilt settled low in her belly as she poured an oversized scoop of kibbles into Ruger's dish and refreshed his water. If the thought of the coming conversation had her passing on the fresh coffee now scenting the kitchen, how was she going to manage eggs? Truth was, she never should've accepted that first invite to dinner. But Grant had just returned to town and they'd started reminiscing about his brother.

God, she still missed Dan.

And so many others. Too many others.

Max, most of all.

Kate pushed the ache aside as she slotted her Glock 9mm into her shoulder holster before grabbing her Braxton PD jacket and badge. As she reached for her phone, it rang.

"Good morning, Lou. I was about to call."

"Mornin' yourself, Kato. But it ain't good."

Damn. She knew that tone. "What happened? Some hunter manage to shoot himself in the foot again?" If so, they were a couple days ahead of last year's schedule.

And a massive stack of paperwork behind given the beer-fueled witness interviews that were bound to follow.

"Wish it was that simple. We got a body. Could be gunshot. Could be somethin' else. Either way, I'm willing to bet my pension it weren't accidental."

Foreboding locked in, along with the realization that she wouldn't be dining with Grant or anyone else that morning. "Why's that?"

"'Cause I'm standin' over the corpse. Or what's left of it. Cain't say for sure. What we got's in at least fifteen pieces."

Shit. She'd prefer a gut-wrenching, tear-stained breakup every morning of the week over this. "Where are you?"

"Off Taylor Hill Road. Halfway up Old Man Miller's drive. You cain't miss us."

"I'm leaving now."

Kate stowed her phone in her back pocket and headed for her desk in the den to retrieve an extra micro data card for her smartphone in case she needed it. She gave Ruger's ears a goodbye tweak and left the dog door unlatched on her way to the garage. Deer season or not, there was no telling when she'd be back to let Ruger out.

Kate climbed into her black Durango, donning the blue Braxton PD ball cap she'd left on the dash as the automatic door opener kicked in. Grant was standing in the drive by the time she eased the SUV out onto the pea gravel.

Kate lowered the passenger window as the garage door settled into place.

Grant took one look at her face and frowned. "Breakfast is off, isn't it?"

"Sorry. Lou called first. Got a case."

"Dinner?"

She shrugged. "If this is as bad as I think, I'll be grabbing that on the run too."

"I can stop by to check on Ruger."

Kate shook her head. "He'll be fine. I'll call you as soon as I can."

Grant looked as convinced of that as she felt, but he nodded and she was off.

It took Kate a frustrating twenty minutes to weave her way through the maze of wooded and winding back roads—some paved and some not—before she reached the entrance to Miller's drive. The rotting two-bedroom shack at the far end of the narrow gravel lane had been abandoned since Jakob Miller died of a heart attack in the checkout line of the town's sole hardware store the day Kate graduated high school.

Despite her father's wishes, she'd blown off the old man's funeral. At the time, she'd been too intent on signing the papers that would secure her enlistment in the Army—and her subsequent escape from this dead end of a tobacco-spitting town.

Her dad had been livid. But then, so had she. Not only had he, once again, tried to dissuade her from following in his footsteps by becoming an Army detective, he'd actually admitted to her face that he just didn't think she could hack it.

The fight that followed had been ugly. Her departure the following month, even uglier.

Kate shoved the memories into the recesses of her heart as she spotted the trio of police cruisers where Lou had promised. She tucked her Durango behind his sheriff's sedan. Her boss' silver hair and terse frown met her as she climbed out.

"You made it in record time. Thanks, Kato."

Yeah, well, she might've violated a posted speed limit or two along the way, but who was counting? "What've we got?"

"Fifteen jumbo—as in yard-waste sized—brown paper bags, the tops all folded over and stapled. The first two were torn open by Scooter Ball. He and his son were headed to their deer stand when they spotted the sacks. Scooter decided to poke his nose in

—and lost his breakfast for the effort. He was still heavin' on and off when he roused me outta bed. He and his son are at the station, scratchin' out a formal statement." Lou dipped shaking fingers into his ever-present tin of chewing tobacco as he finished. The size of the wad her boss shoved in his mouth attested to just how rattled he was.

Kate studied the overgrown thatch of trees crowding both sides of the gravel lane to give him time to collect himself. If the killer was still out there watching for his own warped gratification, he'd be long gone by the time she retrieved Ruger and his super sniffer. "You mentioned pieces on the phone—as in, an arm in one bag, a foot in another?"

Lou spat a stream of blackened spittle into the trees. "Based on the hand and forearm I saw, looks that way. Both parts look to be from a man. No idea if they're from the same one. I just verified Scooter's account, then backed off to call you. But here's the really weird part: the pieces were sliced up and shrink-wrapped like they was on display in the goddamned refrigerated meat counter at the local market. Not sure what that means, but I do know enough to know the twisted son-of-a-fuck that done it falls into your bailiwick, not mine."

Given the mass graves she'd processed in Iraq, not to mention the single kills she'd picked her way through before and after, Lou was probably right. Burglary and drug-related crimes were a dime a dozen in Braxton's neck of the woods. Premeditated murder, not so much. There'd been a grand total of two in the previous decade. Since Lou had leaned on her dad to solve both, she had a feeling he'd be looking to saddle her with the lead on this.

"So, ready to take a look? I just got off the horn with the state police. Have a couple more calls to make, includin' one to the governor's office to give 'em a heads up, just in case. I'll join you when I'm done."

Kate shot her frazzled boss a sympathetic smile, then stepped around his stocky girth to head for the makeshift crime scene barrier created by her two fellow deputies and the cruisers they'd angled across the lane.

"Morning, Owen; Seth."

"Back at ya, Kato. Figured Lou would hand this to you." Kate might've been offended by the senior deputy's comment—were it not for the palpable relief in Seth's stark gray stare.

Owen's mirrored it.

Kate accepted the pair of latex gloves and paper crime scene booties Owen offered and donned them. "How long before Tonga shows?"

"Dunno. Doc shoulda been here by now. Lives less'n half the distance away as you."

True. But the aging medical examiner was a stickler for the speed limit. No doubt a result of the plethora of so-called joyriders that had ended up on his slab over the years.

Seth's hulking bubba build swung toward the sound of fresh tires joining this particular party. "There's Tonga now."

Kate checked the remaining photo storage capacity on her cellphone as the ME parked his meat wagon. She had plenty of room. By the time Tonga had reached her side, she was ready to begin her initial canvass of the scene. Unfortunately, Owen had been so unsettled, he'd forgotten to brief the ME—at least, properly.

Despite the circumstances that'd brought them there, Kate smiled a greeting, then tipped her chin toward the thermometer Tonga had pulled from his bag. "You can re-stow that, Doc."

His ebony brow furrowed. "Why?"

"You'd need a body to sink it in. All we've got is bags with parts."

It wasn't until Kate stepped between the cruisers that she realized how accurate the assessment had been.

The paper sacks were as Lou had described—fifteen in all, each yard-waste sized and plain brown—but there was little else. As murder scenes went, this one was beyond odd. Definitely staged to create a particular effect. Not only were the sacks laid out in an eerily straight line up the right side of the road, each appeared equidistant to the next, with roughly ten feet between. The sacks looked new too, with a succession of crisp elementary school "lunch bag" folds across the tops.

Hell, even the staples were evenly spaced and dressed down, like a row of eager third-graders at their desks, awaiting a cherished teacher first thing Monday morn.

Kate took the stack of tented evidence markers from Seth, then headed for the first bag. The ME waited as she placed a marker beside the already opened sack and snapped a photo.

"Ready?"

Kate nodded.

Tonga reached inside and retrieved a man's left hand, shrink-wrapped and hermetically sealed in clear plastic as Lou had stated. Kate carefully folded and flattened the sack, waiting for the ME to lay the appendage on top so she could take several close-ups. The flesh was eerily clean. But for a bit of seepage at the raw end, bloodless. There was no wedding ring, nor evidence suggesting one had been recently removed. But there were a number of reddened creases and thin cuts encircling the skin at the base of the severed hand.

The marks were distinctive. Definitive.

"The guy was bound before death—" Kate traced a gloved fingertip over the shrink wrap. "—with plastic flex cuffs."

"Are you certain?"

"Absolutely." She'd seen those marks during every terrorist roundup she'd participated in while in Afghanistan and Iraq. Here, now, those marks meant one thing—and it wasn't good. If their killer had drugged his victim to subdue and/or move him, the poor soul had come to long enough to realize whatever was about to happen and had fought for his very life...only to lose.

The weight of the coming investigation crushed in as Kate left the ME at the first sack to continue up the lane. She stopped at each subsequent bag, setting out markers and snapping exteriors of the sacks and surrounding gravel as she scanned for anything that appeared out of place. Not only did she come up empty, save for the faint boot impressions Lou and Scooter Ball had left around the first two bags, she couldn't find evidence anyone had even been there. It was as if the sacks had somehow materialized at the side of the road on their own.

Kate crouched low to study the area around the final bag. The gravel rocks were light gray from even weathering, with no discernible tire tracks, boot or shoe prints to be found. She couldn't even find depressions that suggested the wandering by of the massive eighteen point buck Scooter and his son claimed to have spotted in the area. It was as if nothing alive had made an appearance since Old Man Miller left to purchase that ball-peen hammer thirteen years ago.

Kate headed back to the ME. He was at the fifth sack, laying a shrink-wrapped upper arm out on the flattened paper.

"This bastard is evil and very, very sick." Tonga's tortured stare met Kate's as she crouched beside him, the man's warm South African accent at odds with the ice-cold fury carved into his leathery features.

"Worse—he's smart, Doc. Not only did the killer possess the forethought to cover his tracks, he's intelligent and capable enough to have drained the body of blood before severing the limbs somewhere far from here." Meaning whoever had done this could be at it again, carving up another body as she and Tonga spoke.

But where?

"He may have medical training." The doc tapped a latex-covered finger over the plastic at both ends of the sectioned limb. "See how he cuts cleanly and with confidence? He knows what lies beneath the flesh and how to separate the joints without nicking the bone."

"Or he could be a hunter experienced at dressing his kill."

Like the ME, Kate had noted the clean, steady lines. But, while they could've come from a scalpel, they could also be the result of a thin, razor-sharp boning blade. And there was the shrink wrap. The plastic was freezer-grade and lightly textured on one side, like the type used with one of those food vacuum-packing machines thrifty homemakers and hunters used.

Finally, there was the time of death and its potential significance.

Had some reformed Bambi-killer decided to make a state-ment against an unrepentant sinner by displaying the body here, all but on top of a deer stand at the height of hunting season?

It was worth considering.

The ME nodded. "I agree. He could be an experienced hunter."

She prayed so. The Bambi-lover theory might be the only thing standing between this crime scene and the discovery of a second, meticulously sectioned body. Unfortunately, given the particulars she and Tonga had noted, it was more likely they were on the verge of a timely repeat, no matter the motive, and they both knew it.

"Shall we proceed?"

"Sure thing." Kate offered an arm to the aging ME as he stood.

"Thank you, young lady."

Kate held her tongue as she returned the doc's smile. At thirty-one, she doubted she passed as a kid anymore, even to a man on the verge of retirement. But there was no point in reminding Tonga, not when he'd come to know her as the teenage daughter of a local deputy who did her algebra outside the autopsy suite while waiting on her dad's "work".

Just as well. The doc's indulgent humor disintegrated with each subsequent unbagging. By the time they'd pulled the upper torso out and laid it on its slightly flayed-open front to photograph the reverse, Kate's mood had sunk deeper and darker than the ME's.

Like her, their victim was a combat vet.

She might not have had a chance to roll their mystery man's prints, but between the half-dozen bullet and shrapnel scars, the excellent level of physical conditioning of the chest and limbs, not to mention the detailed 101st Airborne "Screaming Eagle" tattoo that covered the entire upper back, they were most likely dealing with the remains of a former Army soldier between the ages of twenty-five and thirty-five.

All they needed now was a face and name to go with it.

Tonga's sigh was heavy with dread. "I'll get the last one."

"No, you opened the previous three." He was the worse for wear for it, too. The endless string of drunk-driving, drug-related and natural-causes deaths hadn't prepared the ME for this. Pulling out coldly sectioned human limb after limb had taken its toll on the South African giant, each shrink-wrapped piece peeling off another layer of his surprisingly tender soul.

Kate knew the feeling. For her, the rude awakening had come at nineteen. She'd been a cherry military policeman on her first tour in Afghanistan. She could still close her eyes late at night and feel the scorching heat on her skin, smell the ripening muck that had once passed for human fluid and flesh invading her lungs as she canvassed the aftermath of her first IED explosion. A black plastic garbage bag in one hand, the damned-near unidentifiable remains of a squadmate in the other as she bent down, again and again, to pluck up the disjointed fragments of flesh and bone scattered about the road like the burnt and bloodied leavings of some twisted Mardi Gras parade.

The sludge that had been simmering in Kate's gut since before she'd woken that morning began to churn.

"Are you unwell?"

She dragged on a smile. "Not at all. Look—Seth's waving to us. Why don't you head over and see what he needs while I verify the contents of that last bag?"

Shame mixed with the gratitude in Tonga's eyes—but he took the escape as Kate headed for the final sack.

One missing head laid out on the road, and they were done with the worst of it. The eyes would be the hardest. They always were. God willing, they'd be closed.

Kate braced herself as she knelt to pop the final row of staples. But as she reached inside to carefully cradle the head that did indeed await her, a wave of nausea crashed in, damned near swamping her. Instinct merged with an unexpected riptide of terror and she jerked to her feet.

The nausea worsened.

Threatened.

For the first time in her career, she was a split second from heaving all over her evidence. Instinct kicked in again as Kate spun to the right and bolted into the trees lining the road. She was still sucking in huge gulps of blissfully cool air to combat the nausea that continued to threaten when she felt the palm on her back.

Patting. Soothing.

Lou.

She kept her eyes on a spindly pine, desperately trying to focus on the fragmented lines in its bark and *not* the perfect, scarlet slash at the base of that shrink-wrapped head.

"Kato? What the devil was in there?"

"*Nothing!*" Scratch that—and calm down, damn it. "It's a head, Lou. Just a head."

So why did merely picturing it—a simple, solitary head attached to a face she'd never even seen before today—make her want to vomit all over again?

And her lungs. Why wouldn't they cooperate?

Kate clamped down on the dive watch wrapped loosely about her wrist and began to twist, forcing herself to draw her breath into her lungs, then push it out with each steady sweep. The exercise in tactical breathing helped. But it was the constant, scraping friction that gradually hauled her out of the past, slowly but surely anchoring her in the present.

Lou's hand pressed into her shoulder as she straightened, then disappeared as she edged away.

"You want me to call the doc?"

The irony of the ME having to hurry over to soothe her nerves almost caused Kate to smile. Almost.

She found the strength to face Lou. "I'm fine. Must've been the pancakes I had for breakfast."

It was a lie, and this man had known her long enough and well enough to call her on it.

Lou swallowed it anyway. He patted her smooth cheek for good measure. "S'okay, kiddo. This is my first freshly severed head too."

That was just it. When she'd stared into that bag, she'd had the distinct impression this *wasn't* hers.

2

THE SYMPATHY PERMEATING Lou's face had Kate turning away to focus on the dusty lane—and that final, waiting sack. The vacuum-packed head was still secreted within. Not that it mattered. She could still see that perfect, scarlet line where a fellow soldier's neck had been neatly separated from the rest of his body, and she could still feel the ever-present muck as it began to bubble up, yet again.

"Kato?"

She pulled the morning air deep into her lungs, praying the pungent mix of fallen leaves and loblolly pine would soothe the throbbing panic. It did.

But the unease remained.

The case. Focus on the case, damn it.

Begin the brief.

Kate dragged her rusty training to the fore and turned to face her boss. "The good news is we're most likely dealing with a single victim. Skin tone, body hair texture and color, not to mention the consistent dimensions and impressive musculature of the limbs—it all points to a single corpse. Plus, while we can't rule out a woman, based on the sheer strength it would take to subdue and move this particular victim, along with a few psychological factors, odds are the killer's also male. As for the bad: this guy's organized, Lou. Smart. Logistics and time are on his side and he knows it. Make no mistake; he's an expert at killing. Animals, people. He can stalk and take down either, and easily. Hell, he should. He's had enough experience—especially with people."

"How can you be so sure?"

Kate pointed toward the macabre collection strung out along the lane. "Our victim was Army. There's a Screaming Eagle tattoo on his back, meaning he was with the 101st Airborne at some point. On his front: two sets of small puncture scars above the heart. Most likely the result of prongs jammed into his chest from insignia awarded upon completion of his military courses. Given the Screaming Eagle, my money's on Airborne and Air Assault. Then there's the collection of old bullet wounds and shrapnel scars. This guy saw action—a lot. Finally, though he's no longer active duty, he was no couch potato." Brief though her glimpse had been, the length of the man's hair confirmed the former; the impressive muscle tone of his limbs, the latter.

Lou nodded as he refreshed his chew. "You're sayin' our victim was a top-notch man hunter in his own right."

"I am. But as to whether or not an avid pursuit of Bambi drew him into his killer's crosshairs, I have no idea. Yet. But it's certainly possible, given the dump's location and timing."

"Had the same thought when I saw how close those bags were to Scooter's stand. I had Scooter's son take me to their site before Nolan drove 'em to the station. There's no sign the slicin' and dicin' took place there, and I'm assumin' there would be."

Lou was correct. She was all but certain Scooter and his son had simply stumbled across the dump site. She'd have Old Man Miller's shack and the surrounding property scoured, but she doubted they'd find anything. The kill zone and carcass prep area may or may not be one and the same—but both were located elsewhere. Experience suggested miles elsewhere. Anyone with the patience and means to stage a scene this antiseptic was too thorough to risk placing it closer. Too bloody smart.

Not to mention that Scooter Ball's deer camp consisted of a three-sided run-in that barely protected him from the elements. Whoever had cut up that body had had four walls and a door.

A hefty sound and smell buffer.

"See anything else that points to some sicko activist?"

Kate caught the hope in Lou's eyes. She and Tonga weren't the only ones praying for a one-off nut job.

"Perhaps." Kate rubbed at the knot forming between her neck and shoulders. "But it's more what I don't see. Aside from the dismemberment, there's no evidence of trauma. No fresh punctures, gunshot wounds, contusions or broken bones. Other than a number of slices from being flex cuffed, there's nary a fresh mark on the guy. That, combined with the lack of blood, is a serious flag. Someone new to exsanguination might've sliced the vet's jugular or carotid before hanging him upside down to drain his blood. But our guy's experienced enough to know that simply stringing a carcass up after gutting is enough for gravity to do its thing—which, given the rope burns at the victim's ankles, appears to be all the killer did."

It took a good four to five hours to drain a deer. God only knew how long it took to drain a man.

Had the bastard clocked it?

Her dark sigh spread into the surrounding trees. "The most telling part may be the internal organs."

"What about 'em?"

"They're missing—along with the victim's penis, scrotum and windpipe."

Lou's curse split the air. A stream of tobacco-fouled spittle followed.

Kate nodded. As any serious hunter knew, the removal of that specific trio of body parts constituted the initial steps in field dressing a deer. First, the hunter ensured the animal was dead. Next, he or she laid it on its back. If it was a buck, the hunter removed the genitals; a doe, the udder. A shallow slice up the front all the way to the base of the animal's jaw exposed the windpipe and internal organs—which the hunter then removed to prevent tainting of the meat.

Had their killer removed the parts out of habit? Or had the removal been deliberate? And why discard the bulk of the victim's body out on this particular road? For the extreme animal-rights, PETA-level shock value?

Then why exclude the organs?

Because he'd deemed them unimportant? Or had packaging them proved too messy?

Or did the killer possess a perverse taste for organ meat? Had he reserved the innards for his own deviant use?

As revolting as the latter theory was, the presence of those brown paper bags supported it. Upon her arrival, they'd all but resembled a tidy row of oversized lunch sacks, with an odd "to go" feel.

Surely that image was significant, at least to the killer?

From the horror on Lou's face, her final, morbid line of thought had seared through the sheriff's brain as well. His jowls took on a decidedly green tinge as he spat his chew onto the bed of pine needles at their feet.

"Are you thinkin' the son-of-a-bitch *ate*—"

"It's possible." Though she prayed not. "Either way, we'd best keep the suspicion close, at least for now."

Once the shock wore off, Scooter and his son were bound to

talk. Given the way the body parts had been packaged, equally disturbing speculation and supposition were certain to follow.

And if a local hunter or group of hunters should stumble across an unknown woodsman who hadn't yet had a chance to wash off the results of a more traditional field dressing? Braxton could end up with a lynching on its hands, or worse.

And that didn't take into account the deliberately organized booze-fueled posses that would likely form.

Lou retrieved his tin of tobacco and studied it, then frowned as he shoved it back into his pocket. "I'd best get to the station and make that call to the governor. I'll take Scooter and his son aside soon as I get there. Let 'em know there'll be hell to pay if they open their traps about what they found and how they found it before we give the all clear."

Kate snagged one of the evidence markers she'd pocketed earlier, and bent to place it beside Lou's puddle of expelled tobacco for crime scene exclusion. "You might want to give Feathers a call too. Maybe even re-deputize him for a spell."

As kids, Lou, Bob Feathers and her dad had been inseparable. The three-way friendship had taken up where it had left off following her dad's inexplicable decision to trade in his career as one of the Army's best investigators to scratch out a living writing speeding tickets in bum-fuck nowhere after her mom's death. While Kate could do without the trips down memory lane that would inevitably accompany the deputy's recall, Feathers' presence could only be a net positive.

Bob Feathers still held the state's meth lab takedown record. His knowledge of every remote cabin and mobile home in the surrounding eight counties was formidable. They'd need that to locate the killer's slaughterhouse, along with Feathers' unparalleled familiarity with every deer camp and makeshift tree stand from the Ozarks to the Arkansas River.

Lou accepted a second evidence marker and hunkered down

to set it next to the birch that bore the remaining traces of his chew. "Heard tell Feathers got back from visitin' his kids and is already bored stiff with retirement. I'll give him a call." The sheriff stood. Turned.

Relief fled as Kate spotted the request simmering amid her boss' muddy stare. She cut him off before it could reach his lips. "The governor's bound to suggest the state crime lab take point. Might be best if we hand the whole thing off now."

It made sense, damn it, and Lou knew it.

The vet's body, such as it was, was headed to Little Rock. Even if Tonga insisted on autopsying what was left first, they'd need the state lab's specialists to see the investigation through, not to mention access to their array of specialized equipment— toxicological and otherwise.

Given the lack of bruising, it was extremely likely their killer had used drugs to take down his prey. But with the bulk of the victim's blood and internal organs missing, there was an excellent chance toxicology would come up dry. That left the recovery of microscopic evidence in, on and around the remains. This case would hinge on it; she'd stake her former reputation on it. Like it or not, Lou needed the state lab.

And *she* needed Lou to need someone else to run point regarding the rest—desperately.

Unfortunately, Lou was Lou. Backwoods sheriff or not, he was still a cop. Unless it undermined the case, Lou would fight to keep the lead within his department. Especially with the biggest case of his career. And with her credentials under the department's collective belt, there was no way Lou would believe another detective—state level or not—could oversee this investigation better.

Kate could see that too, swirling around amid the indecision in those muddy pools, and it was getting to her. Even if state took over, they'd still need a liaison within the Braxton PD and, unfortunately, she knew that too.

It was what she didn't know—make that, what she couldn't remember—that scared the shit out of her. If a handful of arguments with Grant were enough to stir up the rot in her gut, what would working this case do to her sanity?

She crossed her fingers—hell, her soul—and pushed it. "I really do think it's best if Feathers—"

Lou shook his head. "The vic's Army, Kato. You've already established that. That's somethin' Feathers and the other deputies just won't get. Nor will the folks at the state crime lab. Yeah, I know. They got a couple Air Force and a Marine vet over there. But you done told me about the subtle differences between the branches. We cain't afford to miss the smallest thing on this." He jabbed a finger toward the parts lining the road. "Not with the twisted fuck that done that out there."

Duty warred with panic.

If she pushed harder—confessed all—Lou would let her off the hook. He'd probably even understand.

The dive watch on her wrist grew heavy as Kate stared at that collection of coldly packaged flesh. She forced herself to weigh the remnants of her own mutilated psyche against the snuffed-out life of a fellow soldier.

A fellow combat vet.

The watch grew heavier as the inevitable sank in. She managed to stave off the urge to twist it as she nodded stiffly and led the way back to the road. "Let's see if we can't get an ID so you have something positive to give the governor. I'd also like to get someone's eyes on Old Man Miller's property asap, including his shed and barn. I doubt the killer's set up shop so close to his chosen dump, but it needs excluding."

Lou's relief at her acquiescence to taking point was unmistakable, along with the resurgence of that suffocating sympathy.

He was studying the shredded side of her face, too. Something he hadn't done in over a year. For the first time since she'd crawled home from that hellhole, Kate wondered just how much Lou knew about what'd happened over there. And how he'd discovered it.

Grant?

Now was not the time to probe for answers...had she even possessed the courage.

Kate reached the gravel lane and that still-bagged head. She knelt down beside it as Lou continued on toward the cruisers to order the search of Old Man Miller's property and retrieve the MorphoIDent. One good thing about vets: their fingerprints were in the system. If she could get a clear capture through the plastic shrink-wrapped around their victim's fingers, they'd have an ID within seconds. If not, she'd have to give Tonga first crack at the victim after all—at least his hands.

But first, the head.

Kate braced herself as she reached into the sack. She managed to ease the head out without losing her nerve. Her stomach was another matter. Again, nausea threatened as she studied that stark red line. Tactical breathing reigned as she waited for it to ebb. Several rounds later, it did—but an odd, almost painful cramping had supplanted the sloshing.

Why?

More importantly, why did that simple line of red consume her? She'd seen her share of decapitations before. Granted, all of them had been decidedly past their prime. She'd even bagged an obscene number personally. But those heads had been rudely ripped or hacked from their owner's necks.

Was that it, then? Was her fascination rooted in the surreal simplicity of that perfect line? Or did it go deeper?

Her wrist began to itch.

"Kato?"

She flinched—and nearly lost her grip on the head.

"You sure you're okay?"

She stalled for time, carefully positioning the back of the victim's head on the flattened sack and snapping a photo before she stood. Pinning a *Go Army; been there, done that and got the tarnished Silver Star to prove it* smile to her lips, she faced her boss. "I'm fine. It's just...been a while."

The itching grew worse.

Kate spotted the compassion bleeding into Lou's eyes and snatched the MorphoIDent from his hand.

"Thanks, boss."

Executing an about-face, she headed for the flattened sack bearing the victim's right hand before Lou could argue. They were in luck; the textured side of the plastic was opposite his palm. Less than a minute later, she had a match.

Kate tilted the MorphoIDent's screen toward the sheriff as he joined her so he too could compare the driver's license photo that had registered to the slightly distorted features of their victim's face.

"Yeah, that's him. Poor bastard."

She clicked through the corresponding stats. "Name's Ian Kusić. He lives—lived—in that hodgepodge of trailers out by Jackson Road and Plum Creek."

Lou jerked his chin toward the still-flashing cruisers at the head of the crime scene. "You'd best beat feet and see if there's a spouse or live-in that needs notifyin'. Then start pokin' through his life. We need leads like a skunk needs stink. Take Seth with you. Owen can stay behind to protect the integrity of the scene and assist CSU in processin' while Tonga loads up the vic's parts. You're right, Kato. We might as well have 'em sent straight to the state lab for autopsy. I'll give 'em a holler after I call the governor's office."

Kate nodded. "Sounds good. But Seth should stay. Tonga's

more unsettled by this whole thing than he'd like to admit. He could use Seth's assistance in packing the remains for transport."

The ME could use the deputy's moral support too, but that wasn't why she needed to go it alone.

"You sure?"

"Absolutely." Walking through that trailer and picking apart another vet's life was going to be hard enough.

No way in hell was she bringing an audience.

KATE NEARLY REGRETTED HER FELLOW DEPUTY'S ABSENCE AS IAN Kusić's trailer came into view. The double-wide had been exiled to the western edge of its tree-studded acreage at least thirty years before, and it showed. That said, its wheel-less, sagging belly clung valiantly to stacked cinder blocks far enough away from the other half-dozen trailers, yet close enough to the surprisingly lush, winding creek beyond to be billed as "private, with a view" by some enterprising landlord.

But it was still a depressing pile of crap.

With its pitted exterior so warped and rusted, Kate was half afraid the mild breeze swirling through the dried grass and fallen leaves would send the structure crashing in on itself before she had a chance to gain entrance. She could've used Seth's bulk after all, if only to hold up the roof.

Or not.

The pair of Afghanistan and Iraq Veteran stickers book-ending the dented bumper of an equally dilapidated Chevy pickup caused the unease to return. Claustrophobia joined in, knotting tightly as Kate parked her Durango in the rut of dried mud behind the truck. It knotted tighter as she spotted a Bluetick hound bounding out from the cluster of trees to the east. A thirty-something woman sporting a tangle of russet curls and a neon orange hoodie brought up the rear.

Damn. Seth's non-stop banter would've helped deflect the inevitable curiosity.

Too late now.

Kate exited the Durango. Dressed in jeans and a department tee, she took the time to don her Braxton PD uniform jacket and ball cap. Grabbing a fresh set of latex gloves and crime scene booties from the case she kept in the back seat, she stuffed them in a pocket as the hound reached her. Though she was within her jurisdiction, she didn't recognize the dog or its mistress. Not surprising. Socializing with the surrounding town and rural folk had been even less of a priority since her return to Braxton three and a half years ago than it had been in high school.

The Bluetick appeared friendly enough. And amusingly enthralled with Ruger's scent. The mutt was still frantically sniffing at the legs of her jeans as the woman approached.

Kate patted the Bluetick's head with one hand as she retrieved her badge with the other. Bracing herself, she turned her face squarely into the woman's view. "Mornin', ma'am. Deputy Holland—I'm with the Braxton PD."

The woman's bright blue stare held Kate's for all of two seconds, then dropped. Not to Kate's credentials. To the four-inch mottled scar that bisected her entire right cheek, along with the complementary smattering of pocks and smaller scars left behind by the molten shrapnel that had once ripped through her face, neck and torso. No surprise there. Four years on, she was almost used to the absolute absorption her rein-vented features tended to generate in her fellow man, woman and child. Hell, she preferred it.

Open stares, even the downright rude ones, beat stiff silence and awkward avoidance every time.

Kate waited for the fascination to run its course.

Based on the pink splotches staining the other woman's significantly smoother cheeks as her gaze shifted to accommodate a sudden and intense interest in the door to Kusić's trailer, it had. Unfortunately, Kate had also spotted the tinge of revulsion curdling the woman's features.

It beat pity, right?

Right?

Kate kept her tone cool, clipped. Professional. "Ma'am?"

The woman resumed eye contact—reluctantly. "Sorry. Leena Paquet. My husband Delbert and I own this property. Are you here for our tenant?"

For? Odd choice of prepositions.

Kate pocketed her credentials as the Bluetick resumed its sniffing, this time at the heels of her boots. "Are you referring to Ian Kusić?"

"That's him."

Kate nodded. "Ma'am, I'm afraid Mr. Kusić's dead. I'm here to determine his marital status and to seal off his residence."

The tenuous eye contact strengthened. It was quickly followed up with a frown. "Whatever for? How did Ian die?"

"I'm not at liberty to say. Was Mr. Kusić married?"

"No."

"Do you know if he had a housemate? A significant other?"

"No and no. At least, Del and I ain't seen anyone since he and his latest piece had their final falling out."

Final? "Did Mr. Kusić and his girlfriend argue regularly?"

And had domestic abuse been an element? It would explain the landlady's odd choice of prepositions. Possibly more.

Kate's interest spiked upon the confirming nod. Granted, female lovers tended to *not* settle their disputes using methods which left behind the coldly partitioned results she'd logged out on that gravel road, but Ian Kusić's penis had been missing —and the plastic used to wrap the remaining pieces of the corpse did appear to be the type used in a food prep appliance.

"Do you know his girlfriend's name?"

Leena shook her head. "Never had the displeasure. All I know is she's a bottle blond who prefers too much makeup on her face and not enough fabric on the hind end of her shorts."

The Bluetick snorted as if it agreed.

Kate had her doubts regarding the hound's master, since Delbert's avid appreciation of said hind end—silent or otherwise—would explain the distaste pinching his wife's lips.

Kate kept the suspicion to herself as the landlady bent to scratch the Bluetick's head. "About that final fight; do you remember when it occurred?"

Finely plucked brows furrowed as Leena straightened. "Nine days ago. I know because Del and I had just returned from his mom's in St. Louis. It was so loud that I almost had Del dial 911. But then Ian's screen door slammed, and that little red convertible the banshee drives tore up the lane as she left, spitting gravel everywhere. Like I said, ain't seen her since."

"Do you know what the fight was about?"

The woman stiffened. "Honey, I *don't* poke my nose in where it don't belong."

In other words, she'd been too far away to make out the words. Shame. Kate withdrew a business card from the slot behind her credentials and held it out. "If you or your husband remember anything else, please give me a call."

"Fine." The landlady stuffed the card into the hoodie's kangaroo pocket.

"Ma'am, I don't suppose you or your husband have a key to Mr. Kusić's residence?"

Leena nodded firmly. "Sure do. You'd be surprised what tenants will do to a place if you don't check up on them." She patted that same pocket. "Got it right here."

Kate took a turn scratching the Bluetick's ears, intent on soothing mistress more than hound. At least until she had tacit permission to enter the premises with that key—sans search warrant. "Did Mr. Kusić keep a dog?"

"No."

Nothing to impede her entrance then. If she was lucky.

Leena pursed her lips. "I did see him feeding a stray cat off and on. I made him keep it outside since he was too cheap to fork over a pet deposit. Them things stink, if you ask me—what with their crap boxes and spraying. It gets in the carpet and the walls. Not to mention the fleas, the hair and the dander. Clings to everything. And those claws." The woman shuddered. "Damned things shred everything in sight, including—"

People.

The unspoken word lurched between them, as cold and ungainly as the stare that had dropped to the mutilated side of Kate's face. Scarlet stained the landlady's own flawless cheeks, clashing with the neon orange of her hoodie. Leena's stare hit the ground, where it remained. "Do you, uh, need—"

"Just the key. Please."

The silence returned. Kate left it hanging—ripening—as the landlady retrieved a ring of keys from her pocket and worked one free. Gaze still nailed to the ground, she handed it over.

Kate opened her mouth to thank her, even offer up an inane comment to smooth things over, but it was too late.

Leena had spun around and begun a stiff march across the field. Several shrill whistles and a peeved shout followed before the Bluetick deigned to trail after her.

Though the landlady's rigid spine faced her, Kate still had the westward windows of the remaining cluster of trailers to contend with. Mindful of her potential audience, Kate headed for the rear of Kusić's abode. Like the front of the trailer, it appeared to be a fistful of bolts from condemnable. She stopped beside the set of cracked and weathered two-by-six steps leading up to the back door to don her crime scene booties and gloves.

The board at the top groaned as she keyed the lock. It didn't budge. Either the lock was frozen or it'd been changed—and recently, given the landlady's confidence in her ability to access the trailer.

Kate twisted the knob on a whim.

It gave.

The killer? Had he abducted Kusić from his own residence and left the door unlocked, accidentally or otherwise?

Or had he returned to the scene?

Kate switched her phone to mute, then slid her 9mm from her shoulder holster, offering it first glance inside.

Astonishment reigned as she followed her weapon into an unoccupied living room. While she hadn't expected *Deliverance*, neither had she anticipated *Lifestyles of the Loaded Bachelor.* A wall-mounted plasma flatscreen with massive speakers held center stage, with a dark-chocolate leather couch and sleek coffee table opposite. A floor-to-ceiling display cabinet filled with models of every high-end car known to man anchored the opposite wall. The matching pair of leather recliners rounding out the room would've cost her dad a year's paychecks to park his tush within.

Why would someone who could afford to kit out a place like this live inside a rusted trailer?

The view was nice, but not that nice.

Privacy? If so, for or from what? And was the need for isolation tied to the man's death?

The urban-wannabe remodel was recent too. No doubt while the Paquets had been in St. Louis. The smell of *new* confirmed it. And there was the landlady. With the woman's admitted penchant for spot snooping and obvious gift for gossip, she'd have undoubtedly mentioned the remodel if it had occurred before then.

The mystery deepened as Kate continued her initial sweep of the trailer. The master bedroom and bath were likewise decorated to the hilt, down to the king-sized waterbed and black satin comforter in the former and the fresh paint and glistening sink and shower fixtures in the latter. The spare bedroom had been converted into a computer station-cum-recording studio of sorts, with an impressive array of guitars and two electric keyboards lining the walls in lieu of a bed.

But, still, no untimely visitors.

Unless Ian Kusić's killer had squeezed himself beneath the floorboards, the trailer was clear.

Kate holstered her 9mm, curiosity throbbing as she exited the kitchen. Like the laptop and instruments in the spare room, the oak cabinets appeared new. The financial records on this guy were bound to be fascinating.

What the devil did Kusić do for a living? Had he come into an inheritance? Won the lottery?

Heck, why bother remodeling at all? Surely it made more sense to move?

Kate crossed the plush carpet and tugged on the cord hanging from the living room window's pleated shades. Kusić's rusted truck greeted her. Why hadn't it been replaced with a man-sized version of one of the cars in that display cabinet? Because it had yet to be delivered? Or, in light of the trailer's crumbling exterior, had Kusić been intent on keeping *down* appearances? At least as far as the outside world was concerned. But again, why?

Drugs? The trailer was parked within spitting distance of the I-40 corridor. Corpses of men and women in that particular line of work had been known to surface with missing parts from time to time, though usually a lot closer to Mexico.

Yes, times were changing. But a double-crossed heroin kingpin wouldn't waste time staging that dump site. He'd have simply shot Kusić, possibly hacked off his head as a statement, and been done with it. Likewise, a double-crossed customer wouldn't have enough brain cells left firing to pull off that pristine scene.

Was the killer a recovering addict, then? Or had Kusić pissed off one-too-many emotionally and financially, cleaned-out loved ones?

One thing was certain. Kusić hadn't made the money to outfit this place by working for Uncle Sam. Not unless he'd received a battlefield promotion to general at the ripe old age of twenty.

Kate turned toward the hall, intent on firing up the laptop she'd spotted to scour it for clues. She stopped at the couch instead, her attention snagged by a pair of professionally designed memory albums tucked away on the shelf beneath the coffee table. Odd. Most people didn't print photos anymore, let alone collect up enough to paste in an album. Perhaps she wasn't the only one to have inherited an old 35 mm from her mother, along with the curiosity and stubbornness to use it.

Intrigued, Kate retrieved the uppermost album and opened the cover. An inscription greeted her.

Ian,
We're so proud of you.
Love, Mom & Dad

THAT EXPLAINED THE ALBUMS. AS FOR THE INSCRIPTION, KATE knocked the green-eyed monster off her shoulder and flipped through the succeeding pages—and wished she hadn't.

While the album was filled with countless photos of Kusić and his friends, nearly every one oozed Army. There were shots of the man as a seasoned sergeant in the thick of things all the way back to his swearing in as a lanky, still-unshorn private. The insignia on his dress uniform confirmed Kate's suspicions regarding Kusić's Airborne and Air Assault quals. He'd also qualified expert on his rifle.

Ironic considering that, according to the man's military occupational specialty school graduation photo, Kusić had been a 68 Kilo. Otherwise known as a lab tech. Any knowledge the vet possessed regarding drugs—legal and otherwise—had been earned the hard way. Given the settings of several other photos, Kusić had once been up to his neck in needles, microscopes and blood in at least four of the busiest combat hospitals the US Army had run in both Afghanistan and Iraq. From the legion of mile-wide grins and arm-in-arm poses, Kusić and his buddies had thrived on the resulting adrenaline. That sweet rush that came with knowing you'd given your all for your comrades, and knowing they hadn't hesitated to put their collective asses on the line for you—and would again.

Kate's own past crowded in. The memories.

And then, those goddamned, gaping holes.

She slapped the first album onto the coffee table and grabbed the second. She flipped through the pages, pausing at a photo of Kusić hugging a decidedly older, grayer version of himself. Judging from the banner in the background, the photo had been snapped at one of Kusić's homecomings.

The jealous monster crawled back up on her shoulder as Kate confronted the pride glowing in Kusić senior's face.

She turned the page on both, leafing through the remaining

photos until she reached a written citation near the end of the album. Kusić had been awarded the Meritorious Service Medal while deployed to Bagram hospital eight years earlier. Kate turned the page, skimming two other citations and an effusive attaboy from Kusić's final commanding officer before she reached the write-up for which she'd been searching: his Purple Heart.

Despite that expert badge, Sergeant Kusić had wielded a test tube for the Army, not a rifle. So how had a 68 Kilo earned that generous collection of bullet and shrapnel scars she'd noted out on Old Man Miller's road?

It seemed she and Sergeant Kusić had run afoul of the enemy in an eerily similar fashion. Ambush. Like her, one blissfully ignorant moment Kusić had been riding in a military medical convoy with his fellow soldiers, only to take jarring flight the next on a shitload of instantly expended explosives.

The citation in Kate's hands disintegrated as the memory of another shattered Humvee slammed in. Only this one had been flipped completely over in the blast. Within seconds she was back in that sweltering hell, suffocating on the stench of burning rubber, pinned between a buckled roof and her smoldering seat, half-blinded by the pain slicing through her face and the blood dripping into her eyes. The latter hadn't been hers. It had belonged to her best friend, Max.

Despite a shattered collarbone, she'd managed to retrieve her sidearm and take aim at the bearded face hunkering down beneath the edge of the crumpled door of their Humvee to fire her first bullet of the day.

Bullseye.

The fading light from those eyes had barely registered as she'd worked to twist her battered torso and hips far enough around so she could use her boots to kick the bastard out of the way. Somehow, she'd succeeded in dragging Max's unconscious body and her own broken, sorry ass out into the Afghan coun-tryside...where the rest of the bastards had been waiting.

Kate snapped the album shut and dumped it on the table as the sludge began to churn deep inside.

She closed her eyes and worked to quell it.

It was no use.

Against her will, her right hand came up, her fingers auto-matically finding the dive watch on her left wrist and beginning to twist as she headed down the hall to Kusić's spare room and that laptop of potential clues. She was about to enter when her fingers stilled. Her entire body followed suit.

There.

She forced her fingers to trade the band of Max's watch for the textured grip of her 9mm as she caught a second muffled thump farther down the hall.

Shit.

From the moment she'd spotted that Screaming Eagle tattoo, she'd known she had no business working this case. She wasn't a hard-charging Army detective anymore; she was a backwater, speed-trap monitoring deputy—and had been for three years now. She never should've caved beneath Lou's pleading. But she had. And now her fucked-up brain had caused her to miss something vital.

Because she wasn't alone.

3

Kate eased the 9mm from her holster as she turned toward the master bedroom. She crept forward, pausing at the half-closed door to ensure her cellphone was still muted, catching two more thumps as she returned the phone to her pocket. Glock front and center, she nudged the bedroom door open another two inches and slipped inside.

The room appeared empty...until another thump reverberated from beyond the foot of the bed.

The closet.

She had closed it, hadn't she? Because a good three inches of shadowed air now separated the edge of the mirrored door from its frame—and there was definitely motion within.

Adrenaline pulsed as Kate skirted the waterbed. She used her right boot to slide the door completely open as she drew down on the intruder. "Police; freeze!"

A panicked fumble reverberated from behind the pair of plastic green storage crates...and a meow.

Crap.

Kate swallowed her adrenaline and a healthy dose of humiliation as she shoved the 9mm into its holster. A sleek, black-and-white face with dark yellow eyes poked up from behind the oversized boxes. The cat meowed again, loudly. It was pathetic. Hungry.

And not supposed to be here.

For all the landlady's snooping, Leena had managed to miss a cat she'd officially nixed, along with the delivery of enough high-end, man-cave gear to keep a newly single Kusić from prowling the neighborhood for at least a year.

What else was the man hiding?

And where were the cat's water, food and litter?

A closer inspection of the bathroom yielded two of the three. The water dish was tucked behind the toilet and was bone dry. The litter box, however, was boldly in the open. It was also disguised as a sleek, whitewashed table that doubled as a towel holder and magazine rack. A discreet cutout on the far side allowed the cat to do its job in private. The plastic flap and thick charcoal filter kept what would've otherwise been an impressive odor from leaking out.

Kate opened the door and studied the enclosed pan. Based on the contents, Kusić's cat could have been alone a solid week, depending on when the man had last cleaned.

Not the narrowest of timelines, but it was a start.

Another meow echoed through the room. Yellow eyes blinked up at Kate from the doorway, expectant. Evidently examining a cat's box meant she was obligated to feed its user. Either that, or it was desperate. Kate reached out to pet the cat, drawing back as it pinned its ears and hissed.

"Fickle, aren't you?" A sound assessment, given the creature's willingness to trot contentedly after her as she headed out of the room. She and the cat were two feet from Kusić's kitchen and potential vittles when his doorbell rang.

"Hey, Holland? You in there?"

Seth.

Evidently Lou had his own ideas regarding his department's personnel assignments, because his senior-most deputy was not assisting the coroner with the remains as she'd suggested. Instead, Seth was risking the precarious soundness of the victim's landing.

Kate unlocked the door. "Sorry. I came through the back."

"Probably for the best, with all those avid eyes lookin' on." Seth closed the door on the gawkers that had gathered near the cluster of trailers to the east.

Kate waited as the man donned his protective booties and gloves. She knew it was coming. The mood she was in, she needed it.

Seth didn't disappoint as he turned to take in the living room's decor, his jaw dropping as he spotted the flatscreen.

Kate smiled. "You know what they say—the bigger a man's TV, the smaller his penis."

Seth's snort warmed her for the first time since she'd parted with Ruger that morning. "Thought that was 'truck.'"

"That too." Her smile spread as the deputy's hands came up to stroke the silky leather of the closest recliner.

Awe tinged his sigh.

"Wait 'til you see the guitars. I swear Jimi Hendrix owned that Fender. At the very least, his spirit drooled on it."

"Sweet Momma, forgive me. I have envy." Seth pulled his palms from the recliner to scrub his face. "Guessin' I got no business in havin' it, either. Not after what happened to the poor bastard. Find anythin' else in here? Like somethin', anythin', that points to a motive for what we saw?"

"Not yet. But the decor's not the only thing that doesn't add up. The landlady has a key, but it doesn't work. Not that it mattered, because the back door was unlocked. Something I doubt Kusić would've done in light of what's worth stealing. But there's no sign he was abducted from here. Nothing upended, no blood, no wallet, no cellphone—and his truck's out front. It's as if he left willingly...but he didn't."

Seth nodded. "Hate to add to the confusion, but Lou called as I pulled up. There's no record of a huntin' license in Kusić's name. Also, the boys scoured Old Man Miller's place. Other than that sick display, there's nothin' unusual on the property—house and outbuildings included. Finally, Lou says to tell you it's a no go on reinstatin' Feathers."

Her disappointment must've been visible, because Seth shrugged.

"I know. Man's a walkin' encyclopedia for every hidey-hole in the state. Unfortunately, Feathers has got his own crisis to wade through."

"What happened?"

"His son-in-law was out ridin' ATVs with a buddy when his flipped. Feathers set out last night to join his daughter's vigil at the hospital. It don't sound good. Feathers said he'd head back as soon as he can. Meanwhile, we're to call and pick his brain anytime, day or night."

"That'll be enough." It had to be. Because she was truly stuck with this. And, so far, she didn't have a single decent lead.

Kate headed for Kusić's coffee table and the album she hadn't realized she'd dumped on the floor. She retrieved it and smoothed her fingers over the photo in the cover's cutout. It was a formal shot of Kusić in his Blues. She studied the photo, only to flinch as something warmed her shoulder.

Seth. He'd followed her across the room. His right hand was missing its crime scene glove as it squeezed gently. Odd. She didn't feel the instinctive urge to back away.

Neither, apparently, did Kusić's cat. The fickle feline had closed in on Seth, rubbing against his legs. Seth ignored the cat as he smoothed his thumb across her good cheek.

"You okay? You seem...lost."

She found an honest smile from somewhere deep and long forgotten, and bumped it up to her lips. "I'm fine. Just a bit mired in it all."

Seth's sigh warmed the air. "I know what you mean."

He didn't. He couldn't. But she didn't contradict him.

What would be the point?

She'd worked too hard to keep the worst of it from her fellow deputies and everyone else in this town. Hell, she was still desperately trying to keep it from herself.

Seth must've sensed enough, because he'd stepped back to scoop up the cat. He snuck a peek beneath the ball of fluff and grinned at Kate. "It's a she."

Kate's smile deepened as Seth allowed the cat to snuggle up against the front of his Braxton PD jacket. She suspected he'd engineered the moment to give her time to unscramble her thoughts and get them back on the case, but the cat didn't care.

The hussy was now rubbing her head against Seth's neck and jaw, and purring for all she was worth.

"That decides it. You find the cat food and some fresh water. I'll be in the bedroom. I need to look at something."

Or rather, inside it.

Seth nodded, setting the cat down to re-don his glove as Kate used her phone to snap a close-up of the photo of Kusić in his Blues. Seth headed into the kitchen as she advanced on the plastic green storage crates on the floor of the master bedroom closet. They were long and flat, and plenty roomy if a man had decided against a gun safe, but still wanted to keep his hunting rifle and ammo clean and dry.

Though she held slim hope this was about Bambi, she had to rule it out.

Kate knelt in front of the upper box and lifted the lid. Inside she found a hand-carved Remington nicer than her grand-dad's...along with two 9mms and a Soviet-made 7.62 AKM assault rifle with a folding double-strut stock and a thirty round magazine.

She retrieved the AK-47 and cleared the chamber. Circa 1980s, it had probably been left by some Russian soldier when his country had bugged out of Afghanistan, only to be picked up and used against the next army that came calling post 9-11...until Sergeant Kusić had decided to bring a souvenir back from the war.

Honor and spot checks at the battle end of combat tours were supposed to prevent the practice, but it happened. Especially since airlines didn't search the gear of soldiers on their way home.

As military sins went, it was mortal.

First the decor, then the cat, and now this. What else was Kusić concealing?

Kate returned the AK-47 to the makeshift gun locker and hefted the crate out of the closet. Curiosity surged as she turned back to the second box. More weapons?

Not even close.

Kate blew out her breath as she stared at the face of America's first millionaire. Make that, faces. There were lots and lots of him. Not quite a million, but more Benjamin Franklins than she had squirreled away. The crisp hundred dollar bills were still bound with paper currency bands. Kate thumbed through a stack and multiplied the result by the total bands on the others. The result caused her to whistle.

A second, deeper, whistle echoed hers. "I was about to brag that I'd found more than the cat food, but *damn*—" Seth's gaze shifted from the AK-47 to the money. "—you made out a helluva lot better than I did. There must be fifty thousand in there."

"Double it." Kate retrieved the small pad of paper wedged between the bills and the side of the crate.

Yes.

"What's that?"

"A lead." Though she increasingly doubted Kusić's murder was about Bambi, it might well be connected to drugs, at least obliquely. She held up the blank prescription pad. "Belongs to a Dr. Bill Manning. Know him?"

"Nope."

"Me, neither. The phone number's out of Little Rock."

Kate retrieved her cellphone. She switched the volume on, and snapped a photo of the pad before passing it to Seth. "Bag this, along with his arsenal and the money. I'll track down the doc. If we're lucky, I'll locate and reach his practice before he leaves for the weekend."

Conversations regarding the illegal selling of prescription drugs almost always went better in person...for the cop.

"Sounds good." Seth reached down to snag her hand and draw her to her feet.

"Thanks. Give Lou a heads up on the money so he can inform the governor's office. And ask him to send the crime scene unit here when they're done at Old Man Miller's." Even if Kusić's killer had been inside, she doubted he'd left evidence. Not with that antiseptic crime scene. But it was worth a shot.

"Roger. What about this?" Seth held up a photo of a woman with sleek blond hair and a carefully made up face. "It was beneath a Guillermo's Pizza magnet on the fridge."

"Front and center?"

He shook his head. "Shoved around the side, near the wall."

Blond hair, seriously dark brows. The contrast suggested a dye job. "Probably his ex. The landlady claims they had a falling out nine days ago. Hold it steady?" Kate snapped another photo, this time of the woman's picture. "Bag that too. And ask the landlady if it's the ex. If so, a name would help. If she doesn't know, her husband probably does."

She'd bet that tidy stash of Benjamins on it.

"Also, contact the station and see if Carole's making headway with the data dumps. The phone beside the bed doesn't have caller ID, so we'll definitely need his carrier to provide a list of who he's been chatting with lately. I didn't come across a cellphone, either. Let's cross our fingers Kusić had one on him when he was taken and the bastard didn't realize it." Though, as meticulous as this guy was, she doubted it.

Their best bet was probably that laptop she'd spotted—but only if the killer had been in email contact with Kusić.

Again, with this guy? Not likely.

"What about the cat?"

The minx had rejoined them and resumed its purring love affair with Seth's legs. Kate tossed the man a grin for his coming troubles as she headed for the door.

"Looks like she's decided for you. Unless a relative steps up, she's yours. Call me if you find anything else. Bye."

Kate's smile lingered as she reached the front door to the trailer. She paused on the landing to remove her gloves and protective booties, shoving them in her pocket as she headed into Kusić's rutted drive. She made the mistake of glancing at the bumper stickers on his truck as she climbed into her Durango.

Her smiled faded.

She refused to allow her newfound confidence to follow. She'd made it through that trailer without imploding. She'd make it through the coming days of the investigation. It was like picking a path through a minefield: one careful step at a time.

Fortunately, the next was easy.

Kate accessed the internet browser on her phone and typed in *Bill Manning, MD*. She clicked on the leading link and scanned the man's bio. Midway through the second sentence, her confidence shattered. The doubts set in. Claustrophobia followed.

Bill Manning did practice in Little Rock. In fact, he was the head of his department—at the Fort Leaves veterans' hospital.

An Army shrink.

Like it or not, one all-too-quick phone call later, she had an appointment.

IT WAS WORSE THAN KATE FEARED. FORT LEAVES WAS CRAWLING with vets. And she was still in the parking lot.

The only blessing she'd been able to come up with during the thirty-minute drive was that Little Rock had two VA facilities. Grant worked at the one across town. The chances of her running into him and having to force a friendly chat outside a shrink's office of all places were close to nil. Thank God.

So pull the pin. Lob the grenade.

Sure, she might blow off her own head. But then it would be over, wouldn't it? She could low crawl back to the warm, tidy foxhole she'd dug for herself in Braxton, issuing tickets and making the occasional meth or drunk-driving bust.

Just like her dad.

That got her to kill the Durango's engine. It even had her abandoning the SUV altogether. Dread settled in, cold and low, as her boots ate up the walkway, growing heavier with each step. All too soon, she'd reached the hospital's courtyard. She forced herself to breach the doors. US Army crowded the seats of the inner lobby. Based on the tattoos she noted, a handful of sailors, airmen and Marines had joined the soldiers currently marking time in medical purgatory, the entire lot deemed too old and/or too damned damaged to continue serving their country.

Like her.

Kate headed for the bank of elevators, grateful when the

closest opened immediately. She waited for a lab-coated physician to exit, then entered the blessedly empty lift.

"Hold the door, please!"

Great. She should've taken the stairs.

"Thanks, ma'am."

"No problem." Kate turned to support the wall as a shaggy, thirty-something vet maneuvered his wheelchair inside. Based on the *De Oppresso Liber* script peeking from beneath the sleeve of his tee, he'd been Special Forces. Cop or not, she should've ceased cataloguing his features then. But she didn't. The band on her chest tightened as she noted the jagged scar on the left side of his face. It was almost as long and livid as hers, though without the charmingly abundant collection of pocks and smaller scars that complemented the remainder of her face and neck.

Like the majority of the civilians she'd met, she dropped her gaze. Another mistake. The vet's legs were missing.

Her wrist began to itch.

She clamped her fingers around the dive watch and started the twist. It didn't help. By the time the lift reached her floor, respect and common courtesy were openly battling desperation.

The second the doors opened, the former lost.

Kate skirted the vet's wheelchair with a muffled, "Excuse me," and rudely exited first, double-timing down the hall. She kept going, twisting, until she'd located the shrink's office and was forced to let go of the watch to open the door.

She entered the outer office, deliberately ignoring the bowed heads and sightless stares of the half-dozen patients scattered about the rust-colored chairs and skeletal couches of the waiting room. It was the only way she could keep her frayed nerves knitted together as she made a beeline for the glassed-in reception counter.

An older woman slid the window open and beamed out at her. "Good afternoon. How may I help you?"

Kate retrieved her credentials. "Deputy Holland, Braxton PD. I'm here to speak with Dr. Bill Manning."

The woman's smile melted into disappointment. "You must be the officer who phoned. I'm sorry, but Dr. Manning was called out on a patient emergency ten minutes ago. I have no idea when he'll return. Will another doctor do?"

"Unfortunately, no." Kate retrieved a business card and passed it through the window. "Please tell the doctor I need to speak to him as soon as possible. It's important."

"Of course. If it helps, Dr. Manning spends Saturday mornings catching up on paperwork. He should be in by eight." The receptionist held up Kate's card. "But I will see that he gets your message today."

"Thank you."

Kate kept her stare well above the tops of the patients' heads as she turned to depart—and stumbled to a stop.

Surely that wasn't—

But it was.

Kate stared at the collection of vivid, cobalt-blue Afghan pottery perched along the wall shelf, transfixed. For several moments, the air refused to enter her lungs—and then, suddenly, it was ripping in and then back out with terrifying speed. Bile churned through her belly as sweat popped out along her pores. Within seconds, her T-shirt was damp and clammy.

Please, God. Not now.

Where was Ruger when she needed him? Because she *did* need him. Desperately.

Dreading the coming meltdown, she forced one foot in front of the other until she'd flat-out bolted from the room. Air still

searing through her lungs, she slammed into something hard—
and harder.

It took a moment for the metal edges of the wheelchair
biting into her thighs to register with her brain, along with the
raw ends of the missing legs of the man inside it.

Shock reset her lungs. Her scattered thoughts took longer,
but soon they too coalesced, only to be supplanted by a fresh
wave of humiliation.

The elevator. Her seriously rude exit.

"I am so sorry."

The vet actually laughed. "Not a problem. Been a while since
I've served as speed bump to someone so pretty."

Pretty? Had he seen her face?

But, yes, he had noticed her scars. Because he was staring
straight at them. Not as Kusić's landlady had stared. Nor even
how Kate had glanced at his in that elevator. In fact, he didn't
appear horrified or mesmerized, or even mildly curious.

The man simply...looked.

For some inexplicable reason, that simple stare from those
dark, fathomless eyes diffused the bomb ticking within.

Kate drew in a fortifying breath and met the vet's smile with
her own. "Thank you for the compliment. It's a lie, but not one I
can make an arrest over."

The man opened his mouth as if to argue, then shook his
head and chuckled instead. "Don't know about you, soldier, but
I've been incarcerated in this building too damned long. I could
use some joe before I break loose. You?"

She blinked.

His brow lifted. "Coffee. You remember? Liquid. Black. Able
to dissolve the tires of a Humvee in two seconds flat? The stuff
that kept you vertical and moving mostly forward at oh-dark-
thirty when you were so tired you'd have crawled in the sack
with a viper if it meant five more minutes of shut-eye?"

She remembered. She'd just forgotten...this. The easy camaraderie that sprang up between soldiers within moments of
meeting. That was all this was. The man wasn't coming on to
her. He was simply a grunt who wanted to shoot the shit for a bit
with someone who'd been where he'd been, seen what he'd
seen, and survived anyway. It was pleasantly familiar, and oddly
compelling. Like him.

Despite that scar and the inescapable need for that chair.

"Oh, my God! *Kate? Katie Marie Holland? Is it really you?*"

And it was over.

Kate turned toward the bullet of fizzing energy headed her
way. Elizabeth Vogel. Other than Grant's brother Dan, the sole
true friend Kate had possessed in high school. And with Dan
dead, Liz was due the only high-school reunion left possible.

The vet shrugged as Kate turned back. "Looks like you've got
some reconnecting to do. Feel free to take a raincheck. I'm here
every Monday, Wednesday and Friday, about this time."

"Thanks. I will."

"I'll hold you to it, soldier." The man spun his chair around,
flashing his grin at Liz as he took off down the hall. "Have a great
weekend, Doc. And congrats, again!"

"Thanks, Steve."

Kate lost sight of the vet as slender arms were flung around
her. Liz's familiar mass of strawberry curls tumbled in, smothering her.

"Oh, wow. I can't believe it's you. I was afraid I'd never see
you again. How have you *been?*"

Kate gave her old friend a mutual squeeze and stepped back.
Breathed.

Lied. "Fantastic."

The precise moment that soft blue gaze settled on her scars,
Kate felt it. But then it was gone. It moved on, brightening along
with her friend's smile. Pretending. As if its owner wanted to

believe that the mottled flesh polluting over a third of Kate's face, and the darker wounds that lay beneath, didn't exist.

Though they both knew painfully well that they did.

Kate appreciated the fantasy nonetheless. Nor was she eager to shatter it. Not here.

Still rattled by that pottery, she swerved into the path the wheelchaired vet had plowed, leaving room for Liz to accompany her, preferably right out of the hospital.

Despite this kinder, gentler blast from her past, she was done with this place.

Kate consciously brightened her own smile as they walked. "So, what about you, Lizzie-Lace? If I remember correctly, you hightailed it out of Braxton three days after I did, equally determined never to return."

The dimples Kate had been so jealous of at sixteen vanished, along with her friend's smile. "Things changed. My dad's been sick. Alzheimer's. Early onset."

"Oh, Liz, I'm so sorry." Kate knew Liz's granddad had been diagnosed in his early fifties. But her father too?

"Yeah. He was diagnosed my senior year of under grad. I transferred to UAMS and moved home to help my mom. She died two years later. Heart attack. It took me a bit longer to graduate, but I managed. In fact, I just finished my residency—and I've accepted a staff position. You're looking at Fort Leaves' newest psychiatrist."

That explained the vet's congratulations.

Kate added her own as she paused at the door to the stairs. There was no way she was getting trapped in another elevator with another vet. Not today.

"I'm truly sorry about your folks. They were always so great to me." Especially Liz's mom after the woman had discovered that Kate's mother had died shortly before she and her dad had moved to Braxton. "How's your pops doing?"

Liz shrugged as Kate opened the door. "He has good moments and bad. Right now we're wading through a patch of bad. But enough of that." Her friend's irrepressible smile returned, piercing the gloom as they entered the stairwell. "I want to hear about you. Tell me everything I've missed since you stopped taking my calls and answering my emails."

Kate winced. She should've seen that coming. After all, this was Liz. The woman was nothing if not forthright. Fortunately, she was also forgiving. "I apologize for that. I was wading through a dark patch myself back then."

Namely, her first tour in Iraq. Her first mass grave. It was something she still didn't talk about, lest the accompanying horror ooze in.

Maybe the holes in her brain were a blessing in disguise. Eventually, all the ugliness might just seep right out.

Liz shook her head as they reached the second landing. "Don't worry about it. I could've tried harder to pin you down. A mistake I plan on correcting right now. Do you have time for lunch? The cafeteria's special usually isn't, but the sandwiches are okay. They're on the other side of this door."

Kate wavered. With her sole lead dealing with a patient emergency, she should return to Kusić's trailer. If only to keep Seth company 'til the crime unit arrived. But she'd missed breakfast. And there was that prescription pad she'd found warming the sides of all those Benjamins. Liz might know Dr. Manning. With a few careful questions, she might be able to glean a feel for the man before they met—even know up front if the shrink had a history of "losing" his scripts, or if this batch had actually been stolen.

"I can manage a sandwich. I don't have long, though. I'm in the middle of something at work."

Liz glanced at her Braxton PD jacket as they entered the

cafeteria. "I see that. I'm assuming you decided to get out of the Army after...what happened."

Kate's stride faltered. Why, she wasn't sure. Liz was bound to remark on her scars eventually, even if they'd both been actively trying to pretend they didn't exist.

Impossible now. Not with her right cheek all but throbbing and Liz's ivory ones turning scarlet.

Silence reigned as they entered the line to select their sandwiches. Kate added two apples and an extra bottle of juice, since she wasn't sure when or if she'd find the time for dinner. She'd yet to receive a call regarding the autopsy, but it was bound to happen soon, given its priority.

Kate reached the register first, and paid for both meals as Liz found a quiet table in the corner.

The moment they sat, Liz leaned in to give her hand a squeeze. "I'm sorry. I didn't mean to put you on the spot, and so awkwardly. I guess it's different when it's a friend. It's just... What I'm trying to say is, I've been with the VA for a while. I did my residency here and, well, your...experience has sort of become an unofficial case study on crisis and memory among the psychiatric community."

In other words, the whispers Kate had worked so hard to ignore during her four mandatory weeks of mental waterboarding disguised as therapy had spread beyond Walter Reed and the Army. She and her missing marbles had become water cooler fodder for the shrinks across the VA system, too.

Lovely.

She could count on two fingers the number of times she'd opened up regarding what she did and *didn't* remember about that ambush and her subsequent escape from her captors eleven hours later. Old friends or not, she'd be damned if she'd be adding a third finger today. Especially in a public cafeteria.

Liz seemed to understand. Even better, she appeared determined to change the subject too.

Twin dimples heralded the return of that jaunty smile as the
woman leaned forward, her giddy, *I've got a secret* whisper thick-
ening the air as it had back at Braxton High at their old lunch
room table. "You'll never guess who else moved home."

Why not? It beat discussing herself. "Who?"

"Grant."

Kate was thankful they were sitting or she'd have stumbled
again. "Grant Parish?"

The dimples deepened. "Yup. Or, as they say around here,
God's gift to single doctors, nurses and patients alike. Not that
he's noticed. I think he's seeing someone."

He was. Her. Until they had a chance to talk, anyway.

She might've volunteered the former, had she been able to
get a word in edgewise. Liz was so anxious to smooth things
over, she was babbling a mile a minute. Kate forced herself to
swallow her shock long enough to pay attention.

"—deployed to Iraq, too. Though I guess you wouldn't have
run into each other, since he was a surgeon. Or would you?
Anyway, he got out right before Dan was killed in Afghanistan.
Grant returned home to help their dad through the funeral,
then went to work up in Fayetteville for a bit. He moved back
down here a year and a half ago, but we only ran into each other
recently."

The shock must've finally reached Kate's face anyway,
because Liz blanched. "Oh, God—Dan." Her eyes welled up as
she scraped the curls from her face. "You didn't know he was
dead, did you?"

"Yeah, I knew."

She'd seen Dan's name on one of the countless Killed in
Action lists that had reverberated through her email when she'd
been CID. At the time, she'd been working her second mass

grave. The victim-to-investigator ratio had been so obscene, she'd barely had a moment to squeeze in an overseas call to Grant's father, Abel, before returning to catalogue the corpses in that godforsaken pit. As a fellow soldier, she'd hoped Dan would've understood.

But the pain and the guilt lingered.

"Liz, I know about Grant, too. I was the one seeing him."

"Was?"

"Am." For another few hours, at least. A day, tops. Ah, Christ —*Abel*. She'd lose Grant's dad in the breakup, too. She hadn't thought of that. Hadn't wanted to. "It's...complicated."

"Oh, Katie. With you, it always was. That's why we love you so much." The high school camaraderie returned as Liz leaned closer to deliver another conspiratorial whisper. "Based on what little I gleaned from Grant, he's firmly hooked."

Lord, she hoped not. It was going to be hard enough resetting them to basic friendship. Especially since Abel had taken such delight in their moving past it.

And yet... Why hadn't Grant mentioned running into Liz? He might have five years on them and been in college at the time, but he'd known they were all close from the moment Dan had become the third sword in their naive version of the Musketeers. Confusion fed her growing unease. While Liz and Grant both worked for the VA, their respective facilities—not to mention specialties—were miles apart. Which would've accounted for them not running into each other until...just how recently?

Suspicion multiplied as she watched Liz settle into her chair to unwrap her sandwich.

"When did you two reconnect? Where?"

Liz took a bite. Chewed. The years fell away again beneath the damning certainty—within Kate. Liz wasn't hungry; she was stalling.

There was only one thing that would make Liz clam up

regarding Grant. He might work across town, but he was also a patient—right here at Fort Leaves. Though she doubted Grant was crawling onto Liz's professional couch, he was definitely sprawling out on someone's.

Was *that* why he'd been hounding her lately? Did he hope to nudge her up onto a matching cushion? If so, he was seriously mistaken.

This was also a discussion best saved for later—and Grant.

Kate pushed her untouched sandwich aside and retrieved her phone, intent on broaching the subject of another potential patient. Tapping through the photos she'd taken at the trailer, she stopped at the one of Kusić in his Blues.

"I need you to look at someone. He may be a patient. But it's possible he's simply a friend of one. Either way, I think he lifted something from one of your fellow psychiatrists."

Liz set her sandwich down. "Is this why you're here? Are you trying to locate a missing vet?"

Kate shook her head, but held her tongue as she slid her phone across the table.

"Oh, my gosh. That's Ian Kusić."

"You're treating him?"

Liz shook her head. "As far as I know, no one is. He is a vet, but he works here. In the lab. I can't believe Ian would steal. He's been nothing but professional when I've dealt with him. A stellar tech. And the patients love him."

"He's dead."

Eyes wide, Liz slumped in her chair. "What happened?"

"All I can say for now is the cause was not natural." A doozy of an understatement. But given Liz's profession, she had to understand the need for discretion.

"Are you saying he was *murdered?* Oh, Lord. Is Bill okay? I called his office earlier, but he wasn't in."

"Bill?"

"Dr. Manning. You mentioned a possible theft from a fellow psychiatrist and you were standing outside Bill's office when I noticed you."

Kate nodded. "I'm sure he's fine." She hoped. "According to the doc's receptionist, he's dealing with a patient emergency. I'm simply tracing the final moments of Kusić's life. Speaking to the people he spoke to. Trying to determine what happened."

Liz shook her head. "I doubt I can help. As I said, everyone liked him. Ian—" Her gaze shifted. Narrowed.

"What is it?"

"It's probably nothing."

"Liz, I'm so low on leads, anything will help."

"Well, I did see him arguing with someone. Sergeant Fremont, as a matter of fact. But that was a week ago."

"Fremont? Is he a patient?"

"Of course. You know him. You two were talking outside Dr. Manning's office."

"Just to be clear. The vet I spoke with—the one in the wheelchair—that's Sergeant Fremont? Do you have his number?"

"Yes. I mean, no. Yes, that was Fremont. But he's currently homeless. He doesn't have a cellphone. He can't afford one and he definitely won't accept 'charity', as he terms it. His contact number rings at a local shelter. Their staff takes messages."

"About that argument with Kusić. Do you know what it was about?"

"No. But Fremont was livid. And he's one of the most easygoing men I've met. I mean, the man was Special Forces, you know? He can hold his temper. But not that day."

Kate brought up the next photo. The one she'd taken of the picture Seth had found tucked around the side of Kusić's fridge. She slid her phone back across the table. "Do you know her?"

Liz nodded. "Abby Carson. She works—worked—with Ian. I've seen them in the cafeteria. I think they dated awhile, but it was over by last week." She shrugged beneath Kate's questioning brow. "Body language. Occupational hazard."

Kate knew the feeling. She was about to say so when her phone rang. It was Lou. Hopefully, he had good news.

Namely, a suspect.

"Hey, boss. What've you got?"

"You don't want to know. Hell, I don't want to know."

Shit. What they had was another body. It was in the sheriff's voice. Kate glanced at Liz. Her friend was finishing her sandwich...and listening intently. Discreetly.

Deciphering body language wasn't the woman's only professional skill.

Kate stood and turned to walk several paces from the table before lowering her voice. "How bad?"

"Same as before. Gravel road leadin' to nowhere. This one runs by that patch of land Beulah Winters donated to the county a few years back. I'm lookin' at another fifteen paper sacks strung out in line, one hacked-up body part per. At least that's the prevailin' assumption. The woman who stumbled across 'em only opened one. The rest are waitin' on Tonga and you."

Kate glanced at her watch. It was just past four. The sun would be setting in under two hours. "I'm at Fort Leaves, following a lead on Kusić. I'm leaving now." Kate cut the call and pocketed her phone as she returned to the table where Liz was scribbling out a number on the back of a business card.

"I have to go."

"No worries." Liz held the card out as she stood. "My private number's on the reverse. Call me when things quiet down. Please. I'd love to reconnect."

"Me, too." But with two carved-up bodies in six hours? There was something she wanted to do more.

And it didn't stop with just catching this bastard.

4

KATE BROUGHT her SUV to a halt behind nearly every vehicle in the Braxton PD and scanned the distinctive trio of towering loblolly pines to her right.

Lou was wrong. This wasn't another gravel road leading to nowhere. Not to her.

This was almost the precise location of her first knock-down-drag-out with her dad. They'd driven this way to inter her rabbit at the county's only pet cemetery, and ended up stopped in the middle of the road after she'd threatened to jump out while the car was still moving. The fight had started over her mother's death—that and the fact that, ever since, her dad had refused to so much as mention the woman's name. It'd ended when one of her dad's fellow deputies had heard the commotion while chatting with the cemetery's caretaker and driven back to see what the shouting was about.

The present returned with the abrupt knock on her SUV's window, causing Kate to flinch and drop her keys. Concern etched her boss' craggy features as he peered in.

"Sorry, Kato. Didn't mean to startle you."

She scooped the keys from the floorboard and tossed them on the driver's seat as she climbed out. "I was just thinking."

"'Bout the first vic? I'm hopin' that means you got somethin' useful from the VA."

"Possibly." Though in light of this second body, she wasn't as sure. "Ian Kusić worked in the lab at Fort Leaves. The doc who owns the prescription pad I found had an emergency. His receptionist called back just before I pulled in here. The doc can see me tomorrow at noon. I plan to get there early to question any of Kusić's fellow workers who may be around." Both of Little Rock's VA hospitals admitted patients. That meant their labs were staffed twenty-four/seven.

Lou accompanied her up the line of cop cars toward the yellow tape barrier that had already been strung. Liberal use of the portable flashing cherry she'd attached to the top of the Durango had cleared her path all the way to Braxton, affording her desperately needed time. They now had ninety minutes before the sun set and the. evidence-obscuring dark settled in. Nothing like a ticking clock.

"Thanks for holding the scene."

Lou shrugged. "No one was anxious to take your place, not even the gas bag the governor's office sent over from the state police. By the way, he'll be liaising with you directly and providing whatever you request by way of manpower and equipment—or I want to know about it."

Kate tipped her head toward the uniform chatting with Tonga near the meat wagon. "That him?"

Lou nodded.

"Okay. I'll take it from here." Kate accepted fresh gloves and paper booties from Lou, along with a MorphoIDent. Pocketing the latter, she left him beside his sheriff's sedan and headed toward the ME. The uniformed trooper took one look at her face and stepped aside to give her room to speak to Tonga privately.

Ironic, really. Her twisted mishmash of scars might freak the bejeezus out of kids and civilian adults alike, but to vets like the one she'd met at Fort Leaves and her fellow deputies and cops? Her face was the silver bullet of credentials. She might be relatively young and female, but she'd already confronted more than this or any other state trooper likely would in his entire career—and had survived to tell the tale.

Well, she'd survived. Despite what those in Liz's profession preached, it was enough.

It had to be.

Kate snapped on her gloves and donned the booties that matched Tonga's. "Ready?"

The ME shook his head, but he followed her beneath the tape, reluctance slowing his steps as they closed in on another line of jumbo-sized, brown paper sacks. Kate understood his hesitation. She was supposed to have left scenes like this behind when she left the Army. In fact, she'd counted on it.

Though after retrieving and cataloguing the contents of that first set of bags, she no longer knew why. The hate and ugliness in the world never seemed to cease. If not hers, this latest installment would've landed in someone else's lap, forever weighing on that detective's heart and soul.

Steeling herself as best she could, Kate retrieved her flashlight as she and Tonga reached the first sack. Lou must have admonished the trooper, because he'd remained behind the crime tape with everyone else.

Excellent. The fewer boots contaminating the scene, the better.

Kate swept the beam of her light through the late-day shadows that had begun to cloak and shade the gravel around the bag. The rocks closest to them were disturbed.

Tonga pointed to the shoe-sized dips. "You think he's getting lazy?"

She shook her head. "Too shallow. Probably from the woman who stumbled across the scene." Someone strong enough to take down two victims and carve them up might not be tall, but he—or, yes, possibly she—had one hell of a solid set of working muscles. Kate retrieved her smartphone and snapped an exterior photo before shining her flashlight inside the already opened sack. "We've got another right hand, severed cleanly at the wrist and sealed in what appears to be food-grade plastic."

Unfortunately, the textured side was fused to the victim's palm. If the left hand had been sealed in the same fashion, they might not be getting an ID until they got the parts to the lab for detailed processing.

Tonga withdrew the hand, leaving Kate to flatten the sack. He laid the hand on the bag while she withdrew the Morpho-IDent from her pocket. As she'd feared, she couldn't get a decent capture. She pocketed the device as Tonga traced his fingers over the thin cuts encircling the base.

"More flex cuffs?"

Kate nodded as she absorbed the evidence of a second terrified and futile struggle.

She and Tonga shared a sigh as they stood and headed for the next crisp, oversized bag. As with the remaining sacks, the top was still folded over and neatly stapled. Kate snapped another exterior shot and reclaimed the MorphoIDent as the ME unbagged the victim's left hand.

Damn. The killer had fused the textured side of the plastic to this palm too. By accident? Or in an attempt to delay identification? Since the latter meant the asshole was learning, Kate hoped for the former as she flipped the hand palm down to note the absence of indentation on the ring finger.

Based on the size of the hands and the coarse, blond hairs sprouting from the skin, their victim was most likely male and possibly unmarried. And that was all they had, because, once again, the MorphoIDent failed to grab a decent capture.

Kate shoved the device in her pocket and snapped a close-up before helping Tonga to his feet. She used her flashlight to examine the road as they worked their way to the next sack, and the next. Four bags in, they'd fallen into a sullen, symbiotic routine, with her snapping an exterior, Tonga breaking the seal and retrieving the part, then waiting for her to flatten the sack and take the close-up.

By the time they had the torso laid out, they'd confirmed that the victim was male, but little else. At least, nothing they hadn't already discovered that morning. As with Ian Kusić, this man's vital organs were missing, along with his penis, scrotum and windpipe.

That had to be significant...but how?

Tonga traced the grisly slice that ran the length of the victim's chest. It gaped slightly to reveal the emptiness within. This too was identical to Kusić's.

"Does this mean—" The knot in the ME's neck bobbed as he swallowed. When he couldn't seem to finish it, she did.

"Yes. We're dealing with a serial killer." Just saying it out loud, much less trying to comprehend how so much calculated evil could exist inside one person, caused gooseflesh to ripple across the back of Kate's neck.

Her mood fouled further as the location of that gooseflesh served to underscore the contents of that final, waiting sack: another severed head. Given how unprofessionally she'd handled the first head's unbagging, how was she going to get through this one without losing what little lunch she'd managed to consume?

"Ready?"

This time the cue had come from Tonga, and this time it was her boots that trudged behind his. Tactical breathing supported her through the short journey to the final sack. She quickly snapped the requisite exterior shot. In an attempt to stave off the coming reaction—at least until she was alone in her SUV, or better yet, smothering her face in Ruger's fur—she shifted the flashlight and phone to her left hand to clamp the fingers of her right around Max's watch. The slow, soothing twist began as Tonga reached inside the bag.

It helped.

She continued to twist Max's watch as the shrink-wrapped head surfaced, again utterly and inexplicably transfixed by that line of raw flesh at the base.

"You know him?

Surprised, she glanced at Tonga. "No. Why?"

He pointed to her fingers. They were still twisting. "You seem...unusually upset."

The pronouncement thrummed between them. Thankfully, it generated enough embarrassment to wrench her brain back from wherever it had desperately wanted to go. Kate released the watch and knelt to flatten the final sack. Tonga still held the head. The moment he laid it on the bag, she snapped the photo and clambered to her feet.

"I need to brief Lou, then confer with the crime unit about where to place the flood lamps."

They *were* losing light, damn it.

Tonga, bless him, didn't argue. He simply nodded, his ebony features blending with the coming dusk. "I'll be fine."

She wished she could say the same. Kate gave the severed head wide berth as she made her escape. She forced herself to slow her pace as she headed toward the crime barrier, using her flashlight to combat the shadows infesting the nooks and crannies of the gravel, searching for a miracle in the form of solid, case-breaking evidence with every step.

She came up empty.

Lou met her at the tape, his own resignation stamped amid the exhaustion carved in his face. "It's him, isn't it? The same bastard as this mornin'."

"Yes."

"Please tell me you got somethin' that'll let us nail this son-of-a-bitch."

"Wish I could, boss. He's just too good, and he's getting better. The victim's male. The textured side of the plastic is fused to his palms. I couldn't get an ID. As for the rest of the parts, the vital organs, windpipe and genitalia are missing like before. Also, we may be dealing with another vet, or he could've been active duty. I didn't see any tattoos, but this guy's got an impressive collection of shrapnel scars on his torso and arms, and his hair's regulation short with a standard military taper up the back. The rest of his body is—was—in excellent physical condition too."

"It's official, then. We've got a goddamned serial murderer on our hands."

"Worse. Obviously Tonga can't nail down time of death here. But as with Ian Kusić's, these parts are fresh, meaning we've got a killer with hellishly short cooling down period...as in *none*. In fact—" She stopped. The rest was supposition.

"Spit it out, Kato."

Still, she hesitated. "It's more guesswork than anything at this stage."

"That's more than I got to go on." Lou swept his hand behind them, encompassing half their department. "Hell, it's more than any of us got. At least your guesses are educated."

She dragged in a breath and crawled all the way out onto the professional limb. "Okay. I think he killed both men and packaged their parts at the same time, then dumped the bodies during the same trip."

Lou nodded slowly. But she could see the doubt creeping in.

"I know. It sounds crystal ballish. But consider this: the day never warmed up. That means the ground out here's been equal to the temperature inside a refrigerator since the middle of last night, but no earlier, since yesterday was unseasonably warm. That being the case—if both victims were killed, packaged and dumped at roughly the same time—there shouldn't be a difference in the condition of the flesh. To use your analogy from this morning, think meat counter. The longer the dark cuts of pork and beef are displayed, the more blood leaks into the package and the darker the meat gets. The lighter portions get slimy. And heat exacerbates the effects. I've seen both sets of parts up close, and there isn't a noticeable difference."

Which begged the horrific question: how many more of these grisly displays had been left in and around the deserted outskirts of Braxton for them to find?

"I also think the killer sorted the parts from each body at its respective dump site. He then bagged each piece, stapled the top, and set it out before moving on to the next. I know this because the sacks were too pristine to have been jostled during transport. And there's the order. These parts were lined up in the same order as Kusić's, starting with the right hand, then left, ending with the upper torso and head. Yet there are no marks on the bags to indicate what's inside. So how did the killer know? He couldn't have—unless he bagged them on site. And that order? It may mean something, if only to him."

But what?

Kate stared at the state trooper loitering beside Tonga's wagon. "Boss, we don't need a liaise-fest with the governor's office. We need a full-blown task force in place, and we need it yesterday. Hell, a psychologist from the FBI's Behavioral Analysis Unit wouldn't hurt."

The demand for a task force, much less a BAU agent, didn't

have a thing to do with her scrambled psyche. She needed help. Without it, the body count would only rise.

If it hadn't already.

"Understood. Give me tonight, and I'll get it." The steely determination in Lou's eyes convinced her.

"Okay." Kate glanced past the sheriff's shoulder to where their burliest guys were marking time at the edge of the crime tape with the flood lamps. "I need to get those set up, then see if Tonga's learned anything new."

Lou nodded. "Keep me posted."

"Absolutely." Kate headed for the tape and paused to give the okay to set up the lamps. As she bent low to dip beneath, the setting sun caused something to glint just past the edge of the gravel road. Instinct sent her toward it.

Probably a shard from a long-shattered beer bottle some high school kid had tossed from the car on his way to a drunken reenactment of Stephen King's *Pet Cemetery.*

Kate reached the glint.

It was glass. But the green chip was also lying in the middle of the sweetest thing Kate had seen all day. Hell, all year. A partial tire impression. Though the convex curve was narrow in width, it was a good three feet long.

Please, please. Let it be fresh.

Kate chanted the makeshift prayer as she hunkered down, gravel digging into her elbows as she eased the beam from her flashlight along the impression.

Adrenaline spiked.

She laid the MorphoIDent near the tread to mark it and jackknifed to her feet to head back to Lou. She cornered him in front of his sedan. The second he hung up, she lit in. "Who found the bags?"

"An out-of-towner. Name's Glory Thacker."

"Where'd she park her vehicle? At the cemetery? Was anyone

with her?"

"She was alone. And she weren't drivin'. She's some kinda cross-country cyclist out visitin' her aunt—Thelma Payne. The woman says she's been takin' this route past the cemetery most evenin's for a week now. She didn't have her phone while she was cyclin' tonight, so it took half an hour for her to get home. I called you as soon as we hung up."

"Did she see anyone on this road? Headed in either direction?"

"No. I asked. She was alone comin' and goin'."

Hope rivaled Kate's adrenaline, surging to the lead. She noted the distance between the grill of Lou's sedan and the crime tape. There didn't appear to be enough room to squeeze in another vehicle, but she wasn't assuming anything. "So you were the first responder on the scene. And your car's been parked right here since you arrived? You didn't back up, or ask anyone else to move behind you at any time?"

"No and no. Kato, what the heck you gettin' at?"

She forced herself to temper her excitement. It wasn't easy. "It could be nothing." Or the beginning of everything. She waved Lou up to the tape and slipped beneath. "Careful. Step where I've stepped and, for God's sake, stay on the gravel."

She directed her flashlight's beam at the ground just past the MorphoIDent, bathing the slender section of the tread impression she'd discovered in white light.

Lou's hand clapped down to squeeze the blood from her good shoulder. "What are the odds it's his?"

"Pretty good." Excellent, in fact. Kate shifted the beam to catch the impression from another angle. "See the crisp edges on those tiny walls of dirt? It's fresh. Given yesterday morning's rain shower and last evening's wind, I'm thinking it's *very* fresh. Plus, most kids talk their folks into visiting Rover and Fluffy on the weekend."

It was Friday night.

And the only thing of note at the other end of this road was the pet cemetery.

Lou let go of her shoulder and spun around as fast as a man his age and size could manage. "Get a Denstone kit over here for a tread cast. Pronto!"

Kate retrieved the MorphoIDent and handed it to Lou as he swung back. "Boss, we'll need the crime unit to go over this strip of road with a magnifying glass as soon as dawn hits. And send them back to the Kusić scene. Have them comb Old Man Miller's drive and every road and lane that feeds into it." If they were lucky, they'd find a matching tread.

Lou nodded. "I was on the phone with the governor's aide when you found me. He and his boss'll be pissin' over the particulars for hours, but the task force will happen. Tell Tonga to prep these parts for Little Rock, then crate Kusić's. I want both victims at the state lab by midnight. He won't argue. I spoke to Tonga when he arrived. These autopsies need fancy tools and expertise he just don't have."

"Will do."

Kate left Lou's side to make room for the approaching forensic tech tasked with photographing and prepping the impression for casting. She linked back up with Tonga at the victim's torso. He appeared to be studying the tool marks at the base. "Learn anything new?"

The ME shook his head. "Unfortunately, no."

Kate passed on the sheriff's instructions as she assisted Tonga to his feet, then turned around to join the remaining crime scene techs as they began their careful canvass of the remainder of the road. Despite the luminescent bump from the flood lamps, the search yielded zilch. They'd have to regroup and resume at first light.

Until then, more than enough time had elapsed to allow the

Denstone to harden. Kate reached the spot where she'd found the impression as one of her dad's grizzled old hunting buddies carefully packed up the resulting cast for transport.

"Hey, Emmett. How's it look?"

"Sweet." The tech's grin rivaled the flood lamps as he lifted the lid to the cardboard box. "See these lateral grooves at the tire's shoulders? Combine 'em with the number and angle of these circumferential groves running down the center here, and I'm all but certain we're looking at a Starblaze. I'll confirm at the lab."

"Is it unusual?"

"Unfortunately, no. Starblazes are a cheap, all-season tire. They fit a wide range of cars, smaller SUVs and pickups." In other words, one hell of a list.

But there was more. Why else had the tech's grin split almost to his ears?

Emmett motioned her closer as he tucked a magnifying glass in her hand. "Here's where you plant one on my cheek, Deputy, 'cause we just may have this bastard." He pointed to the right of the cast, midway down. "See this inch-long sliver here? That's a clean slice in the rubber. And see this depression here? Something's caught in the tread. A small rock or the like. And the void here? That's another gouge, though this one's more a missing chunk of rubber at the tip of this groove. All three flaws are within a palm's width." He encouraged Kate to spread her free hand to verify his makeshift measurement. "See?"

She did—and promptly bussed the man's whiskered cheek as he'd predicted. "Emmett, you're a miracle worker."

Kate held her breath as the man hefted the evidence box and carried it down the road with all the care and reverence its contents deserved.

Emmett was right. Starblazes might be a dime a dozen, but a Starblaze with this particular trio of flaws was the equivalent of a vehicular fingerprint. All she had to do now was find the vehicle that went with it.

Unfortunately, that was easier said than done.

Six hours later Kate was still fixated on tires. She and her fellow deputies had spent nearly every moment of those hours combing through gravel bathed in the blinding light of flood lamps. Other than the grisly packaged parts of their second victim, that tread impression was the only thing they had to show for their efforts. They'd still be searching if Lou hadn't called a halt.

His new orders were for sleep.

Despite her reluctance, she'd willingly complied. Lou's rationale was sound. Rest was something they were all going to need in the coming days if they hoped to remain sharp enough to catch this bastard.

Kate succumbed to a bone-weary yawn as she turned her Durango onto her private lane. A quarter mile farther, she turned again, taking the left arm of the Y that led to her split-log home. As expected, Ruger was waiting, the slight hitch in his gait masked by the moonless night as he loped down the lane to meet her. He spun around as he reached the driver's door to race her SUV to the garage. Kate punched the remote and waited for Ruger to enter, then pulled in after. He returned to her door as she exited the Durango, eyes sharp and tail thumping vigorously from side to side despite the hour.

The Shepherd let out a loud *woof* as she spread her arms so he could launch himself into their nightly hug.

"I missed you too, buddy. I truly did." She laughed as he bathed both sides of her face with his tongue, equally. "Good day, huh? Better than mine, I'll bet."

His second *woof* rattled the chimes attached to the door that led to the kitchen. Ruger clamored down from her arms and pushed through the flap, whining as he waited none too patiently for her to lower the garage door and follow him inside.

The wooden cuckoo clock she and her mom purchased on a trip to the Harz Mountains heralded midnight as Kate dumped her phone, flashlight and 9mm on the counter. Ruger had already planted his mammoth paws beside the fridge and was nudging his nose into the seal of the door. He knew better than to break it. He'd done so on his own when she'd been late about a year ago, and gobbled the treats within until he'd made himself sick.

He hadn't violated that seal since. Unfortunately, while the lesson had included a heck of a bellyache, it hadn't included patience. His sharp bark underscored that fact now.

"I know, I know. It's past snack time."

Three hours earlier, her own hunger had turned to cramps even an endless supply of cop coffee couldn't ease. Ruger scooted backwards as she opened the fridge to retrieve the over-sized tub of sliced cheddar. Guilt bit in as Kate spotted the Styrofoam clamshell that held her leftover burrito from dinner the night before. Dinner she'd shared with Grant.

He hadn't texted her all day. Clearly, he was trying to give her the time and distance he'd failed to provide this morning.

Doubt crept in.

If her suspicions were correct, and Grant was seeing a shrink, perhaps she should wait to break things off. Although facing off with some quack who thought he understood the shit-storm of her life hadn't worked for her, that didn't mean it wouldn't help him. She might be ready to punt on their relationship, but she did want Grant happy. Healthy. Someone who'd survived that hellhole ought to be.

What if last night hadn't been about her at all?

What if Grant had broached her POW experience in order to talk about his own tours in Iraq, and his lingering guilt over his brother's death?

If she hadn't shut him down so quickly and completely, Grant might've told her about his meeting with Liz...and whoever else he'd either seen or was seeing at Fort Leaves.

Ruger's pointed whine forced Kate to realize she was still staring into the open fridge.

She closed the door on the clamshell and set the tub of cheese on the counter. Peeling off several slices, she tore the cheddar into sections and lobbed them at Ruger. His succession of happy half-groans and growls warmed the kitchen, and her, as he snatched each piece from midair.

It was gone too quickly, at least according to Ruger. His tail thumped hopefully as she returned the tub to the fridge.

"Sorry, bud. There's food in your bowl if you're still hungry."

His head slumped to tell her what he thought of that. Kate held firm and he finally shuffled toward his bowl. Her own belly resumed its cramp as she refilled his water.

There was still that burrito.

Food or shower? It was a tough choice.

The shower won.

Kate dug her credentials from her pocket, as well as the business card Liz had given her. She was about to set them on the counter when Ruger's ears perked up. A moment later, he growled. Unlike his earlier vocalizations, this one was low and deadly. And meant just for her.

"What is it, buddy?" Coyotes again?

A good twenty seconds later, she heard it. Not coyotes.

A car.

Kate considered Grant—until she heard the engine rumble up the right side of the Y of her private lane. The side that dead-ended at her empty cabin.

Squatters?

It wouldn't be the first attempt.

Kate slipped her credentials in her pocket and swapped Liz's card for her flashlight and 9mm. Based on her previous experience with a group of meth-head, would-be freeloaders, she chambered a round and shushed Ruger. He took the order in stride, patiently waiting for her to unlock the glass double doors that led to the backyard. Within seconds, they were off the deck, Ruger on her left as they slipped across the clearing to thread through the surrounding woods.

Kate slowed her pace as she reached the outer edge of the trees that separated her primary home from the cabin.

There were no lights visible.

But there was an SUV.

It was parked beside the cabin, facing away from her. She couldn't tell if someone was in the driver's seat or not. It was too dark. Ruger shaved the distance between them down to her jeans and his fur as they crept forward. Kate stroked his head once, then tapped his shoulders to signal him to wait as she continued on. Glock raised, she breached the tree line. The SUV's engine roared to life as she reached the gravel drive.

The vehicle shot backward, tires squealing then spinning as it executed a sharp stop followed by a whiplashing one-eighty-degree turn. She clicked on her flashlight, but the SUV's driver had beaten her to the punch, blinding her with the vehicle's brights as he switched them on, gunning the engine as he headed straight for her.

Shit.

Kate dove back into the tree line, sucking in fallen leaves, pine needles and dirt as she hit the ground. She sprang to her feet, coughing violently as she whirled about—but it was too late. The SUV was already halfway down the lane, plate obscured.

Figures.

Within seconds, Ruger was at her side, barking his head off and visibly torn between giving chase and remaining behind to protect her. She won...but he wasn't happy about it.

Kate stroked her hand down the Shepherd's hackles and he quieted. Once more glued to her side, Ruger accompanied her out of the trees and into the lane. Kate reached the spot where the SUV had executed its one-eighty and holstered her Glock.

Great. The SUV had torn up the edge of her cabin's lawn. She swept the beam from her flashlight over the damage at her feet—and froze. Blinked. Her free hand on Ruger's back to hold him in place, she knelt and adjusted the light to double check what she thought she'd seen. For the second time that night, gooseflesh rippled across her neck. The tread she found matched the impression she'd located six hours earlier.

She spread her palm, as Emmett had encouraged, to estimate the distance between the small slit, the elliptical depression and the triangular void that waited.

The trio fit.

Coincidence?

She'd rarely believed in them. Three years with the Army's military police and another six with CID hadn't changed that. Nor had the last three with the Braxton PD.

Kate stood and pointed to a spot several feet from the impression. "Ruger, sit. Guard."

He complied.

Irony ratcheted in as she left Ruger to protect the impression while she headed for her garage and the spare Denstone kit she kept within. She might not know who was slicing up bodies and leaving the results strung out along Braxton's back roads, but there was an outstanding chance he knew her.

5

———

Soft. Cold. Wet.

Ruger.

Kate shot upright, pushing through the fog of sleep to assess her surroundings—herself—as she realized the Shepherd was trying to wake her, and why. The ragged breaths ripping in and out of her lungs. Her heart pounding so hard and fast she feared her ribs would crack. The twisted sheets. The ice-cold perspiration soaking her T-shirt.

Night terror.

Her second one in as many nights. This time she couldn't lay the blame at Grant's feet either. Not all of it.

Stress.

According to the blowhard she'd been forced to see at Walter Reed and the stack of internet articles she'd amassed on her own since, night terrors were brought on and exacerbated by episodes of severe tension and anxiety. Score one for the doc and the internet. Between that display of cobalt blue pottery at Fort Leaves and the grislier, bookending finds out on Braxton's gravel roads, she was swimming in it.

She was also swimming in sweat.

Ruger, bless him, didn't care as he lurched up onto the bed, his massive body landing across her lap. She returned the compliment and unconditional love by burying her face in his fur. It took a good minute for her breathing to calm. Several more for the familiar muck that had been swirling in to ebb.

She finally straightened and ruffled the Shepherd's ears. "Thanks, buddy. I'm okay now."

The lighter patches of brown in his brows furrowed, as if to convey that he wasn't quite as convinced.

Kate withdrew her 9mm from under her pillow anyway and slipped out from beneath the Shepherd to stand. Ever the intuitive one, Ruger bounded off the bed and followed her out of the room. Kate glanced at the dial on her dive watch as they headed down the hall. It was just past three-thirty a.m.

She shifted direction, heading for the living room instead of the kitchen and Ruger's trusty dog door. After nearly getting mown down by an SUV with a potential serial killer at the wheel, she wasn't taking chances with the only family she had left.

She peered through the trio of glass slats in her front door to scan the porch and modest clearing beyond. Once she was sure they were empty, she caught Ruger's stare.

"Stay close, okay? *Close.*"

Kate opened the door and waited as he bounded off the porch and into the middle of the yard. Either he'd understood or he'd sensed her mood because he halted there. Once Ruger had finished his job and was safely inside, she relocked the door and headed for the shower. Oh-dark-thirty or not, she was still coated in sweat.

Kate stripped down as she waited for the water to heat. The watch strapped to her wrist caught her attention.

Her mood.

Other than Max's watch, everything she'd brought back from

the Army was sealed away in a footlocker. Was that why she couldn't seem to move on?

Was Grant right? Were Kusić and vets like him better off with their memories, photos and the rest of their military trappings out in the open, surrounding them?

Was that how others had made it across this eternal, soul-wracking divide? By truly embracing the darkest part of the suck, instead of ignoring it?

And, yeah, hiding from it?

The thought simmered as Kate showered, taunting her with the possibilities. The faintest flicker of hope.

She dried off and donned a fresh Braxton PD tee and sleep pants, then crossed the hall before she chickened out.

Ruger stood by her side, staring at the door to her father's room alongside her. She wasn't surprised. Canine or not, he always seemed to know. Understand.

Even when she didn't.

"Well, buddy, do we go in?" It wasn't as though Hypnos was intent on tiptoeing her way. If anything, tonight had proved that the god of sleep was running like mad in the opposite direction.

Ruger's soft *woof* decided it.

Kate twisted the knob and pushed the door open. She flipped the wall switch. Dust motes swirled up beneath the overhead light, dancing amid the stale air as she and Ruger entered the room together. A thicker, more stubborn layer of dust coated the footlocker she'd dumped at the base of her dad's bed upon her return to Braxton three and a half years earlier. Neither the room nor the trunk had been opened since.

She'd have willingly given the remaining honors to Ruger were he not hampered by his lack of opposable thumbs.

Resigned, Kate knelt down and popped the latch on the trunk. The lid creaked as she lifted it.

A fresh swirl of dust clouded the air, choking her along with the memories. She pushed through both.

Setting aside the black velvet case that had been sealed since the day it had been handed to her, she reached for the small album beneath. The worn leather cover eased into her palms like an old, cherished friend—mostly because that was what the album contained. Friends.

Ruger stretched out on the rug beside her as she leaned back against the wall, tucking his muzzle into his paws as she opened the album. Most of the photos had been taken in Afghanistan or Iraq with her mom's old 35mm film camera, though a few of the prints had been snapped during her military schools and courses. One by one, Kate traced her fingers over the faces of her fellow soldiers, some still with this life and others—far too many others—not.

She managed to hold onto her tears until she reached a dozen-plus photos of a sandy-haired Army doctor nearly four inches shorter than her. In every shot, he was wearing the antique dive watch that now cradled her wrist.

"*Max.*"

She hadn't realized she'd breathed his name out loud until Ruger lifted his head.

His nose nudged her thigh.

She scrubbed the tears from her cheeks before they could drip onto his fur. "It's okay, buddy. I'm okay."

Oddly, here, now, sinking down onto the rug to curl up with Ruger and her photos of Max, she was.

SOMEONE WAS KNOCKING ON HER DOOR. NO, MAKE THAT pounding. And Ruger was barking...somewhere. Kate pried her eyes open, her confusion deepening as she realized she was lying face down on a rug...and something harder. Her footlocker confronted her as she sat up.

It was open.

She was still in her father's room.

She scooped the album from the floor and set it on top of the velvet case, closing the lid to the locker as she stood.

"Calm down, Ruger. I hear you."

He must've made one of his nightly rounds of the house after she'd dozed off and gotten trapped on the opposite side of the door. Unless her dad had adjusted it after she'd left for the Army, it still wasn't level. And Ruger was frantic.

He bounded into the room as the door opened, jumping up to lick and nuzzle her neck. "Hey, I'm fine."

As for the person pounding on her front door, she wasn't so sure. Kate hurried down the hall, glancing through the narrow slats as she unlocked the deadbolt.

Lou. Please, Lord, no more bodies.

"Christ, Kato, you scared the shit out of me! I figured you'd be up for your crack of dawn run, so I called—then again and again. But you never answered. So I drove over. I been out here bangin' on this door forever. I could hear Ruger goin' nuts, but you wouldn't show. I was about to break the damned door down."

"Sorry. I think I left my phone in the bathroom last night. I couldn't sleep, so I took a shower. I must've sunk into a near coma afterward to miss Ruger's racket."

Lou reached up and tapped her good cheek. "I can see that. Where'd you doze off—or rather, what did you doze off on?"

Kate traced her fingers where Lou's had been, dipping into a chasm almost as long as her most prominent scar.

The photo album.

"Doesn't matter." She shook her head, attempting to shake off her lingering exhaustion. She understood why her brain was still so fogged when the clock in the kitchen *cuckooed* out six. An ugly hour for Lou, even on the best of days.

Which this wasn't.

"What happened?"

"We got an ID on the second victim."

Not a fresh set of bags, then. Relief swamped her, easing the clenching in her gut. "What's his name?"

"Prints came back to a Jason Dunne. And you were right." Lou dug a memo pad from his uniform pocket to check his notes. "Dunne's a former Army sergeant. Seth got ahold of Dunne's folks up in Fayetteville. Accordin' to the folks, Dunne got out a few years back and took a job at Walter Reed. Somethin' to do with the admin department. He worked there for three years, then wanted to move back to Arkansas, so he transferred to Fort Leaves six months ago." Lou shoved the memo pad home. "So that makes two vets, both workin' outta the same Little Rock VA. I'm wagerin' my retirement it ain't a coincidence."

"You're in the money, then." The VA hospital tie was no more a coincidence than the tread impression she'd found last night after that SUV had tried to run her down.

Before she could brief him, the sheriff cocked his head toward the kitchen. "You got coffee goin'?"

Déjà vu skittered in as Kate spotted the hound-dog hope in his eyes. She'd seen that same look time and again when she was a teenager. Whenever a particularly troubling issue came up at work—especially in connection with the two murders her dad had been tasked with solving—Lou would show up out of the blue, though usually later in the day, and bum a cup of coffee, and her dad would help him talk it out.

They'd talk, and she'd listen.

Sometimes, on a particularly tough case, she swore she could still hear her dad dispensing advice...to her.

"Kato? You okay?"

She pushed through the déjà vu. "Just an old memory." Fallout from that comatose nap on the floor of her dad's room. Either that or dust poisoning. "I was about to put the coffee on. You want some?" Caffeine just might temper the coming explosion.

She hoped.

"Hell, yeah." Lou followed her and Ruger into the kitchen, automatically commandeering his old seat catty-corner from what would've been her dad's at the table. "Guess I had enough adrenaline pumpin' in. Once I made that first unanswered call to you, I didn't even miss the caffeine. For a while there, all I could think was, he's takin' down Army vets. And, well—" Pink tinged his neck as he shrugged. "—you're a vet."

Guilt twinged as that SUV flashed in again. "I still have a few of those pumpkin muffins Miss Janice dropped off at the station. Want one?"

At his nod, Kate retrieved the elderly woman's plastic food container from the fridge. She popped two of the remaining muffins in the microwave and prepped the caffeine while they warmed.

Coffee began scenting the kitchen as she let Ruger out for his morning job. The dog was either smarter than even she believed or channeling her lingering vibes, because once again, he didn't stray from her sight. Kate filled the Shepherd's bowl with kibbles and scratched his ears as the last drops of the coffee splashed into the pot. She filled two mugs and pushed one across the scuffed oak tabletop as she joined Lou.

Her dad had been dead six years now, and she couldn't sit in his chair either.

"Thanks." Lou washed a bite of muffin down with a sip from his mug as he stared at the empty seat at the head of the table. "I still miss the old guy every day, ya know?"

Though she was a bit more conflicted on the subject, Kate

nodded. And it was time to broach an equally dicey topic. "I have something to show you."

She reached behind her to retrieve the oversized cardboard box she'd set on the counter last night before she'd gone to sleep the first time. Sliding the box across the table, she motioned for Lou to check the contents.

He looked inside, then at her. "I don't understand. Did you stay behind with Owen last night and make another cast? I thought we couldn't do that."

He was correct. Casting an impression generally destroyed said impression, which was why photos were always recorded first. "That's not from the Dunne dump site. Though I did pour this one myself...just after I arrived home."

Terror pierced Lou's stare as the implication hit. A split second later, he was on his feet, towering over her. "*What?*"

"Now, boss, I'm fine. So don't—"

"Don't 'boss' me, young lady. I asked, *what*—as in what the *fuck* happened and why didn't you pick up the goddamned phone when it did?"

So much for easing into this with coffee and a muffin. "Hey, I'm happy to fill you in now...but I'd prefer to do it with you sitting—and relaxing."

The red mottling his entire face scared her more than that relentless SUV, bearing down on her. Lou's ticker hadn't been subjected to the best of care, given his lifelong fondness for everything deep fried and salted.

He must have realized she was serious, because he sank back into his chair. He took a deep breath, then another, as his color faded to almost normal. "Let's try that again. What happened last night, and why didn't you call me then—*Deputy?*"

She fielded the second question first. "Because you wouldn't have slept. Besides, I've got my 9mm loaded and within arm's reach twenty-four/seven, and I have Ruger."

"Who couldn't *wake* you."

Kate shrugged. "He got trapped on the opposite side of the door." And since he couldn't open round doorknobs, he'd been stuck. "It won't happen again." At least Lou hadn't pinged on the slip regarding her perpetually loaded and at-the-ready sidearm. She kept going, lest he double back to it. "Everything was fine when I arrived home. I was contemplating dinner when Ruger and I heard an engine. It was headed toward the cabin. I figured it might be meth squatters again, so we went to check it out. We found an SUV. Black, dark blue, possibly green—I can't be sure. The driver had his lights off at first. By the time I switched on my flashlight, his headlights were on, and he was headed straight for me."

"Son-of-a-bitch. You coulda been killed, missy."

Kate let the nickname slide. "Trust me. Even at full throttle, that bastard was slower than a compound of damned near a dozen terrorists, jacked-up on radical jihad."

Not that she remembered exactly how she'd taken out the majority of said terrorists. Lacking her own coherent eyewitness statement, the write-up for her Silver Star had relied solely on forensics. But Lou didn't know that, did he?

The oblique reminder that she'd proven eleven times over that she could take care of herself did the trick. Lou's color and breathing finally returned to normal. He'd be okay letting her out of his sight now.

"This bastard really *is* after you."

Or not. "I don't think so. Not the way you fear."

His color spiked. "The hell he ain't. Kato, this twisted shit has probably been stalkin' you. How do we know this ain't his way? How he done it before, watchin' those other two before he grabbed them?"

"We don't." But even after a night's stunted sleep, her instincts still voted no. Those same instincts that had seen her through multiple tours in Afghanistan and Iraq and gotten her safely home—against some seriously crappy odds.

Besides, the killer hadn't invaded her home last night.

Those damned night terrors had.

Then it happened—the niggle that had been worming its way through her brain since Lou had briefed her on the second victim finally surfaced. "Where does Jason Dunne live?"

"Little Rock. Somewhere near the river. His folks gave the particulars to Seth. Why?"

The niggle began to dance.

"Something else is going on here, boss. I understand the killer dumping Kusić's body in our jurisdiction. Kusić might've worked in Little Rock, but his trailer's just outside town. But Dunne doesn't live here. So why dump his body here?"

"Convenience?" Lou took several sips of coffee. "You said it yourself. The asshole hacked them up at the same time, then dumped 'em together too. There was no thinkin' involved, just his own sick, two-for-one special so's he didn't have to recon the backroads of another outta-the-way town. Hell, maybe he was in a rush to grab his next victim—*you*—and was savin' time."

"It's possible." But her gut resisted. "Except this guy's smart. Methodical. Organized to the anal-retentive level. I think those dump sites are crucial to him. We figure out why, and we may have the key to catching him. Either way, you can relax. I do not fit his sweet spot. His victims might be Army vets, but they're male. I fit the first category, but I'm missing a rather distinctive organ for the second. I think he saw me working this case—on the way to or from one of the scenes, or visiting that trailer—and he got curious."

It's not as though he couldn't have discovered her name easily enough. She might not have worn her uniform shirt and name tag yesterday, but there was only one female deputy in the department. With her so-called credentials, the mayor had insisted on touting them—and her—on the town's website.

Heck, she might even get the mayor to see the wisdom in taking the page down now.

Lou reached for his coffee, but he didn't drink. He rolled the outside of the cup between his palms. "If you're right, that means he's trackin' the investigation."

Kate nodded. And the very fact that he was tracking it opened up a whole new window into the killer's psyche. One they'd all have to be careful not to get dragged through. "We need to watch our backs, boss. *All* of us."

"Yeah. But you're the one he decided to follow home."

So far.

The thought hummed silently between them for several moments before Lou broke it. "I'd feel a whole lot better if you stayed with Della and me. The spare room's made up. Ruger's welcome too. There's safety in numbers, and you know it."

Kate was touched by the concern in his eyes. Humbled. But reality won out. It always did. There was no way she could risk having a night terror at someone else's house. Anyone's. Especially her boss'.

Not even Grant knew she had them. The fear of waking in the throes of a sweat-slicked, heart-pounding horror she couldn't even recall wasn't the only reason she'd never slept over once she and Grant had begun having sex, but it had been the leading contender.

"I'll be fine. Besides, you said the approval for the task force would be coming through today." She slid the second warmed muffin in front of Lou, hoping he'd accept the not-so-subtle change of subject with it. "As soon as it goes live, we'll have so many cops underfoot, a killer this smart will be avoiding Braxton like the plague."

"It's already done."

"That was quick." Especially for a governor known to take a poll before he decided on breakfast.

Lou shrugged. "All due to you. And a leak at the state police." He snagged the muffin, split it in two and polished off the first half. "Our liaison couldn't keep his trap shut. He tipped off a buddy at the Associated Press. Gave 'em damned near everythin', includin' stuff we'd intended on holdin' back, like the missin' organs and genitals—*and* the ID on both victims. The governor's beyond pissed. The gas bag was fired half an hour ago, but it's too late. The story'll be in most of the mornin' papers. The rest by night."

"*Jesus.*"

"Yeah, but somethin' good came out of it. Seems the AP reporter had a contact high up at the VA. The reporter called the VA official for a comment late last night. Instead of respondin', the VA official called his buddy at the White House. With all the scandals about vets dyin' while on endless waitin' lists, seems the president decided he didn't want to look like a commander-in-chief who couldn't give a shit about vets gettin' outright murdered and hacked up ta boot."

"Great." She'd wanted help, and help they absolutely needed. But when had anyone in DC ever truly provided it without screwing something up along the way?

"Don't look so bummed." Lou washed down the rest of the second muffin with the last of his coffee, and set the mug on the table. "This whole snafu is gettin' us not one, but two FBI agents, and one's from the BAU like you asked."

That perked her up. The latter's expertise would indeed be worth putting up with the added headache of keeping federal politicians in the loop—and the time wasted unraveling the knots they'd inevitably cause.

She hoped.

Kate retrieved Lou's mug and headed for the coffee pot. "When do the agents arrive?"

"They should be flyin' in late this afternoon. They're makin' their own travel arrangements. Which is a good thing—" He tapped the edge of the box containing the Denstone cast she'd made out by her cabin. "—'cause we got enough to do with checkin' both crime scenes during daylight for more of these. As soon as the agents get to Braxton, I'll let you know. You're headin' up the task force on our end. I'm sure they'll wanna meet, so y'all can divvy up jobs and resources between us, the state police and the Little Rock FBI office. Also, the data dumps came back for Ian Kusić. Unfortunately, it ain't much. Carole's still combin' through it, but the land-line traffic looks to be normal stuff. So does the cellular data. Here's where it gets bad—Kusić's cellphone went dead a week ago Friday at Fort Leaves. Carole says the SIM card was probably pulled out when he was snatched. No word yet on the man's computer."

Given this bastard's savvy in everything else he'd done, Carole was undoubtedly correct about the SIM. Which probably meant there'd be nothing of note on Jason Dunne's land and cellular lines either.

This case was going to come down to good old-fashioned grunt work.

Kate set the refreshed mug on the counter instead of passing it to Lou. "I'd best get going then. I've got that meeting with Dr. Manning at noon." Afghan pottery or not, it was more important than ever that she speak to the shrink and anyone else at the hospital who knew Kusić and Dunne. "I'll get Dunne's address from Seth and search his place first."

Anything she found could only help formulate her questions for the doc and anyone else who knew the victims.

"Agreed." Lou resealed the cardboard box. "I'll have Owen run this over to the forensics guys first thing."

"I'd appreciate it." Especially since the station was in the opposite direction from Little Rock.

Lou nodded as he stood. "Between the search of Dunne's residence, your meetin' with the doc, and the task force setup, you might not be back 'til late tonight. What are you gonna do about Ruger?"

He had a point. She couldn't leave the pet door unlocked. Not with that bastard potentially lurking around.

"I'll phone Grant. He's off today." Since he'd offered his services yesterday, he shouldn't have a problem with her cashing in a raincheck.

"If he cain't make it, you let me know. I'll be tellin' the men to include our homes in the patrols, especially yours. Whoever has this sector can always stop by to let him out."

Given Ruger's lack of affection for most males, it wasn't her first choice. But if Grant couldn't stop by, Ruger would just have to deal with it.

"Sounds good." Kate crossed the kitchen to retrieve her spare house key. "Just leave this with dispatch. That way, Grant or one of the guys can grab it. Also, since my liaison's been fired, would you have someone call the governor's office for me? I'll need someone to access both Kusić's and Dunne's military records and email them to me. Since the murders occurred here, I doubt there's a connection in their previous careers. But you never know."

"Got it." Lou slipped her spare key in his pocket and hefted the cardboard box. She and Ruger followed him to the living room. He paused at the front door to stare down at her—hard. "You be careful out there. You even think you've spotted this guy, you call me pronto. Understood?"

"I will. You be careful too. And make sure Della keeps the doors locked and that Mossberg 500 she keeps loaded with buckshot close by." It wouldn't hurt for everyone even remotely connected to the investigation to be vigilant.

A crisp nod, and Lou was gone.

Kate retrieved her phone from the bathroom, then headed for her bedroom to dress and don her shoulder holster and its comforting Glock. Given last night's unwanted guest, she added a backup piece above her right ankle and grabbed her Braxton PD jacket and cap, punching Grant's number into her phone as she and Ruger made their way to the kitchen.

Grant's voicemail picked up as she poured the remaining coffee into her travel mug.

Odd. Unlike Lou, Grant was an early riser. Even on weekends. If he'd decided to sleep in, wouldn't he have reached for his phone in case it was the hospital?

Kate left a message regarding her spare key and asked Grant to let her know whether or not he could let Ruger out.

She texted Seth next to request the address for Dunne's residence. Within moments Seth responded, following up with an offer to contact the apartment building's manager to have someone standing by to let her in.

Kate sent Seth her estimated time of arrival and sincere thanks.

Five minutes later, she was polishing off the final muffin from the fridge and grabbing her travel mug as she said goodbye to Ruger. Thirty more, and Kate had hit the dregs of her coffee as she greeted a gradually waking Little Rock.

She parked her Durango across the street from the building corresponding to the address Seth had provided, and took in the ten-story facade.

This was where Jason Dunne lived?

While both victims' abodes abutted water, Dunne's commanded a mid-capital overlook of the revitalized Arkansas Riverwalk district. The gray brick and glass exterior purred loaded, prowling bachelor in a way in which that trailer's interior could only dream, and she hadn't even made it past the doorman. Bemused, Kate locked her SUV and headed for the silver-haired, sixtyish gentleman beneath the striped awning.

The doorman's stare zeroed in on the shredded side of her face long before she reached him.

She gave the man a courtesy moment to absorb the close-up before flashing her credentials. "Mr. Fisher? Deputy Holland, Braxton PD. A fellow deputy of mine gave you a call about one of your tenants—a Jason Dunne?"

Silence.

Kate pocketed her credentials. The doorman hadn't even glanced at them. He couldn't get past the scars.

"*Sir?*"

"Uh, sorry. I didn't mean to stare."

"It's not a problem." It truly wasn't. Not if he let her into Dunne's unit quickly and without a fuss. "As I was saying, Deputy Armstrong gave you a call, roughly half an hour ago?"

The man shook his head, but it wasn't so much a response as an effort to allow his brain to catch up to a conversation it still didn't seem able to register. "Sorry. It's just... Wait—I know where I've seen you. *Holy shit.*"

The man's cheeks turned ruddy as he realized he'd let the expletive slip.

Again, she couldn't care less. Because his stare had finally reached her eyes. It was a start.

He cleared his throat. "You're that soldier-gal. The one that made the papers a few years back. You took down a dozen of those bastards over there, all by your lonesome. Well, I'll be *damned.*" He shook his head again, albeit this time with palpable amazement. "I never met a real live hero before."

She had. And she wasn't it.

She should know. She'd served with more than her fair

share. All she'd done was kill eleven assholes who'd tried to kill her first. That didn't make her much of anything, except desperate and lucky.

But try and convince this man of that.

Kate accepted the man's jackhammer handshake and equally effusive thanks for her service. To argue would've insulted him. She backed off a pace as he released her hand.

"Mr. Fisher, you did receive a call from Deputy Armstrong with the Braxton PD?"

"I did indeed. Yes, your deputy said you'd be by. I did as he asked and phoned Mr. Marlette. He's happy to let you inside. I just need to unlock the place and wait while you look around."

Kate frowned. She was hoping the bout of hero appreciation would afford her an hour or two alone with Dunne's effects. It might've if someone else hadn't been in the picture. "Am I correct in assuming Mr. Dunne sublets the condo from Mr. Marlette?"

"Yup." The doorman ushered her inside the lobby. "Just how did Mr. Dunne die? I mean, he was young. An ex-soldier like you. Still used the gym almost every day. Good man too. Always a heartfelt greeting. Brings home the occasional girl. Real pretty ones too. Though I gotta say, he's been going through them a bit quick this past month, if you catch my meaning. And I'm not sure he was happy about it. Heck, the last one ducked outta here red-faced and in tears. Wouldn't even meet my eyes. For a moment, I could've sworn—"

The doorman halted his diuretic assessment and glanced over Kate's shoulder, as if he was suddenly conflicted about how much he'd already revealed, and what he'd been about to add.

Before she could prod, he shook his head. "As my wife would say, no sense gossiping about the dead. Did I ask how Mr. Dunne died? Your deputy didn't say."

Kate noted the stack of newspapers beside the reception

desk as they headed for the elevator. The doorman must not have read the article hugging the paper's upper fold, or he'd have known as much as she did. More if the article's nauseating title panned out. "Garbage Man Hacking Up and Dumping Little Rock Vets?"

Lovely. They'd named the son-of-a-bitch. Every reporter in the state would be crawling out of the woodwork, trying to one-up each other with every fact and/or speculation they could beg, borrow or outright steal from anyone connected to the investigation. She needed to get in and out of that condo, and over to the VA before one of them beat her to the victims' co-workers.

"Deputy?"

Kate spotted the expectation in the doorman's eyes as he paused beside the lift. *Right*—cause of death. "I'm sorry. I'm not authorized to say how Mr. Dunne died." She offered up an apologetic, one-worker-bee-to-another frown. "I'm just the one tasked with following up."

"I understand."

"When was the last time you saw Mr. Dunne?"

"Oh, gosh. To be honest, it's been awhile." He appeared to give it some thought, and then, "Last Saturday. That's not unusual though, 'cause Mr. Dunne, he works nights." The lift arrived with a ping. The doorman motioned Kate through the doors as they opened. "After you."

A buzzer sounded at the desk, causing him to hesitate before he could join her.

"I can let myself in and look around while you take that. I promise not to touch anything until you join me."

The buzzer sounded again.

Hero appreciation had its rewards after all, because the man nodded. He withdrew a key from his suit pocket and tucked it in her outstretched palm. "Fourth floor, Unit D. I'll follow as soon as I can."

"Take your time." *Please.*

Kate punched the corresponding button as the doors closed, impatiently counting the passing seconds until the lift slowed and they reopened. Dunne's sublet was to the right, a corner unit that provided an expansive view of the river as she stepped through the door. Mindful of the doorman's arrival, she retrieved her protective booties and gloves from her pocket and swiftly donned them before commencing her walk-through of roughly two thousand square feet of yet another man cave.

As with Kusić's trailer, leather, technology and personal excess reigned. The living room and both bedrooms sported wall-mounted plasma monstrosities, and she even noted a dark satin-finished acoustic guitar in a corner. Not to mention a small, but drool-worthy home gym and a private jacuzzi that took up damned near half the man's covered balcony. All that was missing was the cat and evidence of the victim's military life.

Scratch that.

While the cat was still missing, she'd found the Army encased in a seven-inch electronic frame on the master bed's nightstand. The photos rotated through slices of what appeared to be Sergeant Dunne's tours of duty in both Afghanistan and Iraq.

Kate retrieved the frame as a shot of Dunne and a buddy hamming it up in an outdoor Afghan souk filled the screen. Punching the button at the top to freeze the rotation, she studied the market stall on Dunne's left. The one displaying local tribal weapons and knives.

She recognized the slightly out-of-focus vendor.

In Army MP and CID circles, Hamid Kasi had been known for dealing in two categories of wares, those that were routinely displayed in his stalls, and those that weren't. Afghan black tar heroin fell into the second category...along with an impressive collection of black-market Soviet-era weapons and munitions. The AK-47 she'd found in Kusić's closet flashed in.

Coincidence...or a connection?

And was either one enough to have put both victims in the path of their killer?

Though her gut still leaned toward a Fort Leaves link, Kate retrieved her phone and snapped a second-hand copy of Dunne and his buddy at the souk.

She used the buttons at the top of the frame to push through the remaining photos at a faster pace, but none of the others caught her interest or her suspicion.

She returned the frame to the nightstand and opened its drawer. Nothing of interest in there either. The nightstand on the opposite side of the bed yielded a MacBook Air and an iPad. She fired up the laptop, but the contents were password protected.

The iPad wasn't.

She checked the texts in iMessage, but again, nothing stood out. Neither did Dunne's saved documents or his email. Though, strangely, he'd cleaned out his "sent" and his "trash" folders. Who did that?

Intrigued, Kate opened the iPad's browser and clicked on a random item in its history. A six-year-old article loaded from the LA Chronicle's On War page. She started skimming the article, then stopped when she realized she was already familiar with its contents. It concerned a local Afghan woman who'd claimed she'd been grabbed from behind and pulled into a bombed-out hovel off an alley in Kabul one afternoon by a US Army soldier. There, the soldier had raped her. Due to the obscuring burqa she'd been wearing, the woman hadn't been able to ID the soldier—just his unit patch.

The same patch Kate had spotted on Dunne's uniform in one of the photos in that electronic frame.

Had Dunne attacked the woman? If not, had he known the perpetrator? Could Dunne have been blackmailing a former unit mate all this time?

Unfortunately, there was an excellent chance the answers had died with Dunne. Not only had a local Afghan Army interpreter come forward the next day to claim that he knew the accuser and had seen her coming on to his countrymen and foreign soldiers alike, but the woman had also vanished the next night. Evidently she and her brother had taken an evening stroll. It seemed that, at one point, the brother had turned a corner only to realize she was no longer beside him. By the time he'd gotten around to backtracking his steps *two hours later*, his sister had vanished. No further explanation had been offered by the curiously unconcerned brother—or the woman's remaining relatives.

Everyone had wanted the matter dropped. Including the US Army.

And so it was.

Kate made a mental note to request the Army's file on the incident as she closed the iPad and returned it to the nightstand.

Just in case.

Guilt pinched in as she turned to canvass the contents of Dunne's dresser. She ignored it. She hadn't lied to the doorman. Technically, she wasn't touching anything.

Her gloves were.

Unfortunately, her gloves failed to find anything out of the ordinary in Dunne's dresser...until she reached the second drawer. A soft whistle escaped her lips as she moved the man's silk boxers aside to take in an impressive stash of tubes filled with steroid cream.

A habit Dunne had fallen into in the Army?

As with sleeping pills and prescription pain meds, steroid abuse had been on the rise among Uncle Sam's finest long before she'd gotten out, and still was. It also explained the impressive musculature and definition of Dunne's body—in the parts that had been strung out on that gravel road and in the photos that had been taken years ago in Afghanistan. Steroids might also explain that rape in Kabul.

And something else.

What had the doorman implied? That not only had the door to Dunne's bedroom taken on a revolving feel, but that his latest companion had left red-faced and in tears.

Had Dunne displayed violence stateside too?

If so, no charges had been filed as of this morning.

According to the first victim's landlady, Kusić had fought with his girlfriend as well. Had the two investigations revealed an illicit drug connection after all—between the killer's victims? If so, could it explain that cash she'd found at Kusić's?

Kate snapped a photo of the steroids and closed the drawer. She texted Seth, asking if the crime unit had unearthed evidence of steroid abuse at Kusić's trailer, then sent a text to the ME, requesting that Tonga add them to both victims' drug panels.

She pocketed her phone as she headed for Dunne's closet. This time, her gloves came up empty. She moved through the living area next.

It, too, was a bust. As was the kitchen.

Last stop, the spare bedroom.

She doubted anything there would stand out and it didn't—until she reached the windows. Unlike those in the living room and the rest of the condo which overlooked the river, these had a prime view of the streets to the west of the building.

Along with Grant Parish.

Kate rubbed her sleep-deprived eyes and refocused. That was definitely Grant. But why?

What was her almost ex-lover doing near Jason Dunne's

condo at eight in the morning on a Saturday? She hadn't told Grant where she was headed, nor would anyone from the station. Even in the event of an emergency, Lou would've had Grant contact her via her phone, or called her himself.

Kate checked her phone for missed calls. Except for the trio the sheriff made while she was comatose on her dad's floor, she hadn't missed one in days, texts included.

She dialed Grant's number and watched as Grant paused at his SUV to retrieve his phone. A chill slithered in...because he didn't answer.

6

KATE STARED down from Jason Dunne's window, stunned, as she watched her lover pocket his ringing phone and climb into his Bronco. Within moments, he'd started the engine and pulled into the street. As he turned the corner and drove out of sight, her second call of the day went to his voicemail.

It didn't make sense. Why would Grant ignore her? Was he pissed she'd asked him to check on Ruger?

Only that made even less sense since he'd offered to perform the favor twenty-four hours earlier.

More importantly, what was Grant doing here?

Yes, he might've read that article in the paper. But so what? She'd met Grant's friends. Dunne wasn't among them. And while both men were employed by the Little Rock VA, they'd worked across town from each other. Not to mention, Dunne had worked in admin. Grant was a surgeon. Even if they had worked out of the same hospital, he wouldn't have been asked to identify Dunne's remains.

Besides, even if Grant had been asked to make an initial ID pending the arrival of a relative, wouldn't he have been more likely to take a call from her, even initiate his own? Because even if Grant knew about Dunne's death from someone at the VA and not from that article, he would still have known that the man's body had surfaced in her jurisdiction—and made the connection that the case she'd been called out on yesterday morning was part of the same investigation.

Instead, Grant had shown up at the victim's apartment.

Kate rubbed her temple to ease the headache that was beginning to set in. Between last night's shortfall of sleep and this morning's need for speed, the mystery of Grant would have to wait.

The doorman would be joining her at any moment.

But even after Kate resumed her search of the condo's spare bedroom and came up empty, he hadn't arrived.

A good forty-five minutes had passed. Had the buzzer from one early-rising tenant led to another? Or had the press already tracked down Jason Dunne's residence?

If so, they'd be on their way here en masse, if they weren't already crowding the lobby.

With nothing left to search for save electronic and human fingerprints, and DNA, it was time for her to leave.

Kate locked the condo's door and retrieved a crime scene warning sticker. Scrawling her signature below the department's phone number, she sealed the notice across the door and its jamb, then headed for the elevator.

A minute later, she stepped into the lobby in time to hear the doorman arguing into the phone over his refusal to make a statement, on or off the record.

Fisher severed the call and tossed his phone on the counter as she reached him. The stack of newspapers had grown shorter by at least the one now spread out across the lower shelf behind his station. To her disgust, a grainy shot of that second line of paper bags had made it into print just below the fold of the newspaper's front page.

It appeared to be the only surreptitious photo the trooper had managed to snap with his cellphone.

She hoped.

Kate laid a hand on the doorman's quietly quaking shoulder. "Are you okay?"

His reddened gaze met hers, growing redder as he shook his head. "It's not fair. Mr. Dunne was a soldier. He was willing to give his life for this country." Fisher's index finger stabbed the photo. "What kind of monster could do that to someone like him?"

She didn't answer. Fisher wouldn't have liked her reply anyway, because there was no real explanation. The shrinks would disagree, of course, but she'd slogged through too many death investigations to ignore the truth. Some people were just evil.

The doorman seemed unable to tear his stare from that riveting photo, but he nodded as if he'd heard her. Or, perhaps, he too could see the truth.

"Mr. Fisher? I know this isn't the best time, but I need to ask you something."

His gaze found hers. It was wet.

Lord, she hated this part. "It's about Mr. Dunne. I know you'd prefer to respect his memory, but I need to know. Was he having issues with his temper? That last girl you saw leaving? Did he...attack her?"

The doorman's sigh was riddled with guilt. "I should've reported it, shouldn't I?"

Yes. But there was no sense dragging this man through hell. Fisher had crawled halfway there on his own.

She set the condo key on the counter. "I doubt it had anything to do with his death." She hoped. "But I do need it confirmed. Information like this helps us piece together the bigger picture to get to what and who caused his death. What-ever you tell me won't make the papers. Not from me."

"Yeah, he was rough. I don't know if he did more, but I do know he hit the poor thing, at least. I could see the marks from his knuckles."

"Do you think it was the first time—and the first girl?"

"I do. It's just a feeling, though. I can't prove it."

Unfortunately, neither could the woman in Kabul. And, now, no one ever would. Kate sighed as that box packed with Benjamins nudged its way back into her brain as well. "About the condo. Do you know if it came furnished?"

"Yes. I showed the place when the rental agency couldn't make it. Almost everything in there belongs to Mr. Marlette. I assume that's why he ordered me to stay with you."

"Sir, as far as I'm concerned, you did."

A furnished unit explained the rich, but spartan vibe. And there was the timeframe. According to Seth's conversation with the victim's parents, Dunne had moved to Little Rock six months earlier. Not long enough to expand much beyond the basics if he was working a hectic schedule.

"You wouldn't happen to know how much he was paying in rent, would you?"

"For a corner unit? Three thousand, easy. More, since it was furnished."

Wow. A prime view of the Arkansas River commanded more than she'd assumed, and definitely more than she had. And when she tossed in that home gym and private Jacuzzi on the balcony? The place should've been far too plush for a VA admin employee as well.

Her suspicion must've shown, because the doorman shrugged. "I think his family comes from money."

"Did Mr. Dunne say something to that effect?"

"No. Just another feeling. That, and his car. It's not in his slot, but he drives—drove—a Stingray convertible."

Muscle man, muscle car, muscle apartment.

It wasn't a definitive connection, but it dovetailed into what she'd seen in Kusić's man cave. Especially if the doorman's feeling of family money turned out to be just that—a feeling.

Kate made a mental note to have Seth get the Stingray's registration information and put out an all-points bulletin to locate it, if he hadn't already. She'd also have Seth call Dunne's folks back and see if they were underwriting that car and the rest of Dunne's lifestyle.

Either way, had someone noticed that lifestyle? Was the killer a co-worker or a patient at Fort Leaves? Someone who'd become aware of Dunne's pursuit of material goods, along with the pursuits Kusić had worked harder to keep hidden? The killer could even have been an unequal participant in whatever had been funding said pursuits and had become resentful.

But her instincts voted no.

If the deaths had been simple murders, either scenario might've made sense. Kate stared at the grainy photo in the paper. Those bags were about something else. Something deeper.

But what, damn it?

The desk phone rang, flashing the call sign of a local TV station in its caller ID window.

The doorman ignored the phone as he retrieved a business card from his breast pocket. He laid the card on the counter and nudged it toward her. "You need anything else, Deputy, call. I'll pick up for you. So long as you promise you won't rest 'til you catch this bastard."

Kate nodded. While she couldn't guarantee that she'd catch the guy, she could promise that she would keep up the hunt for as long as she was able.

She traded Fisher's card with one of hers. Retrieving her phone, she swiped through her photo stream until she reached the one of Kusić in his Blues. "Sir, have you ever seen this man with Mr. Dunne?"

He studied the photo. "Is that the other victim?"

"Yes. His name's Ian Kusić."

"No. I've never seen him. Sorry."

"Not to worry. It was long shot." Kate started to turn toward the door, then stopped.

Speaking of long shots. She stepped up to the counter, waiting as the doorman refolded the paper and shoved it out of sight. "Mr. Fisher, when I was upstairs, I saw someone in the street. A doctor. Did he come inside? Ask for me?"

"Doc Parish? No. I was about to open the door for him but he stopped shy of the sidewalk to take a call. He was still talking when he turned around and left."

"I don't understand; you know Grant Parish?" He must, since by the doorman's own admission, Grant hadn't come in.

The doorman shook his head. "Just his name. He's been by since Mr. Dunne moved in. Usually once a week, sometimes more. Doc Parish is—was—a friend of his."

For the second time that morning, a niggle began deep in Kate's brain. This time, she tried to ignore it—unsuccessfully. It grew stronger as she bid the doorman goodbye and headed outside to climb into her SUV and start the engine.

Deep down, she'd known why Grant had ignored her call. Grant had known Jason Dunne, but for some reason, he hadn't wanted to risk *her* knowing that.

Why?

The question dogged Kate as she drove through Little Rock. It was still dogging her as she reached Fort Leaves and pulled into a sparsely populated parking lot. She was almost grateful for the emotional buffer the mystery provided as she made her way into the hospital.

The lobby was nearly empty.

But it wasn't quiet.

As she'd feared, the press was closing in. Fortunately, the hunt was still being conducted by phone. Unfortunately, fielding the calls involved the combined efforts of all three frazzled hospital employees behind the main desk.

Kate stopped several paces away to wait her turn.

"I'm sorry, sir, but we just can't give out—" The woman on the left skimmed Kate's jacket, palpable relief entering her eyes as she spotted the Braxton PD patch on Kate's sleeve. "—I'm sorry; I have to go." She hung up and waved Kate closer. "Oh, thank God. Please tell me you have news. Better yet, that this is all a truly *horrible* mistake."

Kate spotted the newspaper on the counter. She hadn't had a chance to read that article, but according to Lou, their loose-lipped trooper hadn't held anything back, including the victims' connection to this facility.

"I'm afraid not, ma'am." She retrieved her credentials and held them up. "Deputy Holland, Braxton PD. I have an appointment at noon to talk to one of your doctors about Ian Kusić. I know I'm terribly early, but in the interim I was hoping to speak with anyone else who knew Mr. Kusić or Mr. Dunne."

The woman's face fell. "I wish you'd called. I could've spared you the wait. No one working today knew Jason Dunne. Not even enough to say 'Hi'. He worked weeknights and he was just so new, you know? I can help you with Ian. He worked out of our lab. His girlfriend Abby works in the lab too, but she won't be in until later this afternoon. She has the swing shift."

Kate glanced at her watch. A round trip to Braxton took an hour on a good day. That would leave her forty minutes tops to check in at the station before she had to start back for her appointment with Dr. Manning.

"Do you know Abby's full name? Her address?"

"Carson—Abigail Carson. I can get her address. But if you're hoping to talk to her at her apartment, I should warn you. She's not home. She took the week off to visit her sister in Jonesboro. Abby became an aunt on Tuesday."

"And you're certain Ms. Carson's still coming in this evening? She's not remaining with family?"

The receptionist's blond curls bobbed as she nodded. "Yeah. I spoke to her myself. I told her the director said it was okay if she took some time after...what happened. But she was insistent that she wanted to work. Personally—" The receptionist's voice sank to a whisper as she leaned over the counter. "—I think she's in shock. She was in love with Ian, you know? But they broke up right before her vacation."

"Do you know why?"

The woman frowned as she straightened. "Abby wouldn't say. Can I offer you a place to wait for your meeting? There's an employee lounge in the back with muffins, tea and coffee."

"Thank you. I'll just find the cafeteria." She was still working off her own muffin from earlier that morning. Even a vending machine sandwich would better power her rapidly maturing day. Kate withdrew a business card and slid it across the counter. "If you or your co-workers think of anything you feel I should know, please don't hesitate to call, day or night."

The receptionist nodded as she took Kate's card. "I will. As for the cafeteria—" She used the card to point toward the main hall. "—just turn there and follow the signs."

Kate's phone vibrated as she crossed the lobby. She turned into the suggested corridor as she retrieved her phone to see who'd texted her—and collided with something hard and...vaguely familiar.

Surprised, Kate looked down into the exact pair of dark brown eyes she'd spotted in this very hospital the day before. Eyes that were now openly laughing at her—and himself.

"Well, well, officer. Looks like you're champing at the chance to take me up on that coffee date. It's these gorgeous toes of mine, right?" The man winked at her. Winked.

Unable to resist, she matched his smile. She wasn't sure which surprised her more: that wink or the gallows humor regarding his missing lower legs. "Good morning, Sergeant Fremont."

"Ah..." If anything, his grin deepened. "...*and* she was intrigued enough to seek out my name. This just gets better." He eased the edge of his wheelchair backward. As it cleared her bruised thighs, he tipped back on his wheels and spun the chair around until they were both heading down the hall from whence he'd come. "Shall we, officer?"

It was that lopsided smile. Amazingly, it took the sting out of the scar slashing through his own cheek. "Shall we...what?"

"Coffee and a chat. I believe you promised me both."

She had. Not only did she actually want to share them with this man, but given what Liz had revealed yesterday, it would be prudent in light of her growing investigation.

Her phone vibrated again.

Kate checked the incoming text. It was from Tonga, letting her know he'd received her request to expand both victims' tox screens to include steroids. With nothing left to impede coffee and an impromptu interview, she pocketed her phone.

"Caffeine it is, Sergeant. But it's not officer. Or even Deputy Holland. For a fellow former grunt, it's Kate."

"Kate, it is. And it's not sergeant anymore, either. It's just Steve."

Since he knew the layout of the hospital better than she did, Kate followed as Fremont led the way.

She glanced down as he paused for her to precede him into the cafeteria. "I am curious as to how you knew." He'd appeared so certain yesterday.

"That you were Army too?"

Kate nodded. With most former soldiers, there were clues. Hair still rigidly in regs, or defiantly no longer anywhere near them—like his. There was also the lingo they used and, of course, the innate perfect posture, even while at ease.

The sergeant hadn't spoken to her long enough for her vocabulary to have given her away. And she was a deputy. A profession that would account for her posture.

Fremont must've been in tune with her thoughts, because he shook his head as she accepted the chair he'd pulled out for her at a private bistro table for two. He swung his wheelchair around and pushed the second seat out of the way so they could sit across from each other. "It's your eyes."

"Excuse me?"

All trace of teasing had fled, and his were somber now. Dark. "It was the look in those baby greens of yours in that elevator on our way up yesterday afternoon. And again in that hall when you catapulted out of the shrink's office."

Peachy.

The worst of it was, he was spot on. She had catapulted. But earlier, in that elevator? "Was it that obvious?"

"To civilians? Probably not. But to those of us who've been there and don't really care to talk about it—ever?" His nod was slow, resigned. "We've all seen that look in our own eyes often enough. Why do you think we avoid the mirror?"

Kate sighed. "I know why I do."

He didn't respond for several moments. Then he shrugged. "Okay, I'll bite. Why?"

Confusion struck at his genuine curiosity. "Isn't it obvious?"

Her confusion deepened as the man leaned across the tiny table to trail a finger down her most prominent scar.

"Because of this?" He shook his head as he straightened. "Those are sleep wrinkles, Kate. They don't do a damned thing to dim beauty like yours—unless you're a blind bastard to begin with." That incorrigible grin of his dipped back in. "Which, of course, I'm not. Though it could be the uniform. I confess, I always did have a thing for them...especially on women."

That earned him a laugh. "Really? Then why go Special Forces? I don't think I need to tell you, there still aren't too many women in and around that specialty, especially in country."

"True." That crooked smile was downright contagious. "But the cute ones seek you out in droves when you're off the clock. At least until I misplaced the lower half of these." He leaned back in his wheelchair to slap his thighs. As with most amputees Kate had seen, what was left appeared out of proportion with those sculpted shoulders and arms. He shrugged. "But enough about me. It's your turn. What's a gorgeous cop like you doing in a moldering place like this, two days in a row?"

The smile faded from his face as the somber tide returned. "Or do I already know the answer?"

Unfortunately, he did. And so did she.

"You read the newspaper."

The sergeant nodded. "They're hard to miss when you actively seek 'em out at night to use for cover and concealment, especially when it's cold. But in this case, the horror of it was still tumbling through the hospital grapevine when I arrived."

"Unfortunately, it's all true. I'm attempting to track the victims' movements. Piece together their last days. See what pops."

"Got anything yet?"

"Not really. What little I have uncovered leads to you."

Her earlier confusion had passed to him. She could see it

furrowing through the space between his brows. "Sorry, I don't
— ahhh... Ian Kusić. You heard about the argument."

"From what I understand, it was hard to miss."

His smile made a brief reappearance. This incarnation was
grim. "I should hope so. I was trying to make a point."

"And that being...?"

Hesitation replaced the confusion.

"Sergeant?" She'd used his rank deliberately, hoping a subtle
backslide to CID agent/enlisted interviewee footing would work
in her favor. It might've, if the man across from her hadn't spent
years in the field, honing his own particular set of skills.
Damned Special Forces.

He shook his head. "*Steve.* Thought we'd agreed...*Kate.*"

"My apologies."

He shrugged. "It's your job."

"Does that mean you're going to help me do it?"

The hesitation returned.

Just when she was certain he'd refuse, she felt him waver.
Sigh. "What the hell. I caught him stealing."

Not what she'd expected. But perhaps she should've. The
first time she'd collided with Fremont's wheelchair had been
outside the shrink's office.

But Fremont was still visibly loath to rat out a fellow vet,
especially a murdered one. He'd need prodding.

"Was it a prescription pad?"

The furrowed brows returned. "Son-of-a-bitch. He was
stealing drugs, too?"

"I don't know. I found a pad of scripts at his place. Obviously,
it wasn't his." But if that pad wasn't what Fremont had caught
Kusić lifting, what had the lab tech been into? And would it
explain that stash of money?

"Steve, I need to know—what did Kusić steal?"

"Blood."

"Excuse me? Did you just say...blood?"

The sergeant nodded.

"Why?"

"Hell, if I know."

For some reason her brain was still having trouble processing the concept. "How?"

That earned her another grim twist of his lips. "The man worked in a lab; how do you think he was taking it?"

"With a needle?"

Fremont nodded. "And a phlebotomist's vial—or vials. In my case, five of them were drawn that last time. *One* had been ordered by my doc."

O-kay.

Kate sat there as the accusation sank in. There really wasn't much else she could do, let alone say.

"Look, I know how crazy this sounds. But I'm not the only one he stole blood from."

That perked her interest. "How many others?" And would they verify this bizarre allegation?

"At least three that I know of."

"I'd like to speak to them."

The sergeant shook his head. "I doubt they'll be down with that. All three are homeless. Given the way the VA's been treating them and every other vet, they're not exactly trusting of The Man at the moment, if you get my drift."

She got it, but could she even believe it? *This?*

Good Lord...blood?

Why could Kusić even want it? So he could leave it at the scene of some future crime to throw off suspicion? It wouldn't work. The anticoagulants in the vials would be detected, something a lab rat like Kusić would know. Had he hoped to moonlight as a black-market supplier to wannabe vampire nut jobs? Except he couldn't have swung that either. Fremont was talking about vials of blood. Not pints.

Kate almost smiled at the absurdity of it...until another niggle took up residence at the periphery of her brain.

It burrowed deeper.

Pulsed.

Kusić's body had been completely drained of blood before his parts had been packaged. As had Dunne's.

Sergeant Fremont leaned closer, staring into her eyes as if he could see her thoughts churning. Considering.

Was this a connection?

"I could talk to them for you. Maybe even see if I can track down any others. Ones who *will* talk to you."

It was tempting.

But on the remote chance the accusation was true *and* somehow connected to those deaths, there was no way she was letting another vet anywhere near this killer.

Much less one who could no longer maneuver the way he used to be able to maneuver.

"I can't ask you to do that. In fact, I forbid it. Even if this is connected—"

Fremont stiffened. Stared at her. Hard. "I'm not an invalid, Kate. I'm just missing a couple limbs. You, of all people, ought to be able to see beneath the scars."

Before she could apologize, yet another niggle burrowed in. This one caused her to stiffen.

Missing limbs. Vets.

Someone who loved a vet? Someone so grief-stricken over his father, brother or son's missing parts that he'd enacted a horrific plan of revenge to reconcile his own grief?

The theory fit...and it didn't.

"What is it?"

She blinked. "Sorry?"

"You've made a connection. About your case." He reached out to gently tap a finger beneath the corner of her right eye. "I can see it, right in here."

She smiled. "Your tax dollars at work."

"You going to share the results?"

No. But since he knew this place and the people who staffed it better than her, she did offer up another name. "Jason Dunne. Did you know him?"

"Dunne. That's the second guy you found, right?"

"Yes. He worked in admin here at Fort Leaves. Walter Reed before that. He also served in Afghanistan—according to some photos I found, at the hospital on Bagram, possibly elsewhere."

Fremont shook his head. "The name doesn't strike a bell. I'm not surprised. I did split my tours between Afghanistan and Iraq, but most of my fun was gleaned well outside the wire. You got a picture of the guy?"

Kate retrieved her phone and pulled up the DMV photo Seth had sent her during their text exchanges earlier that morning. She pushed the phone across the table and waited while the sergeant studied it.

He pushed the phone back. "Yeah. I've seen him. I'm usually here in the mornings, sometimes afternoons. Though the bus stops running about eight, I like to clear out by five to reach the shelter in time for dinner. But a couple Thursdays ago, I was working late with someone on the ward." Fremont tipped his head toward the phone. "Those blond curls and bucketload of freckles? I saw him then."

"I don't understand." She'd assumed Fremont was just a patient. "You work here too?"

So why was he eating and sleeping at a homeless shelter?

The sergeant shook his head. "I just volunteer. But it gives me something to do. Fills the days. So, it's good for me; good for them. Don't get me wrong. They've got some decent folks working in the clinic gym and on the 3C ward, but sometimes a civilian just can't relate enough to really motivate the troops, you know?"

"And that's where you come in?"

His grin flashed. "What can I say? It's my charming, effervescent personality. Inspires 'em almost every time. And when it doesn't, I shove my proverbial boot up their ass."

Kate smiled as memories of her drill sergeants drifted in. She could easily picture this man's face among them. Her amusement deepened.

"You should join us."

Her amusement fled. Instantly.

"Me?"

"Why not? We can use help. The more the merrier, so to speak."

Come back here? To a VA hospital? On a regular basis?

Silence locked in.

Tension thickened it—in her.

"You don't have to decide now, Kate. Just...keep it in mind."

"I will."

But she wouldn't, and they both knew it.

Worse, he'd already forgiven her.

She retrieved her phone and stared at the blank screen. Anything to escape the stark, knowing compassion still simmering across the table. "About Mr. Dunne. Did you notice anything unusual when you saw him that night?"

Fremont knew damned well she'd changed the subject deliberately. But he let it slide. Shrugged. "Not really. He and a bunch of others were coming out of that shrink's office upstairs. The one we collided in front of. They, ah, run a PTSD group therapy session out of there in the evenings."

Grant.

She had no business thinking about him now, much less

obsessing. But she couldn't help it. Was that how Grant knew Dunne? And why he'd not only spent so much time with the man, but decided to *not* mention it?

Kate tapped the phone to rouse it from sleep and swiped through dozens of photos until she found the one she'd taken the day Ruger had grudgingly let Grant toss him a ball.

She zoomed in on Grant's face and nudged the phone across the table. "Was he in that corridor too?"

The sergeant looked down at the photo, then up. He didn't answer.

"Steve?"

This smile failed to reach full potential. Probably because her not-so-subtle "we're friends" reminder had been as deliberate as her attempt at CID agent/interviewee had been.

"Please. It's...important."

He sighed. "Look, that's not a question I have the right to answer. Helping a murder investigation is one thing. But this? I might not partake in share-fests myself, but that doesn't mean I don't understand vets who do—and usually don't want to be pegged as attending. I gotta respect that."

"Please."

"Christ, lady." Another sigh filled the corner of the cafeteria. This one was darker. Resigned. "Shit. Yeah, that guy was hanging out around the door too."

Nervous energy flooded Kate. She had to stand. Move.

Now.

Before she sprinted from the cafeteria, possibly the hospital. "I'll, ah, get the coffee."

Given how long they'd been sitting here without it, it was a poor excuse. But the sergeant honored it with a nod.

"I'll be waiting."

Kate talked herself down as she headed for the stainless-steel urns. First her friend Liz, now Sergeant Fremont. It was true. Grant was doing the one thing they'd both sworn they'd never do. He was spilling his guts to a shrink. And others. That's why he'd started pushing her to do the same.

But damn it—so what? Fremont was right. Just because she'd gleaned squat from her mandatory share-fests, didn't mean Grant couldn't benefit. He had his own demons to fight. Ones that had been tormenting him since his tours as a surgeon on the front lines, wading through the dangling flesh and oozing fluids of the dead and dying. How could she even think about begrudging him peace?

She shouldn't.

She *wouldn't*.

Kate filled two Styrofoam cups with coffee and headed for the register. She paid before she realized she'd failed to ask if the sergeant took cream or sugar, or if he even preferred his coffee caffeinated. Too late now.

She turned toward their table—and stopped. Fremont wasn't alone. A petite brunette and towheaded toddler stood beside him. The woman was clutching Fremont's hand and smiling as she spoke, despite the tears staining her cheeks.

Fremont murmured something and she released his hand. Wiping her tears, she nodded firmly.

Kate's heart squeezed as the sergeant ruffled the boy's hair. Familiarity didn't always breed contempt. Sometimes it bred envy.

The ugly pinch of green clamped harder as Kate watched the sergeant grasp the boy's tiny outstretched hand and solemnly shake it.

A husband. Kids. From that first, damning glance in the mirror four years earlier, she'd been forced to realize that she'd never have them. She'd even accepted it.

Or so she'd thought.

The pinch turned painful as Fremont leaned forward to lift

the tyke into his lap. The boy grabbed the wheelchair's arms with chubby fists, chortling loudly as Fremont tipped the chair backward before gently tick-tocking them from side to side.

"Ma'am?"

Kate glanced behind her. She was holding up the food line. "Excuse me."

Embarrassment followed her to the table. Kate nodded to the woman and child who'd joined the sergeant as she set one of the cups of coffee on Fremont's side of the table.

"Kate, this is Zoe Brandt. She's married to the soldier I mentioned. The one I was working with that night on the ward. Zoe, meet Kate Holland. She's former Army too. She's now a hard-charging deputy with the Braxton PD."

Zoe smiled. "It's so nice to meet you. I know you know this, but your man? He's amazing. It's taken three months, but my Bobby doesn't think about hurting himself anymore. He's all about the future now, getting fitted for his prosthetics and getting out of here so we can begin rebuilding our lives." Zoe reached down to scoop the boy from Fremont's lap. "He's even talking about having a brother or sister for this guy."

"That's wonderful." Kate didn't bother correcting the woman's assumption that she and Fremont were anything but the acquaintances they were. Possibly because it felt as though they'd known each other for longer than a day.

And, yes, it was nice to meet another woman who simply took the ruined side of her face in stride. Why embarrass her?

"Well, we have to go. Bobby's waiting. I just had to stop and thank you again. Say bye-bye, Eric. Let's go see Daddy."

Kate joined the sergeant in returning the boy's chubby wave as he and his mother departed the cafeteria. Fremont rolled up to the edge of the table to retrieve the cup of coffee she'd brought over as Kate reclaimed her chair.

"Thanks."

"I should've asked how you liked it."

"Army black and piping hot." He used the Styrofoam cup to salute her. "In other words, this is perfect."

Kate took advantage of the quiet that settled between them as they nursed their coffees to study the sergeant as he took his second and third sips...and he noticed.

"What?"

She flushed. "Zoe. She mentioned her husband's prosthetics."

"And you want to know why I'm sitting in this chair."

"Yeah."

"Luck of the draw. Shrapnel from the IED that took my legs also hit my spine in a decidedly pissy spot. I can't use prosthetics."

It wasn't fair. He clearly did so much for others. But when was war ever fair?

Hell, when was life?

"I'm so sorry."

He shook his head. "Don't be. I'm damned fortunate, and I know it. I still have a few things to do on this earth, and I was blessed to come home with enough parts intact to be able to accomplish them...just like you."

Silence cloaked the table, intensifying the moment.

The implication.

It hadn't just been that distant stare the day before in the elevator. "You know...who I am."

His smile slipped in sideways. "Honey, anyone who spent any time over there and returned home with enough faculties left to turn on the nightly news knows who you are. Not too many women came back clutching a Silver Star in one hand and a dozen haji scalps in the other to prove they deserved it." He shrugged. "Though I am sorry I didn't let on earlier that I knew. I didn't want to put you on the spot."

She appreciated that. But, "It wasn't a dozen. It was eleven. Or so they tell me."

His brows rose.

Her wrist began to itch. She ignored it. Along with her shock that she was even broaching this. "I don't...exactly... remember all of it."

"How much do you recall?"

"The ambush. My first kill." The clawing desperation as she'd dragged Max's body to a covered position. Or so she'd hoped. "Something bashed into the back of my skull, here." She fingered the spot instinctively. "I went down hard. Cold. I woke up in a mud hovel, stripped of my weapons." Stripped of every blessed thing. Including her clothes and her skin. The latter in several key places. "I'm not sure how much time had passed. My ribs were cracked, my right collarbone shattered." She smoothed her fingers over the worst of her scars. Those that were visible. "My face was flayed open. My cheek, shoulder and torso were still bleeding."

Among other—lower—places.

The silence crowded back in for several long, interminable moments. And then he splintered it.

"How many?"

She stared at the man. Just stared. Surely he didn't mean— could *not* be asking—

But she'd already totaled her kills for him, so he was.

"Kate?"

She shook her head against the gentle prod. Closed her mind. Her heart. "I don't—"

He leaned forward, trapping her with that fathomless stare, as cleanly and completely as she'd been trapped four years ago. "Chief Warrant Officer Holland, I asked a question. I expect an answer. How many of those bastards *raped* you?"

7

———

THE QUESTION RIPPED THROUGH KATE, all but screaming inside her as Sergeant Fremont waited for her to acknowledge it. Just as her battered breasts, bruised thighs—and worse—had screamed for acknowledgement when she'd regained consciousness in that sweltering, mud-brick hovel.

How many of her captors *had* raped her? And how many times had they come back for more?

Somehow, she managed the truth. "I don't know." That nauseatingly vivid Afghan pottery invaded her brain. "I only remember the last one who tried. He was a kid, really. Fourteen, fifteen tops. I didn't know if he'd already taken his turn, and was returning for seconds. I didn't care. He was carrying one of those cobalt blue jugs they make over there. He said it contained water. He ordered me to clean myself so I wouldn't contaminate him while he had his fun. All I saw was a potential weapon and the wooden door cracked open behind him."

"You broke the jug and used it."

She nodded. "The handle was solid. Plenty sharp enough." The splintered end had cleaved through the kid's carotid like warm butter. A split second later, both she and her latest would-be rapist were bleeding. But he was dying.

Those huge brown eyes had just stared at her, unblinking as he'd grabbed at his neck. Astounded.

"What happened after you escaped?"

She reached for the memory—but, as usual, blackness swirled in instead. She sank into the abyss, embracing the numbing warmth that cushioned her fall.

"Kate?"

She stiffened as the room snapped into focus. Fremont was touching her, his callused fingertips soothing the top of her right wrist as she twisted the dive watch around her left. The buckle had dug into her skin so deeply, it had left a bracelet of raw scratches in its wake.

Kate jerked her hands to her lap and locked her fingers together.

"Are you okay?"

"Absolutely." It was a bald-faced lie, and they both knew it. But it was easier than the truth.

Safer.

The self-doubt returned with a vengeance. What was she doing here, voicing things she had no business voicing? And to a veritable stranger? For God's sake, she was screwing Grant and she hadn't been able to admit to a fraction of what she'd just shared with this man. What was it about that crooked smile and steady compassion that made her want to spill it all before she'd even realized she'd opened her mouth?

She had to get out of here. Before the entire bucket of filth slammed over and came sloshing out.

She was still sifting through her shredded nerves for a plausible excuse when her phone rang.

She snatched it from the table, not even bothering to read the caller ID. "Deputy Holland. How can I help you?"

"It's Debra Yarbrough. You said I could call?"

The name didn't register, but the voice did. It was the receptionist she'd spoken with in the lobby. "Of course. Did you remember something else?"

"Yes—no. I mean, Abby Carson just arrived. Ian Kusić's ex? She's pretty out of it, but no one has the heart to send her home. I don't think she realizes how early she is."

Kate pushed her cup of coffee aside, ashamed at the strength of the relief coursing through her as she stood. "Would you mind asking if she's up to speaking with me?"

"I already did. She says fine. But, well, she keeps crying. It's a miracle she made it here without having an accident."

Intrigued, Kate watched as the sergeant pushed his Styrofoam cup to the side. He withdrew a small memo tablet and pen from one of the storage pouches attached to his wheelchair. As he began writing, Kate refocused her attention on her call—and the valid reprieve it offered.

"Ma'am, I understand Ms. Carson's upset. Anyone would be. But it may help her to talk things out." Especially with someone who may be able to use the woman's insight to help find the bastard who killed her ex.

"That's why I called."

The sergeant recaptured Kate's attention as he tore the uppermost page from his tablet. He folded it and pushed the resulting square of paper to the center of the table.

"Deputy? Are you there?"

Kate turned her back on that tempting square and its owner. "Ms. Yarbrough, where can I find Ms. Carson?"

"Are you still in the cafeteria?"

"Yes."

"She should be at the lab by now. It's on the same floor. Hang a left as you exit the cafeteria and follow the signs. I'll call the lab and let them know you'll be arriving."

"Thank you."

Kate tucked her phone home as she faced the table, intent on offering up her excuses.

Fremont beat her to the punch. "You have to go."

"I do. I need to interview someone asap." She stared at the square of paper. Was she supposed to take it?

The sergeant nudged it forward. "That's my number. Well, the phone rings at Saint Clare's, but they take messages. If you decide you want to talk—really talk—with someone who's been there, done that and has the missing legs to show for it, give me a call. I do my best to check in daily."

Temptation won as Kate snagged the square and shoved it in her pocket. Just because she'd accepted the man's number, didn't mean she intended to take him up on his offer.

"Thanks." She tried to add more, but the words clogged in her throat. She returned the sergeant's nod and made her way across the cafeteria. Rattled or not, it was time to put the past in its place and concentrate on the present.

Her case.

The receptionist had been spot on. The path to the lab was clearly marked. Kate followed the signs and arrows through the mostly deserted maze that formed the hospital's main floor until she reached her destination.

A lanky black gentleman in a hospital coat appeared to be waiting for her. "Deputy Holland?"

"Yes?"

Despite bloodshot eyes and the lines of exhaustion bracketing his mouth, the man's handshake was firm. "Neal Roche. I head up the lab. Debra Yarbrough called to say you were coming this way. I thought you might want to speak to me."

"I do."

"Do you mind if we talk here? I wasn't sure if you'd want Ian's co-workers overhearing, and Abby's resting in my office. I know she doesn't need to hear the details. Not now."

"This is fine." Kate flashed her credentials. "As your receptionist may have mentioned, I'm with the Braxton PD. I take it you're aware of the particularly heinous nature of these murders?"

The man's sigh was resigned. "Unfortunately. I read the paper an hour ago."

"Did you know both victims?"

"Yes, though not well. Ian Kusić worked for me, of course. He was friendly, especially with the patients. But he tended to be circumspect about his personal life. As for Mr. Dunne, I only met him in passing. I understand he was new and worked evenings. I work weekdays. I'm only in now because of the call I received. I wanted to arrange grief counseling for those who knew the men and get the details posted as soon as possible."

"I understand. Regarding Mr. Kusić, do you know how long he's been missing from work?"

The supervisor rubbed his temple. "No. Ian put in for vacation a month back. I asked the staff. The last time anyone can be certain they saw him is a week ago yesterday, the day his vacation began. He was in a good mood as he left the lab."

"Do you know where he went on vacation, or where he intended to go?"

The man shook his head. "Like I said, Ian was tight-lipped about his personal life. I respected that. Of course, Abby may know. You could also try Grant Parish."

Astonishment ripped in. "Did you say Grant Parish?"

"I did. Dr. Parish is a surgeon at our facility across town. He stops—stopped—by the lab now and then to talk to Ian. I've also seen them dining in the cafeteria, so Grant may know Ian better than me. I can get his number for you."

"That won't be necessary." He was on her speed dial. Though

why, she was no longer sure. Clearly, their relationship was rockier than she'd assumed if Grant knew both victims well enough to dine and visit with on a regular basis, yet hadn't bothered to so much as mention either man's name.

Though her present, uppermost concern centered on that PTSD therapy group. Had Ian Kusić been a member as well?

If Kusić had, there was an excellent chance the group had formed the killer's nexus.

Which meant Grant and the remaining attendees could be in immediate danger.

Kate resisted the temptation to excuse herself so she could dial Grant's number. "Mr. Roche, I'm sure you're aware that Mr. Kusić was an Army veteran. Do you know if he attended group or private therapy for PTSD?"

The supervisor frowned. "I know he served. But, no, he never mentioned therapy, or even the need for it. Why? Is it important?"

Kate pushed her suspicion aside. With Grant ducking her calls, there was no way to confirm anything until her interview with the shrink. "It may be nothing. You mentioned that Mr. Kusić was well liked. Were there any complaints against him? From his co-workers, other staff, patients, or a possibly a patient's relative?"

The supervisor smothered a yawn. "Sorry. I caught a midnight movie at the Rave with my son last night. Now I wish we'd waited. As for complaints against Ian, there weren't any. Which was a bit unusual—and refreshing. Sick patients can get testy. That said, I did hear rumors a few weeks ago about a blow up he supposedly had with a patient. But I never got a name, and when no one came into the lab to file a formal complaint, I wrote it off as gossip."

"What about overly friendly fans? Did Mr. Kusić complain

about a patient or relative of a patient who stopped by the lab, followed him around the hospital, or to his car?"

The man's stare grew wide. "You think Ian knew his killer? That he and Mr. Dunne were stalked here at Fort Leaves? Sweet baby Jesus, as if those paper bags weren't enough."

Kate agreed, but she shook her head. "Mr. Roche, I don't yet know how the men were targeted. I'm simply asking the standard questions for an investigation like this. Please keep that in mind. While the staff should take precautions, it would do more harm than good for your co-workers to speculate on the specifics, let alone a particular person. Understood?"

They didn't need a full-blown panic.

The supervisor blew out his breath. "I understand, and I apologize."

"There's no need. This is a trying time for everyone involved, and while I believe guarding one's tongue is best until we know more—" Kate retrieved several business cards and passed them to the supervisor. "—if you or a co-worker think of anything, no matter how minor, that may shed light on either murder, I'd appreciate a call."

The man pocketed her cards. "I will. You should probably speak to Abby now. A nurse administered a sedative before your arrival. It'll be kicking in soon. It won't knock her out—Abby didn't want that—but it'll relax her enough that her answers may be affected. She's in my office, through there."

Kate wished she'd known about the sedative earlier. She'd have altered the order of her interviews.

She thanked the supervisor as she opened the door he'd indicated. The office was modest, with an executive desk anchoring the far end, along with half a dozen pieces of medical equipment. A gray couch braced the wall to her left. The blond from the photo on Kusić's refrigerator was seated in the middle. Tortoiseshell glasses framed eyes that briefly met Kate's before slipping away to stare down at the fingers knotted tightly together in the woman's lap. Those eyes were twice as bloodshot and a dozen times puffier than the supervisor's had been.

The woman didn't acknowledge Kate as she closed the door. She continued to stare at that knot of fingers. From that initial glance, Kate couldn't tell if grief had glazed those blue eyes, or the sedative the supervisor mentioned.

"Ms. Carson?"

That glazed gaze finally shifted to Kate and stayed there. More specifically, to the Braxton PD insignia on her jacket. Fresh tears spilled over and down, welling up at the base of those tortoiseshell frames. Definitely grief. The woman didn't bother wiping as she resumed the silent study of her fingers.

Kate stepped closer. "Ma'am?"

"It's true, isn't it? Ian's really dead."

"I'm afraid so."

Swollen lips trembled. The woman finally unwound her fingers to raise a hand, then lowered it, repeating the motion as if she was stuck in a loop and couldn't figure out what to do with her own body.

Kate closed her own hands over those trembling fingers and guided them to the woman's lap as she sat beside her.

The woman thanked her quietly and finally met her stare. She was so lost in torment, Kate's mutilated features failed to register. Instead, a fresh wave of grief trickled down.

"Ma'am...are you sure you're up to speaking with me?"

Her answering nod was fractured, but firm. "I know it sounds crazy, but I need this. I *need* to help. And it's Abby. Abby Carson."

Kate shook her head. "It's not crazy. It's...normal."

If anything about this could be normal, it was that. The quest to know, to help, had driven her through each of the murders she'd worked with Army CID, including those mass graves. And those crimes hadn't been personal to her.

"Before I start, is there anything you'd like to know about the circumstances of Mr. Kusić's death?"

Abby's attempt at a polite smile failed miserably. "Thank you, but no. I shouldn't have, but I read that article in the paper. I think I need time to let all that awful...stuff sink in."

"I understand. I've left my card with your boss. If you decide you'd like to discuss anything later, just call."

"I will." The woman removed her glasses and scrubbed her cheeks with shaking palms before re-donning them. "So, detective, what do you want to know?"

"It's Deputy Holland. But feel free to call me Kate. What I'm attempting to do today is trace both men's movements. I understand you dated Mr. Kusić. Did you know Jason Dunne too?"

"Just Ian. He transferred here about a year ago. I was hired a few months later. We worked together for a while before he asked me out, and it...kind of went from there."

"Were you two serious?"

The woman's lips thinned. "I thought so. But I wasn't enough."

"There was someone else?"

"No." The woman scraped her tousled hair past her shoulders as she shook her head. "It was some*thing.*"

Ahhh. "What was Mr. Kusić's drug of choice?"

Surprise cut through that reddened stare. "How did you know?"

"I found the pad of empty scripts."

"Oh. I guess it doesn't matter then."

Kate waited, hoping Abby would add to that intriguing declaration on her own.

It took a good half a minute and a deep, hiccupping breath, before she did. "We broke up a week ago Thursday. Ian had been acting odd for a month or so. Distant, silent. But that last night, he was downright mean. I'd found his stash in the pocket of his discarded jeans. Oxycontin. The name on the bottle wasn't his, so I believed him when he said it was an old habit that had gotten its teeth into him again. He swore he'd kicked it before and, since he hadn't been on the stuff for long this time, he could easily kick it again. I wanted to believe that. I did believe it. In him. For a night."

"What changed?"

"You have to understand; Ian was a good man. A hero. Before he got a job with the VA, he served in the Army. But he was tortured by something he saw in Iraq. The pills, they helped him deal with the memories—the nightmares."

Again, Kate waited. Experience had taught that she'd get more if she allowed Abby to face her shattered dreams on her own schedule. When the woman finally blew out her breath and retreated into the corner of the couch, Kate knew her patience had paid off.

"Five years ago, some soldiers were in a market in Mosul when an IED exploded. Several soldiers had to be flown to Germany. One wasn't hurt—not physically. But he suffered all the same. To take his mind off what happened, he got involved with a local woman and deserted, only to be murdered a couple days later by terrorists."

As soon as Abby mentioned the Iraqi woman and desertion, Kate knew where the story was headed, but she let her finish uninterrupted.

"It was terrible. The soldier was strung up in the window of a bombed-out building and tortured. Those bastards sliced his abdomen open and let his intestines spill out onto the dirt—and then they set him on fire. Ian was part of the search team that found the soldier and cut him down. That's why he started using the oxycodone the first time, and why he started again. The nightmares, they just wouldn't leave him alone."

Silence thrummed as Abby crossed her arms, almost daring

Kate to argue with the unspoken absolution of her ex. She needn't have worried. Kate had seen too many soldiers slither down that same hole, dusted with drugs and despair. She might not agree with the method of escape, but she sure as hell understood the siren that'd enticed them there.

But unlike the majority of soldiers who'd gotten hooked on prescription meds during the treatment of their physical wounds, Kusić had swallowed his on his own. He'd had a choice. Far too many of her fellow soldiers in arms hadn't.

Did Dr. Manning know about the oxy and the reason for its abuse?

She was actually looking forward to interviewing the shrink.

But first, she had this interview to finish. Abby Carson's true demon had finally clawed its way to the surface. The evidence was in the woman's stare as it shifted toward the opposite wall, then the desk and medical equipment at the far end of the room. Kate knew that stare like she knew the thick, mottled scars and ugly pits that formed damned near half her face, neck and torso.

Avoidance.

Unfortunately, she couldn't honor it. It was time for Abby to admit to what this was really about. That breakup had had nothing to do with oxycodone. Ian Kusić had done something that had caused Abby to walk out, even though she was still in love with the man. The landlady's comments, combined with the fresh grief trickling down past Abby's glasses to soak her cheeks, revealed that much.

"Abby, what did Ian do?"

That damp gaze slipped back. "He scared me."

"How?" But she knew. She'd interviewed too many battered women to not recognize the monster coming into focus.

Abby had to name it. For both their sakes.

Fingers slipped beneath the woman's frames in an attempt to stem the fresh tears, and failed. "The morning after I found the pills, I woke determined to help him. He was in the shower when the phone rang. As I reached the kitchen, the machine answered. The message was odd, but I recognized the caller. When I picked up the phone, Ian knocked it out of my hand. I told him the doc sounded upset. Instead of apologizing, he slammed my head into the doorjamb and threatened me if I touched his phone again. He was still yelling when I grabbed my keys and left. We both worked that day, so I went out of my way to ignore him until my vacation began. I haven't seen him since." She rasped out the rest. "I still have the lump."

Kate absorbed the woman's story. Not only did it mesh with Sergeant Fremont's characterization of the tech, the picture that was emerging bore striking similarities to Jason Dunne's. The steroids, the stolen pad of scripts and the oxycodone abuse, the violent lashing out toward women, that AK-47 and the hefty stash of Benjamins. Hypocritical behavior for two decorated war vets who were supposedly extending their so-called selfless service in one of the nation's VA hospitals.

What else were the men hiding? And why did she suspect that the clusters of misbehavior were somehow linked to their deaths?

"Abby?"

"Yeah?"

Kate frowned. Given what she'd put this woman through, how did she phrase this? "Mr. Kusić had a lot of...nice things in a not-so-nice residence, especially for a tech with his salary."

"Some relative left him money. I thought he should invest in a starter house closer to work instead of buying and fixing up that dive, but it wasn't my place to tell him."

Another family-money fable. Kate suspected a shadier source. Especially since the former tended to get deposited in a bank or brokerage account, while the latter often made its way under a mattress...or inside a plastic storage crate in a bedroom closet.

Even more curious, "Are you certain Mr. Kusić owned that trailer?" Not according to the landlady.

Another lie? Except the locks *had* been changed.

His ex nodded. "I know Ian was going to make an offer. But I suppose he could've changed his mind, or maybe it didn't go through. He was still working on it when we...broke up."

"About his vacation? Do you know where he was going?"

"No. He was supposed to go to Jonesboro with me. My sister had her C-section scheduled this past week. I thought if we went our separate ways, he'd realize how much he'd hurt me, and I don't mean physically. I guess I hoped he'd beg me to take him back. But, well..." She swallowed a soft sob.

"He never got the chance."

"Yeah."

Given what she'd managed to piece together, Kate doubted Kusić would've put Abby ahead of much. But she'd be damned if she'd admit it to a grieving woman. And there was that photo. Yes, it had been shoved to the side of the fridge. But Seth hadn't found it in the trash. That was something. She just doubted it would've been enough, even if the tech had managed to escape his killer's crosshairs.

"You mentioned an odd message on Mr. Kusić's machine. Do you remember the words?"

Abby slipped her fingers beneath her glasses again, this time to rub her eyes. She blinked as she lowered the frames, struggling to focus. "He wanted Ian to call him before he left for work. He also said he agreed; they had to be careful. Then Grant said they were running out of time."

Grant? Kate leaned forward. "The caller who left the message on Mr. Kusić's machine was Dr. Parish?"

"Yeah. I thought...I...mentioned that." Another blink, and another attempt to focus. Both took longer this time.

The expression Kate had noted upon her arrival had returned. Only tears weren't behind this glaze. It was the sedative the supervisor mentioned. Whatever the nurse had given Abby was kicking in hard, because the woman's eyelashes were drifting down. Abby Carson was fading, and fast.

This interview was effectively over.

Kate checked her watch. Just as well. It was almost time for her meeting with Dr. Manning. And past time for answers.

Kate guided Abby down until she was stretched out on the couch. Retrieving a man's woolen coat from the brass tree beside the door, she used it to blanket the smaller woman.

"S-sorry. I th-think I n-need—"

"Sleep. It's okay. You're safe. Your co-workers are right outside. Remember what I said. I left my card with your boss. If you want to talk later, about anything, just call."

"'Kay."

Despite the lab supervisor's prediction, the sedative they'd given Abby to settle her nerves had knocked her out. Or maybe it was the grief. Either way, the woman was sound asleep before Kate stepped into the hall.

She closed the door on the gentle snores and headed for the bank of elevators near the lobby, only to change her mind and turn into a stairwell. Retrieving her phone, she tapped out a text to Seth as she climbed, asking him to verify the trailer's ownership and have the ME test Kusić's remains for oxycodone—then added a request to have patrol let Ruger out, now that she knew Grant was ignoring her.

Her phone pinged as she reached the shrink's floor. Ruger's scheduled bladder relief was a go—and Seth already had the 411 on the trailer. Seth's conversation with the landlady's husband revealed that Kusić had purchased it. The previous owner just hadn't yet found the balls to inform his wife about the title transfer—and the cash Kusić had paid.

So the tech had preferred to buy a dump on the outskirts of nowhere with a forty-minute drive to work instead of a sleek starter home to match his toys.

Curiouser and curiouser.

Kate located the shrink's office and paused to draw a steadying breath. She could do this, damn it.

Keep your eyes front and center. *Don't* look at that damned shelf.

She dragged in another breath and reached for the handle. Before she could use it to open the door, a sixty-ish man with thick, shoulder-length silver hair beat her to the task from the opposite side.

"Deputy Holland. A pleasure to finally meet you."

"Dr. Manning?"

"Correct. And you're right on time. Excellent." His smile was warm and...weirdly sympathetic.

Kate chalked up the oddness of the impression to her nerves. After all, she was standing inside a shrink's reception room, speaking one-on-one with that same shrink—something she'd sworn the day she'd separated from the Army that she'd never do again. And there was that floating shelf to her right with its chilling collection of cobalt blue pottery, conveniently placed at eye level. As much as she'd tried to convince herself that she'd be able to ignore it, she was failing spectacularly.

Against her will, the fingers of her right hand found the dive watch and began the slow, soothing twist. It helped...until the doc paused beside a slender jug. Short of turning her back on the man, there wasn't much she could do but look at him.

So she did.

Or, rather, she tried. The world had narrowed. Within

seconds, she couldn't see anything but that jug, including the shrink who appeared to be speaking to her.

What the devil was he saying?

She felt something grasp her upper arm.

"Kate."

She flinched...and managed to meet that steady stare. It helped that the doc had somehow guided her past the row of pottery without her realizing she'd even moved.

"Would you like to ask your questions inside my office?"

"Please." She was too relieved to worry about the desperation that had bled into her response.

The shrink's hand fell away, leaving her to realize she was still gripping her watch. Twisting. She forced herself to sever the connection as the doc motioned for her to precede him.

By the time they reached the pair of leather club chairs facing his desk, her breathing had evened out. Kate claimed the seat on the right. Though the office was warm, she didn't dare remove her jacket. After her reaction in that waiting room, there was no way she was volunteering a view of the fresh scratches she'd just added to her wrist.

The shrink rounded his desk, pointing to the large stainless-steel thermos as he sat. "Coffee? I bring it in on the weekends. There's a stack of Styrofoam cups on the table behind you."

Kate shook her head. "I'm good."

That smile again. The compassion within was unmistakable. Damning. Along with the doc's uncanny ability to avoid looking at the mangled side of her face without appearing as though he was consciously doing so. It was clear Manning *knew*—and not just what had happened to her, but how she really felt about it.

To date, other than that conversation she'd just had with Sergeant Fremont, there was only one other human on the planet with whom she'd even broached that subject. Grant. If she hadn't believed Fremont about her soon-to-be ex-lover's share-fests in this very room, she did now.

Grant was seeing Manning professionally—and discussing *her* while he did it.

Kate talked herself down from the edge of fury for the second time that morning.

So Manning knew. It was humiliating, yes. But what did it change? Fremont was right—anyone who could turn on the news had a shot at realizing who she was and what she'd done— even if she couldn't recall the crucial details. True, they wouldn't have the insight Grant had clearly provided the shrink, but she refused to let the violation of trust get to her. Instead, she'd do what she always did when confronted with the leaky sieve inside her skull. Ignore it. Ignore Manning.

At the very least, she'd ignore that *relax, you're safe with me* stare. Because she wasn't.

She never would be. "Dr. Manning, exactly how did Ian Kusić gain possession of one of your prescription pads?"

The man stiffened. Compassion fled his stare. Wariness replaced it.

Satisfaction filled Kate. While that wasn't the opening salvo she'd have preferred, it had done the trick. And given her the upper hand in the process.

"Well?"

Manning shook his head. "I don't know."

"But you did know the pad was missing?"

"Of course. I realized it was gone about a month ago, but I didn't know who took it. Are you certain Mr. Kusić had it?"

Kate retrieved her phone and accessed the photo she'd taken of the pad. She pushed the phone across the desk and waited as the shrink tapped the screen to zoom in on the credentials.

He frowned as he shoved the phone back. "It's mine, but I have no idea how he got ahold of it."

"I understand you run a vet-based group PTSD therapy session on Thursday evenings for hospital employees?"

"I do. But Ian Kusić doesn't attend. I'd never even heard the man's name until I read the paper this morning."

Shit.

If Kusić hadn't attended those sessions, her latest theory regarding that group was a bust. Narrowing down where, why and how the killer had targeted his victims was critical—if she had a hope in hell of determining who was next.

And warning them.

"What about the second victim? Jason Dunne was new, but I believe he attended your staff vet/PTSD sessions?"

From those furrowed brows, she'd surprised the shrink again. "Indeed. Jason Dunne did attend. But how did you know? The members of that particular group insist on anonymity. That's why the meetings are held at night."

Was that why Grant had kept his silence with her?

At this point, she didn't care—not about that. "A patient saw Mr. Dunne outside your office several Thursdays ago as a session let out. Dunne was standing beside Grant Parish."

The doc blinked. As jolts went, she was three for three. His terse frown confirmed he'd reached his limit. "I'm sorry, Deputy. I'm happy to discuss Mr. Dunne and even speculate with you regarding Mr. Kusić. In light of these murders, I'm as determined as the next staffer to assist you in catching their killer as soon as possible. But I can't discuss Dr. Parish's participation, or lack thereof, in any therapy session."

Ironic, considering he and Grant seemed quite comfortable discussing her.

She opened her mouth to respond, only to close it as the shrink continued.

"Though, of course, that confidentiality would naturally extend to you if you were to join the group."

This time, she blinked.

The doc nodded. "My offer is sincere. You're more than welcome to join us on Thursdays. As a police officer at first, if you must. But only if you agree to remain with the group after your investigation is complete...and fully participate."

What the hell had Grant said to this guy? "I was told the group was for VA employees."

"It started that way. But we've added vets who aren't employed by the VA. And since I facilitate the group pro bono and on my own time, you wouldn't have to enter the VA patient system. Indeed, no one does. The group's sole goal is to provide support for returning veterans. That's it. Trust me—" He folded his hands on his desk and leaned forward. "—you would be welcome."

She might've surprised him, but he'd utterly flabbergasted her. She was also beyond pissed. Not at him. As a shrink, Manning was merely running to type. No, she was pissed with herself. By exposing the bent cards in her deck out in that waiting room, she'd left herself open for this. Wide open.

"Thank you, but no. I don't mean to be rude, but I've had as much therapy as I can stomach for one life."

The man nodded gracefully—and let it go.

Thank God.

Kate retrieved her phone from the desk and settled into her chair. "Since you're willing to discuss Jason Dunne, could you tell me about his mood this past Thursday?"

"I wish I could. Unfortunately, he missed the session. One of the other members thought he might've come down with the flu, since he'd texted that member early Tuesday to warn him he'd be missing work the rest of the week."

"I don't suppose you could provide that member's name, so I can get the exact information in the text?" Otherwise, she'd have to wait for the data dump—if there was anything useful. Given the results of Kusić's, it didn't look promising.

"I'm sorry, but as I said—"

"—membership is confidential."

"Exactly. I will ask if he'll speak with you. But I suspect you could confirm the information with Dunne's supervisor."

She could. And would. She'd have her fingers crossed while she did it, too. If the supervisor had the same story, her investigation might just be moving forward. Sick people tended to call to bow out of work, not text. Killers intent on posing as sick workers who were actually victims tended to do the opposite.

"Is that all, Deputy?"

"Unless you're willing to discuss what Mr. Dunne brought up in those therapy sessions, yes."

"I'm afraid the content—"

"—is confidential."

His smile returned. "Yes. And as I'm sure you know, barring a court order, patient confidentiality survives death. But please believe me. If I thought anything said would help, I'd be inclined to mask the information within a few oblique clues. Unfortunately, Mr. Dunne's concerns were far too common with too many of our nation's vets."

"I understand." More than this civilian, however motivated and apparently genuinely sympathetic, could know.

Kate retrieved several business cards as she stood. She stacked them on the edge of the man's desk as he too came to his feet. "If you or any members of your group think of something that may help, please don't hesitate to contact me."

The shrink nodded as he rounded the desk with his own card. Instead of dropping it in her outstretched palm, he folded her fingers up around it. "I'd like you to feel free to call me too. Anytime. Day or night."

It was everything she could do to not yank her hand from his and dump his card on the blotter. Instead, she offered a crisp nod. "Thank you for your time, doctor."

"Wait. I have something. I suppose there's no harm in asking you to return it." The man withdrew a set of keys from his trousers and used one to unlock the center drawer of his desk.

Kate's curiosity blossomed as he rifled through the mess within.

"Could've sworn I left it—ah, here it is." He rounded the desk to drop something solid and sleek into her palm.

A phone?

It was clear he assumed it belonged to Grant. He must, given that Jason Dunne was gone. You couldn't return something to a dead man. But Grant carried a smartphone. This bargain basement number belonged in the nineties—or strapped to an IED on the other side of the globe. It was a goddamned disposable burner. She ought to know; she'd confiscated enough of these cheap-ass things during her time in anti-terror.

And it was Grant's?

"With Dr. Parish on vacation this past week, I haven't been able to return it. And with everything that's happened, I doubt I'll have the time now. Perhaps you'll do the honors?"

Vacation?

Suspicion continued to slam in, and on multiple fronts—until the horror of it was inescapable.

It wasn't possible. Damn it, it just wasn't *possible*. She knew the man. She'd been crawling into bed with him for months. But the facts were inescapable.

And mounting up.

Two phones. One, she'd wager her badge, was untraceable. A week-long vacation her so-called lover had forgotten to mention —*while* he was screwing her. A job in the VA facility sister to one where both victims worked. That Grant knew said victims intimately, yet had left them off the friends' list he'd frequently brought up. Grant's own fucked-up psyche, compliments of three back-to-back tours as a trauma surgeon in Iraq. The fact that Grant was an older brother to yet another soldier who'd been so blown to shit in Afghanistan that they'd had to bury Dan in pieces.

She still refused to accept it.

Damn it, she couldn't.

For Christ's sake, she'd been dancing with the devil since she was an eighteen-year-old MP out on that Afghan road, scooping up the remains of her first squadmate. She knew evil. If Grant was responsible for carving up those men and lining up their coldly-packaged pieces, she'd *know*.

Wouldn't she?

8

"DEPUTY HOLLAND? ARE YOU OKAY?"

No, she was *not*. Kate wrenched her attention from the phone in her hand. "Dr. Manning, are you certain this belongs to Grant?"

The shrink nodded. "It was in his chair a week ago Thursday, wedged behind the cushion. I didn't find it until after he left my office. By then, Dr. Parish had left the hospital. I wasn't able to reach him before his vacation began the following evening. Though I suppose I'd just assumed it was his. Are you saying it's not?"

Kate powered up the cellphone. Antiquated technology or not, the phone was password protected.

So much for an easy explanation.

She slid a professional smile into place as she stared the shrink squarely in the eye. "It's Grant's. I'll ensure he gets it." After she had one of the guys at the lab crack open the SIM card and comb the contents to make sure it was his—and, if so, figure out what Grant was doing with a second phone. "I appreciate your time. I'm sure you have a busy day ahead, so I'll let you get back to work."

Kate tucked the phone in her pocket before the shrink could see through her smile and spun around to leave, only to catch sight of the tattered and singed Islamic flag mounted above the grouping of chairs to the right of the door.

Ice-cold dread slugged in, stopping her in her tracks.

She was dimly aware of the shrink spouting something about the flag being a gift from a Special Forces team he'd worked with in Afghanistan, but she couldn't respond. Hell, she couldn't even *breathe*. It was as though every cell in her body had been paralyzed, save those of her heart. That traitorous organ was pounding so hard, it put a howitzer to shame. When the shrink joined her in front of that half-shredded flag, she swore he could hear it slamming against her ribs.

Surely he could see the sweat.

The perspiration had popped out over every inch of her flesh, coating her with slime. Her uniform shirt and trousers were drenched—and the dread in her belly had morphed into full-blown shrieking panic. Nausea had crashed in as well, along with a succession of short, frantic gasps for air that couldn't quite fill her lungs.

Yet, still, she just stood there, frozen.

Until the shrink touched her arm.

Just like that, every cell in her body regrouped instantly, and with a vengeance. She had no idea where she was headed as she twisted her arm free and bolted from the room. Her mindless sprint carried her across the deserted reception area. It wasn't until she'd breached the outer door that she realized the bile still churning through her gut was intent on its own violent—imminent—breaching. Her boot falls echoed along the antiseptic corridor as she raced toward the bathroom she'd spotted on the way in.

God willing, she'd make it in time.

She slammed through her third door, then her fourth as she

lurched into the closest stall and knelt to purge the sludge that had been bubbling up since before Ruger had woken her from that first night terror the day before.

The heaving continued until there was nothing left inside but the frothing dregs of acid and the burn of absolute confusion.

What the hell had just happened?

Her body had threatened to betray her before, but she'd always been able to control it. At least while she was awake.

Was this to be her new normal?

If so, how on earth was she supposed to solve these two murders and bring the killer to justice? Keep her job afterward?

Deputy Holland of the Braxton PD might not be much, but it was all she had left.

Ruger. Lord, she needed him. She craved his warmth and his unconditional acceptance more than she ever had before.

Unfortunately, that solid source of unlimited hugs was at least a half hour away.

Kate reached for the roll of toilet paper, grateful it was full. An inch shy, she caught the swish of the bathroom's outer door and paused. The subdued scuff of rubber soles on tile followed. It wasn't until she heard the gentle pull of air through someone else's lungs that she realized she hadn't closed the stall door.

Whoever had entered the bathroom stood directly behind her.

Kate grabbed the paper's tail and wadded off enough to dry her mouth. Flushing the evidence of her latest weakness, she stood and turned to face her audience.

Elizabeth Vogel stared back. From the compassion suffusing her old friend's face, Liz had caught her frantic dash in here and extrapolated the rest.

Her humiliation was complete.

"Are you okay?"

Aside from a damp uniform and clammy skin, she was fine now. Mostly. "Yeah." Kate thought about adding an excuse, then decided on a radical change of subject. Anything to kill that oozing pity. "Didn't know you worked weekends."

Liz glanced down at her worn UAMS sweatshirt and faded jeans. "Normally I don't, especially dressed like this. I just stopped in to check on a patient who's become so overwhelmed, he's now suicidal."

Kate ignored any and all questions that statement begged. She had a suspicion the answers would only lead directly to where she was desperate not to be.

Instead, she stepped out of the stall. Liz followed her to the row of sinks.

Thankfully, the hospital hadn't gone completely green. Paper towels were plentiful, as was the gush of water that filled the basin in front of her. She rinsed out her mouth, then nudged the left cuff of her jacket aside to remove her watch before scrubbing away the vestiges of her disgrace.

Her fingers bumped the watch as she finished, knocking the dial face down into the sink. The engraving on the reverse flashed briefly as it settled.

To Max
Happy 18ᵗʰ
May all your dives
be in calm waters.
Love, Dad

SHE SNATCHED THE WATCH FROM THE BASIN AS LIZ JOINED HER, carefully securing the band to her still-dripping wet—and raw

—wrist. The pity had returned. At least this time it was tempered due to its reflection in the mirror.

"Do you want to talk about it?"

The offer was gentle, and dangerously seductive. It tugged Kate back through the years to when she and Liz had been the best of friends. Liz had been the one she'd leaned on then. The one who'd listened as she'd grieved for her mom and what might've been. The one who'd ferreted out all her secrets and had still loved her. The one who'd sworn that nothing was too much.

Unfortunately, they weren't kids anymore.

"Kate?"

She closed her eyes, desperate to block out that sharpening stare before it chiseled off another piece of her soul.

Even if she'd wanted to succumb, where was she supposed to start? With the return of those night terrors? With that pottery? With the rapes she didn't remember enduring, and the nine terrorists she couldn't recall slaughtering? With the two she *did* remember killing? With that fourteen-year-old kid? Or how about her baffling reaction to that flag just now? Or those coldly mutilated bodies strung out along the backroads of her own town...and her growing suspicion that her lover was the monster she was seeking?

"I'm fine, Liz. Lunch just didn't agree with me."

For a moment, she was sure her friend was going to call her out—until Kate's phone rang.

She turned away as she grabbed her phone, more grateful for the interruption than she'd been in that cafeteria with Sergeant Fremont. And that was saying something.

"Deputy Holland."

"It's Seth. We got another set of bags linin' yet another goddamned road to nowhere. This set's near the end of Fox Run, just past Carriage Hill Drive."

Her gratitude evaporated.

A curse slipped out as she braced herself against the wall. Seth couldn't have been more wrong. Like the first two dump sites, Fox Run was not some road to nowhere. Not to her. It was the one road she'd been actively avoiding since her return to Arkansas damned near three and a half years earlier.

"Kato?"

"I'm here. Where's Lou?"

"On his way back from a face to face with the state police. He'll be here in roughly twenty."

"Let him know I'll be another ten behind him." Kate severed the call as she swung around to face Liz.

The pity had vanished. Terror replaced it. Her friend's arms were locked across her chest as though she was desperately trying to hold it in. "You have another body, don't you?"

"Yes. But I'd appreciate you keeping that to yourself for now." At least until the press caught on. "I hate to do this to you twice in two days, but—"

"You have to go." Her friend's chin wobbled as she attempted a nod. "I understand. Please be careful."

"You too."

Kate meant it more than Liz could know. The woman might not be a vet, but she worked here. If this third victim followed the employment pattern of the first two, there was an excellent chance Liz had already come into contact with the killer...and would again.

Especially if her suspicions about Grant panned out.

Seth's apology was in his eyes and tumbling off his lips as Kate bailed out of her Durango. "I am *so* sorry. I'm a bloody moron. I swear to Christ, I wasn't thinkin'. I'm—"

"*Forgiven.* So, stop. Please. Seth, you've had a bit more on your mind this past hour than my dad's death."

He swallowed hard. "You sure?"

Kate pushed yet another painful chapter of her past aside as she patted her fellow deputy's barrel chest, directly over his wildly thumping heart. "Absolutely. Now, what've we got?"

He sucked in a huge gulp of air, then pushed it out on a sigh. "Fifteen bags, just like the others. I had the tape strung, but I haven't let anyone past the perimeter, includin' the crime scene boys. Figured I'd wait for you or Lou to give that order. Still waitin' on Tonga to show. He was due half an hour ago."

"What about Lou?"

"Dunno. He shoulda been here by now, too."

Probably traffic. Roads across the state had already begun to clog due to the Razorback-Longhorn game scheduled for that evening.

"Not to worry. There's a lot we can do while we're waiting for Tonga." She waved her fellow deputy toward the barrier he'd established. "We'd best get started."

Kate accepted gloves and booties from Seth as they made their way up the line of police vehicles. The former occupants were clustered near the yellow tape, quietly chatting as they waited for instructions. Kate nodded to a pair of techs as she donned her protective gear.

Seth's assessment of the scene was spot on. The dump site's layout appeared identical to the others, down to the precise alignment and spacing of the neatly stapled bags.

Kate dipped beneath the perimeter and waited for Seth to join her. "Who found them?"

"Man named Alan McLee. He and his wife live near Jonesboro. They were supposed to pick up his in-laws for an early dinner before headin' home to watch the football game. He got turned 'round tryin' to find their house and found the sacks.

He'd seen the paper so he called it in without peekin'. Course his reticence might've been at his wife's urgin'. She was still hysterical when I got here."

Excellent.

Not the wife's emotional state. The potential for a virgin scene. Kate had to give the reporters credit. Due to their loose lips, the entire set of bags had remained untouched by anyone but the killer. Though with the bastard's meticulous handling of the others, she doubted the edge would amount to anything.

But there was always hope.

Gravel crunched beneath their boots as she and Seth made their way toward the line of bags, carefully checking the stones for anything that appeared out of place.

Nothing did.

Kate retrieved her phone as they drew level with the first sack, intent on snapping a photo, only to have her concentration hijacked by the simple stone cross several yards off the road. God help her; she could make out the engraving.

The name.

From the set of Seth's head and shoulders, he was staring as well. Regretting.

There was no need. In light of his faux pas on the phone, this was likely his first time confronting the marker too, at least this closely. Seth had been hired two months before her and a full year after an unidentified motorist had killed her father during what—until then—had been a routine traffic stop. A pair of high-school seniors had gotten buzzed that night off a six pack stolen from their folks and challenged each other to a drag race down this very road.

Her dad had been struck while writing the ticket and died before the older boy finished dialing 911. Neither kid had been able to ID the vehicle that hit him. All they'd known was that it had been a dark sport utility vehicle—a description vague enough to encompass half the SUVs in the state, including the one she'd confronted behind her house the night before.

Kate broke free from the past in time to catch Seth's wave and realized he was motioning one of the crime scene techs forward, silently ordering the guy to bring a suitable cover to conceal the cross.

"Wait." She drew an invisible line from the stone marker to the leading sack. It was perpendicular to the line formed by the row of bags. "Look at how they're arranged."

Seth frowned. "You think it means something?"

Other than that the killer was an even sicker son-of-a-bitch than they'd already determined? "I doubt it. But have the cross dusted for prints and tell Nester and his team to note any depressions or debris surrounding it."

"Roger."

Kate headed for the dormant grass buffering the road as Seth departed. She reached the edge of the gravel, her chest tightening painfully as she stopped. Much as she wanted to chalk up the sensation to staring at an accident marker with her own rank and surname, she had a feeling the ache was born more of those four letters carved in the center.

Jack.

Kate stiffened as a hand settled on her right shoulder.

Tonga. Despite the gravel, she hadn't heard his approach.

"He was a good man." The ME's grip was as warm and soothing as the lilt in his voice. "I still miss him. We all do."

"Thanks." Kate pulled herself together enough to manage a stiff smile as she faced him. It faded as she spotted the first bag less than three yards away. "You ready to do this?"

He shook his head. "But we must."

Tonga was right. They'd be racing against the coming dusk for the next few hours. Kate retrieved her phone and forced herself to snap a photo of her father's cross before following the

ME to the middle of the road. She accepted the stack of evidence markers he'd brought and tented the first into place.

Tonga waited as she shot the exteriors, then popped the bag's staples and reached inside, leaving Kate to flatten it. Surprise thickened the air as he laid a right hand on top. As expected, it was severed at the wrist and shrink-wrapped with food-grade plastic. But this hand was different.

It was smaller than her own. Slender. And while the nails were unvarnished and trimmed to the quick, they appeared neatly buffed as though they'd had a recent manicure.

"Doc, our latest victim may be a woman."

"Agreed."

But if so, who was she? Had she worked at Fort Leaves? And had she been a vet? The answers would have to wait. As with Jason Dunne, the victim's fingerprints were sealed to the textured side of the plastic—and, hence, distorted.

Curiosity carried Kate to her feet. She assisted the ME to his and retrieved the evidence markers as they headed for the second sack. There, they resumed their grisly roles, with her placing the next numbered marker and snapping the exterior photos while Tonga broke the seal.

Moments later, a slender left hand—sans wedding ring—lay atop its now-flattened sack. This palm was sealed to the textured side of the plastic too. There would be no immediate ID—and no easy answers to the questions brimming within.

Resigned, they forged a path to the remaining sacks to continue the rhythm they'd fallen into all too easily. By the time they'd unbagged the flayed torso and noted the rude display of size C breasts, they'd confirmed gender. But the lack of tattoos, old shrapnel wounds and other scarring didn't solve the vet mystery. The woman could've been non-combat arms, or just plain lucky.

Kate braced herself as they reached the final sack. The

unbagging went smoothly enough. But, again, the sight of that clean line of severed flesh at the base of the head unnerved her more than the previous fourteen unbaggings combined.

"Are you okay?"

She nodded. "Still just...affected."

The ME nodded.

Kate concentrated on the features above that scarlet line. Despite the plastic's distortion, short brown curls, a heart-shaped chin and elfin features were obvious. She couldn't quite nail down the woman's age, not without removing the plastic. Something Tonga and the state ME assigned to assist would do after the parts had reached the lab in Little Rock.

As for Tonga, he appeared deep in thought.

"What is it?"

The ME tipped the head to get a better look at the circle of slightly seeping flesh beneath the neck. "I can't be certain until we get this woman to the lab. But based on the condition of her parts, I believe she may have been killed within hours of the previous victims."

Damn. If he was correct, it was more important than ever that she discover the connection between Ian Kusić, Jason Dunne and this woman. In fact, it was critical. If all three bodies had been dumped during the same trip, the killer might've already called it quits—at least in their neck of the woods. If so, the bastard might be fleeing the state, and soon. If he hadn't already.

Lord only knew if they'd be able to track him down then.

Before Kate could question the ME further, her phone pinged. The text was from Seth. "Lou's here."

And he had company in tow.

Tonga nodded. "You brief him regarding our discovery and my initial impressions. I'll get the woman ready for transport once the official photographer has finished with her."

"Okay." Kate took advantage of her return trek to scan the dirt and packed clay just off the gravel for signs of fresh tire treads. Once again, she came up empty.

At least with evidence.

Her thoughts were another matter. Something had begun to niggle deep in the recesses of her brain as she closed in on that cross for the second time. She ignored it. Whatever it was, was too dark and twisted to pull into the light.

Not here. Not now.

Not with a fresh batch of stomach acid beginning to froth and churn.

Kate reached the tape and ducked beneath, catching sight of Lou as she straightened. He stood near the front bumper of her SUV with two other men. One was roughly six feet tall and light-haired, the other an inch shorter and dark. Both had their backs to her, but the blond turned as Kate moved down the row of vehicles. She didn't recognize him, but she could discern the cut of a federal agent's suit anywhere.

The cavalry had arrived.

Even better, there was something wonderfully familiar about the second man's posture. It was in the set of his shoulders and in the tilt of his dark head.

"Joe?"

He turned and smiled.

Despite the fresh collection of parts and that simple stone cross, Kate smiled back. "My God, it *is* you." Joe Cordoba. They'd worked so many cases together she'd lost count, but at least a third had been during her final tour in Afghanistan. "Are you still with CID?"

Or had Joe joined the FBI as he'd tended to threaten whenever things had gotten really bad over there?

"Yeah, I'm still cleaning up messes for the Army." Her old

friend hauled her in for a crushing hug as she reached his side. "How the hell've you been, Holland?"

She pulled away to absorb those familiar, dusky features. "I'm getting better by the second. Who'd you piss off to pull this case?"

"Not a soul, I swear. Heck, I dragged the knee pads on all by myself and hunkered down for some very selective ass-kissing. You know how fast news travels, especially when it's rotten. That your first two victims were vets came down the pike late last night. I knew if the pattern held, we'd get involved eventually, so I copped to knowing you and offered to liaise on behalf of the Army."

Kate included Lou in her stare. "Well, you can't screw up worse than the last liaison."

Lou flushed.

Joe frowned. "Yeah, heard about that prick. How bad's the fallout from the article?"

"So far, so good." Hopefully, their luck would hold.

Or not.

She'd spoken too soon. Kate matched her former fellow agent's frown as she drew Lou's attention to the distinctive antenna and dish array of the TV van half a mile down the road and closing quickly. Lou shifted to catch Seth's eye as the deputy approached. Seth didn't even break stride as he continued past them while calling out an order to extend the crime scene perimeter far enough to keep the press in that van and any others from recording their conversations.

Lou turned toward the blond. "Kate, this is Special Agent Ed Walker, FBI; he's a psychologist with the BAU. Ed, this is Deputy Kate Holland. As I'm sure you've realized, she's also a former Army CID investigator, who apparently knows Agent Cordoba."

Knew him? She'd been at the man's wedding. Which was a

small miracle, since she'd had a hand in organizing Joe's joint CID/MP bachelor send-off the night before.

Kate kept that to herself as she turned more fully into the FBI agent's personal space to shake hands and genuinely welcome him to the state and the case. She didn't have a problem with shrinks-turned-profilers, so long as they kept their mental voodoo focused on the investigation and off her.

Joe must have prepped Walker, because the BAU agent didn't bat an eye as he took in the far side of her face.

Lou caught her gaze. "You and Tonga get anything new?"

"Yeah. This victim's a woman. We won't be able to get an ID until the body reaches the lab. Same issue as with Dunne." She included the newcomers in her explanation. "The plastic this guy uses to vacuum-pack the parts is textured on one side. Since the first victim had the clear side fused to his fingers and palms, we were able to get an ID at the scene. Not so with victims two and three."

Walker's dark blue stare narrowed thoughtfully. "He's learning."

"Based on how meticulous this bastard's been, I agree. Also, due to the condition of the parts, our ME suspects that all three victims were killed within hours of each other. So unless this guy's got some morbid assembly line going, he's killing with little to no cooling off period. This also means the victims may've been snatched within hours of each other, possibly a day or two. That would fit with what I've been able to piece together regarding the first two victims' timelines. No one's seen Kusić since he left for vacation a week ago Friday. His cat box contents suggest the same. The last known contact with Dunne came two days after Kusić was last spotted, late Sunday night—but that came via a text to his boss, claiming Dunne had the flu. As far as I've been able to determine, the last time he was actually seen was the day before by his doorman."

The killer's timing was critical for several reasons, not the least of which was that a group roundup suggested revenge. If this bastard was working off a list...had he exhausted it? If not, how many more names were on it?

How many more meticulously hacked-up victims would they find?

Kate turned to the sheriff. "Boss, we need Fort Leaves to conduct a staff headcount tonight to ensure no one else is missing. Physical verification, only. Calls, if they know the person extremely well, but no texts. It may also help us ID our latest victim sooner."

Lou nodded. "Seth's already lit a fire beneath digital forensics. I'll get him on this pronto. Carole did get the lowdown on Dunne's landline and cellphone. Same as Kusić. Nothing unusual on either—and Dunne's cellphone goes dead near his condo shortly after that text was sent to his boss about him needin' time off 'cause of the flu. As for his laptop and iPad, they're workin' on 'em, along with Kusić's. They hope to have somethin' soon. What about the interviews you had today? Did you find a connection between the male victims?"

"Possibly. It may be nothing, but—" Hell, she couldn't even put her finger on how or if it impacted the men's deaths. "—not only do we have the man toys in that trailer, along with the AK-47 and that stash of Benjamins, it turns out Kusić was abusing oxycodone. In fact, the oxy may have been the motivation for the stolen scripts. Kusić got hooked dealing with the fallout from an Iraqi search and rescue mission that ended with grisly results five years ago. According to his ex, he'd kicked the oxy on his own, then started using again a month ago—right around the time Dr. Manning noticed his missing pad. As for Dunne, I found steroids in his apartment. Based on the amount and my interview with his doorman, they appeared to be personal use. Plus, Dunne has a potential connection to an unsavory incident as well—though in his case it occurred in Afghanistan, and Dunne may have been the perpetrator in his. Either way, Tonga's added steroids to Dunne's tox panel. Meanwhile, Dunne's lifestyle also shows an infusion of serious money that's yet to be explained."

Lou shook his head. "I'm still stuck on the drugs. I don't see the connection. Oxycontin and steroids are two different animals."

But from his expression, the BAU agent had made the leap. "Both men had something significant to conceal, something that could have cost them their jobs."

"Exactly. And then there's the two incidents from Kusić's and Dunne's pasts. Granted, the events occurred in two countries, a year and nearly fifteen hundred miles apart—hence, I seriously doubt they're connected. But they need ruling out. Especially since both involved local, Muslim women and US soldiers, if obliquely. As for Kusić—" Kate caught Joe's stare. "—remember the Tanner Holmes case?"

"The sergeant who fell for an Iraqi local and deserted?"

"That's the one."

"Mike Barnes worked it." Joe glanced from Lou to Agent Walker. "There was a soldier who went AWOL in Iraq 'bout five years back, only to be captured by terrorists damned near the second he stepped outside the wire. He was intent on running off with some local he'd met and fallen for. If I remember correctly, they never found the girl; she'd disappeared. But they did find the soldier a couple days later, strung up in a bombed-out building, gutted and burned to a crisp. A seriously fucked-up way to go."

Kate was forced to agree. "According to Kusić's ex, he was on the SAR team that found the body. That's why Kusić turned to oxycodone the first time, to forget. We need to see if you can access the case file, read through it and see if anything pops. As for Dunne—do you also remember the local Afghan woman who reported a rape in an alley in Kabul six years ago only to disappear the next day?"

"The one with the shit of a brother?"

"Yeah, that's the one. I seem to recall that she couldn't describe her attacker's face, just his unit patch." Kate retrieved her phone and pulled up the secondhand photo she'd taken of Dunne and his buddy in front of that Afghan souk. "The same patch Dunne's sporting in this pic. Do you know if he was a suspect in the rape?"

"No idea. Hell, I don't even know who worked that case—but I can find out." Joe tapped the screen of her phone, directly over the slightly out-of-focus souk vendor she'd recognized in the original photo. "Is that who I think it is?"

"Yep. Hamid Kasi. And get this, that AK-47 we found in Kusić's trailer? It's Russian. I don't know if that's a connection, but it bears scrutiny too."

"Damned straight it does. And I'm on it, just as soon as we've finished here." Joe tapped the secondhand photo again. "Would you forward that?"

"Sure thing."

"Thanks. Any other weird connections?"

Just the ones concerning Grant. But she wasn't ready to voice those just yet.

Yes, she had witnesses who claimed Grant knew both male victims. And, no, Grant hadn't shared that with her. Nor had her soon to be ex-lover shared his recent vacation status. Or the existence of that second phone—if, indeed, it was his. But none of it was enough to bring him in for questioning. Not officially. Unofficially, she planned on tracking the man down and grilling him until she was satisfied.

Tonight.

If she wasn't successful, she'd be hauling her concerns to Lou's door at the crack of dawn.

"Nope, that's all the weirdness for now. Though I'm sure we'll be adding to it soon enough." Kate ignored the news cameraman and reporter already rigged for sound as they scrambled out of the van and bellied up to Seth's extended crime barrier well behind the line of police vehicles. "Lou, we need to get those bags to Little Rock asap. We need this woman's name and history—most importantly, if she was a vet and/or worked out of Fort Leaves. We also need to know what, if anything, she's been hiding."

As much as Kate detested putting the victim on trial, pawing through the woman's dirty laundry might lead them to her killer a lot sooner.

The BAU agent nodded his agreement. "Agent Cordoba and I spoke during our flight. If it's all right, I'd like to examine the body parts and speak to your medical examiner. If your ME is willing, I'll also assist him in preparing the body for transport and ride with him so I can examine the other bodies as well. Meanwhile, Agent Cordoba will examine this scene and the others. Afterward, he'll review the case files. We'll also need to make sleeping arrangements. Deputy Holland, your sheriff suggested you may be able to help us out there?"

Suggested, her ass. Kate didn't need to see the guilt threading through Lou's eyes to know he'd been plotting this from the moment she'd shown him that tread impression from her cabin. She valued her privacy, and Lou knew it. It was the reason she'd stopped renting the cabin after the last crime tech had moved out.

She'd have been doubly irked with the end run around her bodyguard refusal, if Joe wasn't part of the package.

"Please, call me Kate. I'm sure Dr. Tonga will be happy to let you tag along. We do have a motel in town, but I wouldn't let a rabid coon stay there. The sheriff's right. I have a place where you can flop. My dad and I built a cabin behind our house fifteen years back. My last renter left a year ago, so it's a bit musty—but it's clean and roach-free."

Joe ignored a hail from a reporter as he turned toward the crime scene. "Sold. Especially if your Dr. Tonga can deliver Agent Walker to the cabin after they finish with the bodies. We don't have transport yet, so I'll need to bum a ride with you."

"Not to worry." This from Lou. "I'll have someone at the station set you both up with somethin' by tomorrow."

Lou fell into step beside Kate, leaving Joe and the FBI agent to follow behind as they walked toward the tape. He lowered his voice. "I already had those two in the car when I got the call about this location. Are you—"

"I'm fine, boss. Really. We'll talk about it later."

"Okay. You've got my number."

She did. And she appreciated the unspoken offer of his shoulder. Even if she had been tempted to take him up on it, the best thing she could do right now was ignore that cross and the reason for it, until she had cause to do otherwise. It was the only way she'd survive this.

Unfortunately, Lou had reached the inner barrier and stopped to stare at the first sack...then the marker.

Kate cut him off before he could voice it. "I already asked Seth to have it dusted. There's nothing else to do but keep the possibility in mind and wait to see what pans out."

For Christ's sake, half their department was milling around. She could not *do this* right now.

To her relief, Lou let it go. As he hooked a left to speak with a tech, Kate made her escape. She immediately ducked beneath the tape and motioned for Joe and the BAU agent to follow as they finished donning their protective gear.

She and Joe stopped at the first sack. Agent Walker kept

moving toward Tonga. As with Lou, Kate watched as Joe noted the position of the leading body part with respect to the stone cross. He squinted at the engraving, then her.

"*Holy shit.*"

That was all he offered. Since they'd been pulling each other's hide out of the fire when she'd received that pithy Red Cross death notification four and a half years ago, it was enough.

"Yup." And so was that.

They headed for the second bag in silence, automatically spacing themselves for a more complete inspection of the road, even though a dozen techs were doing the same in front of them. What one person missed, another spotted. Anyone who'd survived their first real crime scene understood that.

They paused at each shrink-wrapped part, still not speaking. Joe preferred it, and so did she.

There was enough spinning through her brain during walks like this; she didn't need another's thoughts added in. Unless someone noticed something significant, there was time enough to discuss impressions later, after her own had time to ferment.

To her frustration, that same strange nausea rolled through Kate's belly as they reached the head. That damned scarlet line. Why did she feel as though there was a message inside it, just for her?

It was crazy. *She* was crazy.

After her rude genuflection before that hospital commode earlier, she probably had proof. There was a good chance she was half off her rocker and simply too stubborn to accept it. At least with Joe here to lean on, she might not have to. If she did end up having a complete meltdown, there was someone nearby who she could trust to see this through.

The thought helped ease the nausea.

Joe was studying her intently as she drew in her breath to

soothe her tattered nerves. She pulled her fingers from the band of the watch she hadn't realized she'd been twisting.

"You okay?"

"Yeah. You never quite get used to it, do you?"

"Christ, I hope not."

As crushing as the past two days had been, Kate agreed. What would it say about them if they could?

Upon Joe's signal that he'd seen enough, they retraced their steps down the gravel strip.

Lou waited just outside the tape. "Nester finished scourin' the edges of the road. Other than one from the sedan owned by the couple who found the bags, there ain't any fresh treads."

"That's right." Joe glanced from Lou to her. "The article mentioned something about an impression located at the second site."

Lou stared at Kate—hard.

She sighed. "I found its twin afterward. At my place. Last night, after I returned home from the Dunne scene."

"Are you saying this bastard followed you *home?*"

Kate winced as the heads of several techs swiveled their way. "Louder, Joe. I don't think the reporters heard you."

"Holland—"

"Nothing happened. Even if the guy was looking for some extra fun, he wouldn't have found it with me. I was locked and loaded."

"Nothing happened, my ass. The fact that he was there is very much *something.*"

Jesus. Joe could be twice as loud and three times as protective as Lou. How could she have forgotten that?

He closed in on her. "I saw the name on that cross. Not to mention that a green MP on his first scene would've noticed the alignment between it and that first, hacked-off hand—a hand that belongs to a *woman,* mind you. There's a decent chance this son-of-a-bitch is developing a hard-on for you—if he didn't start this entire fucked-up scenario with you already in mind."

She couldn't argue with any of it. The moment she'd noted that marker's alignment with the first bag, she too had begun to suspect some sort of sick, symbiotic strategy.

But what did that change?

Absolutely nothing.

Joe loomed closer, blocking out even Lou's girth. "Do you have a personal connection to either of the other dump sites?"

She clamped down on her tongue and her temper—until the mottled side of her face twitched, betraying her. "Damn it, Joe. I live in this town. I police it. Hell, I went to high school here. Of course I have connections—all over the place. But none like that cross. If the guy does have me in his sights, it's most likely a last-minute, extra twist to get his jollies. His own charming way of inserting himself into the investigation. It's clear he did his research on this town. That had to have extended to our department. And the lead page of our website connects to the memorial write-up on my dad. It would take a moron to fail to notice that a current deputy bore the same last name—something we all know this bastard isn't."

She held her ground beneath that same molten stare she'd seen incinerate privates and generals alike. But she wasn't either. Hell, she wasn't even in the Army anymore. She was a civilian deputy and, as she'd said, this was *her* town. *Her* case. And Joe Cordoba damned well knew it.

He backed down, and off. For now.

She wasn't stupid. He'd be bringing up the subject again just as soon as they lost their audience.

Fine with her.

Kate shifted her stance, only to discover a livid Seth six inches behind her. He'd had her back just now, literally and figuratively. Nice to know. "Seth, you busy?"

"Not at the moment."

"Special Agent Cordoba needs a lift to the other scenes. Once he's finished his walkthroughs, bring him to my place. But swing by the station first and grab a copy of anything not yet entered in the electronic case files."

Her former fellow agent took a step toward her. Kate wasn't sure if Joe intended on arguing with the change in plans or apologizing. She shook her head to ward off both scenarios.

Joe and Lou were dead on the money about one thing. This case was jerking her strings. Damn near all of them.

At this rate, it was only a matter of time before she snapped.

She needed to decompress. A decent night's sleep would be ideal. Barring that, a thirty minute power nap would help. So long as it was preceded and then followed by a series of soul-balming hugs from Ruger.

A shower wouldn't hurt either. The dried sweat from that humiliating panic attack in Dr. Manning's office still infested her clothes. If she had time, she might even head to the cabin and open the windows and doors to air it out.

Seth snapped off his gloves and swapped them for his keys. "You ready, Agent Cordoba?"

Joe took the hint and followed Seth to the deputy's Braxton PD SUV.

Kate's crappy night and crappier day must've been on her face, because Lou cocked his head toward her own SUV. "Go home and relax 'til your briefin' with Cordoba, then take the night off. Toss a ball to Ruger. Grant never stopped by the station to pick up your key. Seth volunteered to let him out, but then he learned about this, so I doubt he got the chance. I'll call if somethin' comes up. But since you won't stay with Della and me—*or* let me post a deputy inside your place—stay alert and make sure you lock the damned doors. And keep that 9 mil loaded and close by. Ruger, too."

"I will. Thanks, boss."

Kate crawled inside her Durango before guilt changed her mind. She'd been in the business too long to not know what happened when the lead detective burned out. Ian Kusić, Jason Dunne and that unknown woman lying in pieces out on the road deserved more. Not that the two additional news vans and that swelling gaggle of media vultures would get it—or care.

Kate jacked up the Durango's radio to better ignore the cameras and microphones pointed her way, all of which scraped along her window as she eased the SUV through the narrow opening Seth had left for official vehicles in the outer perimeter.

A series of flashes nearly blinded her and almost caused her to run down the photographer who briefly stepped in front of her grill to snap photos of her face through the windshield.

After that standoff with Joe, she had a feeling her ugly mug would be making the Sunday paper, along with her name, rank and so-called heroic past—and a column full of speculation.

It just kept getting crappier, didn't it?

Her empty stomach growled in agreement.

So much for heading home. She had barely enough food for her and Ruger in her pantry, and none that could be popped in an oven or microwave without a lot of time and thought. The latter of which were both in short to nonexistent supply.

Kate headed into Braxton proper. It took ten minutes to reach the grocery store. Ten more to toss an assortment of bags and boxes from the frozen-meals section into her cart, along with an extra tin of coffee and an assortment of fresh fruit in case Agent Walker didn't share her and Joe's addiction to rising-crust pizza and caffeine.

She chalked up an additional twenty minutes attempting to clear the "quick" register. For every item in her cart, half a dozen residents stopped to share their horror over the murders. Kate fielded questions and soothed concerns before extricating herself as politely as she could.

By the time she made it home, twilight had bled down to full-on night. Kate parked the Durango in her drive and released a pent up sigh as she switched off the engine. She thought about retrieving her phone and affording Grant yet another opportunity to ignore her voicemail, but decided to pop the hatch and deal with the groceries instead. Besides, Ruger came first.

She could hear him from out here.

Strange—the Shepherd was in the house where she'd left him, but he appeared to be going nuts. Kate abandoned the SUV, the fine hairs along her arms snapping to attention at the change in Ruger's tone as she jogged up the darkened walk. She'd heard that tone only once before.

Ruger wasn't so much barking, as snarling...and the sounds were emanating from the back of the house.

Her dad's room?

How the devil had he gotten in there?

A split second later, the intent in his snarls clicked in and she realized it didn't matter. Ruger was trying to warn her of a bigger problem.

Someone was inside their house.

9

KATE EASED her 9mm from her shoulder holster as she crept around the back of the house to peer through her father's window. Ruger was trapped inside the darkened room, frantically clawing at the door. The only other time Kate had seen him this upset was the night she'd conducted an off-duty traffic stop with Ruger in tow. The driver had been so jacked up on flakka, he'd body slammed her when she'd asked him to walk the line. Ruger had turned so feral, he'd actually cracked the Durango's windshield as she'd brought the man to his knees and cuffed him.

Kate eased her phone from her pocket with her free hand and thumbed the first entry in her speed dial. Two rings in, Lou's voice filled her ear.

"Kato, you're psychic. I was just about to call. One of the—"

"I'm behind my house. Ruger's trapped in Dad's old room, and he's going nuts. I think someone's in there. I'm heading in—"

"No! *Wait.* I'll have backup there in—"

Kate severed the call. She muted the phone and swapped it

for her keys as she and her Glock crept toward the double doors at the far side of her shadowy deck.

Wait?

Not bloody likely.

She'd seen what that monster could do. If he was inside her house, she was *not* affording him the chance to slice up Ruger. Canine or not, Ruger had singlehandedly kept her from swallowing her gun after she'd returned home.

Several times.

Kate peered through the kitchen window as she passed. Everything appeared normal in the glow from the light she'd left on for Ruger that morning, save for his frenzied racket. He was determined to shred his pound of flesh. So was she.

Kate reached the double doors and glanced through the slats of the embedded mini-blinds before unlocking the door on the right. Glock front and center, she slipped inside, clearing the mostly darkened house room by vacant room, saving her dad's for last. Ruger's snarling barks and deep growls provided cover for any stray sounds she might be making.

To her relief, she reached her father's door without noting a single item out of place, let alone extraneous people.

But he'd been here.

Ruger was quite insistent on that point.

She turned the knob to the bedroom door and jerked back with a millimeter to spare as a still-snarling Ruger tore out of the room and down the hall. She entered the bedroom to clear her dad's connected bath and closet, then made her way to the living room. Re-holstering her Glock, she switched on the inside lights and outside floods before returning to the kitchen to find Ruger scouring the windowsills, doors and floors with his frantic nose.

Finally satisfied, he bounded over to her, barking his displeasure at the entire experience.

"It's okay, buddy. He's gone now."

Ruger must not have believed her, because he shadowed her to the front door and out onto the cedar porch.

There, his ears pricked up and his head cocked.

As usual, it took several more moments for Kate to hear it —them.

Sirens.

Cavalry had arrived twice in the same day.

This latest herd came in the form of two Braxton PD SUVs tearing up her drive and sliding to gravel-spitting halts. Owen and Seth squelched their sirens as Lou's sedan brought up the rear. Despite his age and more impressive girth, her boss managed to climb out and meet her in the walkway first.

Owen and Seth were seconds behind the sheriff, along with an equally frazzled Joe.

Kate held up her hands. "Everything's okay. The house is clear. Sorry I called for nothing."

"*Nothin'?*" The cold air Lou dragged into his lungs did little to calm his raging temper. "Damn it, young lady, I shoulda foreseen this. Until we catch this bastard, I want a uniform planted in front of this house twenty-four/seven."

"No."

"Kato—"

"I said, *no.*" She met his glare with her own. "I mean it. No bodyguards. There's no need." She jabbed her index finger into Joe's chest as he stepped up beside her boss, his posture set to support him. "You trapped me into letting this man sleep in my cabin, his cohort too. That's plenty of backup."

"It's not close enough."

"It is." She lowered her hand to pat Ruger's head. Easily accomplished, since the brawny Shepherd was still glued to her right leg. "Not only do I have this guy for warning, I have this." Kate shifted her fingers to tap the re-holstered 9mm as she met the stares of Owen, Seth, Joe and Lou in turn. "All of you know I won't hesitate to use it."

One by one the men backed down. They didn't have a choice. Not if she refused to offer one.

"Owen, Seth, thanks for showing up. I appreciate it. But please don't miss dinner on my account. Joe, sorry I interrupted your walkthroughs."

He shrugged. "I'd just finished. We were grabbing the paperwork when the sheriff called."

Owen and Seth headed for the floodlit drive. Joe followed. As the deputies climbed into their SUVs and fired up the engines, Joe accepted a thick folder from Seth. He tucked it under an arm and paused beside her Durango's hatch to heft the waiting grocery bags. He carried everything up the walkway as the deputies departed.

"I'll just put these inside."

Kate nodded, grateful more for the privacy he was offering than the labor, especially after her tantrum at the crime scene. "Feel free to pick out a pizza and preheat the oven. Coffee's in one of the bags; pot's on the counter. Make yourself at home."

"Will do."

Within seconds, only she, Lou and Ruger remained. The silence all but pulsed between them.

"Hon—"

She cut him off as she leaned forward to wrap her arms around his shoulders and hug him tightly. Lou's fury had faded to fear—and he was not a man who feared much. She could feel the remainder bleed off with his shudder as he squeezed her back. "*Jesus*, Kate."

She nodded into his neck. "I know. It's okay, boss. *I'm* okay. I promise." She eased a bit of room between them so she could look him in the eye. "But I do need my privacy. Lord knows you're not putting a guard on Seth's door tonight—or any of the other deputies—so don't insult me by insisting that I need one." Not to mention that out of all of them, she was the one who'd demonstrated that she could take care of herself. Eleven times over. "Besides, I called. I've proven I'm not foolish enough to forgo backup."

"You went in before it arrived, damn it."

"Ruger was inside. What would you have done?"

He held her gaze for a solid minute before purging his remaining tension with a sigh. "Same thing." He glanced down at Ruger.

Ruger stared back.

"Damned mangy mutt." He softened the pronouncement with a gentle tweaking of fuzzy ears.

Ruger slobbered on Lou's fingers in return, then whirled around and bounded across the floodlit clearing and into the trees to take care of the business he'd been holding all day.

Kate headed down the stone walkway toward the Durango's still-yawning hatch. "So, how am I psychic?"

Lou blinked.

"When you picked up the phone, you said I was—"

"Right. Got so worked up, I plum forgot. We got an ID on the woman."

"That was quick." Even with the game-night traffic directed away from Little Rock, Tonga must've put the pedal to the metal to get to the state lab this soon. Even then, he'd have had a bit of prep work before he could get the parts into an autopsy suite to unbag the hands.

Lou reached the Durango first and closed the hatch. "We haven't confirmed it with prints, but we're sure. Nester took one look at the woman's face and hightailed it off the road to puke. Another second, and he woulda contaminated the scene. Her name's Andrea Silva. Late twenties, early thirties."

"I take it he knew her well?" A rhetorical question at best. As with the rest of the department, that had been Nester's third head in two days—and his first vomit.

"Yep. She was married to a fellow crime scene tech when Nester lived in Hot Springs. Back then Silva worked at the Hot Springs Medical Center. She wasn't a veteran, but she was a surgical nurse. Accordin' to Nester's cousin, who was close to the woman, Silva moved to Little Rock two years ago. She doesn't work outta Fort Leaves, but the other VA hospital in town."

Kate frowned. So while the woman wasn't a vet, she had worked with them—in the operating room. Jason Dunne had worked admin. Kusić had been a phlebotomist in the lab. And all three had worked in the same medical system, albeit across town.

An illegal weapon. Stolen scripts, mail-order steroids, possible vials of stolen blood...and a serious chunk of money.

How the devil did it all fit?

"Kato?"

"Sorry. Just collating information. Why did Silva leave Hot Springs? Because of the husband's job, or hers?"

"Ahh...that would be the psychic part. You asked about secrets. Andrea Silva and her husband had two girls. They were four and five when Nester knew them. A few months before Silva and the girls moved to Little Rock, she filed for divorce. Next day, she changes her mind. 'Bout a week after that, her husband up and dies. The whole department thought the death was hinky, but no one—includin' the ME—could prove foul play. But durin' the investigation, rumors came to light. Seems the dead husband was asked to stop helpin' with his church's childcare just before Silva filed for divorce. Some of the moms told the pastor he was a bit too friendly with the kids...'specially the little girls."

"Did anyone file charges for molestation?"

"Nope. But that don't mean it didn't happen."

True. Not to mention, "A nurse could get away with murder if she was smart and patient enough...and motivated."

"Agreed. Hell, the need to keep two little girls safe? That's a pretty good motivator if you ask me. Cain't right say as I wouldn't a done the same thing in her place, neither."

Not only did Kate agree, but Silva definitely had something to hide.

An oxycodone addiction. Potential rape and steroid abuse. Murder. Though that last upped the ante significantly, it fit the pattern.

But how did the fact that all three victims had something to hide connect to their deaths?

Kate scanned the edges of the floodlit clearing, searching for Ruger as she considered possibilities, only to discard them as she located the white flash of the underside of his tail. He was fifty yards to her right, just inside the trees.

She relaxed against the Durango. "Did someone call the hospital and confirm the woman's employment?"

"Owen. Like the others, Silva hadn't been to work in a week. In fact, her supervisor got a text message early Monday morn sayin' she was sick."

"Let me guess. The flu?"

"Yep. In the supervisor's defense, it is goin' 'round right now, along with the stories 'bout how the vaccine missed the mark this year, so folks are comin' down with it."

Which meant their killer kept up to date on the news.

Good. Kate hoped her ugly mug did make tomorrow's paper. Her scars were distinctive enough to taunt the bastard straight to her door. Better her than another unsuspecting vet or a VA provider with kids to keep safe from a depraved father.

She hadn't exaggerated earlier. She and her 9mm *would* be waiting.

Lou's phone pinged. He checked the screen and frowned.

"Governor's aide wants an update. Course it wouldn't occur to the man to get his butt up here and get the facts in person."

"You tell him that?"

"Hell, no. With our luck, he'd snap a few pics and swipe what little evidence we did find to hawk on eBay."

She'd have smiled, but for her suspicion that Lou was right. "If you need to go, boss—do. I'm fine."

Reluctance wracked his features.

"Look, I didn't want to admit this, but I probably overreacted. I fell asleep in Dad's room last night. I don't remember closing the door after you woke me this morning. Ruger and I never go in, so I suspect he snuck inside to nose around. That dragon's tail of his probably smacked the door shut behind him and, after being trapped for hours on end, he lost it."

"You *never* go in?"

That would be the part he'd focus on.

Worse, as Lou's visible reluctance gave way to worry, she realized that her lapse had allowed him to make the leap to the one shame she'd hoped to keep to herself. Namely, that today was also the first time she'd faced that cross out on Fox Run.

Ruger chose that moment to come bounding across the floodlit clearing, hitched gait and all. She could've hugged him for the timely distraction alone as he slid to an overzealous stop and spun around to plant his rump in the gravel beside her.

Moments later she realized why he'd resumed his self-appointed guard duty, as another SUV rumbled up her drive, this one carrying Ruger's least-favorite human.

Grant.

He hadn't even reached the house yet, and the Shepherd was already growling. Weird.

"Ruger, hush."

The Shepherd complied. Reluctantly.

Lou retrieved his keys as the dark blue Bronco pulled up

beside her black Durango. "Guess that's my cue to get lost. I should warn you though; the governor's head lackey's been pushin' for a press conference. I managed to put him off this afternoon—but that was before we found the third dump site."

"Hold him off a bit longer. At least until Agent Walker's had a chance to study the evidence and create a profile. I'd rather go with BAU's instincts regarding what information to release than some wannabe kingmaker who may be more concerned with his boss' re-election than catching this bastard."

"Agreed."

Kate remained fused to the Durango's hatch as Lou climbed into his sedan. The damning tidbits she'd been collecting all day regarding Grant dropped into her gut like jagged stones as Lou fired up his engine and cut a tight one-eighty to begin his return to town. Unfortunately, Lou's departure forced her to turn and face Grant, whether she was ready or not.

He was wearing the same green cable knit sweater, jeans and lumberjack boots she'd noted from Jason Dunne's window that morning. The deep lines etched in and round his hazel eyes and mouth were unexpected.

"Missed you."

Really? After a day of active avoidance, that was what he chose to open with?

She waited for more. Something worth her response.

He'd read her mood accurately, because he sighed—and offered a bit more. "Bill Manning called. He said you stopped by his office to interview him about the two murders in town...Jason Dunne and Ian Kusić."

"I did."

"He also said you left in a rush, very upset. He tried to follow, but got waylaid by a call. Are you okay?"

"I've had better days." Definitely better cases.

Easier interviews.

Kate held her tongue and growing temper in check as she reached into her pocket. Her fingers closed around the prehistoric phone. If Grant had spoken to Manning, its current location had probably cropped up. She wouldn't be able to crack open the SIM card now. Not without a warrant.

She tugged the phone free and held it up—but not out—forcing Grant to move forward to retrieve it.

To her surprise, he didn't. If anything, his entire body appeared to be frozen in place. Including his breath.

"What's wrong?"

"W-where'd you get that?"

"Dr. Manning. It slipped out of your pocket during therapy at Fort Leaves, a week ago Thursday night. The doc would've called your office to let you know but, apparently, you were on vacation."

"*Shit.*"

She carved out a half-smile. "Yeah."

"I can explain."

He probably could. But she wouldn't be buying it. Nor would some impromptu spin change anything. Even without the contents of those paper bags drilled into her brain, his behavior definitely signaled the end to the two of them.

"The phone belongs to my dad. His cancer's back. He's dying."

"*What?*" Abel? No, damn it! Not again. She and Liz had supported Dan through the man's first bout. It had been truly awful. Kate wrapped her arms about her midsection as she fought the surging memories—and renewed panic.

Suspicion set in as both began to fade.

Why hadn't Grant told her before now? He knew she adored his dad. So why the delay?

Grant stepped closer. He ignored the phone to slide his fingers along the skin of her good cheek.

She tensed.

Ruger growled. Emphatically.

But Grant's fingers settled into the curve of her neck and stayed put. "I'm sorry I didn't tell you sooner, but I didn't know how to say it. Scratch that. I didn't *want* to say it. Voicing it made it real." He flicked his gaze toward the phone. "I bought him that because he still insists on his walks. I was afraid something would happen and he'd need help. Of course, he keeps leaving it everywhere. And I keep picking it up, and handing it back. A lot of good it does, as you can see."

Guilt filtered in with the ache. "Grant, I'm so sorry. Your dad —he's amazing."

As for Abel's elder son...Kate inched away from those fingers, from Grant, and slumped against the side of her Durango. As her stare slid down, it instinctively zeroed in on the right rear tire of his Bronco. The tread didn't match the Starblaze pattern from those impressions.

Relief burned in.

"Is everything all right?"

"Absolutely." What was she supposed to do? Admit what she'd begun to suspect? It would only add to his hell. "I called this morning. Twice. You didn't answer. And you didn't call back."

"I'm sorry. It's been a lousy day. I woke to that article in the paper. They didn't name you, but I knew it had to be your case. I wasn't sure if you could talk about it and, well, I was in shock. I knew both victims. Jason Dunne and I served together in Iraq. He started at Fort Leaves six months ago. He'd joined Manning's group and swore it helped, convinced me to give it a shot. I suppose I needed to make sure he was really gone, so I went to his place. That's where I got your call—right after I hung up with Dad's nurse. He'd had a bad night and I wasn't in the mood to talk."

"And Kusić?"

Grant shrugged. "Not much to tell there. Ian and I had been having our own private sessions, usually over lunch. He knew my brother from Afghanistan, but I didn't particularly like him. Out of respect for Dan, I tried to get him to join the group. But...Ian had bigger issues."

"Oxycontin?"

Another nod. "And Xanax. It's a nasty combination to withdraw from. That's why I took vacation. Ian was supposed to take leave with his girlfriend. I tried to convince him to stay behind and get cleaned up instead. I have privileges at a local, non-VA clinic. With an IV and meds, I could've had him off the oxy and Xanax by the end of his leave. When he refused, I decided to spend it with my dad."

"Did Ian and Jason know each other?"

"I don't know."

"What about Liz Vogel? Why didn't you tell me you'd seen her?"

That one caused Grant's neck and cheeks to turn red. "We ran into each other a couple weeks ago outside Manning's office after a group session. I knew if you discovered the particulars of our reunion...let's just say, you haven't exactly been open to the idea of therapy."

No, she hadn't.

But she wasn't fond of lies either, even those of omission. Especially from a lover.

Unfortunately, that was the least of their problems. His tire treads might not match, but she'd looked.

That said it all, didn't it?

She held up the phone. This time, Grant took it.

"Thanks."

"Don't thank me yet. Your day's about to get worse. We're not just dealing with two murders. We've got three. We found

Andrea Silva today. Same sick slice-and-dice. Same row of bags strung out along a little-used gravel road. And I hate to tell you this, but you were my best connection."

Grant stood motionless, staring at her.

At first, she thought he was pissed. That he'd felt she was being flip, or even accusatory. Until she heard him draw a slow, tortured breath into his lungs. Then another. That was all he did. All he appeared capable of doing.

"Grant?"

"I...I knew her too. I've worked with her. Andrea is—was—one of the best OR nurses at my facility. I haven't seen her lately, but she was good people."

Kate waited for him to add more, but he just drew another labored breath and stared at...nothing. When he finally spoke, she swore it was more to himself than to her.

"It's true, isn't it? Someone's killing us off."

"I'm afraid so. Can you think of anyone who might be capable of going after VA staff in so heinous a manner? A disgruntled or emotionally tortured patient, or perhaps a relative of a patient?"

He shook his head. But he was still caught up in his own thoughts, obviously not focused on her.

"Grant, why would someone steal blood?"

That caused his attention to lock in. "What?"

"Blood. Why would someone steal it? Not units intended for transfusion, mind you. A smaller amount, as in a few vials."

It was long shot, especially with his current mood. But he was a doctor. Surely, if anyone would know, he would?

"Kate, I don't understand. What does a vial of blood have to do with those murders?"

"Probably nothing. But a patient claims Ian Kusić had been drawing more blood than ordered by physicians at Fort Leaves. But only from certain patients. Can you think of a reason why?"

He raked his fingers through his hair. "Hell, I can think of a thousand. Everything from DNA research to leukemia testing. But nothing that would get the man killed. Did you ask his co-workers? Maybe he was assisting with an unauthorized research project."

"I haven't had a chance." His ex-girlfriend had fallen into a drug-induced slumber and she'd been too busy returning to Braxton to assist with the third crime scene to question anyone else.

"I'll do it."

"*No.*"

"Why not? I don't mean to be insulting, but if a co-worker did notice Ian drawing extra blood and figured out why, it's not as though you'd understand what he was working on."

Wow. Intentions aside, that was insulting.

"Thanks, but I'll risk my stupidity. After all, there's a guy out there stalking VA employees, stringing them up and hacking them into tidy sections after they've been bled dry. I might not understand ninety percent of what comes out of your mouth in an operating room, but I doubt you could take this bastard down with a single shot from a 9mm at over a hundred meters, let alone track him down to get him in your sights."

"You're right—and I'm sorry." He shoved the sleeves of his sweater up his forearms as he scowled. "Christ, what a mess."

Excellent assessment.

Kate stared at the blood dripping from the impaled heart that had been inked into his arm during his first tour over there. Fellow fucked-up vet or not, he'd also reminded her of why the two of them were at the end of their run.

Hell, she was beginning to wonder why they'd begun. Lonely or not, they should've stayed "just friends".

Grant stepped closer, reached out. "Kate—"

Ruger's growl stopped him short. His words, and that hand.

The Shepherd's third vocalization since the Bronco's appearance. This growl was still reverberating deep inside the dog's throat. And it was getting louder.

Deadlier.

Lord, Ruger was pissed today. To the extent that she was beginning to wonder if this man *had* been inside the house earlier, despite that absolving tread.

"Grant—"

His phone rang.

"Just a sec." He retrieved his smartphone and stepped back as he glanced at the screen. "It's dad's nurse. I'm late for dinner and she needs to leave. I know you're swamped, but if you joined me —even for an hour—we could finish this."

She had every intention of doing precisely that, just not how he assumed. But dumping the man in front of his father —a man whose cancer had not only returned, but progressed to terminal—was not her idea of the right time. She'd visit Abel soon, but not with his remaining son in tow. "I can't. We're setting up a task force. I've got an FBI agent sifting through evidence at the state morgue as we speak so he can work up a psychological profile, and a fellow investigator from my CID days burning pizza in my kitchen while he waits for a briefing."

"The Army already sent someone in? Anyone I know?"

She had no idea. Nor was she in the mood to facilitate an introduction. "Joe Cordoba. We worked together a lot, most recently during my last tour in Afghanistan. He caught the flash traffic that came through and volunteered to fly in."

"Doesn't ring a bell. I'd best be going anyway. Dad's mood can turn dour by dinner. By his own admission, too much time alone with his thoughts."

She didn't wish Grant goodbye, much less feign disappointment as he climbed into his Bronco. She glanced down at Ruger as he drove off. She'd been in her drive for half an hour, and the Shepherd hadn't budged from her side.

Ruger's steady stare tracked the SUV's fading taillights, then swung up to hers.

"Okay, so you were right about the guy." In her defense, she could count on three fingers the human males Ruger did like.

A noise suspiciously close to a human snort emanated from his snout.

"Very funny." She scratched his ears to show her appreciation for his having had her back. Again. "What do you say, buddy? I smell pizza. You ready to eat?"

Ruger took off like a shot, beating her up the walk and onto the porch. He sniffed at the tantalizing air, chuffing and groaning in anticipation as she opened the door.

Joe greeted them from the kitchen's arch, one of her striped dishtowels hooked over his forearm. "I see you've still got that internal Holland food timer. And—surprise, surprise—your drooling dog inherited it. Unfortunately, the pizza's still got a couple minutes left in the oven."

"Mind if I grab a shower? Five minutes, tops." She could still feel the sweat from that panic attack stiffening her clothes. And there was the dust and grime from that last scene.

That stone cross.

"Sure thing. It has to cool anyway."

Ruger plopped his massive form across the hall's entrance as she continued to her room. She peeled off her Braxton PD jacket and backup piece and dumped them on the foot of the bed. Fresh undergarments and navy blue sweats in hand, Kate entered the bath. She shut the door and let the water heat as she stripped off her uniform. Laying her 9mm beside the sink, she groaned as she stepped beneath the blissful spray.

Too many tours in combat zones had her scrubbed, dried and dressed in under the promised five. She tucked her 9mm in the rear waistband of her string-tied sweats as she made her way back up the hall.

Ruger stood as she reached his side, escorting her to the kitchen table where Joe, a pair of paper plates, two napkins, mugs and an already-sliced deluxe pizza waited. Thankfully, Joe had chosen the spot opposite her dad's. The day she'd had, she'd have been forced to ask him to move.

Joe closed the folder he'd retrieved from Seth's SUV and shoved it aside as she took her seat.

"You weren't exaggerating. That dog of yours takes his guard duties seriously. I tried to lure him to the kitchen with a slice of cheese I found in the fridge, but he wouldn't budge. I was about to walk it to him when he suggested in no uncertain terms that I reconsider."

"Sorry. Ruger had a rough start in life a few deer seasons ago, hence his name. I think he holds that inept hunter's bullet against most men."

"No worries. He's not as bad as the ball of fluff Elise took in during my last deployment. That poodle has twice as much hair as your guy and is barely the size of his paw."

"It's a teacup?"

"Uh-huh. Yappy thing, too. Especially when I'm forced to drag it and a plastic baggie around the designated dog yard outside our apartment so it can crap."

Kate laughed at the idea of a pained Joe carrying a poop baggie and a tiny, yipping French poodle. She continued laughing simply because it felt so good to let loose. She knew he'd given her that image to diffuse the remaining tension between them, and it made her appreciate him all the more. Nor did she doubt the story.

Joe and Elise had been sweethearts since junior high. They'd met outside the girls' bathroom after Elise tried to make it inside to give herself a shot of insulin. Unfortunately, she'd passed out first. To hear Elise tell it, if Joe hadn't needed to use the facilities in the middle of earth science that day, she'd have been dead before the next bell rang. Joe had been her designated knight in shining armor ever since.

A role he'd taken seriously through six rescued cats, three rabbits, two ferrets, countless fantail goldfish and a sadly mute, haphazardly feathered cockatiel. And now, apparently, a tiny, yapping poodle.

Kate flopped against her chair and wiped the tears from her eyes. "Thanks. I needed that."

"Figured as much. That's a rotten scene to process. And to push through three of them in two days? It's a miracle you're not blubbering in the corner, rocking back and forth."

"We've seen worse."

"Yeah, but this one was painfully close to home, literally and figuratively." He reached for a slice of pizza.

"You don't know the half of it."

His hand paused over the crust and waited.

Kate squared off the plate he'd set out for her, then rearranged her napkin. Finally, the cup of coffee he'd poured. "That first scene you visited? The cross at the side of the road? You were right. That's where my dad was hit. Where he died. I...uh...haven't been out there since I got back."

Joe retrieved the slice of pizza beneath his hand and laid it on his plate. "From Afghanistan?"

She nodded.

"Kate, it's going on damned near four years."

Yeah, well, "It's kind of a long story."

"One of those chapters deal with why you didn't take emergency leave and fly back for the funeral?"

Yup.

She kept the confirmation to herself. And Joe, being Joe, knew enough to let it drop. Or maybe he simply remembered her toasted blather from the night he and Max had pulled her out of an underground bar in Kabul a couple hours after she'd received that pithy note from the Red Cross.

She was fairly certain it was the latter when Joe's hand repeated its path to the pizza. He set this slice on her plate and sat back to retrieve his coffee. "So, you going to fill me in on the case, or what?"

With a subtle transition like that, how could she not?

Kate retrieved her laptop from the computer desk in the den. She set it on the table so they could access the files the department had been amassing on all three murders. As she pulled up the first, she passed on Lou's information about Andrea Silva, along with the detail that Kusić had been mixing Xanax with the oxy. Though she and Joe had worked both those mass graves together in Iraq, she held off on the crime scene photos until the bulk of the pizza had been demolished.

Joe toyed with a piece of crust as she finally loaded the photos, only to dump it on his plate.

"Jesus. Is it just me, or do you get the feeling you're standing at the meat counter in a grocery store?"

"That's what Lou said."

Knowing Joe would study them later, she clicked through the remaining photos as swiftly as she dared and pushed the laptop aside. As she reached for the folder Seth had provided, she realized Ruger was still sitting beside her chair, patiently waiting for his portion of her dinner.

Kate flipped one of her pizza bones in the air. Ruger dutifully caught it in mid-descent. Joe held out a crust of his own as Ruger finished chewing.

Ruger simply stared.

"Not gonna budge, huh? Buddy, I could tell you stories about how I saved your mistress' hide. She's in my debt, you know."

"Really? Would you like to re-tally that score right now?" He knew full well she'd have to add a mission into her column that involved a certain house they'd cleared in Ramadi as MPs, a house Joe's ass wouldn't have left alive if it hadn't been for her.

"Hell, no. I'm good." He was still chuckling at the mutual memory as her phone rang.

They both sobered.

"It's Tonga, my ME. Grab the coffee. We'll head out back." Kate opened the deck door to let Ruger stretch his legs as she accepted the call. He'd been cooped up all day. "What've you got, doc?"

"Agent Walker and I are at the state lab. Dr. Tolman has the preliminary results from the toxicology tests on Jason Dunne. He was able to confirm Mr. Dunne's steroid abuse; the man was negative for oxycodone. Unfortunately, the samples from Ian Kusić were compromised. Dr. Tolman is retrieving new samples personally. They'll be tested as soon as possible."

"What about Xanax?"

"Mr. Dunne was negative. Were you expecting a different result?"

"Not with Dunne. But I spoke with a VA surgeon who knew Kusić." Kate shook her head as Joe paused near a cushioned lounge chair. It was Ruger's. Sitting there would put him on the dog's poop list for life. "The surgeon says Kusić was using oxy and Xanax."

"I'll let Dr. Tolman know. But first, I have more. We also found traces of doxacurium in Mr. Dunne's tissues. DOX is a surgical paralytic...but there were no traces of anesthesia."

She caught Joe's eye as he set their coffees down on the cedar table. "Are you saying the killer paralyzed Dunne, but deliberately failed to knock him out?"

The bastard had *wanted* Dunne awake?

The hell with Ruger's feelings. Kate took two stunted steps

and dropped into the dog's chair as the implications of Tonga's information reverberated through her gut. "*Jesus.*"

Joe returned his coffee to the table and stood. "Everything okay?"

She waved him back down to his chair. "Is there anything else, doc?"

"I'm afraid so. We also found signs of intubation in the mouths of both male victims, so they were breathing for some minutes following paralysis. How many, we don't know. We haven't begun to examine the third victim, but I suspect similar results. I will, of course, keep you appraised. Also, we still are no closer to the precise cause of death for any of them."

Hell, in light of what they now knew, the victims could've died of terror.

She drew a deep breath and purged it. "Okay. Thanks." Severing the connection, she stared blindly at the phone, unwilling to join Joe at the table to finish her coffee.

Thankfully, they'd already eaten. She wouldn't have been able to stomach pizza either.

"What's wrong?"

"The men." She stood and reluctantly headed for the table. "They were intubated and given a paralytic to keep them breathing and immobile, but that's it. No anesthesia, no pain meds. They had to know what was coming—and probably watched and felt the opening slices."

How long did it take to pass out from pain?

Four years was a long time. She couldn't remember. Or maybe she just didn't want to.

Kate dumped the phone next to her untouched coffee.

"You okay?"

"No." She was fed up and she was tired. Damn, was she tired.

Joe shoved his coffee aside and covered her hand with his. "How much sleep did you log last night? Two hours, three?"

"Sounds about right."

"That's it." He tugged his hand from hers and stood. "Let's go."

"Where?"

"Me, to this mystery cabin of yours. Where I will read until I am sick to my stomach and my heart as I wait for your ME to drop off Agent Walker. And you, Deputy Holland, are going to bed while you can still get there under your own power."

He was right; she was beyond beat. She wouldn't be able to contribute squat until she'd logged a decent night's sleep.

"I haven't aired out the cabin."

"I'll do it. I'll drag a chair outside if it makes you happy, while I read and wait for Ed."

"Okay." She headed into the kitchen to retrieve the keys as he brought up the rear with the coffee. "Sheets and blankets are in the closet. Just pull off the dust covers and stuff 'em in the laundry room. Close and plug in the fridge, and in the morning I'll drop off some things to put inside. The kitchen has a few dishes, dry goods and an assortment of soups. The bathroom's still stocked from a witness we were supposed to house a month back, then never did." She located the keys and a spare flashlight in her junk drawer and dropped them in Joe's waiting palm. "The keys are identical. One for you, one for Agent Walker. Call if you need anything else."

"I won't. You sleep. That's an order, soldier."

"Ha." She smacked his arm as he hefted the laptop and Seth's folder. "I don't take orders from grunts anymore. And since I'm now a lowly civilian taxpayer, technically *you* work for *me*."

"In your dreams, Holland. You sure you don't want me to set up shop on your coffee table? I can crash on the couch when I've hit my limit of gore."

And take a chance the night terrors would win out for the third night in a row? "Ruger snores. He'd keep you up."

"For Christ's sake, I'm serious. This bastard has a bead on you."

"I appreciate the love, especially since you're the most happily married schmuck I know. But the fact that Andrea Silva *isn't* a vet lends even more credence to the fact that this guy's fascination with me is recent—and that he's most likely eyeing everyone in my department. As for me, he's done his initial recon; I'll give him that. But he doesn't know what makes me tick, and he sure as hell won't be able to get close enough to include me in his games. He made a critical mistake tonight. Ruger has his scent. If he shows up, Ruger will know it's him, and then I'll know it."

"You just make sure you act on that knowledge. If that mutt alerts, you shoot first and ask questions while I'm mopping up the mess."

"Absolutely."

"Good. Now where's this cabin?"

"If you'd taken the right side of the Y instead of the left when you and Seth screamed up my drive, you'd have gotten there." She accompanied him to the deck and pointed to a generous gap in the floodlit tree line. "The shortcut starts there. My dad felled enough oaks and pines after we moved in to make the path obvious. Just follow the ribbon of leaves and pine needles smack into a split-log cabin a third the size of this."

She waited for Joe to reach the path, then brought her thumb and index finger to her mouth to generate a piercing whistle that had Ruger racing out from the underbrush. She waited as he barreled into the house before locking the doors and checking the latch on his dog flap. Only then did she extinguish the exterior lights.

"Well, I'm good to go. How about you?"

Kate took Ruger's *woof* as a "yes", and padded down the hall, exhaustion weighing her steps. She retrieved her Braxton PD jacket and backup piece from the bed and tossed them on the dresser. Dumping her phone and 9mm on the nightstand next, she leaned over to draw the covers from her pillow—and froze.

Ruger was right. Despite the impromptu and quite plausible story she'd constructed for Lou earlier that evening, someone had been in her house. In her room.

Leaning over her bed.

The proof was winking up at her.

Her Silver Star. The one some droning, faceless general had hung on her uniform while she was imprisoned at Walter Reed. The same Silver Star she'd shoved in its case five minutes later with that damned Purple Heart and dumped in her duffle bag and, eventually, the trunk in her father's room...where it had remained for the last three and a half years.

It wasn't there now.

It was pinned to her pillow.

10

SHE WOKE from her third night terror in as many days. As usual, Ruger was at her side, gently nudging her.

Heart still pounding, Kate buried her face in the Shepherd's warmth as she struggled to slow her ragged breathing. In, out. In, out.

Over and over.

It took a good minute, but eventually her heart began to settle and the panic eased. It was only when she pulled away from Ruger's neck that she realized she was on the floor of her bedroom closet. Not only had the terrors returned, she was sleepwalking.

Good God, not again.

The walks had begun at Walter Reed. She'd woken one night to find one of the nurses assigned to her recovery standing over her, attempting to comfort her as she cowered in the corner of some unknown doctor's office. She'd begged the nurse to keep the incident to herself. Not only had the woman ratted her out, it had happened again and again. A patient lounge, the corner of some dimly lit stairwell, the visitors' bathroom on an upper floor. Soon it had become routine for her to wake anywhere but in her bed.

Her shrink had warned her during their final session that, unless she found someone she could confide in and dealt with what she could and couldn't remember from those eleven hours of captivity, the night walks and terrors wouldn't cease.

But for a while, they had.

Because of Ruger.

They'd slowed to a trickle from almost the moment she'd found the Shepherd lying in a pool of his own blood out behind her cabin. Ruger had insisted on crawling into bed with her that first night after she'd brought him home from the vet. Even then, with his own wounds still raw and seeping, his mere presence had somehow managed to ease hers. Until now.

Was she losing it again? As much as she wanted to deny the possibility, she couldn't.

That goddamned Silver Star.

Kate opened the closet door and scrambled out. Ruger followed, hopping up onto the middle of her bed as she clung to the edge. The medal was on the dresser where she'd dumped it the previous night, its once gleaming surface and attached red, white and blue striped ribbon now smudged with the remnants of black fingerprint powder.

It was devoid of prints.

She hadn't even been able to lift her own, let alone those from the general who'd pinned it to her uniform...much less the killer who may or may not have attached it to her pillow.

Of course, if the killer had been in her house, he would've also had to have been smart and adept enough to maneuver Ruger into another room while he rifled through her footlocker. He would've then had to have been savvy enough to lure Ruger back into her father's room before heading across the hall to pin the medal to her pillow. A man that methodical would've worn gloves.

But then, why wipe the medal clean? Because he was that paranoid about potential evidence?

She prayed so. The alternative suggested she was losing her grip on reality...or worse.

Was she stalking herself?

If she couldn't remember climbing into her closet in the dead of night, much less grabbing an AK-47 upon her escape from that hovel where she'd been raped and using it to slaughter a room full of terrorists, who was to say *she* hadn't wiped the medal down and pinned it to her pillow? As much as she hated to admit it, the scenario was equally as plausible as a killer entering her house and sanitizing that piece of tin, even though he was already wearing gloves.

Unfortunately, Ruger was the only one who knew for sure if her remaining marbles had shattered completely, and he wasn't talking.

But he was snoring.

Loudly.

Kate eased herself off the bed and padded out of the room. She checked her watch as she reached the kitchen, and groaned. It was barely four in the morning. She poured fresh grounds into the coffee machine and set it to perk before heading for the shower. If she couldn't sleep, she might as well wash the latest slick of sweat from her flesh and plow through any new reports that had been added to the department's files before she reviewed the rest.

Her puttering must've broadcasted her intent, because Ruger poked his nose in the bathroom while she was waiting for the water to heat.

Kate scratched his ears. "You need to go out?"

His answering *ruff* had her turning off the water and

detouring to the front porch where she waited for him to do his business. It took less than a minute. She let them inside and locked the door behind them, then returned to the bathroom to resume the flow of water and strip off her sweats.

Ten minutes later she was dressed in a navy blue Braxton PD polo, jeans and boots. Ruger followed her to the kitchen table where she'd already set up her laptop, and stretched out beside her chair to resume his snores.

By the time Ruger woke, her neck had begun to ache.

No wonder. The cuckoo clock across the kitchen had begun to chirp out seven a.m.

Ruger sat up as the bird finished, and cocked his head to the side.

"What is it, boy?"

Several moments later, she caught the rumble of a diesel engine. They had company. Ruger's tail whipped back and forth as he stood to whirl about. Only two people warranted that level of enthusiasm, and she was already here.

Kate closed the laptop and stretched as Ruger headed for the front door, huffing his impatience the entire way.

"I'm coming; I'm coming."

She crossed the living room, unlocked the door and swung it open before their visitor could knock.

"Morning, boss."

Lou frowned over the stack of files and pair of oversized food containers in his arms. "Did you even bother to look through those glass slats?"

Kate grabbed the files before they could slip from the sheriff's arms. "Didn't have to. Ruger could smell that contraband you brought a mile up the drive."

Even if she hadn't caught a whiff of the jumbo bacon and cheddar muffins that were his wife's specialty, there was no mistaking Ruger's dance. His tongue already hanging from his mouth, the Shepherd tracked the container's every move as he waltzed from side to side—regardless of the fact that just one of those lovely little heart-stoppers would have him producing enough gas to fuel a rocket to Mars.

Lou had the grace to flush as he followed Kate to the kitchen. "Sorry. Wasn't thinkin'. With all that's been goin' on, Della's been bakin' non-stop to keep from worryin'. I gotta get rid of the results somehow. If it helps, I got blueberry scones in here too. And I hope you don't mind, but I called the cabin. Agent Walker and your friend will be here in ten. Figured we could get through the mornin' brief outside eye-and-ear range of them damned reporters."

"They're in town already?" On a Sunday?

"They never left. Seen two of the vans parked at the motel on my way here. What are the odds a little roach reunion with their six-legged cousins will have 'em scurryin' outta town by brunch?"

In her experience? She'd prefer to buy a lottery ticket.

Setting Lou's files on the table, Kate headed for the coffee pot. She refreshed her cup and poured one for Lou, adding fresh grounds and a second pot of water before she brought the coffees and a stack of paper napkins to the table. She lobbed a bacon bomb Ruger's way as she sat. She wouldn't be home to smell the results, anyway. "Anything new?"

Lou lifted the uppermost folder from the stack. "Finally got the data on the first two victims' phones."

Kate waved off the file. "I read it a couple hours ago online."

Lou studied her face as she retrieved a scone. "That explains them circles under your eyes. Thought I gave you orders to go to bed."

"I went. Just couldn't stay there."

From the set of his brows, it was clear he'd assumed her sleeplessness lay at the foot of that cross. She didn't correct him.

Better he chalk up her insomnia to unresolved issues with her dad, than admit to the sleepwalking and night terrors. Not to mention that Silver Star. Knowledge of any or all of the above would only punch Lou's worry into hyperdrive.

Or he'd have her committed.

Right now, she couldn't afford either.

But neither did she have the patience or the nerves to dip into the anger, regret and guilt that surrounded her father's memory.

The cavalry had come to her rescue once again.

Kate stood and followed an alerting Ruger to the double doors that led to her deck. By the time she had them unlocked, Joe and Agent Walker were stepping out from the trees at the end of the wooded path. Both men waved.

Kate waved back and granted Ruger permission to take the run he was champing to make. He took off like a shot, rounding the far side of the clearing as the men reached the middle. A brief stop to sniff at something, and Ruger was shooting back around to her. The Shepherd was seated—and panting—at her side as Joe stepped onto the deck to offer Kate a morning hug.

She and the BAU agent settled for a handshake and followed Joe into the house.

Her old friend joined Lou at the table. "Morning, Sheriff."

"I told you, son, it's Lou." He tapped the plastic tubs in turn before sliding a napkin to Joe. "Muffins have cheddar and lots of bacon in 'em. The scones are lemon-blueberry."

By the time Kate had poured two additional coffees and carried them to the table, Walker had appropriated her father's seat.

She swallowed the urge to suggest he move to one of the two remaining chairs and resumed her childhood seat.

Kate passed Joe the folder Lou had mentioned earlier. "It's the phone company data from Kusić's and Dunne's cellphones.

We're still waiting on Andrea Silva's, but I'm betting we'll see similar results."

Joe frowned. "Let me guess. The phones went out of service near Fort Leaves or their homes around the time they disappeared."

"Yup. And it was near the homes."

"Damn."

She, Lou and Walker nodded in agreement. While they still might be able to glean information about the killer's movements from the nurse's phone, there'd be no further clues from Kusić's or Dunne's, not with the batteries long since removed.

Lou snagged a muffin. "There's somethin' else. I had Nester call his cousin last night and grill her for everythin' else she knew about Ms. Silva. While Silva and her girls were livin' in a modest enough home in Little Rock, the kids have a live-in nanny for after school...and they both attend Pulaski Prep."

"On a VA employee's salary?" Kate let a whistle slip. "Are we sure they're not on scholarship?"

"Yep. Owen woke up the headmaster. Silva paid on time and outta her personal checkin' account."

"So she had extra money coming in too." Based on Pulaski's tuition, quite a bit. Kate retrieved the yellow legal pad she'd been using all morning and turned to a fresh page to scratch out more notes. "So we have three victims: an admin type, a lab tech and a surgical nurse. Two men and a woman. Both men are white and vets; the woman is of Hispanic descent and a civilian. The men work at the same hospital, but all three are current VA employees. All three victims also appear to be concealing something serious enough to cause each to lose his or her job if it came to light—and could possibly send them to jail. Finally, they're enjoying extra income from an unknown and, most likely, ongoing source. Did I miss anything?"

The men shook their heads.

Kate passed the BAU agent a napkin as he reached for one. "Ed, I have to confess. I'm desperately hoping you had a chance to form an initial impression at the morgue."

"I did. The online reports helped flesh it out. I hope you don't mind, but I used the printer in your cabin." The FBI agent opened the folder he'd brought and passed out copies of his assessment. "This is preliminary, of course. But as you can see, I agree with Kate's overall assessment of the scenes. The murders occurred somewhere remote. Housed where the killer could take his time and know he would not be interrupted. He's most likely male, in his mid-to-late twenties to early forties, physically strong, intelligent and highly organized. There does not appear to be a sexual nature to these crimes. I believe the killer is motivated by revenge and is operating off a specific list. This is supported by the fact that his victims are of differing ethnicity and gender, as well as Kate's encounter with the SUV bearing the same tread from the Dunne scene, along with the killer's possible break-in at this very house last night. Both times he could've attempted to stay to hurt her, but he did not. Like Kate, I believe he's toying with her due to her position as the lead investigator. If he were to kill her, he would lose whatever satisfaction he's experiencing. However, this final element—Kate—may or may not be sexual in nature."

That Silver Star flashed through Kate's brain.

It was definitely *not* nice to know that if the killer had pinned it to her pillow, it was probably because he'd used it as fodder to help him get his rocks off first. The thought put a whole new light on its cleanliness—and turned her stomach in the process.

Kate shoved her uneaten scone to the middle of the table as Lou turned toward the BAU agent.

"Any idea who we're lookin' for?"

"Not yet, Sheriff. I too believe the possibility exists for a connection to a disgruntled patient or relative. But there is something about the scene that does not fit that theory."

Kate nodded. "The parts." They bothered her too. "The way they were so precisely lined up. Not to mention the almost fanatical lack of blood—and the missing organs. I still think their absence is key. And those goddamned paper sacks." She just couldn't get the "one, to go" feel out of her head when she stared at them.

None of it shouted disgruntled patient.

Joe added his nod to hers. "I agree with everything but the organs. I think this guy left them out because of the mess. Everything is so pristine. Kate, if your ME is right and those bodies were sliced up on the same day, the organs would've started to break down by the time you found all three sets. I think this guy's smart enough to foresee the decay factor, and plan for it. Or rather, to plan for it to *not* be part of his tidy little display. Ed?"

The BAU agent shrugged. "At the moment, both sub-theories fit. We'll need more to narrow it down."

So long as "more" wasn't another body. Kate reviewed the notes she'd scrawled while Walker had delivered his assessment. A phrase jumped out at her: operating off a list.

List.

Adrenaline spiked, burning through her exhaustion.

Not a list of intended victims. *Patients.* "Wait—think about who we have job-wise. An admin type, a lab tech, and a surgical nurse. What if our victims were operating off a list too? Remember the news a while back about secret wait lists for treatment at VA hospitals around the country? What if our victims had a list of their own, right here in Little Rock? Only this list was not a reflection of the true wait times in central Arkansas, but a list that allows certain patients—patients who can pay for the privilege—to bump to the top? Since we have a surgical nurse in the mix, it may even involve surgeries that were occurring sooner than they otherwise would have."

Joe leaned forward, clearly intrigued. "That would explain the extra money. Most soldiers don't have a lot, especially if they're using the VA system. But some do, or have relatives who do and might be willing to part with it to get their favorite soldier bumped up. Hell, even if the kickbacks were pricey, it'd be cheaper than paying for a civilian surgery. Plus, I've heard some VA waits can pass the year mark, and longer. And that's just to get an initial appointment."

Lou grabbed a bacon muffin and tossed it to his biggest fan—Ruger. "Hell, with waits like that, who wouldn't pay?"

Who, indeed?

Kate drummed her fingers over her notes. "Except we appear to be dealing with a killer motivated by revenge. If so, we should be looking for someone who couldn't pay." Minutes ago, she'd assumed they were searching for a patient who intersected all three victims. If this new preferred-list theory panned out, the killer may have been directly connected to just one. Or at least, one at a time.

If they'd been dealing with a needle in a haystack before, the haystack had just grown to a mountain.

Kate ignored Ruger's request for a third muffin as he turned his puppy-dog brows on her. "It still doesn't explain the stolen blood."

Walker dipped the corner of a scone in his coffee to soften it. "I presume you're referring to the extra vials mentioned in one of your follow-up memos?"

"Yes. I broached the subject with a physician. While so little blood could be used in any of a thousand areas of medical research, the physician also suggested the research might be unauthorized. Hence, the need to take it on the sly."

Then again, those stolen vials only connected to Ian Kusić. The list theory potentially connected all three victims.

So why wouldn't her gut let those vials go? Because of her conversation with Sergeant Fremont? The man was so passionate in his belief that the theft was important, he'd been willing to risk his life to find out more.

Perhaps there wasn't more. At least with regard to the murders.

Kate waited for the BAU agent to swallow his bite of scone before continuing. "Why Braxton? Why dump the bodies on our roads? Kusić lived in our jurisdiction, but the others didn't."

"That could be all there is to the location. The killer may have selected Braxton because he was familiar with the area— his comfort zone, if you will. But it's equally possible that during his reconnaissance on Mr. Kusić, he decided the town's rural nature would better allow him to maneuver unnoticed during the dumps than, say, the outskirts of Little Rock."

It was as she'd told Lou last night, then. The bastard had placed Andrea Silva in line with her father's cross on some warped, impromptu whim. She wasn't the cause.

Thank God.

Her phone rang. Surprise overtook Kate's relief as she read the number on the screen. It belonged to the receptionist from Fort Leaves. The same receptionist who'd called to give her a heads up when Kusić's girlfriend had arrived early for work.

Did she have something new?

Kate excused herself and headed for the living room to keep from disturbing the others. "Deputy Holland. How may I help you?"

"It's Debra Yarbrough. I'm not sure you remember me; I work the desk at Fort Leaves. I hope I didn't wake you. But, well, you said I should call if I thought of something, day or night."

"It's fine, Ms. Yarbrough. I'm up. In fact, I just finished a briefing with my fellow investigators. Have you thought of something that might assist us?"

"Maybe. I— Wow, this is weirder than I thought it'd be. I feel stupid mentioning it now."

Kate let Ruger out the front door, fully aware that she was still trying to make up for his getting trapped in her dad's room.

"Ma'am, whatever you have to say, I won't judge. I promise." With the leads they *didn't* have, she couldn't afford to.

"Well, you asked if I knew of a connection between Ian Kusić and Jason Dunne."

"And you do?"

"I don't know. I mean— Okay, here it is. A lot of hospitals don't handle the bulk of their own staffing. It's contracted out. I was hired through a company out of Little Rock called Madrigal Medical. They're located downtown, in the Baymont business building. Fourteenth floor. Have you heard of it?"

"Yes."

"Then you've been to their offices?"

"Just the ground floor." Really, only the lobby. Once, almost three years earlier, to let one of the high-rise's security guards know what his teenaged son had done. And, again, after she'd arranged for said son to dig his way out of the hole his grief and stupidity had helped him dig.

"Well, Ian Kusić used Madrigal to get his job too."

"And Jason Dunne?"

"I don't know. But that nurse in the paper this morning? Andrea Silva? I think she may have been hired through Madrigal."

"But you're not certain?"

"Well, I didn't know her. We've never even met, not officially. But I had some paperwork to fill out at Madrigal. I stopped by their offices last Tuesday before work. Andrea Silva was leaving the offices as I arrived. But here's the odd part—when I got back down to the parking lot, she was still there, standing beside a car, arguing with someone."

Kate's interest perked higher as she stepped onto the porch to see if Ruger had finished his job. He hadn't. "This someone, was it a man or a woman?"

"A man."

"Would you recognize him again?"

"Sorry. He had his back to me. But that's why I remembered her when I saw her picture in the paper. She stood out. She was facing me when they were arguing, and I swear she looked like she was trying not to cry. Is that the kind of information that will help you?"

"It might very well be." Of course, it could be nothing. The only way to find out was to investigate. "Thank you, Ms. Yarbrough. Was there anything you wanted to add?"

"No, that's it."

"Then let me thank you again. And please don't hesitate to call if anything else comes to you."

Kate hung up and swiped through her phone's contacts as Ruger finished and bounded up to the porch. Not only did she still have the security guard's number, but when she dialed it, she also discovered that the guard was just coming off the night-shift at the high-rise. And more than willing to hang around to return the favor she'd done for him and his son years earlier.

Kate ended her second call of the morning and opened the door. Ruger followed her inside.

She entered the kitchen in time to catch Agent Walker's offer to file the warrant for access to Fort Leaves' records on behalf of the FBI. If they were lucky, they might be able to use them to determine which patients had crossed their victims' paths. And since the VA and FBI were federal agencies, Walker should be able to hack through the red tape faster than the Braxton PD.

Joe stood. "Meanwhile, I'll track down Kusić's and Dunne's

Army records. It appears they connected with the killer after
they got out, but we'd better rule out an active-duty link."

Kate nodded. "Sounds good." Since Andrea Silva had never
served, she agreed with Joe's assessment. But he was right. It still
bore ruling out. "I've got something to check out in Little Rock.
It's probably nothing, but since we have so damned little to go
on, it's worth a trip. I should be back in a few hours."

Lou polished off his coffee and came to his feet as well. "I'm
headed to the station to check on things and brief the rest of the
team. Folks will be pourin' in tonight and tomorrow to kick off
the task force. We'd best be ready. I'll bring these two with me so
they can pick up their car keys. Carole's arrangin' the local transport for everyone. I'll call the governor too and let him know Ed
recommends holdin' off on the press conference a bit longer.
Kate, Seth should be in by now. I can give him a holler if you're
needin' someone to tag team it in the city."

She shook her head. "It's better if he adds another set of eyes
to the Little Rock PD search of Silva's place. I'll join him as soon
as I can. Until then, I'll be making the rounds of a certain
building with a security guard I know. A building that's...not
exactly open today."

"Ahh." Lou shot her a wink. "In other words, no witnesses
required—or desired."

"Precisely. I'll let you know if it pans out. Also, the woman
who just phoned me? She knew the third victim's name. Andrea
Silva was ID'd in this morning's paper. If our loose-lipped
trooper was still in the mix, I'd suspect him. Since he's not, we
have another leak."

Lou scowled as he followed the others into the living room.
"I'm on it."

Kate retrieved her 9mm, jacket and backup piece as the men
left, then refreshed Ruger's food and water before tweaking his
ears and locking him in the house.

Half an hour later, she'd reached Little Rock. She turned her Durango into the lot attached to the high-rise that housed Madrigal Medical and parked beside a cluster of vehicles, surprised to see so many, so early on a Sunday morning. There were no churches or restaurants nearby. Just a block crammed with two other modern high-rises and several shorter, historic office buildings.

Kate exited her Durango and carefully scanned the tread patterns of the other vehicles as she headed for the Baymont's entrance. None were a match to their Starblaze's. Not surprising. There were a lot of tread designs in the world. Not to mention, Ian Kusić and Andrea Silva were potentially linked to Madrigal through employment, not their murders, though she hadn't ruled that out.

Kate entered the Baymont's glass doors. A cropped salt-and-pepper afro and mile-wide grin met her inside, hand already extended for a shake that was pleasantly firm and twice as sincere. "Deputy Holland, it's been a long time. It's good to see you again."

"You too, Mr. Burgess. I'm grateful you're willing to show me around. I hope the delay doesn't affect your weekend."

"Not at all. And I told you on the phone, it's Cal. Anyone willing to cut my kid some slack back when he needed it most, can call on me twenty-four/seven for the rest of my life, and I'll be there."

Good to know. Though, really, Manny Ramos had done most of it. Three years ago, the Braxton storeowner had readily agreed with her. The plate glass window Leon Burgess had shattered following a Braxton/Sacred Heart basketball game had stemmed less from school loyalty and more from the anger and raw grief left behind in the wake of Leon's brother's death.

"How's your son doing?"

If possible, the guard's grin split wider. "Fantastic! We got the call last week. Leon's been accepted to UT. Starting forward. Full scholarship. He wouldn't have gotten either if it weren't for you and Mr. Ramos. We're indebted to you both."

Kate followed as Cal waved her past the bank's shuttered windows and toward the row of elevators that led to the upper floors and assorted offices that made up the remainder of the high-rise. "Nonsense. Leon admitted his mistake and stepped up to make amends. That goes a long way in my book, and in life."

"True. But a lot of folks wouldn't have tried to get past the how, let alone work so hard to ferret out the why."

Perhaps. But she and Manny had. The wily old storeowner had served in 'Nam. As for her, she'd been hooked the moment she'd discovered that Leon's older infantryman brother had been recently killed a mere thirty miles from where Max and the other members of her convoy had been slaughtered.

How could they not give the kid a break? Especially since Leon had worked damned hard to prove it was warranted.

"Well, I'm proud of him. I know I've told him so, as has Manny, but feel free to repeat it. And let him know we'll be watching his games and cheering next year."

"I will."

They'd passed Cal's replacement at the building's main security desk and reached the row of elevators. Cal motioned for her to continue on. Bemused, Kate followed him around the corner and out of sight of the current guard on duty.

Why? "Is something wrong?"

"I don't know." Her suspicion spiked as Cal glanced over his shoulder, double-checking their six to ensure no witnesses lingered behind them. "When you called and asked to see the Madrigal offices, I didn't think taking you up would be an issue."

"And now it is?"

"Yep. I was about to call you. The CEO pulled up ten minutes before you did. That's his dark blue BMW in the first slot. A couple minutes later, he was joined by another man and a younger gal. I think she's the office manager. They were huddled together and chatting something fierce as they crossed the parking lot, then clammed up the second they reached the lobby. Didn't hear a peep from any of them all the way to the elevators and during the wait. I had the feeling they were worried Felix and I might be listening."

Perhaps there was something to the Fort Leaves receptionist's tip after all. Why else would Madrigal's CEO drive to his office—and have others join him—before nine o'clock on a Sunday morning? He had to have read the paper along with the rest of the state.

Then again, why would the head of the entire company know the names of a lowly lab tech and nurse who'd been contracted out?

Kate retrieved her phone and swiped through her stored photos until she'd located the one of Ian Kusić in his Blues. She turned the screen toward the security guard. "Have you seen this man around here?"

The guard nodded.

"You're sure?"

"As sure as the summers here are soul-sucking hot and even more humid. That guy's been through here a half dozen times at least. And that's only what I've seen. Not to brag, Deputy, but I've got an eye for faces. It's a plus in the security business."

That it was. Kate swiped her way to the driver's license photo Seth had texted her of Jason Dunne. "What about him?"

Cal studied Dunne's blond curls and mug for a good ten seconds, then shook his head. "No. And with those freckles, I would've remembered. But keep in mind, I work nights to be home with the kids after school." The guard tapped the photo. "If this guy came though during the day, I wouldn't know."

Cal Burgess was a sharp man. That had been evident when

they'd met in this same building nearly three years earlier. He, too, had to have read the papers or seen the news, and he knew she was with the Braxton PD. Yet he didn't press for verification that this entire meeting was about those murders.

She appreciated that.

Kate brought up the DMV photo of Andrea Silva. Again, compliments of Seth's texts. "What about her?"

Cal's nod was immediate and firm. "She'd come in a couple times a month. Usually in the mornings, around six or seven. Last time was a week ago Tuesday. I remember, because I almost called the local boys in blue."

"Why's that?"

"Argument. She came and went fine. But when she crossed into the parking lot upon leaving, an SUV pulled up beside her. I couldn't hear anything because of all the windows, but from her gestures, she was mad about something. Then the driver reaches out and grabs her arm. I started for the doors, but the guy let go and drove off. By the time I made it outside, she'd gotten in her car too, and left."

"Did you get a look at the guy's face?"

"No. The visor shadowed it. I never saw the rear bumper, so I wasn't able to get the plate either. But his SUV was dark green. A foreign job—Land Rover. No idea which edition. Does that help?"

"Perhaps. Just to be sure; she arrived around six?"

"Yep. But that argument was half an hour or so later. After she'd come back down."

So he'd witnessed the same argument as the receptionist from Fort Leaves. But with whom had Andrea Silva argued? Her killer? Could he have been so bold as to accost her outside a high-rise with an armed guard on duty?

Given the amount of time the killer had risked on arranging

those ballsy dump sites—three in one night, no less—it was more than possible.

But what had Andrea Silva been doing here in the first place, especially with such regularity? Kusić, too. If the two had been taking bribes from VA patients, had someone upstairs been in on it?

The CEO? Was he here to conduct damage control?

Kate returned her phone to her pocket. "I'll go up alone. But thank you for the information. If you notice anything unusual regarding anyone from Madrigal, please call me immediately." She gave Cal a fresh card in case he'd tossed the one that included her office and private number. "I'd appreciate you keeping this conversation to yourself."

"You have my word."

That was good enough for her.

She kept pace with the guard long enough to round the corner they'd taken earlier, stopping to punch the main up arrow at the bank of elevators as Cal continued on back to the security desk without her.

A lift pinged within seconds. Kate stepped inside.

Fourteen floors later, the elevator slowed to a stop. She schooled her expression as she exited the lift and followed the signs to Madrigal's suite of offices. If she was lucky, her face would repel the trio inside in a way it hadn't even during her initial meeting with Cal Burgess years before, allowing her to deploy one of the best weapons in a cop's arsenal.

Distraction.

The reception area was larger than she'd expected, glossier. And there was something odd about the logo hanging behind the counter. Kate stepped closer to study the white MM centered amid a sideways oval of red. Before she could put her finger on what bothered her, a sleek brunette in a sleeker emerald dress whispered in from the hall on Kate's left.

"We're closed. You'll have to come back on Mon—"

The rest never materialized as Kate turned to give the woman a full-on view of her unzipped Braxton PD jacket, holstered 9mm and not-so-sleek face.

Kate waited patiently as those expertly thickened lashes widened in horror, and then—nothing. Ms. America's Next Top Model contender couldn't seem to tear her stare from Kate's mutilated cheek long enough to acknowledge the credentials held up beside it.

The seconds continued to tick.

Tired of waiting, Kate shifted her face far enough to the right to sever that critical, visual connection.

The woman flinched. Swallowed. "I'm sorry. I didn't realize you were with the...the..."

"Police." Why not? She was in an accommodating mood. For now. "Deputy Holland, Braxton PD." She lowered her credentials, but kept them at the ready. "Ma'am, I understand your CEO is in this morning? I'd like to speak with him."

"May I ask why?"

"No."

Annoyance rippled through those perfect features, leaving a pinched smile in its wake. "Just a moment."

Ms. Model spun around, her spiked heels digging into the carpet with more force than they had earlier, as they ferried their owner back up the hall. Kate returned her attention to the logo as she waited. The same strange sensation of déjà vu returned.

She was certain she'd seen that red and white oval before. But where? In a magazine? A billboard across town?

Possibly.

"Deputy Holland?"

Kate turned as another polished brunette entered the room. Though this one was male, suited up in crisp white and hand-tailored navy blue—and had a good twenty years on the previous, feminine version. Unlike Ms. Model, he also came with an outstretched hand, a welcoming smile and a decided lack of interest in the mottled section of her face.

It was a serious miscalculation.

Especially his smile. That confident curve had ushered in much more than the studied avoidance of her cheek. She'd seen that same smooth smile slide onto the lips of far too many suspects as they'd prepped themselves for the coming interrogation, in the Army and out. Damned near all had turned out to be guilty.

So what was this man hiding?

Kate shifted her credentials to her left hand as her right met the solid grip of his. "Good morning, sir. Deputy Holland. I'm with the Braxton PD. I apologize for showing up unannounced, but I was in town and thought a quick detour worth the risk of a shuttered door. Fortunately, it paid off. Are you the CEO?"

"No. I'm Robert Stern, Mr. Kessler's legal advisor. Unfortunately, Mr. Kessler is on a conference call. Perhaps I can be of assistance?"

A lawyer? Peachy. Shysters ranked up there with practicing shrinks in her book. Make that, down there.

"Mr. Stern—"

"*Robert*—" another brief, easy smile, "—please."

"Mr. Stern. I appreciate the offer, but I'd prefer to wait for Mr. Kessler." She headed for the grouping of taupe leather chairs. "I'll just make myself comfortable."

She stopped beside a glass accent table as the lawyer sighed. "I'm sorry, Deputy, but Mr. Kessler is dealing with a critical situation whilst straddling incongruous time zones. The call is bound to take a while. And others will need to follow. However, I'm certain I can assist if you'll but share your concerns. What can a Braxton PD deputy possibly want with Madrigal's CEO?"

"Murder."

The word hadn't warranted so much as a blink. Impressive.

And even more telling.

"Mr. Stern, I appreciate your wanting to limit my idle time. I confess—lately I haven't had much to spare. I've spent the past few days examining the heinously sectioned bodies of three VA healthcare professionals, and I've been told at least two were contracted out via Madrigal Medical."

That earned her a blink. Unfortunately, the model's had been more sincere. "Good lord, Deputy. The bodies were cut up? That's—"

She plucked the worn newspaper off the table and brandished it. "—right here in this morning's edition." The edition he or the CEO had carried up less than an hour ago...and promptly forgotten about. Though how anyone could with a charmingly insensitive headline like "Garbage Man Bags Third Victim" she'd never know. "Damned if we can't seem to keep the ten-toed vultures from circling those dump sites and scavenging for clues." She closed in on the shyster and dropped the paper into his equally suspect hands. "The names are all there, should you need refreshing. Just below the photo of those goddamned paper bags. And, yes, I did find the bodies of Ian Kusić, Jason Dunne and Andrea Silva drained of their life's blood, hacked up and sealed inside tidy little vacuum pouches."

A hard swallow followed. But, again, the model's had been more sincere. And, worse, sympathetic.

Bastard.

"And I assume you'd like—"

"—to know if any of them were contracted out to the VA healthcare system through your company. *Now*."

"I'll need a moment to have Marilee access our records."

"I'll be right here, Mr. Stern."

Within seconds, the lawyer wasn't.

Too bad he'd taken the paper with him. She was curious to read the rest of the story he'd worked so hard to convince her that he and his boss hadn't. With no other reading material lying around, Kate returned to that captivating logo. She'd seen it somewhere, all right. And not up on a billboard.

Somewhere close. Personal.

Intimate.

But where?

Her musings were interrupted sooner than she'd expected.

That didn't bode well. Damage control must truly be in full swing because, despite his professed ignorance and subsequent request for time, Stern had been ready for the police, complete with a crisp, anorexic manila folder.

Just what was being discussed at the other end of that hall?

Unfortunately, short of ignoring the law she'd sworn to uphold, she couldn't barge in and demand to know.

Damn.

"Here you go, Deputy. Everything I'm legally able to provide."

Kate accepted the folder. A single sheet of paper lay inside. Printed upon it were the names of Ian Kusić and Andrea Silva. The starting date of Kusić's employment—three years earlier— had been typed beside his name. Silva's had two dates separated by as many years and a dash.

Kate glanced up. "Andrea Silva left Fort Leaves?"

Stern nodded. "Miss Silva quit six months ago. She refused to say why, or leave a forwarding address. As you may know, Mr. Kusić was employed by the VA until...recently."

The Silva information did fit with Grant's comment that he hadn't seen the nurse in a while.

"What about checks? Is it possible Ms. Silva stopped by your offices since, possibly to pick up overdue severance?"

Say, last Tuesday morning around six?

"No. Miss Silva has had zero contact with Madrigal since the morning she quit." It was firm. Unequivocal.

Kate might've bought it too, were it not for the fact that one of the Baymont's own security guards and another Madrigal VA hire claimed differently.

"And Jason Dunne? I don't see his name listed."

"That's because Jason never dealt with this company."

Jason?

She decided not to follow up on the potential Freudian slip —for now. A sound decision, given the slight tic that had begun to flag at the side of Stern's jaw. Lawyer or not, the man's patience had been exceeded.

As had her tolerance for nodding politely in the face of copious lies.

"If you'll excuse me, Deputy, the CEO requires my expertise."

She didn't doubt it. "Thank you, Mr. Stern. I appreciate your assistance."

"Then you have everything you need?"

Not by a long shot. But it was plain the rest would require a warrant, and there was no sense tipping him off. As a lawyer, Stern was certain to know how to operate a shredder. If not, the charming and capable Marilee would undoubtedly teach him.

Kate offered her card in lieu of her own honest response. "If you think of anything else, please don't hesitate to call. I'll see myself out."

She could feel the man's glare heating her back as she made her way out of the reception area. Kate took a chance on phoning her boss on her way to the elevator.

Lou picked up as she stepped inside. "You get anythin'?"

She had indeed. She filled the sheriff in on her stunted but telling Q&A with Stern, pleased when her phone's reception held as the elevator continued to plummet. Kate finished with the lawyer's denial regarding Silva's numerous visits after the woman had quit, and the argument both Cal Burgess and the VA receptionist had witnessed.

"And this ambulance-chaser called Dunne by his first name, but not the others?"

"Yup."

"Well, don't that just suggest all?"

Indeed it did. Dunne might very well have obtained his position at Fort Leaves without Madrigal's involvement, but the staffing company's chief counsel knew the man—and well.

"Boss, I need a favor."

"You want Seth to poke through the lawyer's life."

"Yes." The lift slowed to a stop. "Just a minute."

Kate lowered the phone as the doors opened. Sound echoed easily in the lobby, and Cal was no longer manning that security desk. She nodded to his replacement as she passed.

She brought the phone back to her mouth as the Baymont's main doors closed behind her. "We need to know if Robert Stern worked for Madrigal Medical, or was in private practice somewhere around Fayetteville. And have Seth run the man's name past Dunne's folks to see if it rings a bell." The connection could be as simple—and deadly—as a friend of the family.

"I'm on it."

Kate checked the tires on two vehicles that hadn't been in the lot earlier as she headed for her Durango. Neither matched the casts they had at the lab. She was about to hang up when she felt the vibe in their conversation shift.

And then, "How you holdin' up, kiddo?"

Great. She should've guessed Lou would take the opportunity to check on her psyche. It wasn't as though he could've broached the topic of that stone marker and the third body's proximity to it during their earlier briefing with Joe and Agent Walker.

Kate paused beside her Durango and turned to lean her

back against the driver's door, needing the crisp morning air and the wide openness of the lot as last night and this morning came crashing in.

That blasted Silver Star pinned to her pillow.

The complete lack of prints.

Waking up from yet another hazy night terror in a clammy, sweat-slicked ball in the corner of her closet.

"I'm fine, boss."

"Possum shit. I can hear it in your voice."

Yeah, well, what had he expected?

"Yikes. Got another call coming through. Need to go." She hung up before Lou could nail her on that too.

Kate closed her eyes as the lingering adrenaline of a promising lead sank into the smothering sludge that, once again, had begun to bubble up and churn.

Damn it. She could *not* do this. Not here. Not now.

She had a job to do. A murderer to catch.

She spun around and grabbed the handle to her driver's door, tugging firmly before she realized she'd forgotten to use her remote to pop the SUV's locks.

The door opened anyway.

Gooseflesh prickled up her spine as she bent down to scan the Durango's cargo area and back seat through the tempered glass. Both were exactly as she'd left them.

The front seat was *not*.

11

SHOCK GAVE WAY TO SUSPICION, certainty—and, yes, relief—as Kate stared at the pair of military ID tags dangling from the Durango's rearview mirror as she slid into the driver's seat. Though her grip on sanity might be tenuous at times, it *was* holding. Ruger was right. Someone had been in their house. Someone who, despite Ruger's snarlingly determined presence, had deftly retrieved that Silver Star from her trunk, wiped it free of prints and pinned it to her pillow.

She was *not* stalking herself.

But someone was.

The proof was in the name, social security number, blood type and lapsed religious preference stamped into those twin, seemingly innocuous slivers of stainless steel.

They were anything but. Like the watch she'd automatically begun to twist, those tags belonged to Max.

They shouldn't exist. Not here, in Arkansas.

Hell, not even in the States.

Unlike Max's watch and body, those tags had never made it home. She knew, because she'd asked. Begged. According to the fellow CID agent who'd interviewed her following her escape from that compound, the tags had disappeared before the crime scene unit had arrived. Only that hadn't made sense even then, while she was still curled up in the fetal position on that hospital cot. She could understand Max's murder, but why strip him of his tags?

The bodies of the two other soldiers who'd made it as far as the compound had still had theirs around their necks. Hell, the bastards had even left hers in place. How had singling Max out for special treatment fit into his killers' collective jihad? Especially since she'd been successful in sending the entire bunch to Paradise earlier than those assholes had planned.

But these *were* Max's tags.

Any suspicion that they were fake disappeared as Kate spotted the pair of tiny dents along the edge of the tag missing its bumper. She'd created them herself during a friendly tussle in Max's tent the night before they'd left on that last, fateful mission. No one else knew that.

So how had these tags made it from that Afghan terror hold to her Durango's stateside rearview mirror?

Who had strung them up?

And why?

Ruger. Lord, she needed his thick fur and solid hugs. Desperately. Before she ended up twisting Max's watch right through her wrist. The skin beneath had been scraped raw, but she couldn't stop.

Until her phone rang.

The lilting notes pierced the panic long enough for her to retrieve her phone and check the caller ID. It was from Saint Clare's.

Sergeant Fremont.

For some reason, the interruption was enough to reset her brain. She didn't question it; she simply connected the call before her nerves had a chance to betray her again. "Good morning, Sergeant."

"*Steve.* And it is a good morning, isn't it? Because we both made it home to see it."

Kate pulled a fortifying breath of that same morning air deep into her lungs and smiled despite herself. "What's up?"

"Information. Can you make it into Little Rock today? We need to meet. I came across something you should know."

"I'm already here. But please tell me you haven't been poking around, asking about missing blood."

"Okay. I haven't."

Yes, he had.

But had she honestly believed he'd comply with her order to stand down? The man had been Special Forces. A notoriously tenacious branch, down to the last soldier. And something told her this soldier was more tenacious than most. He'd have to be, given how generous he was with his fellow vets, despite the karmic shit that had rained down on his own body and soul over there.

The man was also homeless. And, since she suspected he tended to reserve whatever meager benefits Uncle Sam had deigned to cough up to ease the plight of his fellow vets, most likely hungry.

Kate grabbed the Durango's door and closed it. "I've got a search I need to check on before I head back to Braxton, but I could do with a quick bite." A bit of distracting company wouldn't hurt either.

She stared at the dog tags still dangling six inches from her face. The more distracting the better.

"There's a twenty-four hour diner across the street from Saint Clare's. It's shaped like one of those old metallic Airstream campers. It's called the Silver Bullet."

"I know the place."

"Great. I'm still at the shelter, but I can be there in ten minutes."

Kate unhooked the beaded, stainless-steel chain from the Durango's mirror and rode out a shudder as she slipped the tags into her jacket pocket. "I'm on the other side of Little Rock. Grab a table. I'll be there in twenty."

Between the relatively early hour and the sparse Sunday traffic, she made it in eighteen.

Kate passed the church's crowded lot and pulled into the first in a row of parking slots in front of the diner. As soon as mass let out, the vehicular tide would shift and the entire row and restaurant beyond would be packed with hungry parishioners. But for now, nearly all the Silver Bullet's spots were up for grabs.

So why, as she bailed out of her SUV, did she feel as though someone was nearby, watching?

The sensation was faint, but palpable enough for her to slow her pace as she made her way toward the diner's door, so she could discreetly scan the sidewalk and street beyond.

She was alone. And clearly paranoid.

Hell, after those tags, who wouldn't be?

She shrugged off the sensation and stepped inside the Silver Bullet. The diner's tables were mostly deserted, save for two elderly couples and Sergeant Fremont. He'd staked out a spot to the right of the entrance and swapped out the facing chair with his wheels, leaving the closer seat for her. A slightly pregnant teenaged waitress stood beside him, setting out a pair of black coffees as Kate approached.

"Good morning, officer. Cream and sugar?"

"No, thanks."

"Okay." She smiled at Fremont. "Well, breakfast will be out shortly."

As the waitress left, the vet leaned forward to tilt the spare chair out. Kate removed her Braxton PD jacket and hooked it across the metal shoulders of the proffered seat.

"Thanks."

"I hope you don't mind, but I already ordered. Bountiful Breakfast, times two. Figured it would shave off a few minutes of the wait; plus the spread comes with enough eggs, bacon and toast to feed a squad."

"Sounds perfect." Kate flushed as her stomach underscored the sentiment with a series of gurgles.

"Let me guess: long night, followed by a longer morning."

"Correct on both counts. I imagine you saw this morning's headlines?"

"About the third body? Yeah."

She leaned into the table. "Then you know why I wish you wouldn't go poking around right now. Steve, this guy isn't playing. Not to mention that both men he's taken down should've been able to defend themselves—mentally and physically—but couldn't."

"Trust me, I appreciate the concern. But I also know you'll change your mind when I share what I've discovered."

"Then you've spoken to the vets who claimed Kusić took their blood without permission?"

"Can't. They're gone."

Kate straightened. "All three of them?" Fremont had said the men were homeless. "Did they move on?"

"In a manner of speaking. They vanished. As in, not a trace left to track. Not a one said where he was going, let alone that he'd planned on leaving—and before you ask, none of these guys had family. Not any that cared. There was no one to 'go home' to. That's why they were on the street."

Before Kate could follow that up, the waitress returned with an oversized tray, burdened with two very Bountiful Breakfasts indeed. Forget the squad; they could feed an entire platoon with this.

The table's laminated Formica disappeared with record speed as pancakes, grits, deluxe hash browns, sausage and juice joined the scrambled eggs, bacon and toast Fremont had mentioned.

The two of them thanked the waitress, shamelessly digging in as only two ex-soldiers could while the teenager ferried the empty tray to the kitchen.

Halfway through her eggs, Kate paused. "It's possible a good Samaritan took in one or two of the missing men until they could get back on their feet."

Fremont's snort punctured that fantasy. "No one stops long enough to look anyone in the eye on skid row, let alone extend a truly helping hand, and we both know it. Besides—" He polished off the last bite of his own eggs and started in on his sausage and hash browns. "—two of them left boxes behind. The priest assigns everyone a plastic tub on arrival. You're allowed to put anything inside, and he locks it up for you. Two of the vets took him up on the offer. No one's seen the men for damned near twelve days now. Yet the boxes are there, waiting. Father Popichak was concerned enough that he let me tag along to take a peek. One of the boxes has baby photos, a Purple Heart and some cash—almost four hundred bucks total. You think the guy just forgot it?"

Unfortunately, "No."

"Me, neither."

So why were the men missing? And if not to them, to whom had Fremont spoken, and what had he learned? Kate stacked the trio of pancakes nearest her on top of their mates and jock-eyed the resulting tower across the table. "So what did you discover?"

"Two more vets with stolen blood, at least three vials apiece.

And get this: one of the new guys was in Kusić's vampire seat the day the lab tech left on vacation."

So whatever Ian Kusić had been into, had been on-going. But stolen blood still didn't mesh with her only viable working theory: the list. Four hundred bucks was a tidy sum for a homeless vet, but it wasn't enough to buy a slot at the top of a potentially year-plus surgical waiting list. Not if that trunk of Benjamins was any indication of the going rate. Then, again—

Kate frowned.

"What's wrong?"

"Nothing." Or, perhaps, something. Eventually. "Stolen blood doesn't fit with what we've been able to learn about the other two victims." Just the tech.

But this wouldn't be the first time she'd uncovered evidence of unrelated criminal activity during an investigation. And while time-consuming, such detours often led to the fleshing out of a case in other areas—and to connections she might not have noticed if she'd ignored seemingly extraneous clues.

"Did Kusić take anything besides blood from any of the men —including you?"

To her surprise, Fremont nodded. "Yeah, medical histories."

Kate forked a piece of scorched pepper out of her hash browns. "I don't understand. Kusić was a phlebotomist. Isn't that his job to ask questions while he's drawing blood?"

"About cancer and dementia?"

"Dementia?" That was odd. In eight years, the Army had jabbed more needles into her flesh than an addict could abuse in a lifetime, and she'd never once been asked about the possible physical deterioration of her brain—even as she'd teetered on the verge of a psych commitment at Walter Reed.

Fremont nodded as he retrieved a slice of toast. "Yup. Near as I can figure from talking to the others, Kusić had a list of weird-ass questions he saved for those he stole blood from. Most involved cancer and dementia. Specifically, Creutzfeldt-Jakob's disease. I thought about copping to my dad's ball cancer, but his docs were pretty sure he got it 'cause of 'Nam. A parting gift for operating in and around Agent Orange. In the end, I figured it was none of the tech's damned business, so I didn't say anything."

Kate might've agreed, were she not still stuck on his earlier comment. "Creutz—what?"

"Creutzfeldt. It's a strange one. Had to look it up. It's also called mad cow disease."

Mad, it was. Along with this entire conversation, because it made no sense. Unless— "Did Kusić ask his questions before he drew the extra blood, or after?"

"No idea about the others. Didn't think to ask. But with me, the questions came first. Why?"

She laid her fork on her plate. "I asked a doc about the potential use for small amounts of blood. His suggestions included unauthorized medical research." If Kusić had been collecting under the table for a study, it made sense to lead with any pertinent and perhaps disqualifying questions.

There was no sense in risking his job if the patient didn't fit some predetermined criteria.

But could a study of dementia—or even cancer—yield the kind of money she'd found inside Kusić's bedroom closet, let alone the funds to support the lifestyles of Jason Dunne and Andrea Silva?

Though she suspected not, she'd be putting the question to Tonga and the state's pathologist as soon as possible.

Kate reached inside the pocket of her jacket to retrieve her memo pad and pen, using them to transcribe the gist of their conversation as the vet made inroads into the tower of pancakes she'd nudged his way.

Loath to interrupt the man's enjoyment, she began a sketch of Madrigal's logo. For some reason, it still bothered her.

Fremont paused between bites to wave the tines of his fork toward her drawing. "What's that?"

She added the outline of the company's whited-out MM in the center and used the ink from her pen to color in the rest of the oval. "Something I saw today. But that's not what's bugging me. I've seen it before. I just can't figure out where." She spun the pad so he could get the full effect. "The real logo's red and white, not blue."

Fremont nodded as she twirled the pad back around. "I've seen it." He squinted at the now upside-down drawing for a bit longer. "Madrigal, right?"

"Yes. You know the company?"

"Not really. Just that it has something to do with medicine. I once spent a couple hours staring at that logo on some doc's coffee mug."

She flinched as a white mug with that same scarlet logo flashed through her brain. She'd seen one of those mugs too. In someone's hand, being raised to lips.

An odd jumble of sounds buzzed through her ears as she attempted to focus on the image, only to dissolve into pulsing silence.

"Kate?"

She met that intent stare. Concern had darkened it. For the second time since she'd sat down to breakfast, she flushed. "Sorry. Had a weird, almost déjà vu moment there. You said you'd seen the logo on a doctor's mug. At Fort Leaves?"

He shook his head. "Iraq—Baghdad. I had some time to kill while I was waiting for the docs to patch up a buddy of mine. A lot of time. I can still describe everything in that damned waiting area."

Madrigal staffed active duty facilities overseas? Was that

where she'd seen her mug? Except she'd never been in one in Baghdad. "What about Landstuhl or Walter Reed? Madrigal's a hospital staffing company. Do you happen to know if they contract healthcare workers in either of those?"

Fremont shrugged. "They might. My physical therapist at Walter Reed had one of their freebie calendars on his wall. Had some pens, too. He never mentioned the company though."

Unlike those vials of blood or those potentially missing vets, this connection meshed. Jason Dunne had been at Fort Leaves for the past six months, but before that, he'd worked at Walter Reed—for three years. Possibly long enough to come in contact with Robert Stern and Madrigal Medical.

The heck with Dunne's folks and a Fayetteville connection; there was an excellent chance Dunne and the lawyer had met in DC.

Kate closed her memo pad and stuffed it in her jacket pocket as their waitress stopped by to refresh the coffees. Rather, she tried to pocket the pad, but the wire spiraled along the top caught on something. As Kate pulled it free, the tags she'd managed to forget about until that moment clattered to the floor.

She leaned over to wrap the chain around her left hand, fisting the tags securely within her palm as she straightened.

The vet's brow rose. "Those yours?"

She shook her head. "They belonged to a friend."

"The same one who gave you that watch?"

This time she nodded. Because Max must have gifted it. Still, "How do you know I didn't find it at some swap meet?"

To her chagrin, the compassion returned...and it was threaded with pity. "Because you twist it when you're upset. I may not be a shrink, but I've been around enough screwed-up vets—myself included—to know a crutch when I see one. Hell, we've all got 'em. And they tend to be personal. There's no shame in it."

But there was, especially as he reached across the table to smooth a finger along the raw flesh at her wrist.

"You just gotta be careful you don't clamp down on your crutch so hard, you lose the ability to function on your own without it."

Silence pulsed again, and this time it was not in her ears. She had no idea how to respond, had she even possessed the nerve.

He shook his head slowly, regretfully. "You're not the only one, Kate. There's an entire Army of us, trying to make our way through the fires of redemption, right along with you. All you gotta do is look to the left or the right and reach out for support. Shit, it took me quite a while to scrape up the courage to do it myself."

"Did it help?"

"Some days, absolutely. Others?" He shrugged. "All I know for certain is I have to keep trying. We've all got a mission in this life, whether we're still wearing the uniform or not. That doesn't mean it's not damned difficult at times. Or that you won't fall flat on your face and get sucker-kicked in your kidneys while you're down. You just gotta suck it up—the pain and, yeah, the humiliation—and grab on to whatever you can and right yourself. Then start pushing forward. You do that, and you'll get there. Eventually. And here's the best part: somewhere along the way, you just might realize you started enjoying life again."

Her wrist began to itch. She ignored it and tightened her grip on the tags. "What if...you don't remember what the mission is anymore?"

"Don't remember? Or don't want to remember?"

The tags cut into her palms as she accepted the truth for the first time since she'd woken up in that hospital bed four years ago. "Both. I told you about the kid I killed. There's more, but not much. And it's not good. He had an AK-47. I found it propped up against the wall just outside the cell as I was dragging on the jihad jammies I'd stripped from his corpse. I grabbed the rifle and took off to find the others. I knew three men had survived the ambush. The kid had taunted me with that while I was pretending to wash up, telling me he was headed across the compound to torture my friends next."

Only one of the men had qualified as an actual friend. But that hadn't made her first discovery any easier.

"I found two of the soldiers where he'd promised. But someone had beat the kid to the punch—literally. And then shot them." She raised her empty hand and stroked a fingertip over her right temple. "Right here. The opposite sides of their skulls were missing, but there was enough left of their faces for me to ID them when I got back."

Something she still did in her nightmares, a couple times a month at least. Who knew if the two had been stopping by to visit with her during her night terrors, as well?

"What happened after that?"

Kate stared at the hand still gripping the tags. Its skin was tight and paper white, contrasting starkly with the band of excoriated red above and below the watch.

Max's watch.

She swallowed hard, and followed Fremont's earlier advice. She tightened her grip on the tags, and kept moving. "I searched the buildings in the compound, one by one. There were seven in all. Most about the size of the hovel where I'd regained consciousness. But they were empty. I'd saved the largest for last, figuring that's where I'd most likely die. And that's where the bastards were. I could hear Max inside, moaning as someone struck him. I remember thanking God that at least he was alive as I switched the AK-47 to auto and breached the outer door. That's it. My memory stops there."

Except, for the first time in four years, it didn't.

Kate stiffened as another fragment exploded into focus. Just like that, she was back in that mud-brick hellhole, looking down the sights of her enemy's AK-47, staring at one of those same, bearded enemies at her still-naked feet. The bastard was dead. On his wrist, Max's orange-faced dive watch.

Yet another fragment cut in. Her, bending down to wrench the watch from the bastard's wrist. And then she was locking it around her own, where it had remained ever since.

A plate shattered in the diner's kitchen and the vision disintegrated, replaced by the reality of her raw flesh—and Max's watch. He hadn't secured it to her wrist as she'd assumed. Hoped. Prayed.

She forced her hand open and stared at his tags. Had she taken these too? Had they been in her trunk all along?

But...they couldn't have been. The tags hadn't been lying on the table beside that hospital bed with the watch when her psyche had returned to its shredded self.

"Kate?"

She fisted the tags, drawing comfort and courage from them, despite their bizarre re-emergence in her life. "They called it a fugue."

"They?"

"The doctors. The ones gathered around like vultures when I woke. I was told that, basically, my brain checked out in that final building in that compound. One of the shrinks said I just couldn't handle mowing down nine of those bastards at once." She'd always doubted that. How was that worse than having to kill a kid? To feel his blood sliding over the back of her hand, warming it before it splashed into the dirt? Unfortunately, she hadn't been right enough in her head to argue. Still wasn't. "I came to, so to speak, roughly two days later in a bed at the combat support hospital. I was found by a search patrol while attempting to return to friendly territory. I don't remember that either. But by then, the compound had been located and the bodies recovered. Our forensic guys sketched in the rest. As for my missing hours and so-called heroism, the shrinks at Walter Reed said it might all come back eventually—" She pushed forth a shrug infused with significantly more indifference than she possessed. "—or it might not."

"Do you want it to come back?"

She bent out a smile at that and mimicked the vet's answer to her earlier query. "Some days, absolutely. Others?" She shook her head firmly. "Hell, no." Her sigh bled down into the bits of congealed sausage left on her plate. "Who knows? Perhaps it's better if I don't."

His nod was slow, thoughtful. "Perhaps."

"Really? I figured you'd be telling me to give the shrinks another go at my marbles; see if they can fill in all the chips and cracks and polish them up for the world to see. Another fucked-up vet made whole again—*hallelujah*." She tapped the pocked and mottled scars that took up more than a third of her face and neck. "Well, as whole as possible."

"That's up to you, Kate. But you should talk to a professional."

For some reason, that pissed her off further. "In the interest of full disclosure, *Steve,* I haven't even read the investigation. Didn't want to. As for the write-up for that Silver Star? I only heard that second hand during that asinine ceremony they insisted on at Walter Reed. I shoved the write-up and its corresponding piece of tin in my trunk when it was over and left them there to rot and rust."

The vet leaned forward, pinning her to her seat with that loathsome compassion and its bastard brother, pity. "Why haven't you read it? Hell, for that matter, why haven't you framed that write-up and hung it on the wall?"

"Because it's a lie."

"You just said the forensics—"

"*Fuck* the forensics. Who killed whom is immaterial. Don't you get it? I *failed* those men. So I killed those bastards. One, two, three, or eleven of them—it doesn't matter. Our men are still dead. *Max* is still dead. You think it's so great that I made it home? I've got news for you and your kumbaya shit. My best friend was on that mission. He was the one I heard moaning as I entered that last building with that AK-47. But it wasn't enough. *I* wasn't enough. I didn't save anyone's ass but my own. And let's face it; that is nothing to brag about."

The compassion vanished, along with the pity. Fury took their place as his fingers bit into the arms of his wheelchair. If the man could've stood up and loomed over her, he would have. "Damn it, soldier—"

Her phone trilled, cutting him off. Just as well. The waitress had returned too, alerted by Kate's tirade, coffee pot in hand and a soothing offer of a refill on her lips.

Kate scraped her chair away from the table and turned her back on all of it—especially Fremont—as she retrieved her phone.

It was Liz.

Figured. She'd managed to avoid the Army's shrinks and their psychobabble for four years—until these past three brain-battering days. Why not continue the mental waterboarding with Liz?

Kate accepted the call—and changed her mind. Instantly.

"Please tell me Grant's with you."

The panic lacing her friend's voice jolted Kate to her feet. She was halfway to the door before she realized she'd left her jacket—and the sergeant—at the table. She stopped and whirled back around. "What happened?"

Please God, don't let Grant be—

"He's missing."

No, he wasn't. Not yet. Not without proof, damn it. So, *calm down.* "Did you phone his dad?"

"No. Abel called me. Kate, he's frantic. Abel says Grant was supposed to stop by for dinner last night, but he never showed. When Grant's cellphone went to voicemail, Abel assumed he'd been called to the hospital on an emergency. Then someone from the hospital called Abel this morning. The woman said you guys had ordered a head check on all the staff, and they couldn't locate Grant. His phone's going straight to voicemail. That's why they called his dad. Abel couldn't remember your number so he called the hospital back after he checked the house and barn. Grant must've mentioned that I was back in town, because Abel asked for me. Kate, there was no hospital emergency last night. And no one's seen or heard from Grant since. No one."

Shit. "Liz, don't panic. I'm in Little Rock. I'll be back in town in half an hour. Can you get to the farm?"

"Yes."

"Okay, go. Get Abel calmed down and keep him that way. Grant told me his cancer's back and it's terminal."

"Oh, Lord."

"I know. I'll see you soon." She hung up and grabbed her jacket from the back of her chair. The waitress had left during the call. Kate pulled out her wallet to leave cash, only to freeze as Fremont reached out and laid his hand over hers.

"No."

"But—" The man was homeless, damn it. And despite their argument, a fellow vet.

"I knew you'd try to pay, so I took care of it when I ordered. I get a disability check." He squeezed her hand briefly, firmly. "Now go. You've got my number; call when you've got time to talk about this—really talk. Just let me add one thing first. It's important. You remember it when you think over what we've said. Your friend's death was *not* your fault."

That was the problem. Deep down in the dregs of her soul, she knew it was.

And, now, she was on the verge of losing another.

12

BY THE TIME Kate reached Braxton, four cars were haphazardly racked into the gravel drive of Grant's childhood home. She didn't recognize any of them. She did, however, spot Joe jogging down the steps of the wraparound porch as she vaulted from the Durango. Clearly, he'd taken her phoned plea to drop everything and get here *yesterday* to heart. Thank God.

"Is Abel okay?"

Joe grabbed her arms, steadying her as they met at the corner of the lawn. "Mr. Parish is fine. We've managed to calm him with a little help from an injection your friend Dr. Vogel had in her bag. Don't worry; she said the sedative's mild. Agent Walker's with them. We haven't interviewed the man yet. Mostly because the sedative's just kicked in, but also because Ed and I thought it best to wait for you given your relationship with his son. From Abel's conversation with Dr. Vogel, I understand you two were also good friends with his younger son as well?"

"The best." Los Tres Amigos. The irony lashed in. Here she was, about to climb the steps of that rambling farmstead house where she'd spent a good deal of her high school years. Liz would be inside again, but no Dan—and, now, no Grant. From what Grant had relayed last night, Abel wouldn't be around for long either.

The sludge she'd been swimming in for days surged up and did its best to drag her under, damned near succeeding.

Joe cupped her chin. "You okay? You don't need to do this, you know. Hell, this is perilously close to conflict of interest, as it is."

"Yeah, I do. I know Abel. He's not going to open up to anyone else, except perhaps Lou—and the sheriff's stuck in an ass-covering meeting with the governor and the state police over those newspaper articles." Plus, this was Braxton. Everyone in her department was experiencing a conflict of interest today.

The town was that small. Which made Grant's disappearance all the more horrifying—and suspicious.

She dropped her forehead to Joe's chest as the guilt pummeled in. "It's because of me, isn't it?"

"No!" He hauled her closer and squeezed hard. "Good God, there's no way anyone can know that."

But there was. And she did.

Grant had disappeared somewhere between her house and this one, last night of all nights. The same night Ruger had staked his watchdog credentials on his belief that someone had been in their home, uninvited. "I talked down the threat, Joe, because I just didn't want to accept it. But Ruger knew. And from Ruger's reaction, the bastard left minutes before I arrived home. He was probably hiding in the trees, watching, while Grant and I were talking in my drive. And now Grant's missing, and according to Lou, his cellphone's been cut off. If I'd accepted Lou's offer of a bodyguard then, or even yours to sleep on my couch—"

"*Stop.*" Joe grabbed her chin and forced her to meet the determination in that iron stare. "It wouldn't have made a difference,

and you know it. Come on, Kate. Suck it up and start thinking
like the agent I know you still are. You can do this. You *will*."

He was right. She could do this, and she would. Starting now.
That he'd used the same phrase Fremont had slapped her with
less than forty minutes earlier in that diner, helped.

Suck it up.

Kate pulled the cold noon air into her lungs and did just
that. She released the lapels of Joe's jacket and shoved her hands
in the pockets of her own as she nodded and took a step back.
"Thanks, friend. I'm good to go now."

"You sure?"

"Absolutely." Her fingers had found Max's tags with unerr-
ing, subconscious accuracy. She knotted the beaded chain
around her hand, holding on for support as they reached the
steps to the porch she'd helped whitewash all those years ago.

It could use a fresh coat.

The screen door creaked as Joe opened it.

Kate thanked him again as she entered, then turned into the
living room. The lanky, vibrant man she'd chatted with outside
the post office four short weeks ago was now slumped in his
favorite brown La-Z-Boy recliner, silent, bleak and somehow
aged by an additional seventy years.

It wasn't from the cancer.

It was terror.

Though dulled by the drugs, fear was still achingly visible
amid those pale blue eyes that had somehow become paler, and
in those pinched, quivering lips.

"Katie?"

"It's me, Poppa Abel." She let go of the tags and leaned down
so she could wrap her arms about his shoulders for a gentle
squeeze as she pressed her lips to his lined, papery cheek.
Christ, he was frail. Little more than brittle bones with a bit of
muscle stretched across, here and there. This was definitely the

cancer, and this time it was eating through his body, hard and fast.

How could she have been so blind?

Kate choked on her tears as she straightened. She caught the subtle tip of Liz's head and knew there was something else going on. Something Liz needed to share. Kate turned to where the BAU agent had struck up a quiet conversation with Joe.

"Agent Walker?"

"Yes, Deputy?"

"Would you mind sitting with Mr. Parish for a bit?"

"Sure thing." The shrink redeemed his entire profession as he crossed the room and gently drew Abel into a conversation about the array of photos on the mantle that actually had the old man smiling.

With Abel distracted, Kate led Joe into the large kitchen at the back of the house. Liz followed. Her unease increased as Liz closed the door behind them.

"What's wrong?"

"I'm not entirely sure. But something is." She walked them over to the pine beadboard cupboard Mrs. Parish had designated as the family pharmacy and first aid station when Grant was in diapers. "It's in here. Rather, they're in here."

Kate and Joe waited, bemused, as Liz plucked a succession of pharmacy-grade, orange pill bottles from the cupboard and lined them up along the butcher block counter. There were over a dozen when she finished, all prescribed to a name and address Kate had never seen before.

"Who's Theodore Stewart?"

"Abel."

Kate retrieved a bottle to take a closer look. Abel's name was nowhere on the label. "I don't understand."

"Neither do I. Not completely. As I'm sure Agent Cordoba told you, I decided to be proactive. I brought a selection of sedatives with me. Because you said Abel was out of remission, I took the time to come in here and check his medications to make sure nothing was contraindicated with what I thought would best calm him. I found these."

"And he admits they're his?"

"No. But he didn't deny it. And that's not the bizarre part." Liz tapped two bottles in the middle of the line. "These aren't used to treat cancer. They're immunosuppressants. They're designed to negate a body's normal immunological response to foreign tissue. In effect, to prevent the rejection of said tissue. Or in Abel's case, an organ." She tapped a bottle to the right. "This one prevents infection. A critical precaution for someone taking immunosuppressants."

Kate shook her head as she tried to right her spinning brain. It wasn't that she hadn't understood what Liz had said. It just didn't make sense. "Are you telling me Abel had an organ transplant?"

"Yes. From the scar running down his chest, I'm guessing he received a new heart about a year ago, possibly two. Please note; I'm estimating that timeframe off the scar I've seen on a patient of mine who received one three years ago. But that's not the stunning part."

It was to her. Grant had never mentioned this. Hell, he hadn't even hinted at it.

Liz turned to address Joe. "I don't know if Kate told you, but Abel was first diagnosed with colon cancer when we were sophomores in high school. Fortunately, it was caught early and the cancer went into remission. But the fact that he'd once had it should've prevented him from being placed on the national waiting list with the United Network of Organ Sharing. And when you add on Abel's age at the time of transplantation— well, let's just say he had two strikes against him and you don't get any with UNOS. They abide by very rigid criteria. They must. There are simply too many people who need organs and too few available."

Kate stared at the name on the bottle in her hand. There was only one explanation that made sense for a transplant that shouldn't have been and the obvious secrecy surrounding it.

Black market.

She returned the bottle to its slot in that long line and swallowed the bile that threatened. "I know there's a thriving market for illegal kidneys in certain countries." China, India and Pakistan readily came to mind. "But hearts?"

Even the truly desperate tended not to sell those, because you couldn't walk away from the table once the transaction was complete. Even if he had found someone willing to make the ultimate sacrifice, Abel had never been outside the country. Ironically, Abel had volunteered that himself during that visit outside the post office last month. At the time, he'd been admiring a resident's new passport as he bemoaned the fact that he'd never needed one.

That meant the surgery had taken place in the States, possibly in Arkansas. But that wasn't the most appalling part. There was only one person Abel knew with the skills to track down a black-market heart who would also have been willing to risk his professional reputation and freedom to obtain it.

Grant.

But she had to be sure. She caught Liz's stare. "Did you ask him point blank about the transplant?"

"Yes."

"What did he say? His exact words."

"'Grant took care of it.' Then he clammed up. Moments later, Agent Walker arrived so I didn't push it."

The betrayal cut to the bone as Kate sagged against the maple table she'd dined at a mere six weeks ago with both Grant and his father, three feet from that collection of damning pills.

At the time, she'd have sworn on Ruger's life that neither man—but especially Grant—was capable of such heinousness. But now? With that confession? Worse, with three meticulously hacked up bodies in the state morgue, all devoid of their vital organs?

Ten minutes ago, she'd assumed Grant had been kidnapped and was the next likely victim. Now, staring at those pills, she didn't know what he was. Surely, he was innocent of murdering his co-workers, at least?

Please, Lord. Give her that much.

Instinct and experience combined to warn her she'd likely come up empty.

She'd believed she was the cause of Grant's disappearance. She might be right—but for the wrong reason. She'd all but laid out her investigation for the man in her driveway last night...and he'd immediately vanished.

Had he simply gone off the grid?

The bile rose once more as she recalled that burner phone. The one she'd blithely handed over following Grant's revelation regarding the re-emergence of Abel's cancer. A revelation she now believed he'd had no intention of making anytime soon. He'd deliberately abused her sympathy to get himself out of a jam—with her.

Lest that bountiful breakfast she'd shared succeed in its relentless upward quest, Kate pushed off the table and zig-zagged toward the door at the rear of the kitchen.

"Are you okay?"

She waved Liz off as she continued her dogged path. "I just...need a moment. Alone."

Or a million.

Would any amount of time be enough to pull herself together to face the man who'd been more of a father to her at times than her own? To question him, and treat him like the suspect he now was?

Kate stumbled down the back steps of the house, grateful there were only three. She stared out over the stone patio at the old semi-truck tire swing hanging from the limb of a gnarled oak.

She closed her eyes against the memory of Liz pushing Dan so hard he'd flown off and landed in the dirt. He'd bruised his tailbone so badly he hadn't been able to sit properly for a month. She could still hear Grant laughing.

Grant.

Good God, how *could* he?

Kate lurched off the patio and turned toward the old ramshackle barn that served as a detached garage, desperate for another memory of simpler times, before her childhood innocence and her town had gone to crap. She focused on those that'd begun in this very barn. She and Liz sneaking out here late at night during the summer of their junior year. They'd help Dan open the barn's rear doors and shove his mom's old Buick into neutral so they could roll it out and push it down the lane where they'd finally gather their nerves and fire it up.

She'd spent most of those midnight rides terrified someone would recognize them—most especially, her dad. Now, today, she wondered if her father had known all along and had simply accepted that she'd needed that tiny spark of rebellion.

The bittersweet memories of the past merged with the sour denial of the present to carry her up to those barn doors. She opened the one on the right and slipped inside.

Of course, Mrs. Parish's old Buick wasn't inside. She hadn't really expected it to be. But neither had she anticipated this.

A Land Rover.

The bulk of the British SUV was camouflaged amid the hay-strewn shadows, but it was definitely green...just like the one Cal

Burgess had spotted a week ago Tuesday morning in the parking lot of the Baymont building. The one the security guard had seen driven by a man who'd argued with Andrea Silva.

Kate's nerves bellowed like a wounded calf in the chilly silence of the barn, warning her to turn around.

Close the door. Run.

Go back inside that kitchen and pretend she hadn't seen what she'd seen. What this *was*.

She listened to her cop instincts instead, and stepped deeper into the barn. She hooked Max's dog tags around her neck so she could retrieve her cellphone as she approached the passenger side of the SUV. Thumbing the phone's flash, she prayed with every step that the evidence she'd culled from not one, but two of Braxton's roads did not match the Starblaze tread patterns in front of her.

But they did.

And there was more.

Kate swung away from the Land Rover as the bile that had been threatening finally breached her throat. She slammed her phone onto the barn's workbench and braced herself as she deposited the bulk of that much-too-bountiful breakfast into the hay at her feet.

It didn't help. She could still see that trio of nicks and voids that Emmett had pointed out to her at the edge of the road near the pet cemetery. They were seared into her brain.

Along with those coldly sectioned body parts.

She voided her stomach once more and used a rag from the bench to dry her mouth.

"Feel better?"

It was Joe. Thank goodness. Lord only knew what Liz would think, finding her in this position twice in two days.

Kate traded the soiled rag for her phone and turned to face the man who'd seen her through straights equally as rough as this. "Not really." She waved him deeper into the garage, toward their most recent and damning piece of evidence yet. "Take a look."

Joe switched on the flashlight of his own smartphone as he moved closer to the Land Rover. "What am I searching for?"

"Did you get a good look at the tread impressions back at the lab?"

"Yeah—why?"

The moment his beam hit the tread of the right rear Starblaze, he knew. It was in the sharp pull of his breath. Joe expelled his breath just as sharply as he hunkered down beside her. The pain ground in deeper as she held out her palm to double-check its measure against that distinctive trio of flaws.

"Holy shit, Holland."

"Yeah." No doubt about it. This was the SUV that had left its mark out on the edge of that gravel road beside Jason Dunne's body. The same SUV that had almost run her down at her cabin.

So who had been driving? Grant, or his father?

Did she even want the answer anymore?

Her stomach threatened another rebellion. Odd, because there was nothing left inside with which to rebel.

Not even froth.

And for some reason, she was freezing.

She was dimly aware of Joe taking her phone from her nerveless fingers and helping her to her feet, then leading her out of the barn. She grabbed his arm as he guided her around the corner.

"Wait. We need photos. I have to call Lou and brief him. And the crime unit. And then the—"

"No, you don't. Kate, you're in shock. Hell, so am I—and I didn't grow up in this town with these folks. Just let me get you to that pair of Adirondack chairs I saw out by the patio and I'll make the calls while you...process."

He supported her body and soul the entire way, gently nudging her into the closest chair upon their arrival. She fell back against the slats of the weathered wood, grateful she hadn't removed her jacket. She was so cold now that her hands were shaking, too. She shoved them in her pockets in a desperate attempt to warm them.

"You want me to get Dr. Vogel?"

Kate shook her head firmly. She couldn't see Liz just yet. Nor did she want to go back inside. She knew she had to face Abel—but, again, not quite yet.

Joe nodded. "All right. I'll phone the sheriff. You sit here and let things settle for a minute. Okay?"

"Okay."

She did as ordered, staring dutifully, if blindly, at the scuffed toes of her boots as her former fellow investigator moved far enough away to give her what privacy he could while he made the call that would swing the entire focus of their investigation around to the man she'd been crawling into bed with for the past six months.

How long she sat there, she wasn't sure, but eventually she moved. Breathed. Assessed.

Decided.

It was time.

Time to do what she'd done before she'd gathered up those pieces of her squadmate in the aftermath of her first IED explosion. The same thing she'd done before she'd crawled into those mass Iraqi graves she'd been tasked with processing. And what she'd been forced to do when she'd woken up naked inside that Afghan hovel to find her collarbone shattered, her ribs cracked and her face and shoulder flayed open, and some horny kid wanting to rape her again.

Suck it up, soldier.

Fremont's voice echoed in her ears as she clamped her hands

around the tags dangling from her neck and pushed through the agony and horror long enough to locate the core of strength deep inside that always seemed to be there when she needed it most. She used it to pull herself to her feet.

It was easier than she'd expected. And harder.

But she made it. Kate Holland fell away as she stepped off from that chair. Deputy Holland took her place.

"Thought I told you to rest."

"I'm fine." And she was. For now.

She dragged the dog tags up to the collar of her polo and slipped them beneath. The flattened chips of metal slid like ice down her chest, coming to rest over her heart. And, yet, she'd never felt warmer. Stronger.

There, the tags weren't a crutch, but her own personal talisman. A tangible promise to Max...and herself.

She *would* get through this.

She turned to face Joe and the case. "What did Lou have to say?"

Instead of answering, Joe stared at the outline of the tags between the edges of her jacket. She thought he was going to mention them, until he shrugged. "I got his voicemail. Thought about leaving a message, then decided to try Seth. He says to tell you he'll get through to the sheriff, then round up the crime unit and head over here. You want to wait for him?"

"No." She was ready now. She had a thousand questions ricocheting around inside her brain and she wasn't leaving without answers. She accepted her phone from Joe with a surprisingly steady hand, then turned to march across the patio and up those three steps to the kitchen. "You coming, Cordoba?"

"Right behind you, Holland."

Just like old times.

She took perverse comfort from that as she entered the empty kitchen. Stopping at the pine cupboard, she grabbed the first bottle of medication that wasn't in Abel's name and kept walking. Liz and Agent Walker were seated on the couch beside the La-Z-boy—and one still very weary, shell-shocked old man.

Liz vacated her spot as Kate approached.

"Thanks." Despite those thousand ricocheting questions, Kate set the bottle of pills on the coffee table in front of Abel, then sat down beside him and quietly waited.

It took a good five minutes for him to screw up his nerve. She knew that's what Abel was doing long before he was ready. Dan had gotten that same look in his eyes out in that barn the night he'd finally confessed to her that he wanted to take her to the senior prom "for real".

Unfortunately, she hadn't felt the same. She had even less desire to slow dance with his dad a decade later.

Still, she waited.

Despite the latest pummeling of her psyche, her instincts were still good to go, because Abel finally broke.

"I got the heart almost eighteen months ago. We'd found out I needed it a few months before that. Grant hadn't run into you yet—on purpose, I might add. He was working at the VA in Fayetteville at the time, and still reeling over Dan's death, along with his own years spent stitching up an endless supply of folks over in Iraq. He pleaded with UNOS, called members of the transplant committee personally and insisted that, at fifteen years cancer-free, I oughta be an exception. He told 'em that, other than my failing ticker, I had the body of a man half my age and had a detailed physical to prove it. They still said no."

Abel paused as they heard a car pull up, then sighed as Kate leaned forward to tap the lid to the bottle of pills. She was in no mood to be delayed or distracted.

"I'd accepted it, you know? Death. I guess with Dan gone and Grant avoiding me and the house, I was ready to move on and see Barbara again. Then it all changed. Grant showed up and said he'd accepted a job in Little Rock and that, while he was settling in, someone had heard of my need. Grant claimed a fellow doctor's wife was on life support and the doc was ready to terminate if and only if the heart was a match. Claimed the doc said he'd see it as a sign." Abel broke off again as the shadow of Seth's hefty bubba build passed by the lace-covered window.

Joe left to head off the deputy at the front door.

Kate spotted the growing exhaustion in Abel's stare and decided a prod was in order. "It wasn't a match, was it?"

Abel scowled. "Hell, it wasn't even from a woman. I figured that out a couple months later when I overheard Grant talking about my prognosis with someone on the phone. I guess I shoulda suspected something wasn't right. They knocked me out here at the house before the surgery, on a Friday night no less. When I came to afterwards, I was in an official recovery room, but then they knocked me out again when it was time to come home. Grant never did tell me whose heart I got, but the whole blessed thing was just off, you know?"

She knew. And so had Abel. That the surgery had been illegal, and the rest. The whole filthy business that nailed Ian Kusić, Jason Dunne, Andrea Silva and those missing homeless vets to Madrigal Medical's front door...and Grant's.

There was a list all right. Only veterans, homeless or not, did *not* want to be on it.

But if Grant had masked the location of the surgical site from his own father, Kate was that much further away from discovering where those illegal transplants—and potentially subsequent murders of vets—were taking place.

Hell, she didn't even know where Grant was. All she had to go on was the staffing company.

"Grant works for Madrigal Medical on the side, doesn't he?"

The old man clutched at his thinning hair as he trembled out a nod. "He tried to quit, especially after he met back up with you. But they wouldn't let him go. I don't know who he works for, though. He wouldn't say."

"Do you know if he has one of those vacuum-pack machines to seal food for the freezer?"

Stiff silence greeted that question.

But she'd seen the newspaper on the kitchen table. Like the one at Madrigal, it was today's, and well worn. "Abel?"

He sighed. "I don't know if he has one...but I'd been talking about getting one to put up the vegetables from the garden so I could quit canning. He bought me one for Christmas this past year."

Add on the fact that Grant had been hunting and field-dressing deer since he was in elementary school to those Star-blaze treads and his surgical expertise, and she was on solid ground for a warrant.

So why did she feel as though she was sinking—and suffo-cating—in quicksand?

Kate stood. Not only was a briefing with Seth in order, the resulting distance from Abel could only help her regain her equilibrium. She shot Agent Walker a brittle nod and headed for the kitchen to clear her head. There was no hope for her battered heart anymore. If there ever had been.

Through the double windows above the sink, she caught sight of Joe escorting Seth around the back of the detached barn, and chickened out on the briefing.

It could wait.

One look at that Land Rover would hold her for a lifetime.

Water. She wasn't thirsty, but her mouth was still coated with the vestiges of her rejected breakfast and the dregs of Grant's betrayal.

As Kate reached for a glass, the cacophony of half the department's vehicles barreling up the gravel lane reverberated through the kitchen, shaking the floor and cupboards. She had to give Seth credit. Emmett and the rest of the crime scene unit had arrived in record time.

Kate lowered her hand, bemused, then ticked as she caught sight of the smartphone she'd snagged in lieu of the tumbler she'd sought. A swift click of the phone's power button, and her suspicions were confirmed. Grant had told the truth about one thing. Abel was prone to leaving his phone in odd places, but he wasn't using that bargain-basement burner she'd returned to Grant. Because this phone was Abel's.

"What's that?"

Kate whirled around to find Liz tucking the bottle of pills she'd left in the living room into the beadboard cupboard. "Evidence of yet another lie. Christ, I am such an *idiot*."

"You are not."

"Really?" Kate stalked across the kitchen and slapped Abel's actual phone on the counter so she could wave her hand at those pills. "Then explain how I could've missed all this! And don't get me started on what I found in that old barn."

To her frustration, Liz simply closed the cupboard and leaned against it. "I have no idea what you found. I'm not sure I want to. But I do know this: you, Deputy Holland, are a *great* cop. Heck, you were better at solving mysteries and crimes than most of Braxton's police force when you were fifteen years old. That's why your dad used to run his gut instincts past you to double-check them ahead of his partner—remember? And don't try and tell me he was just humoring you, because we both know he wasn't. But here's something you may not know. When it comes to Katie Holland, the daughter and the woman, you also have the most amazing ability to ignore what's too painful to acknowledge, even when it's stabbing you in the eye. And let's not forget, Grant had an excellent reason to hide what we've both learned today—which he actively *did*."

"But, why? Why didn't he come to me?"

She truly was an idiot, wasn't she? Because that answer was a no-brainer. You didn't tell your lover, who also happened to be a cop, that you were up to your surgical mask and scalpels in a scheme to steal organs from your fellow vets. Because it was looking very much as though that's exactly what Grant and those three victims whose bagged parts she'd helped identify had been involved in.

Damn it, she would've supported Grant through Abel's declining health, just as she had in high school, if he'd only opened up to her. Yes, there was an excellent chance Abel would've been dead by now. But others—how many *innocent* others?—would be alive today, and Grant and his father wouldn't be staring at life sentences. Or worse.

But according to Abel, Grant had been avoiding her since his return to the States. At least a year before he'd discovered Abel needed a heart. "Liz, I just don't understand *why*."

And she desperately needed to.

Her friend pushed a strawberry curl behind her ear and laughed. The sound was born more of frustration than humor. "You really are an emotional ostrich. Grant's in love with you, Kate. I know we were just kids to him at first, but Grant fell hard for you when he came back for Christmas break our senior year. And before you ask why he never told you, it's because he knew Dan was hung up on you too. I still think that's why they ended up following you into the Army, especially Dan. Yes, he wanted to serve his country. But deep down, I think Dan was hoping you'd run into each other a few years down the road, and that being a soldier would help you see him in a different light. A light you understood and respected."

Liz was right. Dan had tiptoed around it the night he'd asked her to senior prom, but she'd ignored it—and him—just as Liz had accused her of doing. She'd assumed he'd gotten over it. Evidently not.

Hell, maybe Dan was right. Maybe she might've seen him differently if they'd run into each other overseas.

But they hadn't. And now Dan was five years dead. Perhaps not directly, but obliquely because of her.

No wonder Grant had avoided her.

Was it possible that if she'd been less of an ostrich she could've headed off the rest? She'd probably be obsessing over that one for the rest of her life.

Kate picked up Abel's phone and switched it on, torturing herself with the view of the old family photo that either Grant or Abel had installed as the phone's wallpaper. Abel, his wife and the boys looked so happy there.

How had it all gone so wrong?

Kate shoved the phone in her pocket and faced Liz. It was time for the truth—and this woman, shrink or not, would give it to her, unvarnished. She just had to ask for it. "Do you think Grant did it? Is he even capable?"

She wasn't referring to Abel's heart, and Liz knew it. Her friend's bright blue gaze glistened brighter as it settled on the worn Sunday paper neatly refolded and centered on the distressed farm table they'd sat around as teenagers.

"Do you know if Grant suffered a concussion over there?"

For the first time, Kate wished she had broken down and swapped war stories with the man the few times he'd attempted to draw her out, even if it had meant offering up the fantasy showcased in that Silver Star write-up. "I have no idea."

Liz shook her head. "Me, neither. I assume you've figured out that he was seeing Dr. Manning. Grant was also participating in a group for vets who worked with the VA. If you can't get access to his medical records, someone there might talk if you get them alone. As a psychiatrist, I'm not supposed to suggest that. But if Grant did suffer a concussion, the damage to his brain could've affected his personality significantly. If true, as his friend, I'd want that bit of mitigating knowledge out there."

Kate nodded, but she didn't agree. She'd processed too many shrink-wrapped body parts to entertain the idea of mitigation at the moment, if ever. "And if there was no concussion?"

"Well, he's not the same teenager and young man we used to know. Iraq changed him. As did Dan's death. I could see that before he opened his mouth. He's...distant now. Guarded. I don't know if he's different with you, but I suspect not."

This nod was genuine. Liz suspected correctly. Grant had tended to be distant with her too. But she was guilty of the same with him, so it hadn't really registered, much less mattered.

She pushed Liz the way she hadn't pushed herself. "And?"

Her friend dug her hands through her loose curls and sighed as she massaged the base of her scalp. "I don't know. There is a significant stressor at play."

"Abel's cancer? That it's terminal this time?"

"Yes."

Kate nodded. "I agree." Though she'd yet to speak with Walker, the BAU agent was bound to concur. As stressors went, that cancer's return was a doozy. For Grant to find out that the illegal heart and whatever role he held in Madrigal's macabre business had been all for naught?

It was more than a stressor.

It was a recipe for revenge.

And according to Abel, Grant had wanted out. But someone at Madrigal had refused.

In his grief, anger and desperation, had Grant seen the murders of his co-conspirators as his only escape? It wasn't as though Madrigal's CEO, that slime of a lawyer Robert Stern and anyone else in on those illegal transplants could call the police and turn Grant in. Was that what the trio had been discussing in that back office at the Baymont this morning?

If so, she and Agent Walker were wrong about the stalking. Grant would have no need. He knew his victims. They would've trusted him. That's why there were no signs of an initial, physical attack on the bodies.

And Grant would have had access to the paralytic drug that turned up on the tox screens.

"Liz, I had breakfast with Sergeant Fremont this morning. He says Ian Kusić had been drawing extra vials of blood from certain homeless VA patients. Those same patients appear to have been questioned extensively by Kusić about potential family histories of cancer and dementia, specifically Creutzfeldt-Jakob's disease—and some of these same men are now missing."

Her friend clutched the closest kitchen chair and shifted to sink into it. "Wow. This really is happening. Right here in Arkansas." She stared at the photo of those oversized bags beneath the fold of the paper. "Yeah, everything you just said fits. When you think about it, a bit of blood is all you need for tissue typing. A sample from the donor and the recipient for comparison. If you have enough markers, and the health histories check out, it's a go. Of course, you'd have to have access to a lab to run the blood work."

Kate claimed the seat beside Liz at the Parish family table, but it was nothing like old times as she flipped the paper upside down and shoved it away from them. "I've got a good lead on the lab." As a medical staffing company, tissue typing was probably the easiest step for Madrigal to abuse. "Have you heard of a company called—"

Her jacket pocket vibrated. For a moment, Kate thought Abel's phone had gone off. But Joe must've bumped the mute button on hers by accident. The caller was Lou.

Kate stood. "Sorry. I need to—"

"—take that. I know." Liz stood as well. "I'll keep Agent

Walker company until the hospice nurse arrives. I need to speak to her, but Abel says she's not due for a couple hours."

Kate withdrew Abel's phone from her pocket and passed it to Liz. "The number's probably in here. Please give the phone to Agent Walker when you're finished."

"I will."

Kate connected through to Lou as her friend left. "Hey, boss. I guess you've heard by now."

"Yeah. Life sucks. But you already knew that."

She did.

"You okay, kiddo?"

"Yup, what've you got?" Because Lou Simms wouldn't be eating up her time at an active crime scene—and that was what this old farmhouse had become—just to engage in chitchat, however much he feared she might need it.

"We're still waitin' on the warrants for Madrigal, but tell Seth the ones for Abel are a go, to include the house, surroundin' property, and especially the Land Rover and the barn it's parked inside. I've expanded the Fort Leaves warrant to include anyone Kusić drew blood from. I'll let you know when that comes in. The one for Grant's condo is approved too. Since it's in Mazelle, their police department will be executin' it. You're free to assist them in an advisory capacity or wait for the report if you can't get away from there. We still haven't been able to connect Jason Dunne to that shyster you spoke to, but the Little Rock PD did find Dunne's Stingray. It was parked in an overflow lot at Fort Leaves. Also, the second round of tox results on Kusić are in, along with the initial financial data dumps."

"Kusić popped positive for oxy, didn't he? But he was clean on Xanax." The drug Grant had sworn the tech was also addicted to.

"Yeah. How'd you know?"

"Educated guess." One that served as yet another nail in the coffin of Grant's guilt. If she'd been in a better mood she might've been impressed with his quick thinking last night in her drive. She reached out and flipped the newspaper over to stare at that eerily straight line of sacks.

Or not.

She shoved the paper away. "Anything interesting in the financials?"

"Not with the first two victims. Though that's not surprisin' since you found Kusić's cash stashed at home-sweet-home. Dunne must've been spendin' his—cash, that is—faster than he could bank it, 'cause it don't show up anywhere. But neither does a history of payin' for that swanky place on the river or the Stingray."

"He may have funneled the cash though a second account and paid his bills through that."

"Agreed. I got Carole on that angle. We did find somethin' of note in Andrea Silva's account."

"That was quick." They'd ID'd the woman's body roughly sixteen hours earlier, on a Saturday night. "How many bankers did the governor's aide have to drag out of bed and threaten with obstruction?"

"Less than you'd think. A third set of those bags in as many days? Let's just say folks are gettin' mighty cooperative."

"That'd do it." Kate headed to the sink to retrieve the glass of water she'd been distracted from earlier. She filled it halfway and finally rinsed out her mouth. "What'd you find on Silva?"

"Her new employer. For the past six months, Silva has received deposits from a company called VitaCell Tissues, Inc. Don't yet know what all they do, but VitaCell's a subsidiary of—"

"Madrigal Medical."

"Got it in one, Kato."

So much for the company pit bull's claim that he had no idea where the surgical nurse had gone after she'd quit the VA. "We need those records for Madrigal, boss. Every sheet of paper and digital kilobyte. VitaCell's, too."

She'd scour the entire batch personally, over and over, until she figured out where those surgeries were taking place.

Until then, God only knew how many vets' lives were in danger. Men and women who'd already given more for their fellow citizens than they should've ever had to give.

Warrant or not, she refused to mark time in this farmhouse, becoming more enraged with Grant and Abel by the second. "Did you happen to get a home address for Madrigal's CEO?"

"I did. It's near Grant's condo in Mazelle."

Excellent. It was time to pay a house call—and God help Robert Stern if he and his legal briefs tried to get in her way.

13

"STOP OBSESSING."

Kate shifted her attention from the burgundy Ram 2500 traveling ahead of her Durango on I-40 South to glare at the man in the passenger seat. Joe met her scowl and raised her a pointed brow, then went back to texting on his phone.

Kate cursed her former fellow agent and his intimate knowledge of her vices as she returned her focus to the road. She was obsessing...now.

The first half of the drive had been much more proactive. She'd filled it with a series of calls via the speaker on her iPhone. The first had been to the Baymont security guard who'd relieved Cal Burgess that morning. Fortunately, Felix had still been on duty and had indeed noted the Madrigal CEO's departure from the building. The guard had been happy to inform Deputy Holland that said departure had occurred roughly ninety minutes prior to her call and had included an offhand comment from the CEO that he was headed home.

Felix had had less information to relay regarding the lawyer —just that Robert Stern and a younger brunette in a green dress had left at the same time as the CEO.

Satisfied that her current plan to beard the bastard in his mansion had a better than average chance of success, Kate had accessed her contact list and had begun to phone everyone she could think of who *might* know where Grant could be.

When none did, she'd moved on to Sergeant Fremont and the number he'd given her to Saint Clare's on the hope that the vet had returned to the shelter following their breakfast that morning. If she could obtain the names of the two homeless vets Fremont had recently located who'd passed Kusić's covert, pre-transplant questionnaire, the Little Rock PD could track them down and warn the men to take precautions, even place them in protective custody if they agreed.

She'd had no joy there, either. Fremont was out. All she'd been able to do was leave a message requesting that he contact her when he returned—and ask him to take care. Though she had every intention of persuading Fremont to accept protective custody too. After all, Grant knew she'd spoken to a Fort Leaves vet about those vials of blood. And there were plenty of witnesses to the coffee she'd shared with Fremont in that cafeteria.

A coffee that may have inadvertently risked the sergeant's life.

It was that disquieting thought that had ushered in the time-honored hobby of self-flagellation. She'd spent the trip since pulling up every moment she'd spent with Grant during the past six months and re-examining them in a new and horrifying light. Especially those they'd spent in his bed.

How could she *not* have known?

Even more terrifying was the suspicion that Grant, subconsciously or not, had wanted her to. After all, he'd all but deposited the bodies on her doorstep. And there was that cross. Were those dump sites less about his knowledge of and comfort with the backroads of their hometown, and more about punishment for her?

If Liz was right, and Grant had been in love with her since high school, it made a depressing sort of sense.

Worse, she hadn't even seen it coming.

Was she an ostrich? Did she have her head shoved so far down in the sand when it came to her personal life that she could miss her own lover's transformation into Mr. Hyde?

Ruger hadn't. He'd had Grant pegged from the moment she'd introduced them. Ruger had even—

"I said *stop.*" Joe's sigh cut through the SUV's chilly air as he clicked off his phone and tossed it to the dash. "That's an order, Holland, and I don't care who works for whom."

"Yeah, well, either way, that order's easier issued than followed."

"I know. But you can't beat yourself up. All you can do is learn from it. Detectives miss things. And the closer we are physically and emotionally to the source, the easier it is to miss 'em too. You know that. You've seen it happen with others. I know, 'cause I was there. People have a special set of blinders when it comes to those they care about, even cops."

True. But something this huge, this awful?

She could almost understand the transplants scraping beneath her radar—but those murders? "There must've been hints, Joe. Shifts in his behavior. I knew him for four years before I left town. Yes, I was a teenager and he was the older brother of a good friend who popped back in during breaks from college and med school. But those breaks added up. Together, they should've provided me with a decent enough benchmark."

"Exactly. You *knew* him—note the past tense—and, as you just admitted, not all that well. Certainly not on a day-to-day basis.

And then you left. So did he. And while you two were apart, for over a decade I might add, you both changed." Joe shrugged. "You just didn't want to see those changes, much less accept them. It's human nature. You wanted life—and him—to be like it was before. Given the absolute hell you went through four years ago, I suspect your subconscious worked doubly hard to believe you hadn't changed either—without you even realizing it."

Kate slowed the SUV to take their exit off the interstate, following the directions from the Durango's GPS unit through the subsequent suggested turn, and the next. "So what are you saying? That my brain kept a virtual pair of rose-tinted glasses lying around, just for the Parish family?"

"Could be. Hell, I'm guilty of donning a pair myself when it comes to my own family. I fully admit, there are days I'd give almost anything to be able to forget what the world looks like beyond them. Especially what those godforsaken hellholes we managed to crawl into, then back out of, look like. Maybe Grant just couldn't find a way to do the same."

"So like Liz, you think Grant held it together though his tours in Iraq only to come home and crack stateside four years later, upon learning of his dad's cancer?"

"You can't rule it out. We're not the only ones the powers that be decided to bounce between war zones like rubber balls—over and over again." Joe snatched his sliding phone off the dash as the Durango took a turn onto a secondary road sharper than she'd intended. "Think about the cases we've worked—suicide bombings, IEDs and VBIDs, fratricides. All those human pieces and parts, and all those goddamned gaping, bloody holes in soldiers and civilians alike where they just didn't belong. Grant had a better view than even we did—inside operating rooms with more hacked-off parts lying around than an over-stuffed butcher's shop. Maybe it was all still simmering around inside him, fucking with his head until it just boiled over. God knows, it's fucked with mine. And don't even try and tell me it hasn't with yours."

She wouldn't. She couldn't.

Because it still did.

Joe shoved his phone in his pocket as they neared the gated community where Madrigal's CEO lived. "I know it doesn't help, but it sounds like it started out small and desperate. I suspect that was deliberate, to reel Grant in before he realized how big a bite out of his soul it was going to take." Joe sighed as she brought the Durango to a halt beside Kensington Acres' glassed-in guard shack. "His dad was dying, Kate. I sure as hell can't condone that first transplant, much less forgive it, but I can understand it. Some people will do anything for those they truly love. We've both been in the cop business long enough to have learned that the hard way."

"True." But he was right. It didn't help.

Kate rolled down her driver's window as the gate guard approached. She kept the mottled side of her face averted as she flashed her credentials to keep the man's attention where it belonged. "Good afternoon. I'm Deputy Holland with the Braxton PD." She tipped her head toward Joe and the badge he was holding up. "This is Special Agent Joe Cordoba, US Army CID. We're here to see Mr. Kessler. Has he arrived home yet?"

"Yes, ma'am. 'Bout an hour ago. You need me to call and give him a heads up?"

She shot the guard a smoothly inclusive, *we're all law enforcement* smile, knowing without looking that Joe was mirroring it. "That won't be necessary, sir. Mr. Kessler's expecting us." If he wasn't after this morning, the man was an idiot. "He's at 12 Westchester Drive, correct?"

"Yes, ma'am." The rent-a-guard tipped the brim of his ball cap, then pointed deeper into the enclave. "Second street is Westchester; it's the sixth house on the right. If you have trouble locating the place, give a holler. The driveways can be a mite hard to see with all them towering trees."

"I will."

Kate rolled up the window and nudged the SUV through the gate before the guard decided to revisit that heads-up call.

"Are people always so trusting down here?"

Kate laughed. "Welcome to the South, Cordoba."

"Yeah, well, with the kind of excitement you got going on, you can keep it."

She was forced to agree. "The guard was right about the trees. They are thick." There were twice as many low-sweeping pines in these woods than in the ones around her house, creating a dense, nearly impenetrable stand, even in fall. Kate cocked her head as they turned onto Westchester Drive. "Did you hear that?"

"The wood chipper? Can't miss it. Rivals a Warthog screaming in for a low-altitude strafing run."

She shook her head as they passed the chipper and a trio of workers shoving tree limbs inside. "No, there's something else, during the ebbs in the grinds."

Two cars were parked at the crest of the CEO's semi-circular drive. In the lead, the blue BMW Cal Burgess had pointed out that morning at the Baymont. Behind the Beemer, a low-slung silver Jaguar. Her aging Durango would only lower that three-story monstrosity's property value, but what the hell.

Kate killed the SUV's engine, her ears perking as she opened the driver's door. There it was again. Mixed up with the gnashing of that ravenous chipper.

Barking.

But not the annoyed or even "on alert" type. It was the same frantic, snarling, *get the hell in here 'cause something's very wrong* tone Ruger had snapped and howled at her just last night.

"Shit." Kate reached inside her jacket and eased her Glock from its shoulder holster as she closed the driver's door.

Joe didn't question her actions or that succinct assessment as he too abandoned the Durango while slipping his 9mm SIG Sauer from his holster. "Sounds like it's coming from around the left side of the house. Possibly the ground floor."

Kate nodded. "You take the right."

She had the left.

She took off as Joe nodded his agreement, sprinting around the stately, red-bricked facade until she'd arrived at the source of that barking. Stopping to peer in between the slats of a low window, she made out what appeared to be a utility room. Inside was a massive, torqued-off Doberman, his leather muzzle hooked uselessly on the handle of the inner door as he bellowed and snarled louder than an entire inner-city dog pound on End of the Road day.

Kate resumed her sprint. Within seconds, she'd rounded the back of the house and hooked up with Joe two feet from a set of French doors that were disturbingly ajar.

Kate nodded her intent and moved in first, spotting two bodies just inside a spacious music and TV room. Ms. Model from the Baymont's Madrigal offices and an equally well-maintained, dark-haired man in his fifties were lying on the floor. Both their throats had been slit from ear to ear, with near matching pools of blood soaked into the plush, cream-colored carpet beneath.

Despite the glazed, lifeless stare in the woman's otherwise perfect face, Kate bent to check for a pulse. She shot a swift shake of her head toward Joe as he bent over what was most likely Madrigal's former CEO.

Joe followed up the press of his fingers with a silent shake of his own.

Damn.

They kept moving.

Joe signaled his intent with his free hand just before he split off into the formal dining room. Kate entered the foyer on her own to find Robert Stern, his throat slashed like the others and lying in a slightly smaller pool of blood amid the polished, black-and-white checkerboard tiles. Like the model, the lawyer's eyes were open—but Stern was still alive.

Barely.

Kate dropped to her knees, jamming her fingers into the pressure points at the sides of the man's neck to try and slow the loss of blood as she whispered in his ear. "Is the killer still in the house?"

The lawyer managed a slight, negative shake and a soft gurgle.

"Joe! Call 911! We got another one, and he's still with us!"

Both hands occupied at the lawyer's pressure points, Kate jerked her head down to his ears. "Did Grant Parish do this to you?"

Stern's mouth worked, but all that came out was another, queasier, gurgle of blood, most of it spilling over onto her hands.

This was not good.

"Don't try to talk. Just blink once if I'm right, twice if I'm wrong. And hang in there—the ambulance is on its way." It would be a miracle if the man lasted that long.

She could hear Joe shouting into his phone as his boots thundered down a set of stairs, but by the time Joe had reached her side, all the lawyer had enough life left to do was stare frantically at her, then Joe, then back at her—before Stern, too, was gone.

"Goddamn it, *no!*" Kate ground down on her teeth as she yanked her fingers from the man's lifeless neck and slammed back on her haunches. "Son-of-a-*bitch*. If we'd left Abel's just two minutes earlier—"

She broke off as Joe's hands clamped over her shoulders for a quick, absolving squeeze—but she wasn't buying it.

There was no absolution for this one. Not for her, and not for the others.

"Joe, we needed him. These three were our only hope for quick answers."

Who knew how long it would take to get them now? To find those three, already-missing vets? To locate Grant before he could murder someone else involved with this filthy racket?

She jackknifed to her feet and left Joe standing over the lawyer's body as she returned to the kitchen she'd barreled through minutes earlier. This time, she was in search of a stream of scalding water and a gallon of soap.

She was still scrubbing her skin raw when a cacophony of wailing sirens overtook the wood chipper. Within seconds, both died out, leaving the pissed-off Doberman to provide his own, jarringly lonely soundtrack to the afternoon's events.

She kept scrubbing as she heard the front door open, then several unknown males speaking. Joe, briefing.

She ignored it all. She just couldn't seem to stop scrubbing.

Until, finally, "You okay?"

Joe.

He was in the kitchen now. Behind her.

She looked up from the flood of water in the sink that had been clear of the lawyer's blood for several minutes now. She forced herself to shut off the faucet and turn around. "No. I'm furious. I know I should be sorry for the loss of life here, and I am. But I have to be honest; I'm mostly livid—and terrified."

But not for herself.

"I understand. But half a dozen cop cars arrived with that ambulance. They're already stringing the barrier tape. There's bound to be a computer somewhere in this place. If we're lucky, the CEO kept the damning stuff close at hand."

"And if not?" Because with legal counsel as slick as Stern had been, she doubted it.

Joe retrieved Max's dive watch from where she'd laid it on the granite counter and held it out. "Then we keep looking. Keep working. There's not much else we can do."

Lord, she hated when he was right.

She snatched the watch from Joe's fingers and wrapped it around her wrist where it belonged. At least with all the scrubbing she'd just done, her right wrist was now as raw as the left.

Nothing like a fresh catastrophe to camouflage her previous meltdowns.

"Thanks. What happened to the dog?" The kitchen was suddenly, echoingly silent.

"One of the cops in the foyer said something about a tranquilizer gun in his trunk."

Ruger forgive her, she was grateful. Her head was pounding through adrenaline withdrawal as it was. Plus, the dog would have to be removed from the crime scene so they could fully process it. Given the Doberman's day, even she wouldn't want to do that without a little help from Morpheus.

"I don't hear the chipper anymore, either."

Joe cocked his head. "Nor do I."

"What say we wander next door, Agent Cordoba, and see if those yard workers saw or heard anything while they were setting up shop?" Any second now, the local boys in blue would be streaming into the kitchen to take over this part of the scene too. They might as well use the ensuing confusion to see what they could glean, then come back to offer up their own, detailed eyewitness statements.

Joe's wink served as her answer, as did the sweep of his hand underscoring the path out of the room.

They retraced their entrance, skirting the first two bodies they'd spotted in the den, then out and around the back of the house, all the way to the silver Jaguar in the semi-circular drive at the front. There, they stopped.

A tall, impressively muscled suit had beaten them to the chipper crew. He was shaking hands with the older of the workers, then turned to nod and wave at them.

"Looks like we've been summoned, Holland."

Kate returned the wave for the both of them. "Try not to piss the man off." She knew full well her friend's true feelings on smaller town cops, despite his ability to shield those feelings from others...when it suited him. "I'd like to get out of here in time to stop by Grant's condo while they're still searching it to see if anything's turned up."

"Roger Dodger."

"Shut up."

To her relief, he did, even to the extent of letting her field the introductions as the dark-haired, muscled suit reached their side. Kate extended a hand. "Deputy Kate Holland, Braxton PD." She turned slightly to facilitate the second set of shakes. "This is Special Agent Joe Cordoba, US Army Criminal Investigation Division."

"Detective Arash Moradi, Mazelle PD." He didn't appear taken aback in the slightest by Joe's federal affiliation, or the shredded side of her face.

She'd almost chalked up the cause to a combination of the Sunday paper and the all-points bulletin for Grant that was bound to have blanketed the state by now—until she spotted the detective's tattoo as he withdrew from his handshake with Joe.

It was small, roughly an inch in width and centered on the inside of his right wrist, just beneath his palm. The simple, black inking consisted of four Arabic letters that, together, spelled out the one word so very dear to nearly every soldier who'd served over there.

Infidel.

Kate nodded. "Afghanistan or Iraq?"

Moradi grinned. "Afghanistan. Matter of fact, last time I was there, I was just down the road from you. Even took a jaunt around the countryside with a bunch of buddies for about eleven hours one day just to seek you out." His grin deepened, along with his palpable respect. "Turned out you didn't need any help finding your way home."

Well, that was debatable. Especially since she was fairly certain she'd yet to arrive.

Home, that is.

At least that's what it felt like, even four years later, standing in an upscale neighborhood in a central Arkansan town, chatting with someone who looked like him. With those distinctive features, he'd have blended in well in Afghanistan or Iraq. Except that name was Persian. His accent and manners, though, were pure Deep South.

As for his part in that search for her, she offered up her own, genuine smile. "I appreciate the effort, regardless."

The detective clipped another nod, and they both let it go at that.

Joe glanced across the drive to where the chipper crew appeared to be wrapping up their labors for the day, no doubt at Moradi's suggestion. "I see you had the same idea as us."

"Figured I'd waylay them early, in case they tried to leave." The detective shrugged. "It didn't yield much. They've been out there with that chipper for over an hour. Between earmuffs and almost non-stop grinding, they didn't hear a thing—not even the dog. They did see the cars pull up though. The BMW, shortly after they started the chipper. The Jag, ten, fifteen minutes before your Durango. Their backs were turned when the Jag turned in, so they can't be certain."

It was enough to confirm that Grant had been on foot, at least during his final approach. The most likely reason: the guard at that gate. If he'd seen Grant coming and going from Kensington Acres often enough to recognize him, the guard's mere presence would've forced Grant to adapt accordingly.

But what about the new bodies? Had Grant planned to kidnap and hack up the CEO, his lawyer and the woman as well? If so, had the Doberman and his misplaced muzzle forced Grant's hand and saved his owner from a nasty postmortem fate?

Either way, who was left?

Grant hadn't been waiting around for them or the police. Who else did he plan on killing?

"Deputy?"

"Sorry. Just sorting the pieces. And it's Kate."

Especially for a fellow former soldier who'd given up a day of his life to search for her.

She glanced at the crew across the street. "Their timeline meshes with the gate guard's estimate on the Beemer. Agent Cordoba and I heard the dog as we pulled up. We rounded the house and found the French doors ajar. The two in the den were already dead; their throats had been slashed. The one in the foyer—a lawyer by the name of Robert Stern—was dying when I reached him. Agent Cordoba called 911 but Stern died within seconds. He wasn't able to name his killer, but he did manage to signal that the house was empty. We suspect—" She broke off, swallowed the surge of renewed muck.

It was one thing to suspect Grant of hacking up those bodies, another to discuss him with Joe. But a stranger? Even a fellow cop?

Damn it. Grant was a suspect now.

She drew her breath in deep and forced herself to act like it. "We suspect Grant Parish, a surgeon with the Little Rock VA. I take it you've seen the APB?"

"I have. I was a block from here, headed to his place to assist with the condo warrant when your 911 call came through. Looks like I've been rerouted here for the duration." Moradi withdrew a small memo pad and pen from his inner suit pocket. He opened the pad to a half-filled page and drew a line beneath the scrawl, then added several more notes. "Robert Stern. So you knew the victims?"

"No. I've been working the body parts cases from Braxton since the start. I had a lead on a possible connection between the victims—that all three may have been hired through a medical staffing company out of the Baymont building in Little Rock."

"The company's name?"

"Madrigal Medical. I met the woman lying in the den at the Baymont this morning. She never gave me her name, but it may be Marilee. I'm fairly certain the man lying next to her is the owner of the house and the CEO of Madrigal, Ben Kessler—but I never actually met him. Stern was his chief legal counsel. I did speak to Stern."

"And were the victims from your case connected to Madrigal?"

"We believe so. Stern denied a solid connection at the Baymont, but we came across evidence since that contradicts a major portion of his story—which is why Agent Cordoba and I came here. I'd intended to question the CEO without prior warning. Unfortunately, we arrived too late to assist. I should be able to say more once I've had a chance to speak with my boss. Until then, that's all I can offer."

Moradi nodded. "Understood."

"You should know: Grant Parish is smart. He's left damned little at the dump scenes in Braxton. Plus, the staggered arrivals of that BMW and Jaguar, along with the timing of the kills in the mansion, the location of the bodies over two different rooms, and the ownership of the house? It all suggests that both men were targets, possibly the woman as well. Also, the alarm was off when we arrived. I'm betting it was off when Kessler and the woman returned, too."

"But you can't be sure."

"No. But there's no sign of forced entry on those French doors, and given what we've learned this afternoon, it's very possible Parish had access to the keys and codes to this place. Again, I'll need to speak with my boss before I can offer more."

Moradi added a final note and closed his tablet. He retrieved one of his business cards and traded it for the one she'd had ready. "Thanks, Kate. Would you mind showing me the position of the doors upon your arrival?"

"Sure thing." She was about to turn around when her phone rang. She glanced at the caller ID, then Joe. "It's Saint Clare's." Sergeant Fremont must've gotten her message.

Joe nodded. "Maybe we'll get positive news for a change. I'll show Detective Moradi the doors and start the walkthrough. Catch up when you can."

"Thanks." Kate accepted the call as the men headed around the mansion. "Steve?"

"I'm sorry; this is Father Popichak with the homeless mission at Saint Clare's."

Too many hours steeped in the ugliness of this case had her gut plummeting to her boots. "Yes?"

"I am speaking to Deputy Holland, correct?"

She blew out the breath she hadn't realized she'd been holding hostage. "Yes, Father. This is Deputy Holland, Braxton PD. Please, call me Kate."

"Very well, Kate. I'm told you left a message for Sergeant Fremont. Something about needing to watch his back. That's why I'm phoning you. I'm worried. The sergeant does odd jobs for me around the mission and the church. He usually stops by my office on Sunday afternoons to discuss the upcoming week's tasks. He missed today's meeting. Since he has been very concerned recently about the welfare of three other missing vets, I thought perhaps I should phone and let you know."

Kate's heart followed her gut to her boots. "Absolutely. When was the last time someone saw him?"

"I was told the sergeant had last-minute plans to have breakfast with a friend this morning. He hasn't been seen since."

"Thank you, Father. Please let me know if you hear from him. I'll do the same."

"I will."

"I'd also like to send a local officer by the shelter today to look through the items in those tubs that you still have. The ones that belonged to the missing vets. We need as much information on each man as we can get."

"Of course. I won't leave until your officer shows."

"Thank you."

Kate closed her eyes as the priest hung up. *Breakfast.* She braced her free hand against the Jaguar as the sensation she'd experienced that morning during her walk from her Durango into the Silver Bullet diner snapped in so vividly; she could feel the same prickling of flesh as it rippled down her neck once more.

What if someone *had* been watching her then?

What if it had been Grant?

Kate turned to face the now yawning entrance to the CEO's mansion as a dozen of Mazelle's crime scene technicians, burdened with their gear, began to file inside. Her fears had come to fruition. Grant was cleaning house. Sergeant Fremont was already either drugged and zip-cuffed to a gurney somewhere, and next on Grant's list.

Or he was already dead.

14

By the time she and Joe made it back to Braxton, the search for Sergeant Fremont had gone from bad to rotten.

Though Kate had called Lou to brief him on the latest developments after she'd spoken with the priest, she hadn't been able to provide anything other than a general description for an immediate all-points bulletin on the vet. Evidently, the VA computer system was down across the entire blessed nation because of yet another inexplicable outage—its third that month alone. The timing of this particular outage couldn't be worse for their investigation, since as a result, she had no photo, no social security number and no home of record for the man.

Hell, she wasn't even sure of the vet's legal name.

"Steve Fremont" hadn't come back in the state DMV. Neither had "Steven" or "Stephen". Due to the nature of his disability combined with his current homelessness, that wasn't surprising. She doubted the man had a current driver's license in any state.

But he might've had one prior to his injury. Lou had their best data tech running those possibilities now.

Hope allowed the tension to ease, if only a bit, as Kate parked the Durango in the police station's lot. It eased a bit more as her boss met her and Joe at the glass doors with a decently thick manila folder. "VA's system's still down, but Carole's been bustin' her hump. These are all the Steve, Steven and Stephen Fremonts she's been able to round up so far, nationwide. Let's take a look."

Lou led the way to their conference room.

Agent Walker was seated at the far end of the rectangular table, an open laptop to his left, a yellow legal tablet overflowing with notes in front of him. He glanced up to nod a welcome, before shifting his attention back to whomever was on the other end of that call.

Kate shrugged off her jacket and tossed it to a spare chair before occupying the seat next to Lou at the head of the table. Joe joined her down the line, setting his laptop on the table as the manila folder Lou had waved earlier landed in front of her.

Kate flipped through the out-of-state DMV photos as quickly as she dared, frowning as she reached the final one. She slid the folder back to Lou. "He's not there."

She turned to ask Joe to access the Army's archives, but he was already hefting his laptop and returning to his feet. "I'm on it. You said the man was Special Forces?"

"Yes."

"Then, archives or not, someone's bound to remember him. I'll interrupt the SOCOM general's Sunday dinner if I have to." He glanced down the table to where the BAU agent was still scrawling out notes while listening intently to his phone. "Sheriff, do you have someplace I can set up where I won't disturb Ed?"

"Sure thing. Hang a right when you leave here and head down the hall. Carole will find you a quiet spot."

"Thanks."

Lou caught her stare as Joe departed. "How you holdin' up?"

"All things considered?" She pushed forth a stiff shrug that said it all. "You?"

She needn't have asked. The shock and profound grief of the day had added at least a dozen lines to Lou's face. "I still can't believe what he and Abel did. Barbara must be turnin' over in her grave 'cause of this—Dan, too."

Amen.

"Anything turn up at Grant's condo?"

"Not yet. Joe and I spent the last two hours shadowing a Mazelle detective around that mansion. Nothing jumped out at any of us. They were packing up the CEO's computer when we left. It should be at the state lab later tonight. The detective phoned the condo search team, but there's nothing there yet either. And no sign of Grant's smartphone, or that burner phone. They did find his laptop. It's on its way to the lab too. Detective Moradi promised to call if anything interesting surfaced."

"Moradi?" Lou appeared to consider the name for a moment, then shook his head. "Must be new. He's the one you shared the case info with, right? You get a good feel about him?"

Kate nodded. "He's former Army. Did a handful of tours over there. Intel and interrogations."

Lou nodded as he reached for the plate of muffins on the deserted side of the conference table.

She shook her head as he nudged them toward her. Despite her humiliating genuflection in Abel's barn, she still wasn't hungry. Must be the worry and the guilt.

"So what about this end, boss? Did Seth find anything else in that barn?"

Lou took a chocolate muffin in her stead and began to peel down the waxed wrapper. "Not yet. But Seth's still processin' the farmhouse. Abel's nurse showed up. She offered to stay the night. I agreed. Seth'll leave someone from the department behind to stay with, but we'll need to figure what to do about Abel soon. Given what he's done, we'll have to bring him in at some point."

Though she hated thinking about it, Lou was right. Terminal cancer or not, Abel couldn't be allowed to just walk away from this, even if it was to shuffle up to his grave.

The fact that he hadn't known at the time would've mitigated things—had Abel come forward when he'd found out. But he hadn't.

Worse, he'd kept his mouth shut about the reoccurring possibility of other victims.

Finally, it just wasn't their call. All cops did was enforce the laws; they couldn't change them.

That was up to the voters and the courts.

Lou must've decided against the chocolate muffin, because he pulled the paper up and set it on the plate. "Before I forget, Tonga called. The initial tox report came back on Andrea Silva. Same paralytic in her system as with Kusić and Dunne."

Shit.

She'd known it was coming, had even tortured herself with that inescapable vision during the ride here: Steve Fremont, a man who'd already given so much to his country, who'd been giving everything he had left to his fellow wounded vets; to think of him lying on a gurney somewhere, paralyzed by some drug as Grant—

Lou's hand covered hers. Squeezed. "Don't punish yourself. It might not even be true. There's a chance the sergeant got waylaid by a friend today and is just late gettin' back."

"Yeah. There's a chance." There was always a chance. Kate caught the shadow in Lou's eyes.

He didn't believe it either.

She tipped her head toward the BAU agent, still deeply

engaged in his notes and that quiet conversation at the opposite end of the table. "Who's Walker talking to?"

"Some kidney doc he went to college with. The woman does transplants. Ed says what happened to Abel occurs more than you'd think. His friend's a member of some kind of international network of like-minded physicians. She and her fellow docs monitor illegal transplants by cobblin' together stats on patients who show up at hospitals and clinics with new organs in place and no paper trail to show for it. While the docs don't swap medical info or forward names to folks like us, they do piece together enough to sketch out a decent picture of the black market. They share that with some bigwig at the UN. Anyway, Ed's tryin' to get the lowdown on Madrigal and VitaCell. Want some coffee while we wait?"

She might've passed on the muffins, but she was always up for caffeine.

Before she could accept, Walker concluded his call. The BAU agent dumped his phone on the table, then his pen. He sat there, staring at his notes as he rubbed his temples, disgust and horror tinging his features a washed-out gray as he attempted to process what he'd heard.

Kate was loath to interrupt the man. Lou, too.

She was about to leave to grab that suggested coffee, if only to give the agent some space, when he stood. Gathering up his pen and scrawl-filled legal pad, he walked along the table, dropping heavily into the chair Joe had vacated.

"Sheriff, Deputy, it's worse than we feared."

She didn't follow. Couldn't. "How can it be worse than murdering homeless vets, and selling off their organs?"

"Because I no longer think that's all Dr. Parish and his cohorts were, and possibly still are, selling. I think they're partitioning up entire bodies, arranging for the immediate sale of the more perishable organs, then preserving and—in many cases—

freezing and storing the remainder of the parts, until they can be sold off piece by piece to the highest bidder."

Lou looked as green as she felt. He shoved the plate of muffins as far away from them as he could, locking his arms over his girth as he sat back. "Explain."

"VitaCell Tissues, Incorporated, is an FDA-sanctioned tissue bank. They recover corneas, heart valves, skin, ligaments, bone and other tissues from human bodies. Much of this is done legally, of course, in surgical suites set up for this purpose and in funeral homes."

Lou stiffened. "Funeral homes?"

"Yes. Technicians come in and harvest the tissues on-site, up to thirty-six hours following death." The BAU agent tapped his notes. "Though there have been instances of unscrupulous techs harvesting from bodies that have been deceased longer. Depending on the condition of the corpse, of course."

Of course—*not*. At least not in her book.

Kate kneaded the base of her skull where the nerves had begun to throb. "I'm guessing there's money in it."

Walker nodded. "Quite a bit. And there is a genuine need for many of these parts. Skin sections, for example, are used to treat burn victims. In fact, skin is supposed to be earmarked for this specific need because it saves lives. But from what Nicole relayed to me, not nearly enough of the skin that's collected ends up there. The majority is reworked for cosmetic purposes. Nose jobs, lip plumping and the like. It can be used to smooth out other areas of the face and body, too. For example, reconstruction to minimize previous scarring. Bone is used too. It can be ground down and used as filler during dental procedures and other surgeries, including implants. Again, some of these procedures are life-saving and/or altering due to the nature of certain deformities, while others are intended simply to enhance a man's or a woman's perceived beauty."

Kate's fingers came up, instinctively tracing the cavern carved into her flesh along the mottled scar covering the right side of her face. A conversation she'd had with a well-meaning physician at Walter Reed flitted in. The doc had been an Army reservist in the midst of her annual training. In the civilian world, the woman headed up a plastic surgery practice and had tried to press her card on Kate.

She'd refused.

In retrospect, rather rudely. At the time, she'd felt judged. Maybe she had been, maybe she hadn't. Either way— Kate stared at the BAU agent as she dropped her hand into her lap. "Thanks, but no thanks. I'll live without the plumping."

Especially now that she'd worry where it came from.

"Sorry—" this from a still visibly queasy Lou, "—I'm stuck on the funeral home part. They slice bodies open right there? Parts they're gonna turn around and stick in someone else?"

"Yes. All a recovery technician needs is a sterile environment. According to Nicole, the tech brings along a portable harvesting kit that's set up at the site to create the necessary sterile environment. The parts are removed and placed inside sanitized coolers. If the body is slated for funerary viewing, it's then stitched up as best as can be, often with sawed off sections of PVC piping inserted to replace any missing bone to give the illusion of structural integrity. From there, the recovered tissue is usually wrapped, labeled and frozen to await transport to the processing facility."

"Jesus, Son of Mary—" Lou planted his fists on the edge of the conference table as he shot to his feet. "—Those damned paper bags; all those carefully hacked-up, vacuum-packed parts. That's why Grant strung 'em out like that along the road. They're supposed to be waitin' for transport. Abel wasn't lyin'. Grant did want out. And whether or not he planned on gettin' caught, he wanted us to know what was happenin'."

Walker nodded. "I concur."

Kate leaned forward as Lou regained his seat. "How much money are we talking about? Tens of thousands per body, or more?"

"Much more. Though the tissue recovery side of the business is billed as nonprofit, it's anything but, especially since even the usual donors and their families are unpaid. According to Nicole, however, the black and gray markets surrounding the tissue processing and the subsequent marketing pipeline are even uglier. Donation might be presented as a compassionate gift but, make no mistake, to VitaCell Tissues and companies like it, it's all about money." Walker retrieved his pen and tapped it along a column of figures. Each entry was nauseatingly large. "A recovery broker alone can make up to two hundred thousand dollars or more per body, depending on the age and condition of the corpse, along with the donor's corresponding medical history prior to death."

Donor. The word tumbled through Kate's empty stomach, making her doubly grateful she'd passed on those muffins.

Those missing vets weren't donors, they were *victims.*

"And when you multiply that figure with transplantable lungs, kidneys, livers, pancreases and hearts carefully selected from military veterans for their ability to become near-perfect tissue matches to someone who would otherwise not be able to receive said organ?" Walker shrugged. "The sky's the limit."

No wonder Kusić had that much cash tucked inside his closet. He probably couldn't spend it fast enough. Not unless he'd wanted to draw undue attention for a government-paid lab tech working in a VA hospital.

Kate suppressed a shudder. "What about the organs? Kusić, Dunne and Silva were missing theirs. You don't think Grant entered them into that pipeline do you? His own co-conspirators?"

But Grant had been murdering his fellow vets ever since Abel had received that stolen heart eighteen months ago. Since then, he'd been helping those Madrigal bastards sell off every extra inch of flesh they could lay their greedy paws on. Why not sell those organs too? Grant probably felt it was justice served.

Walker closed his legal pad and laid his pen on top. "It's possible. It would explain their absence from the bags. Though I fear we won't be able to obtain the answer until we've located Dr. Parish and the setting for all the murders. Those that involved the bags, and the missing vets."

Walker was correct. Worse, they still had no idea where any of it had taken place. At least now they knew they were searching for someplace sterile, or at the very least someplace that could be made sterile.

"The warrants." Kate turned to Lou. "Boss, we need to expand the ones for Madrigal and VitaCell Tissues to include every hard record and electronic data file they have, financial and otherwise. Yes, they'll be doctored. But there has to be a clue somewhere as to where they're running the surgical end of this scheme."

"Agreed. I've got another call to make to Little Rock in—" Lou glanced at his watch. "—ten minutes. The governor's been champin' to light a fire under someone. Let's let him."

Fire.

Son-of—

Kate swung back to Walker. "What about the remains? You said normal donors are prepped as best as can be if they're slated for funerary viewing. But what if they're not slated for burial at all? Those bodies are cremated, right?"

The second set of paper bags.

Grant had strung Jason Dunne's out along the road leading damned near to the entrance to that pet cemetery.

Lou must've read the look on her face, because he nodded. "I agree. If it ain't enough for a warrant, I'll punt that to the governor too and let his people figure out how to work it."

"Work what?"

It was Joe. She'd been so consumed by the possibility that they might have a real lead, she'd missed his return.

Walker shook his head as Joe sat down beside him. "I have no idea. They're speaking in Braxton code."

Kate flushed. "Sorry. The second crime scene—Jason Dunne's. It's just down the road from the county's only full-service pet cemetery...complete with a brand-new crematorium, put in maybe two, two-and-a-half years ago."

And it was large enough to handle horses.

Walker's nod was almost eager. "Yes, that would do. It would be an excellent spot to reduce the remainder of those vets' bodies—and any other evidence—to ash without anyone being the wiser."

Except for them.

If her suspicions were correct.

Lou stood. "I'm on it. Ed, you mind taggin' along? I'll put us on speaker, and you can run through the medical and financial details with the governor and his aide."

"Of course."

Kate turned to Joe as Lou and the BAU agent departed. Joe had brought his government-issued laptop back with him. "Did you find the sergeant?"

He set the computer on the table and fired it up. "I think so. I found a Sergeant Stephen Fremont Wright. He served in Special Forces from 2008 to 2016. He was in Afghanistan and Iraq, and he lost both his lower legs to a VBID."

It had to be him then.

Flush with the possibility of adding a photo to the APB Lou had sent out, Kate spun the laptop toward her. The guy on the screen had blond hair and green eyes, not black and brown. And his face was completely wrong.

"It's not him."

"You sure?" Joe tapped the write-up. "See the—"

"I can read his stats. It's just not him. There must be another Fremont in SF. One with Fremont, not Wright, bringing up the rear." The branch was small, but not microscopic. "Heck, Steve or Steven could be his middle name for all we know. And did you try changing the spelling to—" Her phone rang. "Just a sec." Kate retrieved her phone and glanced at the caller ID. "It's Detective Moradi."

She stood to stretch her legs as she accepted the connection. "Hey, Arash. Please tell me you got something from searching that mansion besides altitude sickness."

A warm chuckle filled the line. "I wish. My guys did finish the initial neighborhood canvass, though. You said you wanted an update as soon as possible."

She had. Did. "And?"

"We found a witness, but I don't think her statement will amount to much. One of Kessler's neighbors left for the grocery store around the time you and Joe were paused at the security gate. She says she saw a man jogging along the back of Kessler's yard before he disappeared into the trees."

That sounded like a lot to her. "Was he blond?"

"She didn't get a good look at his hair, or much of anything else. She thinks it was dark brown, maybe black—but that impression could've been due to the shadows of the trees. Either way, I doubt it's your doc. She only noticed the guy because of his stride. It took her moment to realize what she'd seen, and it knocks your doc out of the running, so to speak. The man she saw was wearing a sweatshirt and running shorts, and had—"

"—*prosthetic legs*. Both of them. From the knees down." Kate wasn't even sure why the words had popped into her brain, much less out of her mouth. But they had.

"How'd you guess?"

Sweet Jesus. Maybe she had been sure—in the deep, dark recesses of her gut where she'd been afraid to go from the moment she'd stared at that face she hadn't recognized on Joe's screen, but should've. Kate braced her spine against the conference room wall before the implications that were reverberating through her body sent her shuddering to the floor.

"Kate?"

"Sorry. Gut instinct. That, and the wrong face in the only possible military record that should match...but doesn't."

She caught Joe's equally shocked stare. On the drive back to Braxton, she'd shared the story that Fremont had relayed to her about his IED and the supposedly shitty spot on his spine where shrapnel had hit. Only now she knew that explanation to be an utter lie—along with the man's name.

But if the soldier on Joe's screen was Sergeant Stephen Fremont Wright, US Army Special Forces, who the hell had she shared eggs with?

"I take it you'd like a copy of the neighbor's statement."

Kate forced herself to focus on the former Army sergeant to whom she was actually speaking. "I would indeed. As for my gut instinct, I don't have a name to go with it yet. I'll let you know when I do."

"Understood. Check your email; the witness statement's on its way. I gotta go. A tech I need to speak to is about to leave. Talk to you later."

Kate stared at her phone as she lowered it, reconsidering everything they'd learned these past few days in light of this new, tectonic discovery. A discovery that had rocked their entire case to the core, and her along with it.

By the time she looked up, Joe, Lou and Agent Walker were

all staring at her. For the second time that evening, she'd been so rattled she hadn't heard the door open.

"Kato, you okay? You look like you've seen the ghost of your dad."

Why not? He was rumored to haunt the station, though usually around midnight, roughly the time when he'd died out on that road. Even if she had run into her father's spirit, she couldn't have been more surprised. "Boss, I just found out I had breakfast this morning with a man who doesn't exist."

Joe swung his laptop screen toward the newcomers. "Meet the real Steve Fremont—who, evidently, Kate has not."

Liz was wrong. She was an idiot. "A blind, self-centered idiot who can't see past her own goddamned scars."

Lou tore his confusion from the screen. "I beg your pardon?"

"I said, I'm an idiot. The first time I sat down with that man at Fort Leaves he actually waved it in my face. He told me flat out that people never bothered to look beneath the scars. He was right." She was one of them. Even with her past and her own mutilated face, she was as guilty as everyone else. "All I saw was the chair—just as he'd intended."

Lou still appeared bemused by her self-directed vitriol, along with the critical element to the vet's deception.

Walker, however, had nodded. "He's been injecting himself into the investigation."

"And brilliantly." She hadn't caught so much as a hint of the man's shadow on the proverbial wall of the cave. Hence, she hadn't been remotely close to seeing him for who he truly was.

The Garbage Man.

Kate dumped her phone on the conference table and slumped into the closest chair. "Damn, he's good."

First, the hospital elevator. Then those two "accidental" collisions with his wheelchair. Coffee in the cafeteria. And then he'd called and invited her to the Silver Bullet where he'd sat across that worn Formica table, carefully laying out the rest, crumb by crumb, luring her down the path he'd wanted her to walk without her realizing it. "An unscrupulous lab tech. Vials of stolen blood. Questions to homeless vets that when added to the rest came back to one answer: organ transplants. He's been following—and guiding—the investigation through me."

Giving her just enough information while garnering her trust so he could make certain she'd ferret out the remaining details he wanted her to discover.

Worse, he'd ruthlessly used her own fucked up psyche against her to keep her and her investigation off balance while he did it.

She stared at Walker. "I'm right, aren't I?"

"Yes. But in retrospect, none of us should be surprised, and all of us are guilty of not considering the possibility. This is not the first time a murderer has attempted to interject himself into an investigation."

Attempt, hell. He'd *succeeded.* "But why not just come forward? He clearly knew about the organ racket. And he knew they were getting them from vets. Given how he hacked up and displayed those bodies, he had to know about the tissue bank too. Why not tell someone? Me, some other cop—*any* cop. The man was respected at Fort Leaves and at Saint Clare's. Someone would've listened. Acted. He didn't have to murder them."

Lou scrubbed his hand through the silver sprouting along his jaw. "In his mind, maybe he did. Sure, this bastard's smart. He's proven that time and again these past few days. But maybe we're givin' him credit for too many brains. You got that Madrigal connection followin' a conversation with a reception-ist. Could be he couldn't quite get to those two or three ring-leaders he killed today without you. Maybe that's what he needed you for."

It was possible. But she didn't believe it. And from Walker's expression, neither did he.

Kate snatched her phone from the table and shoved it in her pocket. "I disagree. I think he's known about all of it for a long time. This whole week feels like the final moves of a long and meticulously executed chess match."

And for some reason, she was his favorite pawn.

Why else had he slipped into her house and gone through her trunk? Pinned that damned mothballed Silver Star to her pillow?

And more.

Kate hooked her fingers to the stainless-steel chain she'd shoved beneath her Braxton PD polo out on Abel's patio, and tugged Max's tags free. "He didn't need me to complete anything. I don't even think he's been forced to deviate from his plan. Not yet. He killed Ian Kusić, Jason Dunne and Andrea Silva right on schedule, and dumped their bodies exactly where and how he wanted to dump them. Then he took Grant. What he has planned for Grant, I'm not sure any of us want to know, but we will, and soon. As for the latest three, I think he intended on slitting the CEO's and Robert Stern's throats all along. The woman may have been an unexpected blip on his radar that he was forced to deal with—and he did. If so, she's the only one."

"But you can't be sure." This from Lou.

"About Stern and the CEO?"

He nodded.

"Yes, I can. He was on foot, boss. As skilled as he is, he never would've gotten even one grown man, let alone two—actively fighting him *or* drugged—out of that gated community without wheels. Wheels he'd have brought, if he felt he needed them. That BMW and Jaguar wouldn't have sufficed. Neither vehicle had tinted windows. The gate guard, along with anyone pulled up next to him at a traffic light, could've looked right in. Not to mention the guard would've recognized the cars."

"But why not plan to slice 'em up and display 'em like the first three? It just don't make sense."

"That, I don't know. But if he'd wanted to, he would've." Kate glanced at the BAU agent. "Any ideas?"

"Not yet. But I agree; he had a reason for the change."

Kate nodded. "This is still about revenge, just not Grant's. Somewhere along the way, this guy has a connection to one or more of Madrigal's victims. We ferret that out, and we'll understand him." She was certain of it. The man she'd seen interacting with that disabled vet's wife and son in the Fort Leaves cafeteria loved his brothers-in-arms, cherished them even. Despite the six murders he'd committed, she didn't doubt that for a second.

But a man, especially a vet, didn't do everything this one had done without a very good, very personal reason.

She sat up straight. "That's it—personal."

Family. Friends. Co-workers. Without the killer's real name, she didn't have a Vietnam vet's chance at a ticker-tape homecoming of locating any of their faux Fremont's friends or relatives. But with a bit of judicious digging with an Army CID-honed spade, they would be able to find *someone's*.

"You've got that look, Holland."

She tapped the laptop Joe had closed. "Yeah, well, you get to do the finger and phone work. I need you to fire that thing back up and print out Sergeant Fremont Wright's record."

"But you said it's not him."

"True. But I think our guy *knew* him. The man I had breakfast with is the real deal." That scripted *De Oppresso Liber* tattoo wasn't just for show. "He was Special Forces. And who works with and hangs out with SF, but—"

Joe nodded. Grinned. "—other SF."

His gaze dropped to the tags dangling from her neck. Kate

fisted them as deftly as she could to prevent him from reading the name. She was hanging by a thread as it was. She didn't need a man with Joe Cordoba's insight tugging on it. With the day she'd had, she was certain to unravel.

To her relief, Joe hefted his laptop and stood. "I'll start my labors at the desk Carole set me up at. It's got a supply of hot coffee an arm's stretch away."

Lou tipped his head toward the tags still secured within her grip as Joe left, and Agent Walker gathered his tablet and pen to return to his own laptop at the other end of the table. "I've never seen you wear those before."

Crap. "They're not mine."

His brow shot up.

"It's a long story. Another day, okay?" Kate tucked the tags home before he could snag them. Knowing Lou, she wouldn't put it past him. And, frankly, she just couldn't deal with the fallout right now.

It must've shown.

Lou's sigh filled the conference room. "It's been a shitty day, Kato, for this whole blessed town—but especially you. It's dinner time. Go home. Spend an hour or two with Ruger. Feed yourself and the mutt. Let him run around a bit, too. He needs it...and so do you. Just do me a favor and be damned careful, okay? I wish you'd let me send someone with you, but since you won't, make sure Ruger stays on the alert—keep that Glock of yours at the ready."

She thought about arguing about the reprieve, but didn't. Lou was right. About Ruger, and her. Besides, those muffins were starting to look good, and she couldn't afford the resulting sugar crash that would hit the moment she caught her second wind.

As for his concerns regarding her safety, they were valid. But whoever she'd dined with that morning had blown his one chance of getting close enough to her to take her down. She had no intention of providing another.

That said, in light of recent developments, Lou had capitulated to her stance on bodyguards far too easily. Which only meant one thing. The moment she left the room, he'd be phoning Seth or one of the other boys and asking her fellow deputy to step up—and extend—the timing of his "coincidental" drive-by of her place. Which, of course, would necessitate her offer of a complimentary cup of coffee inside the house.

Fine with her. And definitely not worth arguing about.

Not if it gave Lou peace of mind.

She nodded as she stood to retrieve her jacket from one of the spare chairs. "Okay. I'll be back in an hour to crack the whip over Joe."

"Take the full two, or you're fired. I hate to be the bearer of obvious news, but you look like you could use five times that. Now get out of here, Deputy."

She saluted the man and left.

Twilight had set in by the time Kate punched the button to lower her garage door. She thanked Lou in absentia for the reprieve as she crawled out of her Durango. Not only did she need this break, so did Ruger.

She could tell from the tone of his barks that he'd had his fill of the day, too.

Kate stepped inside the kitchen, not bothering to remove her jacket, much less close the door as she held out her arms for their nightly hug. Ruger's half was as enthusiastic as ever, but disappointingly brief. He thunked down from her arms far too quickly and spun around, surprising her further as he bypassed the fridge and its tub of cheddar to lope across the den. He came to a nail-digging halt smack in the middle of the mud rug.

There, he waited, impatient for her to follow.

When she didn't move fast enough, he punctuated her boot falls with a series of yips and barks.

"You trying to tell me a big guy like you can't hold his water?"

A string of louder barks underscored her arrival at the slider.

"Okay, okay, I was kidding. I guess I wouldn't want to hold it all day either." She unlocked the glass door and slid it wide. "There. Happy? Go whiz to your heart's content."

Lou's warning in mind, she followed the dog outside. Stopping at the edge of the deck, she closed her eyes and pulled the twilight air deep into her lungs. Even with the year's crop of deciduous leaves beginning to decay into the ground, it just smelled fresher out here than in town.

Cleaner.

She opened her eyes as Ruger let out another round of barks. He was sitting in the middle of the clearing and looking at her expectantly. Obviously, he wanted her to follow.

But why?

The frosted breeze drifting across the clearing intensified the chill already rippling down her spine.

Yet another bark filled the quasi night.

"Okay. I'm coming." She checked her pocket for her phone, relieved she hadn't instinctively dumped it on the counter on her way through the kitchen as she usually did. Her coincidental bodyguard hadn't shown up yet, but her Glock was still holstered snugly beneath her left arm, her backup piece attached to her right ankle.

She doubted she'd need either, but with Grant missing and her unknown breakfast companion still on the loose, she wasn't taking chances.

Besides, though Ruger believed she needed to see something, he wasn't on alert.

Another, sharper bark forced her to pick up her pace. As she reached his side, Ruger turned to lope to the head of the path she'd helped her dad clear of stragglers and underbrush all those years ago. Ruger punctuated this latest pause with his loudest bark yet.

"I said, 'I'm coming', and I am."

Along with her Glock.

Kate slid the 9mm from her holster as she followed Ruger into the thicket, straining for any unusual sounds as she made her way along the darkened path. She couldn't make out any. From his stance, neither could Ruger. The latter reassured her, until she followed Ruger out of the trees, smack into a line of crisp, yard-waste-sized brown paper bags.

There were fifteen in all, strung out along the opposite edge of the pea-gravel drive with the same eerie precision she'd noted on three other backroads around town.

But this road was hers.

There could be only one reason why. One possible victim.

Kate had no idea why she kept walking, but she did. She just kept staring, moving, step by step, buffered by the fog swirling into her brain, until she reached that first sack. It might've been the fog—or perhaps the denial that seemed to hammer in harder with every beat of her heart—that allowed her to kneel down and carefully pop the staples. Or perhaps this had all just become some sort of morbid habit.

Either way, she reached inside and slowly removed the shrink-wrapped hand, and laid it on the sack.

The denial continued to pound through the second sack and the second unbagging, only to falter at the staples of the third, disintegrating altogether as she slowly withdrew the forearm within. One look at the distinctive, snake-seducing sword impaling that blood-red heart, and she could no longer deny the truth.

And, yet, she pushed on.

The cop in her fought hard as she popped each subsequent

row of staples. She knew she was destroying evidence. But she couldn't seem to stop.

And her wrist had begun to itch.

Badly.

If she didn't make that call now, she never would.

It was the certainty that gave her the strength to pause in front of that final bag. To retrieve her phone and punch the top entry in her speed dial list.

"Lou, I'm at the cabin. You can cancel that APB for Grant. He's here...in fifteen pieces."

15

THEY FOUND her at her house. Out on the back deck, sitting at the table in her father's chair. She had no idea how she'd gotten there. The fog had closed in completely, obscuring the entire world. Numbing her. All she knew for certain was that Ruger was at her side, and that she'd shed her Braxton PD jacket.

It was in her lap, wrapped up around something large, round and solid. Liz was trying to take it away from her.

She clutched it closer.

"Katie, please. You have to let it go. You're scaring me. And you're scaring Lou."

"Lou?" She tried to focus on the features fading in and out of the tunneled shadows. But just as she caught sight of a man's worried smile, it was gone.

"I'm here, kiddo. Right beside you. I'd be even closer, but Ruger won't budge enough to give me room."

Ruger.

She looked down. She could definitely make out those warm brown eyes and soft muzzle, even part of the Shepherd's neck. She blinked and caught a bit more.

She blinked again and lost it. Lost him.

Someone tugged at her hands. "You need to give it to me, hon. Please. You have to let it go."

No. She might not know what was wrapped up in her jacket, nor was she sure she wanted to know. But she was absolutely certain she shouldn't let it go. Ever.

I will never leave a fallen comrade.

But she had, hadn't she? Part of him anyway.

And others.

"You sure you can't give her somethin'?" Lou again. But his voice sounded uneven, distant. As if he was moving away from her.

Or was she the one moving?

"No, Sheriff. She doesn't need drugs. She needs time. Patience. She has to process it. Accept it." *Liz.* At least, she was pretty sure that sounded like Liz. Except her friend's soft, clear voice had turned husky and ragged, as though the woman was upset about something and fighting tears. Desperately.

But why?

Drugs. Lou wanted Liz to medicate someone.

Her.

The certainty penetrated the fog still clinging to Kate's brain. The mist thinned a bit as she shook her head. "I don't need pills. Or a shot. I'm fine."

But she wasn't. Somehow, she knew that. This was the same numbing cloud she'd had to push through when she'd woken up in that room at the combat support hospital in Afghanistan. *Fugue.* That's what the doctors had called it.

For some reason, it had happened again. Here, now. Four years later. In the States.

While she was working a case.

Fuck.

Pull it together, soldier. Before Liz was forced to medicate her. Or, worse, lock her in one of those quiet rooms.

The tunnel widened as she fought the fog. Shadows coalesced into discernible swaths of fur and frowns, and then into faces. Ruger. Liz. Lou.

All friends. All family.

What she had left of it.

Kate shook her head as she saw the sheriff whisper something in Liz's ear. "I'm okay now, guys. Just...a little rattled. How —" She licked her lips, stunned to find them parched, even cracked in a few places. "How did I get here? What happened?"

But she knew. Grant. She could still see that tattoo on his arm when her eyes were closed...and when they weren't.

"He's dead."

Liz nodded, the tears Kate had heard now visible in that bright blue stare. "Yes, hon. Grant's dead. You found his body out by your cabin. You called Lou. He called me. That's why we're here. That's why you need to give us your jacket."

Her jacket? Why were they back to that?

Kate stared at the bundle in her lap. The navy blue nylon was wrapped around something heavy. The shape was odd. Round, yet not quite. Suddenly, she knew the reason for that too. *Grant.*

Liz wanted her to let him go. Kate managed a nod. "I need to see it first. Him." She needed to say goodbye.

"I don't think—"

"*Please.*" She heard the desperation in her voice and didn't care. She had to find the strength to do this.

To end it.

Liz's nod was no less shaky than hers had been. It was sincere, though. Supportive. "Okay."

Kate pulled in her breath as she gathered her courage. She could feel Ruger pressing into her knees, as if he was loaning her his strength as she slipped her fingers into the edges of her jacket and slowly unwrapped it.

Despite the plastic shrink-wrapped to that hair and face, she could make out those striking features.

It was Grant...until her vision wavered. And then it wasn't.

"Oh, Max." Hot tears trickled down. They multiplied so quickly, they flooded her eyes until she couldn't see anything anymore. It no longer mattered.

Because she remembered.

She was back in that mud-brick hell, bending down to check for a pulse at the neck of the first of the two soldiers who'd survived that ambush with her and Max. The soldier was dead. So was the second. Both men had been shot through their temples with a large caliber weapon similar to the one in her left hand.

Kate tightened her grip on the AK-47 she'd culled from her would-be second-round rapist and crept out of the hovel where she'd located the bodies of her fellow soldiers.

Within minutes, she'd cleared three more buildings in the compound. Each had been empty.

Max. Where the hell was he?

Another two buildings, and still no sign of him—or the bastards who'd ambushed them.

All too quickly, she had one building left. The only building she'd yet to clear. The largest one in the compound. Max had to be inside, along with the rest of those zealous assholes. Confirmation came in the chorused shouts of "*Allahu akbar! Allahu akbar! Allahu akbar!*"

Another voice cut in behind the chorus as she reached the wooden door. A man's. He was speaking Arabic so quickly, she couldn't make out what he was saying. Just the solid slaps of human flesh smacking against human flesh as they punctuated his shouts. The slaps turned to thumps as someone switched to fists.

The crack of bone followed.

This was it, then. It was now or never.

Since her first deployment, she'd often wondered when and how she'd die. Now she knew. All things considered, it was a decent way to go. She'd die at Max's side while taking as many of those bastards with them as she could.

Kate flipped the AK-47's switch to full auto, pain searing in as she braced the rifle's butt against the pocket of her shoulder and shattered collarbone. Clenching her teeth against the agony, she breached the door.

What she found on the other side was *not* what she'd expected.

Time simultaneously pushed and pulled at her senses, twisting and folding in on itself as it dragged her into a bizarre, almost slow-motion movie that split and sputtered in spots. She caught sight of a bright green and white Islamic flag tacked up against the far wall of the room, a camera held aloft by one of the eight armed and bearded bastards to her left. The ninth stood four yards away, directly in front of her own AK-47 and to the right of a naked, kneeling Max—and this one was brandishing a sword.

Her best friend's resigned mutter drifted across the sweat and blood-laden air as that gleaming blade swung up, crested...and began to fall. "At least I can have that Arlington burial."

And then the soft, chilling click to her left of another AK-47 switching to full auto—and another.

She instinctively turned and fired, sweeping the barrel of her stolen rifle from left to right, picking off the first gunman, then the others in rapid succession, until she'd reached the final bastard still holding that now-glistening sword.

A split second later, he too was dead.

But it didn't matter. Max's head had already hit the woven mat with a sickening thunk that reverberated straight down into her soul...and then his body was falling too.

She stared at that surreal scarlet line of severed muscle and skin at the base of her best friend's head, transfixed—a moment later, almost as an unforgivable afterthought, it started to bleed.

She knew it was over. She had to go. Now. Find friendly territory. But she couldn't. She couldn't leave a fellow soldier behind.

She couldn't leave *Max*.

The next thing she knew, she was dragging off the top of the jihad jammies she'd stolen and wrapping the grimy white cloth around Max's head. She started to turn, only to halt as she spotted the arm of that goddamned murderous bastard flung outward on the dirt, still gripping the hilt of that stained sword. On the bastard's wrist: Max's dive watch. The watch her friend had treasured so much.

She leaned down and wrenched it off, carefully securing it to her own wrist.

Then she picked up her bloodied shirt, cradled the precious cargo within and began to walk.

"You *sure* she don't need somethin'?" Lou again.

She must've really freaked Lou out for him to want her sedated.

Then again, discovering that your most experienced deputy had destroyed a crime scene and made off with a crucial piece of evidence—namely, the victim's head—and was now huddled up on her deck with it, would probably have freaked anyone out.

"I don't need to be drugged. It appears I forgot which continent I was on for a while, but I've got it all sorted now. Promise. Even better, I can report that I've finally found my missing marbles. I just need a few minutes to organize them all and slot them back into place."

From the tension thinning Lou's lips, he had no idea what she was referring to—but Liz did.

Kate was actually relieved.

She mustered a half smile for the man who'd become her

honorary uncle through the years. "In other words, boss, I'm okay. I can let Grant go now." As for Max, now that she'd finally remembered his death—and her part in it—she suspected she'd never be able to let him go.

She tucked the edges of her jacket over Grant's head and gently handed the bundle to Lou. "Take care of him for me. Please."

"I will."

The moment the bundle left her arms, Ruger moved in, sniffing and nuzzling her face and neck, as if verifying for himself that she was truly okay. She wrapped her arms around the Shepherd's firm, steady warmth, the contact soothing them both as Lou came to his feet. "I'm sorry I destroyed the crime scene."

"It don't make no nevermind. Truth be told, Joe and Tonga said you did a damned decent job of unbaggin' it all...considerin'."

She was glad when Lou's phone rang. It saved her the humiliation of acknowledging the stark pity in his eyes. It cut deeper than his anger or disappointment ever could.

"Go on, boss. I know you need to get back to the cabin." There was work to be done. Though she was unquestionably off this detail—for legal and emotional reasons—she wanted the job done by someone who cared enough about Grant to keep in mind the man he'd been, along with the one he'd somehow become. "Just promise me you'll let me know if you guys find anything."

"Done." The sheriff nodded to Liz. "I'll check in soon."

Kate avoided tracking Lou's journey across her darkened clearing. She might've come to tenuous terms with finding Grant's body carved up and laid out beside her cabin, but that didn't mean it was easy to watch someone cart away his remains.

When she finally looked up, she found Liz watching her. Intently.

Figured. "I guess you've been saddled with babysitting the loon."

"Nah." Her friend snapped a cheeky grin. "I volunteered. It's called occupational recreation." Liz knelt in front of Ruger. Finally assured that his mistress was okay, he'd turned in Kate's arms and was now shamelessly head-butting her old friend in an attempt to garner Liz's attention. "Who's this handsome devil?"

Kate ruffled the Shepherd's ears as she stood. "This is Ruger. The one true guy in my life."

"Ruger, huh? Well, handsome—" Liz joined Kate in standing. "—what say we find you some dinner while your mom takes a nice long, hot shower? You are hungry, aren't you?"

Kate smiled as the self-designated Holland household schmoozer let out an eager *woof*. "You've hit on the path to his heart. Try a slice of the cheddar in the fridge. Ruger's pretty picky about who he'll take it from, but it's your best shot."

Liz opened the door and entered the house where she too had spent much of her high school years.

Instead of following, Ruger bounded off in the opposite direction. His reason became clear as he swiftly did his duty before galloping back up on the deck and into the house. Kate had suspected he hadn't left her side during her latest fugue. His copious deposit confirmed it.

Kate glanced in the kitchen as she closed the door to the deck, bemused to find Ruger swallowing a square of cheddar. "Wow. I don't even think Lou won him over that quickly."

Liz tucked a curl behind her ear as she laughed. "It's a shrink trick. Sorry, but I'm bound by a moonless, midnight blood oath." She winked. "I could lose my license if I tell. Now go, take a long, hot shower, Katie Marie. This handsome guy and I have some serious belly-scratching to enjoy."

There was no point in arguing. Not when the two hadn't even waited for her to leave before they got down to business right there on the kitchen tiles. She left Liz and her traitorous, belly-up, tongue-lolling mutt to it and headed for the bathroom. Once inside and stripped of clothes she never wanted to see, let alone wear again, she crawled into the shower, intent on following Liz's instructions to the T.

Namely, making it long and hot.

Fortunately, both elements served to disguise the crying jag she wallowed in as she sank down into the middle of the tub. There she sat, clutching her bent knees beneath the steaming water, grateful the flood was loud enough to drown out her sobs. She cried for Max, she cried for Grant, and she might've even cried for herself somewhere in there while she was at it.

When she was finally ready to face the world again, she donned a pair of worn gray sweats, Max's dive watch and tags, and returned to the kitchen. Liz was lifting a covered sauce pot off the stove as she entered. Ruger must've indulged in one-too-many belly rubs, because he was passed out alongside the table. Or perhaps her rotten night had gotten to him, too.

"Feel better?"

"Yes. Thank you. I needed that."

"Good." Her friend pointed to her childhood place at the table. It, and Liz's old spot, were laid out for dinner. "Now, sit. Eat. Doctor's orders. And don't try to argue. I am not above using those drugs your boss wanted me to shoot into you to force your compliance."

Drugs. One simple word, and the memories pounded back; every moment of her captivity, from when she'd woken in that hovel until she'd stumbled across the patrol which had taken her to the combat support hospital. From then, until she'd come to three days later in that "quiet room", was still pretty hazy. But that hazy stretch was due to the sedatives they'd slipped into her IV. Her body had never dealt well with those, or pain pills.

Except for the part where she'd been knocked unconscious beside that Humvee or when she'd been sedated by the doctors, it had all come back. And it was all so clear, so crisp.

Kate shook her head as she sat at the table, baffled. "How could I have forgotten?"

"Max?"

She nodded as Liz set the boxed mac-n-cheese she'd prepared on a hot pad and removed the lid to serve up two portions. "You didn't forget. You suppressed. Huge difference."

"You knew, didn't you? From the moment we met up again at Fort Leaves."

"Oh, honey, you can't wrap up a severed head with your shirt, bring it into a combat support hospital in the middle of Afghanistan and deposit it on the counter in front of a dozen doctors and nurses as if you expect them to fix it and *not* expect the story to make the rounds. You, Katie Marie Holland, are a legend—whether you want to be, or not."

"I don't understand. Why didn't anyone tell me?"

Liz swallowed a forkful of pasta, and shrugged. "You weren't ready. Not mentally, and not emotionally. Until you were, the knowledge would've done your psyche a lot more harm than good. Since you were out of the Army and away from anyone who might've mentioned it prematurely, it wasn't a critical issue. That said, I had a feeling this case was going to bring it all up and out into the open, and I still wasn't sure you were ready. All I could do was cross my fingers, and be here for you when it did. Let's just say I'm glad Lou found my card on your desk and called me."

Kate shook her head. "I barely remember phoning him. And I certainly don't remember coming back here, but I must have."

"You did. Lou told me he was headed back to the cabin where you'd said you were when you called. But I figured you'd instinctively head home for maximum emotional safety, so I came here. You walked out of the trees a couple minutes later." Her dimple dipped in. "I'm good, aren't I? Remember that when you're handing out referrals."

How could she not?

Ruger's ears perked up. Kate paused in the middle of forking a bite of mac-n-cheese into her mouth. When the dog sat up and headed for the living room, she returned the fork to her plate without indulging and stood to follow.

"What's wrong?"

"We have company." Ruger's hackles were still smooth, his gait easy. "Keep eating. I'll be back in a minute."

She reached the front door and opened it to find Joe's knock still trapped in his poised knuckles.

He scowled at her. "Don't you look before you open the damned door?"

"I cherish you, too, Cordoba." She nodded to the Shepherd seated a quarter of an inch from her side as she swung the door wide. "You can relax. I'm blessed with vicarious bionic hearing." She waved Joe into the living room. "What's up?"

Though she could tell from his haggard face and the weary set of his shoulders, there was nothing. Nothing crime scene-wise.

"I just wanted to stop in and touch base. Ed and I will be accompanying your ME to the lab with the...evidence."

Grant.

His name hung between them, unspoken.

Joe cleared his throat. "Anyway, there was nothing there. The bastard left this last scene cleaner than he left the first three. I figured you'd be beating yourself up for the lapse in procedure, so I wanted to let you know."

"I appreciate the update." The self-excoriation, she deserved. As for the timing, "That was pretty quick."

"Not really. You were...out of it for a while there on your deck. The sheriff said you said something about remembering?"

Max.

She glanced at his watch instinctively, startled by the eleven o'clock hour. No wonder it'd been so dark when she'd come out of that fog. "Yeah, the memories are still jangling around inside my head—" and her heart, "—but they're there. I think. If any of the pieces are missing, I'm sure they'll snap into place with the rest soon enough. At least, I hope so."

"Just give it time. God knows you deserve it. I—" He broke off and stood there, awkwardly staring at her, then tried again. "What I wanted to say was—is—I'm sorry. You'll never know how badly I wanted to tell you."

"I know. Liz explained the prevailing medical wisdom of it all. Which, I suppose, also explains my shrink's insistence at Walter Reed that I find a doc out here. I guess he figured I'd pop the cork eventually, and was afraid I wouldn't know how to shove it back in on my own before everything else fizzed out."

Despite her attempt to lighten the mood, the silence returned, pulsing with the rest. His guilt. Hers.

This time, she broke it. "Tell you what. I'll stop beating myself up over tearing apart that crime scene tonight, if you stop kicking yourself for following some shrink's orders four years ago."

"Then...we're okay?"

"Always, Cordoba. Always."

Relief washed his features, smoothing the worst of the haggard lines. His arms came up to meet her spontaneous hug halfway, only to pause, then drop as his phone rang. He glanced at his caller ID. "I need to take this. I should be getting back anyway. Ed and the ME are waiting."

Kate nodded as she reached around Joe to open the door, closing it as he stepped off the porch, his phone already sealed to his ear. She and Ruger joined a contemplative Liz still seated in her traditional spot at the kitchen table.

"You okay?

Oddly, "Yeah."

"Then why are you frowning?"

Because she'd realized she'd forgotten to ask if Joe had made progress on his search of the real Fremont.

Plus, "It's this case." Liz was bound to find out that yet another man she admired wasn't who and what he'd appeared to be, and frankly she wasn't looking forward to the telling.

Liz took a sip from the soda she'd filched from the fridge. "He's right, you know."

Who? "Joe?"

"Well, Joe is right about you needing to let that disturbed crime scene go. But, no, I was referring to the advice you received from your therapist at Walter Reed." For a redhead, her flush was impressively faint. "I didn't mean to eavesdrop, but it's a small house."

"I know. And it's okay." Though that comment about her ex-therapist's claptrap was not.

"Well, since I did eavesdrop—and since I'm not only qualified to offer advice, but also invested in you enough to push it—I'm going to repeat his. You've had a lot of really traumatic stuff surface tonight. You need to find someone you can work through it with."

"Right." Because her first go round on the proverbial couch had done so much for her. Panic attacks. Night terrors. Sleepwalking. That infuriating itch on her left wrist that just *would not quit*. All of it had started after those quacks at Walter Reed had begun digging around in her head. "Liz—"

"I'm serious. You need a therapist. I'm a childhood friend. I can only do so much. Medically and ethically, my hands are tied. That said, I will be here for you—*always*—when, where and how much you want. But you need to talk to someone apart from me. Someone who can be impartial. A therapist who is truly committed to helping you work through this. I can recommend—"

"Thanks, but I've had my share of—"

"No!"

Ruger tensed as her friend's palm smacked the table. He snapped up to the pads of his paws, shifting his entire body until it was planted firmly between the two of them, his muzzle pointed toward Liz—and she was no longer his new friend.

Kate ran her hand down Ruger's back to let him know it was okay. She was not in danger. He could relax.

But he didn't. Neither did she.

She kept her focus beyond Liz's head. It was the only way to deal with the woman when she got herself into this particular mood. To her shock, Liz grabbed her chin and forced her to meet that molten stare.

"Sorry, but you don't get to shove your head in the sand on this. Not with me. So listen up. What happened to your friend and the rest of those soldiers when you were taken prisoner is *not* your fault. You need to come to terms with that. Accept it."

Kate wrenched her chin away and sprang up from the table. She spun around from Liz and Ruger, then stopped to whirl right back. Liz wanted her to pull her head out of the ground? Fine.

It was time for her old childhood chum to get a good look at just how ugly her scabs and scars really were. "And you know all this because of some hallowed legend? You're so sure I did everything right? The big-bad, female Rambo, wielding the enemy's AK-47 as she managed to stumble her way out of the cell containing the body of the kid whose throat she'd just slit.

You're certain it's not my fault that my best friend died that day? I've got news for you, Dr. Vogel: it *was* my fault. It *is*. Max took a bullet for me during that ambush. But when the chips were down later, I chose to save my own goddamned selfish ass. What's more, I didn't even *try* to save his."

"Really? What do you call going into a building to confront nine terrorists, knowing every single one of them is almost certainly armed to the teeth and ready, willing and eager to kill you? That's nine-to-one odds, Kate. I may be a civilian, but that sounds a lot like trying to me."

"Well, I failed on the follow through. Spectacularly. When that sword came up and I heard those rifle clicks off my left, I chose to turn and unload my magazine there. I should've started with that fucker with the sword."

Liz nodded curtly. "And you'd be dead. And a breath, perhaps two later, so would Max. Shooting that man with the sword wouldn't have changed anything, and you know it. Max would simply have been shot instead. And so would you. You can argue with me all you want, but you know it's true. There was nothing—*nothing*—you could've done to save him. To save any of them. All you could do was save yourself. And, honey, that is *not* a bad thing. Not ever. It is okay to survive. Max would've wanted your survival, just as you wanted his. Right?"

Liz paused, clearly expecting an answer.

Unfortunately, Kate didn't have one to give. Not one that made sense. To Liz, or herself.

Exhaustion gripped her so suddenly and so completely, she couldn't even take those four steps back to the table. She leaned against the counter delineating the kitchen and slid down to the floor instead. There she sat, too tired to reach out to soothe a still-vigilant Ruger as he came over to plant himself beside her.

Liz stood and scooted around Ruger to join them.

Great. She should've tried harder to make it to the table,

because now she was trapped on the hardwood planks between them. Neither appeared inclined to let her budge.

Worse, Liz linked hands with her and refused to let go. "You know I'm right. Especially if those rifle clicks you described mean that those terrorists were getting ready to 'unload' on you."

The tears returned. They were as plentiful as they'd been in that shower, and just as scalding.

Ruger pushed his muzzle into her lap. She clung to him with her left hand as Liz continued to squeeze her right. They sat like that until she finally scrounged up the courage to turn her head and look her friend in the eye.

Those blue eyes she'd missed so much over the years were brimming with tears, too. For some reason, Liz's stung worse than her own.

"I don't even know why I'm yelling at you."

Liz swiped at her own cheeks as she managed the first smile between them. "Because you know I'll love you anyway."

Kate nodded. "Probably."

"Definitely." Her friend's smile deepened. "I told you—I'm good. But in the interest of full disclosure, I should confess I know someone who's better. I believe you've already met him. I know you've been to his office."

The VA shrink, Dr. Manning.

No way. She'd rather tiptoe down an Iraqi road riddled with IEDs every morning of the week than spend an hour trapped in the man's office, absorbing the pity in that penetrating stare.

"I told you, I'm—"

"—fine." Liz shook her head as she sighed. "You're just like him."

"The shrink?" She was actually offended.

Liz laughed. "No. But you've definitely met this guy. In fact, you collided with his wheelchair."

"Sergeant Fremont?"

"Right."

Except her friend was wrong. At least about that name.

Kate tugged her hand from Liz's, and stood. Instinct had her pushing forward instead of backward to fill Liz in on the latest—figuratively, at least. Though she did reach down to help her friend to her feet. "Exactly how are we alike?"

"Well, for one thing, he's very good at appearing to hold it together. But deep down, the man is hurting. He uses his innate confidence to mask the worst of what happened to him over there, especially—" She broke off, shook her head.

"Especially what?"

"I'm not sure. He wouldn't say. Just that the Army had betrayed him. When I asked him how, he muttered something about camouflaged battles and true heroes, and making things worse. None of it made sense. I prodded further, but he just repeated that the Army had betrayed him. I was stunned. He's been nothing but gung-ho and supportive of his fellow vets. When I told him so, he gave me the strangest look and said it wasn't the same thing. I don't understand how."

Kate did. Any soldier would.

Male, female; black, white, brown—hell, even purple—it all faded before the rifle sight of the enemy. In the heat of battle, your comrades-in-arms trumped everything, including Army and country. At times, even God.

But try and explain that to a civilian.

"Anyway, he might not look like it on the outside, but Sergeant Fremont is pretty messed up. And, like you, he keeps insisting that he's dealing with it all just fine."

"I thought you didn't see the man. Professionally, that is."

"I don't. I ran into him one night while he was waiting for the bus. He must've had an especially rotten day, because I'd stopped before, but that was the first time he accepted a lift to the shelter. We chatted during the drive."

She grabbed her friend's arm. "What else did Fremont say? I'll explain in a minute, but I need you to repeat every word that came out of that man's mouth. Don't leave anything out, including your impressions."

"Kate, you're scaring me."

"I don't mean to." Ruger must've picked up on her vibes too, because he'd decided to run his late-night check on the house an hour early.

Okay, according to her mom's chirping cuckoo, not early.

"Just tell me."

"There really isn't much else. I might be a shrink, but I'm not his shrink. I didn't take notes. All he said was that his friend was cheated out of a soldier's death. But he wouldn't say what that meant, much less who, or how."

Tanner Holmes.

What were the odds?

Actually, they were fairly decent—and increasing with each new connection. Namely, the revealing comments their faux Sergeant Fremont had made to Liz.

According to Ian Kusić's girlfriend, the lab tech claimed he'd gotten hooked on oxycodone following the search for Staff Sergeant Holmes. What if that was only partially true? What if Kusić had gotten hooked not because he'd been on that search and rescue detail, but because the tech had been instrumental in selecting Tanner Holmes for his unwitting donation and death?

She'd bet that damned Silver Star that Holmes had been Kusić's first. Kusić had swallowed those pills because of the guilt.

As for Holmes, he'd been branded a deserter. A vile and permanent stain that ranked right up there with traitor in most soldiers' eyes. And a deserter—falsely accused or not—would definitely be cheated out of a soldier's death. No Purple Heart. No flag at the funeral. No toasts from his former comrades in arms. Just the nagging, bitter shame of his memory.

And if it was all a lie, the burning need to correct it.

Kate vaulted to her feet and double-timed across her kitchen.

"Where are you going?"

"I need my laptop. I have to google something." She reached the desk in the den and fired up her computer.

"Google what?" Liz followed her and stood beside her chair. Ruger joined them.

"Not what—*who*. Staff Sergeant Tanner Holmes, US Army." Kate clicked open her laptop's browser, typed the man's name into the search field at the top, and hit *enter*.

Links filled the screen.

She scrolled down to an *LA Chronicle* "On War" article and brought it up. The article was five years old and had been written shortly after Holmes' body had been found hanging in the window of that bombed-out Iraqi building. She skimmed past the description of the man's entrails lying in a scorched nest at his feet.

There, the second-to-last paragraph—it contained a quote by another soldier, a fellow staff sergeant by the name of Thomas Burke. Though stateside at the time of Holmes' death, Staff Sergeant Burke insisted the Army was wrong. Yes, Holmes had met and fallen for a local Iraqi woman; and, yes, the two had put in a request for a visa so they could marry and she could move to the States; and, yes, that visa had been denied due to ties the woman's older brother was rumored to have had with a particularly nasty terrorist—but Tanner Holmes was *not* a deserter. Burke would prove it.

Kate opened a fresh search window. This time, she typed Burke's full name and rank into the waiting blank. Instinct had her adding "Special Forces" at the end.

Liz leaned close to tap the screen. "Who's that?"

Kate held her tongue and mentally crossed her fingers as she hit the return key. Another list of links slotted in. Kate ignored them and selected the "images" tab at the top.

She felt Liz stiffen as a succession of thumbnail photos began to appear. Kate zeroed her cursor in on the first close-up and tapped the trackpad. The face of the man she'd met and breakfasted with as Sergeant Fremont twelve hours earlier filled the screen. "That, Dr. Vogel, is the *real* Garbage Man."

Thomas Burke.

16

LIZ PUSHED TREMBLING fingers through her curls. "I don't... I don't understand. That's a picture of Sergeant Fremont—right?"

Kate sighed as her friend absorbed the fallout from this latest mortar to her crumbling world. She was reluctant to be the one to lob in another round. Unfortunately, "No. I realized he was using an assumed identity earlier this evening at the station when Joe—Agent Cordoba—thought he'd located a photo of Fremont. We were looking for one because I'd received a call from the shelter. The man we knew as Sergeant Fremont had disappeared. I was terrified he was Grant's latest victim, until I received another call from a Mazelle detective I met this afternoon. The Mazelle detective had located a witness who saw someone running from yet another murder scene shortly before Agent Cordoba and I stumbled upon it during the course of our own Garbage Man investigation. But the suspect couldn't have been Grant—because he was wearing prosthetic legs."

Liz's already fair complexion blanched to stark white. "But Fremont—" Her eyes brimmed with fresh tears as she glanced at the photo on the screen. "—*Burke*, can't use prosthetics."

"I think he can. Nor do Burke's skills end there."

Everything she'd noted these past few days fit. Using the trust Burke had built up at Fort Leaves to get the drop on his first three victims before he administered that paralytic to keep them immobile—but awake—as he carved them up. Surprising Grant long enough to do the same to him. Breaking into her home and removing that Silver Star from her trunk and pinning it to her pillow. Trapping Ruger in her dad's old room before he left. Breaking into her SUV while she was inside Madrigal's offices before heading back across town so he could phone her and arrange to meet her at the Silver Bullet for brunch to find out if Max's tags had succeeded in jogging her memory. And, finally, breaking into the CEO's home and trapping yet another snarling dog so he could lie in wait to slit the throats of the three holier-than-thou civilians who'd engineered his best friend's murder and posthumous disgrace.

As a quick-thinking and adaptable Special Forces soldier who'd been vetted by combat in Afghanistan, Iraq and elsewhere, Burke would've been capable of it all.

And a hell of a lot more.

The slump to her friend's shoulders as she stumbled to the couch testified to the fact that, deep down, Liz agreed.

But that wasn't all.

Kate also believed Burke had taken on his faux identity so that he could obscure his own while he spent the past several years ferreting out the members and particulars of Madrigal's illegal organ and tissue racket as he'd honed his skills and gathered the supplies he'd need to take it apart, piece by piece and limb by limb. Literally. Burke had planned these kills down to the slightest nick of his knife. But not for God, Army or country, or even to protect his fellow soldiers and vets—though he might be telling himself so.

He'd done it for cold-blooded revenge.

Kate made her way to the couch. In a depressing turnabout,

it was she who sat down next to Liz to hold her friend's hand for comfort. Ruger had done his part, too, moving in to nuzzle into Liz's lap.

"The good news is, Grant didn't kill those first three VA employees. But he has been killing vets—and he wasn't just taking their organs. He and his co-conspirators at Madrigal have been slicing off every useable bone, ligament, valve and piece of flesh, and selling them through a tissue bank. I think that's why Burke carved up his first three victims—and Grant—the way he did, and why Burke vacuum-packed their parts and set them out in bags along the roads." She'd always felt that "take one, to go" display was critical to the killer's psyche.

Even the missing organs made perverse sense in light of what they'd learned.

"Liz, I know you're the shrink here, but I'm pretty sure Burke has been trying to tell us about Madrigal's organ and tissue rackets all along. Even worse, I think the murders began with active duty soldiers and progressed to vets."

Hell, given everything she'd learned, she seriously doubted Tanner Holmes had even been the first.

Liz wiped at the shock and dismay still staining her cheeks. "*Oh, God.*"

"I know." But as depraved as it was, Madrigal's business model was sound.

What better place to cull organ "donors" than from soldiers serving in various hotspots around the globe? As donor pools went, it was stellar. Military personnel tended to be young, in shape and prescreened for diseases that could and would impede a conventional transplant. With a pool that numerous, Madrigal could guarantee a near perfect match. Or at least as perfect as they were likely to get.

Something for which the truly rich and desperate wouldn't hesitate to pay a small fortune.

As for the pesky fact that a donor couldn't survive without certain organs and/or might balk at losing one they could spare, since said organ loss would signal the end of a career they wanted?

Well, those hotspots were also conveniently located in places where soldiers were not only likely to die, but had done so on a weekly—if not daily—basis. Places where deaths would have been relatively easy enough to conceal. She'd worked enough of those hotspot cases to know firsthand that more than a few evidentiary details got lost in the fog of war.

And if those details had been deliberately obscured by the same medical personnel tasked with signing off on a victim's cause of death?

Kate shuddered to think how many murders had been missed. "You told me in Abel's kitchen that all a lab needs to tissue-type an organ is a couple vials of blood. Soldiers give that every time they turn around." Hence the need for a bribable lab tech and an admin type on the payroll. "But then the wars began to draw down and Madrigal's once ready supply of quality organs slowed to a drip." Which would've made it harder to explain away murders. Until they realized they still had a ready supply; it had simply shifted. "So, they began to target vets." And if they concentrated on those who were homeless or isolated, but still caring for their bodies enough to seek out the VA medical care they were entitled to, Madrigal no longer had to worry about burials. "I suspect they got into the body parts business then."

Why waste the extra parts and potential profit?

Kate left Ruger at the couch to comfort Liz and returned to the desk. Minimizing the window containing Burke's close-up, she re-read the *LA Chronicle* article on Tanner Holmes, stopping at the description of his body's desecration. The staff sergeant's intestines had been found at his feet. It hadn't been enough to hang the man, Madrigal had also had Holmes gutted and burned to conceal the organs that were missing.

Had the coroner known? Had he or she been paid to look the other way?

She'd have to track down the autopsy report and compare the information and conclusions within to the staff sergeant's exhumed remains, but odds were that the answer was a heinous and traitorous *yes*.

Disgusted, Kate minimized the *Chronicle's* article, and enlarged the window containing the close-up of Staff Sergeant Burke. She clicked out of Burke's photo and switched the view to the original list of links concerning Burke. There, she clicked on a headline she'd noted earlier: "Wildcat Triathlete Loses Legs to Afghan IED."

The image the article painted of Tom Burke as a teenage triathlete and subsequent Special Forces soldier—and cross-trained medic—was one of patience, persistence and inner strength. Qualities that would've stood him well while deployed downrange, and also as a determined vet bent on regaining the use of his legs so he could wreak overdue vengeance on those who'd murdered his friend.

The author's admiration for Burke didn't surprise her, but the photo he'd pasted in the article's sidebar did.

It was of the staff sergeant in-country and definitely in his element. Sporting the generous facial hair many SF and SEALs grew during deployments, Burke had been photographed beside a wall of sandbags, dressed in a tan T-shirt and camouflaged trousers stained with the sweat and grime of a recent mission. According to the caption, the photo had been snapped a mere week before her ambush—and six before his own.

Like her, Burke's Humvee had been hit with an IED. He'd lost his legs and suffered a serious head injury in the blast.

Liz's questions regarding Grant and the rare, but potentially deadly shift in personality a traumatic brain injury could bring filtered in, only to be supplanted by those mesmerizing eyes.

Something about their intensity got to her in a way they hadn't in that diner or at Fort Leaves. An eerie sensation prickled in. Perhaps it was due to the mustache and full beard, but the longer she stared at *this* Burke's mouth, the more she swore she could see his lips moving.

"Kate?"

She stiffened as her friend's fingers pressed into her shoulder. The impression vanished.

"Are you okay?"

"Yeah. Sorry. Had a weird moment there."

"Another memory?"

She shook her head. But she wasn't so sure. "I don't know. If it was, it's gone now. Just a sec, okay? I need to take care of something." Kate brought up the clean-shaven close-up of Burke she'd located and used her laptop's software to text the photo to Lou so he could update the APB, then sent it to Joe. She sent the close-up to Detective Moradi as well, adding a request for Moradi to run it past the witness who'd seen someone running from the Madrigal CEO's house.

Kate reopened the *LA Chronicle* article on Tanner Holmes next and sent a final text to Lou and Joe with a link to the article.

"Almost finished." Retrieving her phone, she dialed Joe's number, only to get his voicemail. He, Tonga and Agent Walker were probably already at the state lab, carting in Grant's remains, if they weren't already hip deep in the autopsy.

Kate left a message asking the CID agent to retrieve all records the Army had on Staff Sergeants Thomas Burke and Tanner Holmes.

She dumped her phone on the desk as she finished and turned to find Liz staring at her. "What?"

"You're doing it again."

"Doing what?"

Suddenly, she knew. Kate withdrew her fingers from Max's watch as smoothly as she could. The watch that, given the fresh scrapes on her skin, she'd been twisting for some time.

"That's a classic coping mechanism, you know. Tactile touch. It can be very soothing, even stave off panic attacks."

"Really?" And to think she'd hit on it all on her own. Bully for her.

"Do you know when you use it?"

That was a trick question, right? To get another discussion going so she'd accept the referral Liz had been pushing?

Well, it wouldn't work. "Look, I—"

"When you're thinking about the past, that ambush, that's when you start turning it. I've watched you do it several times since we've met up again, so don't deny it. And, yes, I know you've probably figured that out for yourself. But what I don't know is why you started twisting that watch while you were staring at—scratch that, *mesmerized by*—that bearded photo of Thomas Burke."

"I did?"

Liz nodded. "You did."

That odd déjà vu impression rippled back, giving her pause once more. But she still couldn't put her finger on why. "Got a second?"

Her friend smiled. "I've got all night, remember? I'm the babysitter."

Kate appreciated the attempt to soften the tension, but it hadn't worked. Not with her. She pushed away from the computer desk and stood. "Follow me."

Destination in mind, she was relieved when Ruger took it upon himself to join them as they headed down the hall to her dad's room. Kate braced herself at the door and opened it. Liz and Ruger followed her inside.

Her friend stopped beside the trunk at the foot of the bed, turning around as she took in the dust-covered decor that hadn't changed since the day they'd met. "This is so weird. I can actually feel the fear I felt when we snuck in here to poke through your dad's case files when he wasn't home."

"Yeah, I know." It was probably why her father had built that cabin and moved his desk and files over there.

"So what are we looking at tonight?"

Kate knelt and lifted the lid to the trunk. She withdrew the velvet box inside and passed it up to Liz.

"Oh, wow. This is your medal. Well, the big one."

"Yep. Silver Star." The going reward for killing eleven men in as many hours, and somehow living to bury the tale, at least mentally. "The first and last time I opened that case was after I'd pulled the medal off my chest at Walter Reed. From there, I dumped it in this trunk with the rest of my gear. I hadn't laid eyes on the medal since...until I found it pinned to my pillow last night."

Her friend's lashes flew wide. "Are you telling me—"

"That someone was in my house? Yes."

Liz's knuckles turned white as she and the case sank down to the floor beside the trunk. "Holy moly. Burke?"

"I think so. Ruger's the only one who knows for certain. He was trapped in here at the time. But that's not all." Kate withdrew the dog tags from beneath the collar of her sweatshirt and held them out. "These belonged to Max Brennan. The final time I saw them was the night before we left on that last mission." She pointed to the pair of nicks at the edge of the upper tag. "I put those there myself that same night. Max and I were messing around. No one else knows that. After I came to in that hospital, I asked for these. I was told they were never recovered from that Afghan compound. So how did they get inside my Durango this morning? I found them dangling from my rearview mirror when I came out of the Baymont building in Little Rock."

It was a good thing Liz was sitting or she'd have hit the rug then, along with her jaw. "Oh, God. He—"

Kate held up her hand. "There's more. That photo of Burke? The one where he's in uniform and sporting a full beard and mustache? When I saw that, it was as if he was suddenly inches from my face, staring at me, telling me something over and over. I could even see his lips moving. But damned if I can figure out what he's saying—or said."

If he *had* said something. Despite the return of the memories from that compound, part of her still wondered if—feared—she was doing this to herself.

"Only that doesn't make sense. If I had met Burke, surely I would've remembered him? Plus, why pin that medal to my pillow? And why hang onto a set of tags for four years and then dangle them from my mirror? Mind you, I'm not suggesting he held onto them for me, but he would've had to have found that compound before CID did and retrieved them. While that's possible given the man's particular combat-honed skill set, why would he even want to go to that compound on the sly?"

"Did he know Max?"

"I have no idea. But it's possible. Max was a lieutenant colonel and a trauma surgeon. He knew a lot of soldiers." He'd treated even more.

Kate tensed as Liz reached inside her trunk to retrieve the photo album she'd perused and put back two days earlier.

"Do you mind?"

Yes. "No."

Liz went with the latter as she laid the album in her lap and opened it. She flipped through the pages until she'd reached the man who most likely qualified as the best friend, based on the number of photos he appeared within.

Liz tapped a shot of the two of them searching for souvenirs in an Afghan souk. "Is this Max?"

"Yeah."

She started to flip the page.

Kate reached out to stay her hand. "Hold it." She gripped the corner of the book. "May I?"

"They're your pictures."

True. But there was a photo on the bottom of the page that she'd never really paid attention to before. Possibly because it was a group shot taken in the office Max had shared in Afghanistan, and she hadn't known the other medical personnel surrounding him. But there, on some doctor's desk beside the group was a mug with that now distinctive, red and white Madrigal Medical logo.

Was this the desk and Madrigal cup Burke claimed to have seen? Had he spotted it when he'd rifled through her trunk and mentioned it in an attempt to jar her memory? Had he wanted her to connect Madrigal...to Max?

Given how meticulously he'd planned every other detail, including both their "accidental" meetings at Fort Leaves, it was more than possible.

It was all but certain.

"Liz, I think they did know each other—Max and Thomas Burke. And I think Burke wanted me to know." Why else had he hung those tags from her mirror?

But why would it matter that the two had met? Max had been active-duty military. He hadn't been a Madrigal Medical contracted hire...although that cup did suggest Max had shared an office with someone who was.

Kate groaned as she rubbed her hand over her face. "If I could just remember what Burke said to me."

Because he had said something. That, she'd finally come to accept. Their encounter must've taken place in that quiet room while she'd been less than lucid due to sedation. The more she thought about it, it was the only scenario that made sense.

"Close your eyes."

"What?"

Liz nodded. "You heard me. Close your eyes and take several slow, deep breaths as you try to clear your mind."

"I don't—"

"Who's the detective in this room, and who's the psychiatrist?"

Kate sighed and closed her eyes. She took the directed breaths, bemused when they did help to relax her.

"Now, keep your eyes closed and picture the photo you saw in your mind. The one that jarred the partial memory. Close in on his face. Can you see it? Now move out. Can you make out anything around the man? Clues to tell you where you are? For example, are you inside or outside?"

"Inside. I'm in a small room. It's dim, but I can make out Burke's mustache and beard."

"Okay, that's good. Hold on to that image. Keep focusing on it as we move on to sound and smell. Does anything stand out?"

"Not really. It's quiet." In fact, there was no real sound at all. Just those silent, moving lips.

"What do you smell? Food, sweat, shampoo...deodorant?"

"No, none of that." If anything, the air was clean. Cool. With the barest hint of, "Wait—antiseptic. I smell hospital antiseptic." She was definitely in that quiet room at the combat support hospital. Hope coursed through Kate and, then, she could hear him. The voice in her ears belonged to Burke, but he wasn't telling her anything. He was asking.

Did Brennan tell you anything before he died?

She opened her eyes. "I don't— Why would—" She lurched to her feet and began pacing as the confusion whirled in. "It doesn't make sense."

"Then you do remember something?"

"Yes. Burke kept asking if Max had said anything to me before he died." In fact, that was the only question Burke had focused on, asking it again and again, even when it became clear that she wouldn't—couldn't—answer.

But why would Burke care about her private conversations with Max? How had Burke even gotten past those doctors and into that quiet room undetected?

Hell, why had he gone through such hoops to ask her anything at all, much less if Max had made some grand, final confession?

"Did he?"

Kate spun around. Liz was still seated beside the trunk, holding that album. "Did who, what?"

"Did Max say anything?"

At least I can have that Arlington burial.

Only...that wasn't a confession, grand or otherwise. Hell, Max hadn't even been speaking to her at the time, but himself. Nor did the comment make sense. Not earlier, out on her deck, and not now. Max hadn't even been buried. His body had been cremated as per his wishes, his ashes interred in the Brennan family vault alongside those of his folks and the rest of his ancestors while she was still laid up at Walter Reed.

Kate stiffened as the connection locked in.

I.

A short, seemingly innocuous word. But it wasn't innocuous. In fact, that single pronoun was the key to the entire, horrific ambush—and everything that had followed. Especially when paired with those damning words that preceded it: at least. Max hadn't been referring to his final send-off, but someone else's.

Shit.

Kate crumpled against the edge of her father's dresser as she nodded. "Yeah, Max did say something. A split second before that blade dropped he said, 'At least I can have that Arlington burial.'"

Bemusement furrowed into Liz's brow. "I don't understand. Was he referring to eligibility?"

"Yes."

"But...I still don't get it. Even if your friend hadn't been a POW when he died, he was active duty. Serving in a war zone. Surely he wouldn't have been barred from interment at the national cemetery?"

"You're right. He wouldn't have been." But someone had. And not only had Max known, he'd been thinking of little else at the time.

For damned good reason.

"Tanner Holmes."

The furrow in Liz's brow deepened. "The soldier you just googled in your den?"

"Yes." Max had known that Holmes hadn't deserted—*and* he'd known how the staff sergeant had really died. Which meant Max had also known about Madrigal's organ-harvesting racket...because Burke had asked him to look into it.

It all made sense. Especially in light of Max's mood that last night inside the wire. It had been odd to say the least, more so when he'd asked her to tag along on that mission. But during the drive, his mood had become stranger still. She'd had the distinct feeling Max had been trying to find the words to say something to her. Now she knew what.

And when she added in that cryptic comment Burke had made to Liz during the car ride the two had shared to Saint Clare's shelter?

"Liz, when you told me Burke claimed the Army had betrayed him, you said he'd also muttered something about 'camouflaged battles and true heroes, and making things worse.'"

Her friend nodded. Like her, Liz appeared numbed by the shock of it all.

In the context of Max's final, resigned words, that last part of Burke's statement wasn't cryptic anymore. It was downright damning.

...making things worse.

The more she thought about it, the more certain she became. In fact, it was the only explanation that allowed everything else to fit: Burke had come to Max with his suspicions about his buddy's death. And when Max had uncovered enough to make him believe Burke was right, Max had decided to turn to her.

"That's why Max really asked me to accompany him outside the wire." The only place he could guarantee they wouldn't be overheard, especially by his fellow physicians. Specifically, the one he suspected of colluding with Madrigal. "The night before we left, Max said he wanted to discuss something, but not then —that it could wait until the coming mission. He was scheduled to check on the wife of a warlord the Army was courting. He'd performed the woman's surgery." At the last minute, Max had asked her to come along as an extra set of female hands. Naturally, she'd agreed. The trip would've been worthwhile for the potential intel alone. "But Max was in a strange mood. When I pushed it, I could've sworn he was about to open up, but then he got a call and left to check on a patient. Liz, I think he knew about Madrigal and those organs. I think he'd been poking around for Burke. And he was murdered for it."

Worse, Max had known why he was being killed.

Max had spoken Arabic. Maybe one of the terrorists had unwittingly let something slip within his earshot, or maybe Max had been taunted with the knowledge. Either way, he'd known they'd been sold out. Why else had he mentioned Arlington? Max might've been eligible for interment—but Holmes wouldn't have been. Not after the staff sergeant had been officially branded a deserter by the Army.

"I don't understand. Your friend was killed by terrorists. Your entire team was."

"Yes, and no. They were terrorists. But I now think they were tipped off. Most likely via the coroner. As a doctor, the first thing Max would've done was pull the Tanner Holmes autopsy report. He'd want to review it for himself. He must've spotted a serious inconsistency." In turn, once that report was pulled, the coroner would've figured out that Max was on to him—so the coroner had ratted Max out to Madrigal.

It would've been easy for Madrigal to employ the services of a shadier-than-hell go-between that the company had in its Middle-Eastern pocket. Quite possibly the same go-between who'd facilitated the hanging, gutting and burning of Tanner Holmes' body in Iraq. The terrorists wouldn't even have known who they were really working for. Nor would it have been the first time a bounty had been placed on heads of specific US soldiers. It was the only scenario that made sense.

The coroner would also have known the details of Max's coming medical mission with the warlord's wife.

Plus, "Why else were those two soldiers who'd also survived the ambush shot through their temples? And there's Max—a seasoned trauma surgeon—beheaded. Terrorists or not, he could've treated their wounds for them if they'd kept him alive. Hell, he would have; he'd taken an oath. But they cut off his head without so much as a ransom demand." And there was that flag and that camera.

When she'd entered that final hovel, the bastards had been in the midst of filming Max's death. Granted, posting the resulting video on some agreed upon jihadist website would've added to a growing collection of anti-American terror porn. But if her suspicions were correct, that video would also have provided proof of a job completed—and that whatever blood money promised by the go-between should now be released into a predetermined bank account.

"And, finally, there's me. I got the rapes. I might not remember them, but I got them. I suspect it's the only reason I was kept alive as long as I was." But after they'd had their fun? She was next. "There were never any plans to trade us for other jihadists, much less exploit us for medical services, human intelligence or money. That ambush had been a targeted kill to take Max out, preferably before he confided in me."

She and all those other soldiers had simply been collateral damage from the makeshift weapon sighted in by their own countrymen. From a *physician*, no less.

Talk about fratricide.

Her phone rang from across the house. Though the sound was faint, it caused her and Liz to flinch.

Kate stood and headed for the den, numbed enough to let her friend close the album and return it and that medal to her trunk. With the shock of it all still reverberating through her, she wasn't sure she could've managed any of it.

Better to concentrate on the job. Her case.

That call.

According to her caller ID, it was from Lou. "Hey, boss."

"Hey, Kato. I got the texts and updated the APB with Burke's real name and photo. How about you? Feelin' better?"

Not by a long shot. "Yes."

"Good. Could you send Agent Cordoba back here, then? Ed and Tonga need to get going."

Her stomach lurched, then bottomed out as she checked the dial on her watch. Kate tightened her grip on the phone as terror locked in. "Boss, Joe left my place a while ago. As in almost two hours."

But Ruger hadn't alerted. If Burke had been in the

surrounding woods, surely the Shepherd would've heard something and warned her?

But she'd been trapped in her hellish past. And when that happened, Ruger's entire focus was on her—as it had been when Joe had left.

"Just a sec."

"Sure thing, Kato."

With no time to lose, she bypassed the boots she'd left in the hall bathroom and grabbed her Glock instead. She didn't even stop to tell Liz as she chambered a round. She simply headed for the back door. Ruger followed her out onto the deck, then down and across the clearing.

It was pitch black out now due to the thick cover of clouds that had moved in.

Joe had taken a call as he'd left. An emergency?

It was long shot, but—

Kate brought the phone back to her ear. "I'm back. Where's the car Carole signed out to Joe?"

"It's still here, parked right behind Seth's."

Oh, God. No emergency, then. "I'm entering the path to the cabin now. And, yes, I'm armed." Dried leaves, needles and twigs snapped softly beneath her bare feet, digging into her soles. "I don't see or hear anything out of the ordinary." She glanced down at Ruger, keeping pace at her side. "Neither does Ruger."

"I'm heading in from the opposite direction. You got a flashlight handy?"

"Just the one on my phone."

"Then hang up and turn it on. Seth and I'll be hooking up with you in two, three minutes, tops."

She hung up as instructed and dialed Joe's number instead...and heard ringing from deeper inside the woods.

She bolted toward the sound, twigs and rocks cutting into her feet in earnest as she panted to a halt beside a large oak.

Even in this low light, she could see the glistening swath of blood that coated the bark at the base of the tree. Beneath that, Joe's ringing phone, its crystal shattered.

Joe was nowhere to be found.

Burke had taken him.

17

LOU HAD BROUGHT her back to her deck where he, Liz and Ruger were once again at her side. All too soon, Agent Walker and Seth joined them—empty-handed.

Kate's heart slammed against her ribs as her fellow deputy reached the patio table, the fruitlessness of the search he'd just completed intensifying the hollows beneath his eyes. "I'm sorry, Kate. He's gone. Burke must have Agent Cordoba slung over his back, because his prints are deep. Easy to track."

She slipped her arm around Ruger as the Shepherd scooted closer, grateful as always for his instinctive support.

"But?" Because there was more. She'd heard it in Seth's voice.

"Given the terrain, the prints are damned near in a straight line until they reach Quaker Run. There, they just stop. Right at the edge of the gravel road."

That explained why Ruger hadn't alerted. There'd been no nearby car. And, if Burke had carried Joe, the vet had to have knocked Joe out with that first blow. No audible, drawn-out struggle, and worse, "Burke had get-away transportation waiting."

"Appears so. And since that's the roundabout way to your

place—" Seth shook his head. "I already checked with the guys. None of us took it on our way here earlier."

Which meant they had no make, model or color for the vehicle Burke had stashed—no chance at an updated APB. Which of course, Burke had also planned, just as he'd planned every other move he'd made in this drawn-out, deviant scheme of his.

"Burke was waiting for me, wasn't he? Once you all left, he'd planned on slipping back inside my house. Only this time, he was going to force me to remember."

But Joe had spotted Burke first.

She'd seen what that bastard had done to Grant and his co-conspirators. She'd *held* it. Joe did not deserve that.

If Burke hadn't already slit her friend's throat and left him for dead deep inside those woods.

No one voiced it. But from the unease that had set in, they were all thinking it.

Even Liz.

Walker stepped forward. "Don't despair about your friend. Agent Cordoba's unexpected presence on that path has accomplished one positive thing. It forced Burke to deviate from his plan. That may work to our favor. Especially if Burke decides to keep Cordoba alive as leverage, as would be prudent."

The shrink was right. Burke would be a fool to blow leverage. Something the vet had proven he was not.

Walker returned her slow nod with a crisper one of his own. "Your sheriff shared the link to the article you sent. While we were waiting on Agent Cordoba to return, I pulled Burke's military record. I haven't finished the file, but I did read the summary. The sheriff said you had breakfast with Burke this morning?"

"Yes." Ruger tucked his muzzle into Kate's lap as she turned to include Lou. "I've pieced together the rest of my past. I believe my friend Max uncovered the organ racket after Burke asked him for help back in Afghanistan. Max planned to lay it out for me once we were outside the wire and out of range of eavesdropping ears—but Max never got the chance. Burke visited me when I was sedated following my escape to see if I knew anything." She filled them in on the Silver Star and Max's tags.

She thought about explaining why she'd withheld the information about both. But in the end, she couldn't. It was hard enough admitting to herself that, for a while there, she'd feared she was losing her mind. But she did apologize.

Especially to Lou. "I think Burke used them to try to jog my memory."

The sheriff's frown had grown darker during her briefing, especially as she revealed the developments she'd withheld.

Walker's nod, however, had become firmer. "This all fits with my theory. I believe Burke is frustrated. According to his record, he suffered a traumatic brain injury when he lost his legs. I suspect the portions of his brain that regulate his moral code were affected. He's spent the years since planning every step of his revenge. The recovery of your memory appears to be a crucial element. But as far as he knows, those memories have still not cooperated. This would explain why he left Grant Parish's remains on your property. He hoped to stress your mind further to see if the memories he sought to restore would surface."

"Well, he succeeded."

"But he doesn't know that. Which can only have increased his frustration. And since the sheriff informs me Burke effectually shed his stolen identity at the shelter by failing to show for his meeting with the priest, we can assume he knows that you, at the very least, are now aware of who he is *not*. Unfortunately, this is not enough for Burke. And if he's neared the end of his plan for revenge, and he feels your memories aren't cooperating to his satisfaction—"

"Then you do think he was lying in wait, intent on getting me alone."

The BAU agent nodded. "I do. He may now hold you personally responsible for not remembering after everything he's done to ensure it. Or he may simply want to talk to you, to lay out his grievances with someone he feels is a kindred spirit. The hidden escape vehicle, the location of Agent Cordoba's blood and the shattered phone on that path? It all supports both theories. It's possible Cordoba surprised Burke while the staff sergeant was waiting for everyone to leave so he could confront you alone. But Cordoba's presence on that path forced him to take action—and take Agent Cordoba instead."

She was right. This, too, was her fault.

Another friend lost to this barbaric organ and tissue racket. Just like Max and all the soldiers who died in that ambush, and in that compound later. Unless she figured out where Joe was in time to prevent it, certain death was in his very near future too. If she held any hope of preventing it, there was only one place to start.

The past.

"Agent Walker, I need that copy of Staff Sergeant Burke's military record. I also need Tanner Holmes' record and a copy of the CID investigation into his death—including his autopsy report. I'd also like a copy of Major Grant Parish's records and those of Lieutenant Colonel Maxwell Brennan, along with the CID investigation into Max's death and my own capture."

Liz was right. She was an emotional ostrich. If she hadn't been such a bloody coward in avoiding that write-up of her own POW experience, she might've remembered Max's strange statement during his execution and that subsequent, stranger visit from Burke years sooner—and begun to piece Madrigal's filthy scheme together in time to prevent the bulk of the subsequent deaths.

At least of those homeless vets.

The BAU agent nodded. "Absolutely. When I pulled Burke's record, I discovered that Agent Cordoba had already requested the files for Tanner Holmes following our earlier discussion. They were just sent to his email, so I requested copies as well. I'll forward those to your Braxton PD email address along with Burke's file, as soon as I put in the request for the remainder of the records on your list. If you'll excuse me?" His phone already out, Walker headed for the corner of her deck to place the call.

Kate turned to find her boss brandishing his own phone. She sent Ruger into the yard to do his canine business as Lou wrapped up the human, verbal cop variety.

Lou dumped his phone on the table as he finished. "That was the governor's aide. The warrant for the pet crematorium and all related grounds is approved. I'd planned on executin' it at dawn so we could see what the hell we were doin', but with Cordoba missin', we'll go in once everyone's mustered up and briefed. You, Deputy Holland—" Lou retrieved his phone as he stood. "—will remain here and work those records. We don't need some defense attorney arguin' conflict of interest at trial."

Kate nodded. She fully agreed. So long as there was a trial. "You'll call—"

"Just as soon as I know who's who and what's what. You have my word."

It was enough to tide her over. Kate stood, waiting as Ruger loped across the clearing and up onto the deck even as Lou, Seth and Agent Walker filed off.

Walker gave her a thumbs up as he passed. "The first set's already in your inbox. The rest is on its way."

"Thanks."

Kate opened the glass door and waved Liz and Ruger

through. She turned to make one last check of the darkened clearing, only to discover Braxton PD's newest rookie approaching from the driveway side of her house. Regret tinged the young man's face as he caught sight of her.

"Hey, Moonie. You just missed the sheriff."

"I know, ma'am. I'm here to see you."

The regret deepened, turning awkward as she noticed the small white envelope in his hand. Shit. As junior man, Officer Moonier had most likely been stuck out at the Parish farm after everyone else had left.

"What happened?" She actually hoped the stress of half their department combing through everything on that farm had been enough to send Abel's stolen heart into a full-blown rebellion. It was the most humane of the only two logical explanations for Moonie's presence.

But instead of answering, the officer extended the envelope. Her name had been penned on the outside, via a shaky hand.

"No. Please, tell me that idiot didn't—"

But Moonie was already bobbing his sandy head. "I'm so sorry. It's all my fault. We thought he was napping, but I think Abel heard the nurse and me discussing the discovery of those bags with his son's body inside 'em. The nurse went outside to take a call from her husband afterward. I was still in the living room with Abel when he appeared to wake. He said he needed to use the bathroom. He was only gone for a few minutes. I didn't even realize he'd stepped into the kitchen, let alone that one of the bottles was empty when he left. That envelope was on the kitchen table, on top of the Sunday paper."

"Did he suffer?"

"No, ma'am. He just drifted off to sleep. The nurse didn't suspect a thing 'til his breathing ceased."

Kate took the envelope from Moonie's hand. "Thank you. Let Seth know what happened. It's his call, but tell him I recommend not telling the sheriff until after they execute the coming warrant." The knowledge that Abel had taken his own life because of all of this would only further screw with Lou's head when he needed the distraction least.

"Yes, ma'am."

Kate slumped into the chair she'd recently vacated. She was still out on the darkened deck, trying to absorb the horror of Abel taking the image of Grant's body, hacked and bagged up, to his own death, when Liz came out to check on her.

"Are you okay?"

She shook her head. "Abel committed suicide. He found out Grant was dead and swallowed the contents of one of those bottles of pills before anyone realized it."

Liz braced herself against the door's frame for several long moments, her gaze glistening in the light bleeding out from the den. She finally straightened, nodded silently to Kate, then turned and went inside.

For once, Kate was glad Ruger hadn't come out to make sure she was on her way in.

If he had, she'd have lost it. That was something neither she nor Liz needed.

As it was, the Shepherd's absence allowed her to stitch her guilt and regret together long enough for her to stand and follow Liz. She found her friend at the sink, hand washing the dishes that had begun piling up from the moment she'd left to examine that first set of bags out on Old Man Miller's drive.

She knew Liz well enough to leave the woman to it, and headed for the computer desk instead.

Liz would talk when she was ready. She might as well get started on those files while she waited.

She pushed the envelope Moonie had handed her to the rear of the desk and opened her laptop. She was nowhere near ready to read Abel's goodbye and formally accept his loss, along with yet another piece of innocence from her childhood.

She'd implode in front of Liz for certain.

Accessing her email, Kate found both Burke's and Holmes' records waiting. She clicked on the attached PDF file for Staff Sergeant Holmes' autopsy and began to read.

Six minutes later, she stiffened.

She'd found it. Right there in the write-up attached to those damning close-ups that were more blackened and charred than any collection of autopsy photos should ever be. Max, and possibly Staff Sergeant Burke, had to have noticed the same discrepancy.

As she'd expected, Tanner Holmes' body had been missing organs. Specifically, his kidneys, liver, pancreas and stomach. But the explanation for their absence didn't make sense. The coroner stated that the organs had been most likely dragged off and consumed by wild dogs. But while wild dogs had roamed the bombed out sections of many Iraqi cities, there was no evidence of bite marks on the charred viscera that remained.

In fact, the only marks she could make out in those bile-churning photos had been caused by something slender, sharp and flat—like a scalpel or knife.

Instinct caused Kate to minimize the autopsy and open the laptop's internet browser. She typed the coroner's name and credentials into the search field and hit return. Skimming the list of links, she selected one dated six months earlier; the one titled "Former Iraq Doctor Dies in Bouldering Accident."

Three paragraphs in, she was all but certain the man's death was no accident.

It seemed the coroner was an extreme rock-climbing enthusiast with twenty years' experience. He'd been bouldering in the Gunks in upstate New York early one morning when he'd had the misfortune of slipping on a large level stone and plunging a mere twelve feet to his death. His sole injury: a broken neck. Though foul play had been considered at the time, local detectives had been unable to find so much as a stray boot print. They'd finally determined the man's death to be an accident and had closed the case.

Kate made a mental note to petition for its review as she returned her attention to the files Agent Walker had sent. She opened the CID report on Staff Sergeant Holmes' desertion, only to have the world spin dizzyingly and completely away as she spotted the name in the investigator's block: *Special Agent Joe Cordoba.*

Kate jackknifed to her feet, denial sending nuclear-grade shockwaves throughout her body as she swung around to yell for Liz—but didn't. Liz was already behind her, on the couch, asleep. Ruger was crammed up beside her on the cushions so Liz could hug his body close.

Heart still pounding, nerves screaming, Kate left her friend to the surcease she desperately needed and whirled back to the screen, hoping, praying she'd misread that block...but she hadn't. The implications were fierce and nauseating.

Damn it; it wasn't possible. She'd known Joe for over a decade. Not only was Joe not connected to Madrigal, he was as honorable as they came.

Except...when she'd mentioned Tanner Holmes to him following her search of Jason Dunne's condo, Joe had told her Mike Barnes had worked the case. Obviously, he'd lied.

Grant.

She thought she'd known him too. Hell, she'd trusted that man so completely, she'd let him into her bed.

And there was more.

What had Joe said to her as they'd left the Parish farm with her battered soul still attempting to reconcile the enormity of Grant's and Abel's crimes?

Some people will do anything, risk anything, for someone they truly love.

His wife.

Elise Cordoba had diabetes. Kate had never given it much thought before now, but the seemingly healthy and vivacious woman had been diagnosed while she was still in diapers. Elise had been dependent on her daily insulin injections ever since.

How much of a toll did a chronic disease like that take on the human body?

Kate was almost too terrified to find out.

She forced her own body to resume its seat in front of that tattling laptop. She minimized the desertion investigation and opened a fresh browser window, praying as hard as she had the day her mom had died as she typed "diabetes, organ transplant" into the waiting search bar.

She hit *enter.*

Her prayers disintegrated as link after damning link crowded the screen. She clicked the first one and crossed her arms to keep the muck contained as she read.

She needn't have bothered.

Halfway into the article, she had her answer...and Joe's motive for betraying not only his sacred oath as an investigator, but also his fellow man.

But before she condemned him completely, she needed proof. The kind that would stand up in a court of law.

She knew just where and how to get it.

Kate slipped her phone from her pocket and nudged her stiff fingers into motion once more, opening her contact list. She located Joe's home number much too quickly, and dialed.

His wife answered on the first ring.

Even more damning given that it was barely two in the morning in Fort Bragg, North Carolina. "Hello?"

"Elise? Hi, this is Kate Holland. Remember me?"

"Of course I remember you. Is Joe—"

"Just listen, okay? I know you know what's going on out here. And I know Joe's up to his lying teeth in it. What I don't know is which organ he obtained for you—pancreas or kidney?"

Silence filled the line. The seconds ticked out as it continued to grow and distend, until the truth that spawned it had become a monstrous, breathing thing, coiling through the connection as it prepared to choke them both.

"Elise?"

"Yes?"

"Joe's been kidnapped. He's—"

"*What?* Oh, my God! Kate, you have to—"

"*Stop.* Just listen. Then answer my damned questions— honestly. Joe's life depends on my finding him before it's too late. Even if I can locate him, I'll need to be armed with all the facts or I won't have a hope in hell of lancing a boiling, righteous rage that's been five long years in the feeding. Now, I asked you a question. *Which* organ?"

"Both."

The nauseating scheme shattered on Elise's end as the rest tumbled out, each piece of the conspiracy uglier than the last. "You know I'm diabetic, or I was. I'd begun to show symptoms of autonomic neuropathy. My digestive tract was already affected and my kidneys were beginning to fail. My prognosis wasn't good. With my antigen profile, I was a difficult match. And then the diabetes began to affect my heart. I started fainting for no reason. When I had my heart attack, Joe was deployed to Iraq. He freaked. He called two weeks later with a solution. He said he knew someone in Pakistan who brokered organs. They'd found someone willing to donate a kidney and part of his pancreas— and we were a perfect match. I swear to God I didn't know I'd be getting the entire pancreas and both kidneys. I only found out after my doctor let something slip. Though I'd begun to suspect something was off."

Kate gripped her phone and forced herself to remain calm and questioning, to not test the bounds of physics and attempt to reach though the line to strangle the woman on the other end. A woman she'd once called friend. "You said you *were* diabetic?"

"Yes. That's why I had suspicions. A few months after the surgery, I discovered I no longer needed insulin. Also, my neuropathy and heart issues actually reversed themselves."

So while Holmes lay disgraced, murdered and buried in some swept-under-the-rug, out-of-the-way plot—and his best friend left little more than a seething mass of wounded vengeance—Joe and Elise had been getting on with their rejuvenated, sunshine-and-flowers-filled lives.

"When?" It was all Kate could manage.

"I told you, a few months—"

"The surgery. *When* did it occur."

She heard Elise swallow a fresh batch of tears, before hiccupping on the next. "Five years ago. I flew to Pakistan on June 29th. I was admitted to a hospital in Lahore the next day."

Kate glanced at the date on that CID report, the one which had officially branded Tanner Holmes as a deserter. They matched. She'd located three of the staff sergeant's missing organs...and so had his friend and former brother in arms, Thomas Burke.

"You have to believe me; Joe wasn't there for the surgery. You can check his military records. He was in Mosul. He had—"

"—a murder to cover up." A spectacular Special Forces career to tarnish. And then another murder to plan...this time, in the form of an ambushed convoy—a year later and several hundred miles away—in another war zone.

An ambush which would end up costing the lives of countless additional innocent soldiers. Along with her sanity, and the guilt-stained remnants of her own tattered soul.

And Max.

"Please, Kate, that's all I know. You have to find Joe. I don't know who runs things or how to contact them. Or where they are. I swear on Joe's life. I—"

Kate didn't hear the rest. She'd already hung up.

She stared at the phone in her hand as she finally accepted the truth. Not only was Joe not the man she'd believed him to be, he was up to his blackened, traitorous heart in Staff Sergeant Holmes' murder...and by association, the murders of all the active-duty soldiers and vets who'd been slaughtered since.

Her stomach was still folding in on itself as her phone rang. It was Elise, calling back.

Kate ignored it. She'd already obtained every scrap of information Elise had. She'd be damned if she'd pick up simply to listen to the woman's pleas or, worse, excuses.

She was too busy rearranging the evidence she'd obtained earlier that night. For all his otherwise excellent educated guesses, Agent Walker was wrong about one crucial thing. Burke wasn't fixated on, much less after her. Joe had been his final target all along. Though, admittedly, the former Special Forces staff sergeant wasn't above shoving yet another collection of clues in her face, this time in the form of that last morbid set of bags.

Why else had Burke plunked Grant's limbs out along the drive of the cabin where Joe had been staying?

To jar her memories loose, yes. But those bags had also served as a trail of clues leading straight to that cedar door, all the while bellowing, "Hey, you moron—*here's* the depraved motherfucker you're really after!"

But there was more. Though Burke's intent was now as clear as the crystal face of the dive watch that had been strapped to her wrist for the past four years, she couldn't be sure Burke had been successful. She was no longer certain who had kidnapped whom.

Burke was a trained killer.

But so was Joe.

Had Burke really gotten the drop on Joe as the agent had walked back to her cabin?

Or had Joe managed to turn the tables on Burke and kidnap him?

Because she now understood why Joe had flown to Arkansas, and it wasn't to help her and her department solve this case. His mission had, however, involved the disposition of her investigation. Joe and Madrigal needed a fall guy.

Looking back on Joe's comments since his arrival, she suspected it had originally been Grant. Most likely due to the waves Grant had been making to get out of the business.

Why else had Joe held back on the Holmes investigation? He'd known his name would surface. But with Madrigal's chief counsel and CEO dead, Joe might believe he could kill Burke and still protect his own reputation.

Or not. Despite the possibility that Joe may've gained the upper hand in her woods, her instincts still pegged Burke as the victor.

Kate retrieved her phone, intent on calling Lou to brief him on the latest twist to their case and her life, only to pause as she spotted that small white envelope lying unopened on her desk. She traded her phone for the envelope, knowing full well it contained Abel's suicide note.

It did.

Determined not to succumb to the fresh crop of tears that threatened, Kate withdrew the single sheet of paper folded neatly within...and failed miserably as the tears began to fall.

. . .

DEAR KATIE,

I'm so sorry. I should've come to you. I'd be lying if I said I was only protecting Grant. Truth is, I couldn't face the shame of everyone knowing I'd taken a heart that wasn't mine to take. Most of all, I couldn't face you. Though God may forgive me, I'm not sure you will. That pains me more than you'll ever know since you're the closest to a daughter Barbara and I ever got. Both my boys loved you too, and I know that despite all that's happened, you loved them. Thank you for that.

Just one more thing. When you asked if I'd told you everything, I said yes. Well, I lied. This time, I did do it to help Grant. Now that he's gone, it doesn't matter. Inside this envelope is a bit of plastic. Grant called it a microchip, I think. He's been hiding it in my kitchen. I don't know what's on it, just that Grant called it our Madrigal insurance policy. I hope it helps you take those bastards down. And, please, try not to hate Grant. His biggest flaw was loving his dad too much.

Abel

ENERGIZED BY ABEL'S GIFT, KATE DRIED HER CHEEKS AND retrieved the envelope she'd discarded. Sure enough, there was a tiny piece of plastic wedged into the bottom right corner. It wasn't a chip, though. It was a micro SD card. The kind used in smartphones—like the phone Grant normally carried.

And her own.

Kate grabbed the adapter she kept in her desk drawer and inserted Grant's card, then plugged the adapter into the spare USB port on her laptop, stunned as photo after photo exploded onto her screen. There were hundreds, if not a thousand or more.

Abel had unwittingly handed her the smoking gun to Madrigal's entire illegal organ and tissue racket. Grant had surreptitiously managed to photograph patients, surgeries, medical personnel, medical records, purchasing orders for equipment, drugs and other supplies...as well as interiors and exteriors of a phenomenal state of the art mobile operating theater used by overflow patients and hospitals in disaster relief areas. The latter was housed in a massive eighteen-wheeler with pop-out sides that would put a billionaire's platinum-plated, weekend camper to shame.

Where the hell had Madrigal purchased that thing?

And where was it now?

Kate was forced to thank Grant as she spotted the close-up he'd snapped of the eighteen-wheeler's license plate.

Unfortunately, she'd yet to spot a single photo that gave her a clue as to where Burke might have taken Joe.

Despite her missteps and misplaced trust these past few months—and years—she was still certain Burke had come out on top in the struggle on her wooded path, if only because the photos she was viewing depicted a setup Burke would've given his life to take down. Since she hadn't found Burke's body on that path, she was certain she was hours from finding Joe's.

But where, damn it?

Kate scrolled to the end of the massive collection, wondering if they'd been organized in some sort of logical order. They had. All one thousand, six hundred fifty-two photos had been grouped first. At the very end of the collection of JPEGs sat a lone text file. Its label?

KATE.

The tears returned as she opened the document and began to read. It was a diary of sorts, written by Grant...to her. The first entry reiterated much of what she'd already learned: that Madrigal had lured Grant into their scheme by dangling a heart for his father in his face. Grant had reasoned away his conscience at first by telling himself he was culling from those destined to fall through the cracks of life.

But his conscience had finally gotten the better of him, and he'd come to accept that no one—even desperate, guilt-wracked surgeons—had the right to play God.

Then Grant discovered his father's cancer had returned, and it was terminal. Grant decided that, when the time came, he'd check out of life too. But first, he wanted to give the woman he loved the tools to help herself. Which was why he'd begun attending that PTSD group. But she'd balked. Then the first set of bags had appeared. He'd updated the SD card, added this letter for her and tried to work the case on his own.

...SINCE YOU'RE READING THIS, I'VE FAILED. I'M SORRY. I KNOW THERE'S enough here to prove in court what you've no doubt already come to realize. Madrigal Medical is as filthy as that hole where we found Saddam—and like those missions in that man's country, our vets are still paying the price. Take this card and use it to do what I wasn't strong enough to do. Make sure you access the comments section in each file's info. When applicable, you'll find more evidence there.

When you're done, promise me you'll focus on yourself. You deserve so much more than what life handed you. My only regret is I didn't just tell you what happened to Max and why, once I discovered it. I know you'll never forgive me, but please find a way to forgive yourself. Kate, if you can become whole again, my death will have meaning.

FIND HAPPINESS,
   Grant

RUGER'S MUZZLE SLIPPED INTO HER LAP, STARTLING HER. KATE thought he needed to go out, until she realized he'd simply left

Liz's side to check on his mistress and make sure she didn't need him more. Kate reached down to hug the Shepherd closer—because she did need him. While Liz slept, she'd been awake, fencing with her demons firsthand, still without so much as a clue as to where Burke had taken Joe.

Unless—

Kate gave Ruger a final squeeze and turned back to her MacBook as he settled down to warm her toes.

Grant had said something about checking the comments section in each photo. Had he been referring to each file's "Get Info" window where she, Liz and Dan would paste lyrics when they emailed each other music in high school?

Kate closed the text file, and right-clicked on the closest JPEG file. Scrolling down the dialogue box that appeared, she clicked on "Get Info". Sure enough, the JPEG's comments section contained information Grant had deemed important about that specific photo. The discovery jumpstarted her hope. She scrolled back to the first file in the collection and began checking the JPEGs that looked as if they might help her locate Joe. A solid hour and several hundred photos later, she hit on an honest-to-God lead.

Not only did Madrigal own a clinic in a smaller town between Braxton and Little Rock, Woodgrove was off the beaten path. According to the qualifying information Grant had added, the building served as the after-hours setting for VitaCell's tissue recovery "clean room".

Had Burke found it?

He must have. He'd tracked his targets' movements so closely, he'd managed to kidnap both Grant and Joe as they left her house—the latter with half her department several hundred yards away, still working the former's body dump. What better place for Burke to kill his first three victims and end the life of the Army investigator responsible for murdering his friend than the spot where Grant had slaughtered countless other vets?

Kate grabbed her phone, and this time, she did dial Lou. Unfortunately, her call went to voicemail—as did her subsequent calls to Seth and Agent Walker.

The warrant.

She checked her watch. Sure enough, she'd made her discovery on the cusp of the search of the pet crematorium and its vast property. The men and women on that team were on radio silence and would remain so until they'd breached the facility and cleared every inch of potential threats to their lives.

She had two choices. She could sit here and watch Liz sleep as she waited for the comm blackout to end. Or she could arm herself to the teeth and go save Joe. At the moment, she wasn't convinced he deserved it. But she'd made her choice. Murderous bastard or not, the man Burke was about to kill was *her* former brother-in-arms. They'd had each other's backs for over a decade. She'd save Joe one more time.

And then she'd toss his ass in prison.

For life.

18

TWENTY MINUTES and almost as many miles later, Kate took the I-40 exit that led to the outskirts of Woodgrove. As usual, Ruger was at her side, riding shotgun in the Durango. She wasn't convinced the Shepherd had understood the need to quietly gather supplies before slipping out of the house, but he'd complied. For that, she was grateful.

Liz had begun to stir while she'd penned a note on an oversized yellow sticky, asking her friend to make sure Lou received the attached envelope and micro SD card if she failed to return. Fortunately, the woman had drifted into a deeper sleep by the time Kate had donned her uniform and grabbed her rifle and an extra clip for her Glock, along with several other critical items.

Even so, she hadn't risked calling Lou back to leave a detailed voice message regarding the night's latest discoveries and her pending plans until the SUV had cleared the drive.

Ruger's soft, questioning whine filled the SUV as Kate slowed for their next turn.

"Soon, buddy. Soon."

According to her GPS unit, they were less than a mile from that clinic. Hopefully, the directions spouting from her dash were sound, because even without the dense cloud cover, this section of Woodgrove would've been darker than a moonless night on the Hindu Kush. The topography was almost as bad, little more than a tree-packed stretch of ancient blacktop with the occasional clapboard house tucked far enough from the road that no one would've heard the Durango, had they even been awake.

Another turn, and the lighting and topography hadn't improved, but it didn't matter.

They'd arrived.

Kate scanned the 1970s ranch-style clinic as she drove past, noting the faint glow bleeding through the blinds of the window on the far left, as if a room beyond was occupied.

She pulled off the road and killed the headlights as she tucked the Durango in a copse of trees. Ruger was well behaved enough to wait patiently as she bailed out to retrieve her dad's old .30-30 Winchester rifle from the rear seat, before concealing her backup .38 handgun and spare munitions.

She silenced her phone. "Ready, boy?"

His soft *chuff* matched her whisper.

"Okay, let's go. Ruger, close; quiet."

His demeanor changed with the official commands, becoming tense and hyper-vigilant as he complied.

Kate shifted the Winchester to her right hand, carrying the rifle low and loose as she took off toward the clinic. The running shoes she'd donned in place of her usual boots turned out to be a wise choice. Rubber soles made the trek swifter and quieter than it would otherwise have been.

Ruger kept pace easily, slowing with her as they rounded the corner of the building. A black Explorer sat parked near what appeared to be the clinic's only rear door.

Adrenaline surged as Kate reached the SUV. Not only was the grill still warm to the touch, a blue and white handicapped parking tag hung from the rearview mirror. But the most promising discovery? The generous smear of blood at the front of the driver's headrest.

No soldier worth his Special Forces tab, let alone horrifically hard-earned Purple Heart, would trust his enemy at the wheel of his getaway vehicle. Which meant Joe had gotten in a whack of his own somewhere between that struggle in her woods and now.

But was it enough to give her the edge?

It just might be, because when she pulled on the paddle handle of the clinic's rear door, it gave.

A trap? Or had Burke's brain been rattled enough that he'd accidentally left it unlocked?

She had no choice but to hope for the latter as she quietly stationed Ruger outside the door and ordered him to stay. Ruger wasn't happy, but he complied as she eased the door open just far enough for her to slip inside. She'd entered the rear of what appeared to be the clinic's empty waiting room. There was enough light spilling down the hall to illuminate a waist-high reception counter and several clusters of chairs intended for patients and loved ones.

And she could hear voices.

Relief burned in as Kate recognized both Burke's and Joe's. The vet sounded pissed. Joe was pleading, then shamelessly wheedling, before suggesting an outcome to the night's events and the entire Madrigal investigation that turned her stomach.

"Think about it, man. I'm still CID, and I have connections beyond the Army. Connections that are *very* high up. I can make sure no one tracks you down. Ever. Hell, I can make sure Madrigal tosses in enough money for a comfortable life in the Caribbean. They won't even argue. You just—"

"—aren't interested. Listen, asshole. Not only do I have zero illusions as to how this is gonna end, I don't give a shit. I never have. Hell, *Agent* Cordoba, I welcome it. Like you, I once swore an oath to defend my country against all enemies, foreign and domestic. I never realized I'd have to take the second half of that promise so goddamned literally. So quit sniveling and let's get this done. 'Cause I am more than ready to finish this."

Like it or not, that was her cue.

A stealthy advance on another room, four years and half the globe away, knotted along Kate's nerves as she tightened her grip on the rifle and crept down the hall.

At least this time, she was better armed.

Unfortunately, she still found an old friend kneeling on the floor at the opposite end as she peered around the door. Gleaming tiles formed the basis of the bare-bones surgical suite surrounding Joe and Thomas Burke. Joe's hands were behind his back, probably zip cuffed, though she couldn't be sure from this angle. She could, however, make out the set of high-end metal prosthetics that allowed Burke to stand behind Joe as the vet shoved a stack of gauze pads into the CID agent's mouth with his left hand.

To the right of both men stood a wheeled hospital gurney...and a dangling nylon noose supported by a strut exposed though missing ceiling tiles.

"Hello, Kate. I'm glad you could join us."

She stepped into the doorway, deliberately ignoring the terror flitting through Joe's dark brown eyes as she sighted the rifle's sights in on the head above and behind his. She couldn't afford the distraction. "Don't think I won't pull the trigger."

Burke actually laughed as he secured Joe's gag with a strip of surgical gauze—again, with his left hand. "Oh, I know you will. Which is why I should point out that I've got the muzzle of my trusty 9mm welded to the back of Agent Cordoba's skull." He shoved Joe's head far enough forward with that same muzzle for her to verify his story, and the zip cuffs. "Now, lay that rifle down, nice and gentle, and kick it to me."

She did as ordered. The Winchester hadn't been central to her plan, anyway.

"Excellent. Next, reach inside your jacket and slowly do the same with the Glock in your shoulder holster."

Again, she complied. Neither had the Glock.

"Now your .38 backup."

Shit. That had.

"I don't—"

"It's strapped to your right calf. No, I can't see it from this angle. But if you wore it into that hospital cafeteria, you're wearing it now."

For the third time, she did as ordered—though decidedly more grudgingly than she had the first two.

"And now, finally, the blade. According to Max, you like to keep the pretty little thing strapped to the same leg, but a bit higher up. Mid-thigh, if I remember correctly."

No doubt about *his* memories.

Kate bit down on another, darker curse as she unsheathed the slender blade in question and sent it skittering across the tiles where it spun to a halt amid the now-completed nest of her weapons. She hadn't felt this naked since she'd woken up in that vile, mud-brick hovel.

Thank you, Max—not.

Still, there was hope.

The blow Joe had landed on Burke had definitely been productive—for her. She'd yet to catch a glimpse of the back of Burke's head, but the collar and shoulders of his gray sweatshirt were stained red—and with this much light, she could tell his pupils were uneven. His right was pinpointed.

Burke was concussed.

According to her Army first aid briefings, the damage from TBIs was often cumulative.

But was his latest severe enough to give her the edge here, now, and while she was woefully unarmed?

As Burke shifted—and swayed ever so slightly—she realized it just might.

The man might've jogged through the Madrigal CEO's yard and her own woods quickly and steadily enough to evade capture, but he was experiencing issues with balance now. All she had to do was bide her time and her patience. Wait for the perfect moment. Until then, she'd try reason.

"Tom, you have to let him go."

Her use of Burke's real name earned her a genuine smile, but then he shrugged. "Why? You do know the reason he's here. You must. You made it here in time for the righteous denouement. That means you've pieced together the rest of the case—and your memories. He killed Tanner and he killed Max. He facilitated a shitload of other murders too, and looked the other way on even more. Good ol' Joe. He might not have committed them all personally, but he's the reason those vets are dead, along with the rest of those men in that ambush of yours."

"I know. But this isn't the answer."

"Sure it is. I don't know about you, but I'm an Old Testament man. An eye for an eye. Or in this case, a pancreas and a set of kidneys for— Well, you've finally got all your bullets located, polished up and tucked back in your mental magazine; you get the idea."

"I do." Just as she'd also finally realized why Max had been so determined to get her outside the wire before he laid everything out for her. She'd assumed Max had been worried about another doctor or the coroner overhearing their conversation.

He had been.

But Max had also been worried about Joe.

"Then I take it that you're good to go regarding tonight's mission?"

"No."

The rage Burke had been keeping at bay flashed through his eyes, darkening them, even the one with the constricted pupil. "*No?*"

"Don't you see? Tom, it doesn't matter what you or I want. What matters is what Tanner and Max would've wanted."

Burke stepped so close to Joe, he shoved the agent's torso forward a good forty-five degrees. Unfortunately, that 9mm was still fused to her former partner's scalp. "How the fuck would you know what Tanner would want?"

Kate held her ground and unloaded the only ammo she had left: the truth. "I know because I just spent half the night reading his record. Staff Sergeant Holmes was an outstanding soldier. Sharp, motivated, someone who got the job done, no matter the odds against him. But he was also compassionate, extremely so. I read his letters of commendation, including the one that detailed how your friend motivated his entire company—when he was just a private, mind you—to get tissue-typed on the slimmest of chances that one of those men would be able to donate bone marrow to another private's toddler. Would a man like that want a fellow soldier—no matter how screwed up that soldier is—to die?" She flung her hand toward the dangling noose. "And like that?"

Kate rode the doubt she saw creeping into Burke's face and edged closer. "Tom, there are other ways to gain justice. Better ways. I know you know Grant had regrets. He had to have shared them with you while you prepared to do what you did. And I know he forgave you—because he couldn't forgive himself. But he did something right. Grant has been amassing evidence against Madrigal Medical and VitaCell Tissues. He'd planned on blowing the whistle. I have that evidence in my possession, and it's ironclad. There's no need to kill Agent Cordoba. He's going to jail. And when the truth comes out, there will be justice for Tanner and Max and the rest of those men who died in that ambush—and for the soldiers and vets who died before and since."

For a moment, perhaps two, she thought she'd gotten through to him. That she'd reached the man Thomas Burke used to be before that IED had stolen his legs and his ability to reason clearly.

Then it was gone, and he was shaking his head.

"Sorry, Kate. I tried it your way in Afghanistan. You know better than anyone how well that worked out. It took three years to get things set up here. Had to start with learning to walk again. And, yeah, things got a bit graphic this week. But it had to be. I couldn't afford for everything to get swept under the rug. These people, they had enough power to do it once. They'd find a way to do it again. Hell, they're so fucked up, they were issuing certificates for those organs and tissues they stole from vets and pricing them accordingly, like they were jewelers rating a bunch of goddamned gemstones for auction. Puts a whole new shade on 'Thank you for your service', don't you agree?"

She did.

But before she could do so out loud, Burke shrugged. "Don't worry. There's a package on its way to you from me too. You'll see what I mean when you open it. But know this now: I don't regret what I've done, not even to Parish. Yeah, he had his come-to-Jesus moment. But it was too little, too late. Irony is, I'd planned on framing him and slipping away when it was done. If you haven't found the tire on the Land Rover in his dad's barn— the one that matches the tread impressions I left out by your cabin and where I put Dunne's body—you will. I thought about leaving a third impression, but Max swore you were the best. So

I kept the faith that you'd find 'em—especially after you came across me in the midst of planting the one at your cabin."

"I found them."

That earned her a weirdly proud smile. "See? Max was right. By the way, I wouldn't have hit you. If you hadn't jumped out of the way, I'd have swerved."

Given all that had happened, she actually believed him.

She stopped at the corner of the gurney and tucked her fingers beneath the edge. "Why'd you change your mind about framing Grant?"

Another shrug—but that 9mm didn't budge. "No need." Burke clipped his chin down toward Joe. "I had plans to go after this bastard next. Arrange his 'accidental' death, along with a few, final others. But the good Lord must be on my side, because Agent Cordoba did me the courtesy of showing up here in Braxton. And there was that damned doc. I watched you two together, especially that last time in your drive. Deep down, you knew Parish was bad news. Hell, even your dog knew it. What with your memory not cooperating, I figured I'd take care of things for you. Drop two birds with one shot. Get Parish out of your life for good, even as I used his parts to try and jolt that stubborn brain of yours one last time. And it worked."

It had.

And she'd found her moment. Burke was just distracted enough for her to make her move. Kate tightened her grip on the gurney, but before she could shove it forward, she realized Ruger had disobeyed her order to stay.

Worse, the Shepherd had used his refrigerator-opening skills on the clinic's back door.

She could hear the light *snick, snick* of Ruger's claws as he tiptoed up the hall.

Unfortunately, so could Burke. Grabbing Joe by the neck,

Burke dragged the agent along the tiles as he swerved past her left side to slam the door in Ruger's face.

The Shepherd snarled and bellowed with rage as he threw his body against the door, but it didn't budge.

And then—silence.

She thought she caught another string of snicks, followed by the thump and swish of Ruger pushing through the clinic's door, but she was too busy concentrating on Burke to worry about the Shepherd's destination. Burke had swung Joe around by his neck a second time, forcing her former friend to meet her gaze as the vet half-stumbled, half-lurched the two of them back to that dangling noose.

Burke's balance might be compromised, but his determination held firm as he whirled about to face her. "We're done chatting now, Kate. I hate to point out the obvious, but you're either with me in this, or you're not. And you'd better make your decision quick, because that mutt of yours is getting testy. I'd hate to have to take care of him too."

She took the threat to Ruger as seriously as she took the proximity of that Glock's muzzle to Joe's head. While she had a decent enough understanding of Ruger to know why he'd disobeyed her and opened the door to come inside, she had no idea why he'd given up so easily and left. It wasn't like him.

Had Lou arrived?

Unfortunately, no. Kate bit back her shock as she spotted the now-muted Shepherd. Ruger was outside, at the clinic's window, behind both men. She could make out the dog's golden irises between the slats of the vinyl mini blinds, darting up and down, left and right, as if he was actually casing the room.

"Well?"

Stall—at least until she'd figured out what Ruger was doing —and how to use it. If what the Shepherd saw pissed him off enough, he just might throw himself against that window as he had in her Durango during that impromptu traffic stop the year before. And that might be enough to startle Burke.

Ruger accomplished the task for her, though not the way she'd thought. The sound of his snout bumping into the window was enough to cause Burke to swing his head around. Kate capitalized on the distraction and shoved the gurney forward. It clipped Burke's left hip, causing the vet to stumble and spin into the right wall of the room before he hit the floor.

But as Burke came up, so did Joe.

Her former partner must've grabbed her knife when Burke had dragged him back to that rope.

He'd severed his zip cuffs.

"No!"

But Joe had already retrieved her rifle.

Glass exploded into the room, along with those broken blinds—and Ruger. A split second later, Kate felt more than heard the Winchester's sharp report as she lunged forward. She jerked to a stop as she realized Ruger had beaten her to Joe. Ruger tore his snarling jaws from the agent's shredded and bleeding elbow to re-clamp them around Joe's throat as he knocked the agent to the floor atop those broken blinds.

Kate grabbed her Glock from the pile of glass as she kicked the rifle and remaining weapons across the room, including Burke's own 9mm. Leaning down, her upper right arm began to burn as she snapped her steel cuffs around Joe's wrists. She left the gauze gag in place as she checked Ruger over.

His hide was nicked and oozing blood in a few spots but, otherwise, he was fine. And royally pissed at Joe—who he still held pinned to the floor with his snarling jaws.

"Ruger, guard!"

She spun around to find Burke braced against the wall behind the gurney. Before she could roll it out of the way to cuff Burke with the spare zips in her pocket, he began to slide, leaving a telling swath of glistening scarlet down the wall as his body slipped lower and lower.

"Oh, Jesus." Kate grabbed a stack of the trauma pads from the counter and shoved the gurney aside. She caught Burke's arm as he settled heavily on the floor. "You've been hit!"

He nodded. "Appears so." His left hand came up to finger the seeping hole in the right sleeve of her Braxton PD jacket. It explained why her upper arm was aching like hell. "You, too. Looks like we got another two-for-one special going on this weekend."

"Shut up." Because that pinpointed pupil wasn't the vet's only problem now. His skin was turning deathly pale. The hell with her arm, Burke was losing blood and a lot more of it than she was based on the amount of scarlet coating the wall behind his back. Kate yanked the hem of his sweatshirt up so she could assess the situation.

It wasn't good.

The bullet that had passed through the flesh of her throbbing arm had gone on to strike Burke in the middle of his chest. A dark-pink froth was foaming up from the resulting hole. Worse, his ribs were expanding less and less with each breath.

"Staff Sergeant, you've got a sucking chest wound."

The froth bubbled and hissed as he managed a soft laugh. "Is that all?"

By itself, it was bad enough—but, *no*. The trauma pads she'd tucked against his back were already soaked. Something else had been nicked too. Something even more serious than a lung. If not his heart, one of those "damned vital tubes" as Max had termed them, running in or out of it.

Kate holstered her Glock and grabbed her phone. Before she could dial 911, Burke's hand closed over hers.

She tried to work her fingers free, but his wouldn't budge. "Tom, listen to me. We might be in a clinic, but you need someone who knows what the hell to do with all this gear that's lying around—and *soon*."

He shook his head. "Just let me go. Please. It's gonna happen anyway. I can feel it." He glanced at Joe, still pinned to the floor by a vigilant Ruger. "Consider it a trade. Though why, I'm not sure. That bastard was aiming for you, not me."

"I know." So had Ruger. That was why he'd crashed though that window when he had.

She also knew that Max had noted Joe's name in the Tanner Holmes desertion investigation all those years ago when he'd been looking into the staff sergeant's death for Burke. Max would've known then that Joe was either incompetent—or involved. And he, too, had known Joe well enough to know it wasn't the former.

But she didn't want to talk about Joe right now; she didn't even want to think about him. He wasn't worth it.

But Burke was.

She tried to tug her fingers from Burke's once more. And, once more, Burke tightened his.

"Please...let me try."

"It's too late. I'm already cold. Just sit here with me, okay?"

She opened her mouth to argue—shout, if need be. Then she closed it. He was right. She could feel the ice spreading though his fingers. See the light dimming in those uneven eyes.

His hand left hers, shaking slightly as it came up to cup her cheek and wipe away the tears she hadn't even realized were sliding down. "Hey, none of that. You were right. This end is more fitting. I'd planned on stringing him up and gutting him, the way they did Tanner. But you can use him. He's still got his wife to worry about. I wouldn't have killed her. Not even after I finished with him. It would've been like murdering a piece of Tanner, you know?"

"Yeah, I know."

Burke nodded. "Use her against him. Make Cordoba testify against the rest of those bastards. Just promise me two things, okay? Clear Tanner's record. Make sure the whole fucking world knows he wasn't a deserter."

"I will. I swear it."

He gave her another nod, but this one was slow and uneven. Frighteningly so.

Despite everything that had happened, she wasn't ready to let him go. "Tom, you mentioned two promises. What else do you need?"

"You. I need you to live, Kate. Really live. Max's death was not your fault. I tried to tell you that over there, in that padded room where they stuck you and again this morning in that diner. But I couldn't get through. You've got to find a way to let the past go. Forgive yourself. I know I'm asking a hell of a lot. But Max? If anyone's responsible for his death, it's me. I got him involved. I just couldn't believe Tanner would desert, so I tracked down a mortuary affairs specialist I knew at Dover. The guy was there when Tanner's body was flown back to the States. I guess I just needed a set of eyes I trusted to sign off on Tanner's death, ya know? Except he told me something didn't look right. He'd spotted several scalpel-like cuts in the scorched mess they made of Tanner's innards—but he was ordered to leave before he could investigate. So when I got sent back over there, I brought his suspicions to Max. I begged Max to look into it. B-believe me, the doc would not have wanted you to spend your life flogging yourself for something you couldn't have prevented. T-trust m-me."

Panic surged through her body as Burke seemed to run out of steam. And then his breath caught, before ceasing for several terrifying moments. His lungs started up again on a stunted cough, but the man's breathing was painfully shallow now.

His lips were beyond blue.

Damn it, she just couldn't sit here and watch him die.

She tugged her fingers from his, intent on retrieving her driver's license and a credit card from her wallet. Sealing the plastic to his entrance and exit wounds just might give him enough of a reprieve so she could convince him—

"*No.*" His hand flailed as he tried to retrieve hers. "Please. I meant what I said. It's too damned late for me. But not for you. Let me finish. I won't get another chance."

The tears clogged her throat as she nodded. She returned her hand to his chest. Allowed him to grab on and hold it, as she held onto him while he gathered his remaining strength.

"It's true, Kate. Max's death is on *me.* He called to tell me the Dover specialist was right. And that he'd found something else. Someone. He said he needed to bring you in on it. But I was on a mission when he called. So he left that vague voicemail instead of the proof he'd found—and Cordoba's name. I got back an hour after that ambush. I went looking for you guys the second I heard his message. I found that compound. But I was too late. Max and the others were already dead. And you were gone. But I saw those bastards' bodies in that hovel. I know what happened. There is no blessed way you could've saved him. *None.* So do both Max and m-me a favor. Save yourself."

"Tom—"

"*No.*" He struggled through several more shallow coughs. They finally eased, but there was blood trickling from the corner of his mouth now. Steadily. "The only word I want from you is *yes.* Promise me you'll take that Silver Star out of your trunk. Mount it on the goddamned wall. That thing is proof you made it out in one piece. There aren't nearly enough soldiers who can say that. And, yeah, I know...I know it won't ch-change...overnight."

Her heart clenched as his voice broke, before slipping into a whisper. She cupped her free hand to his face and cradled it as she leaned closer to catch the rest.

"You're gonna have to w-work h-hard, but you'll get there. You're tough, Chief. I believe in you. Don't ever...d-don't *ever* forget that."

She managed a nod. Her throat was so raw and thick, she couldn't speak. She wasn't sure he'd caught the motion before his lashes drifted down, so she sealed his palm to the scars that covered the right side of her face and nodded again, but it was too late.

Burke was dead.

She wasn't sure how long she sat there in the stark silence, listening to her own heart thumping beneath the occasional, muted growl from a still pissed-off Ruger guarding Joe behind her.

Eventually, the sirens overtook both. Lou must've turned on his phone and gotten her message.

Once again, the cavalry had arrived. But this time, it was just too goddamned late.

THE PACKAGE BURKE HAD REFERENCED IN THE CLINIC ARRIVED BY courier the following morning. Between Grant's photos, the cellphones Burke had culled from his victims and the four-year diary which detailed the vet's recovery and growing desire for revenge—along with every unsavory fact Burke had managed to uncover about Madrigal Medical and VitaCell Tissue's side businesses—they were able to take down the entire grisly operation, including a US senator and federal appeals court justice.

Joe hadn't been exaggerating; he could've pulled off Burke's disappearance and funded a Caribbean retirement to boot. As it was, the former CID agent was on his way to the US Disciplinary Barracks at Fort Leavenworth. Joe had copped a plea, trading his freedom to assure Elise's.

Kate hadn't bothered to stop in and see him off.

As for Lou, he'd finally stopped yelling at her when he'd realized both she and Ruger required a few stitches.

Almost two weeks later, they were both healing nicely, and Kate was well on her way to making good on her first promise to Thomas Burke. The Army was in the midst of clearing Staff Sergeant Holmes' name and posthumous reputation. Even better, Holmes' remains were on track to be excavated and reinterred at Arlington before the year was out. She'd had Burke's ashes scattered over the countryside as per the request Burke had also enclosed in the package he'd mailed to her.

As for her second promise—

Kate stared at the pair of black coffins in front of her. The closer one belonged to Grant, the farther one to Abel. The funeral had finished an hour ago. The minister, Lou, Seth and the rest of the department had left soon after—including, to Kate's surprise, Detective Arash Moradi from Mazelle.

Liz was still at her side though.

Along with Kate's guilt.

She wasn't sure she possessed the strength to turn around, walk out of the graveyard, climb into her waiting Durango and make good on that second promise to Burke.

But she had to try.

"It's almost eleven. I could use some lunch. Interested?"

Kate shook her head. But she did look up and finally meet her friend's reddened stare. "I have something I need to take care of. How about dinner later tonight? My place, say around six?"

"You bet." Liz smiled, carefully linking arms with Kate's rapidly healing one as they turned together to cross the cemetery so the men waiting to finish with the graves could take over. "But only if I get to cook."

Kate laughed. It came out rusty, but it felt good. "On behalf of Ruger—and especially Ruger's stomach—I accept."

After all, the Shepherd was the real hero of it all.

They reached the parking lot all too quickly. Kate was grateful when Liz paused beside the Durango.

It forced her to get inside and start the engine.

She pulled out of the lot, setting aside her memories of Grant and Abel as she reached the highway. She'd honored the good times while she was at their funeral, but it was time to let both men go—and let Max back in.

The night Burke had died, she'd returned home from that clinic to find a seriously stressed-out Liz sitting on her couch and Max's records in the inbox on her computer, still unopened. Once Liz had calmed down and left to check in on her dad, Kate had finally faced the write-up for that fateful day four years ago. Attached to the write-up had been a transcript of the video the terrorists had been making when she'd stumbled into that room moments before Max's beheading.

Burke was right. As much as she hated to admit it, there wasn't anything she could've done to save her friend. But somehow, the knowledge hadn't helped.

Maybe Liz and Burke were right, and what she was about to do today would help. At the very least, it might give her a place to start.

Kate turned off the highway as she reached Little Rock. Several more turns and she arrived at her destination: Fort Leaves.

Scraping together her courage and her nerves, she parked the Durango in the hospital's sparsely populated, Saturday-morning lot and smoothed her fingers over the set of dog tags she'd received two weeks earlier as she got out of the SUV.

With the tags' help—and Max's spirit—the trip into Fort

Leaves and up one of the hospital's main elevators was easier than it had been the first few times she'd been here.

She reached her floor and that outer office before she was ready though, tensing when the door opened before she had a chance to knock. The man she'd come to see stood on the other side, holding that towering, stainless-steel thermos he'd had on his desk two weeks earlier.

His lopsided smile was a bit baffled, but friendly and welcoming. "Deputy Holland. I didn't expect to see you today. Then again, I know from experience how things can crop up during the course of an investigation, even on a weekend."

"Good morning, Dr. Manning. That's...not why I'm here. The case, that is."

"No?" The shrink's snowy brows shot up, but they were suddenly and embarrassingly full of hope.

It gave her the courage to continue.

Kate nodded at his thermos. "I'm guessing you finished your paperwork. I don't want to hold up your plans—and it is short notice—but...do you have time to talk?"

"Absolutely. Come on in."

The door to the outer office swung wide as Kate took a deep breath and followed the shrink inside.

Thanks so much for reading my work. I hope you enjoyed it! As you know, an author's career is built on reviews. Please take a moment to leave a quick comment or an in-depth review for your fellow readers

HERE.

**Are you ready for
Kate's next gripping adventure?**

IN THE NAME OF:
*He'll do anything for his country
...even murder.*

CLICK HERE for details on IN THE NAME OF, Book 2 in the
Hidden Valor Military/Veterans Suspense Series.

~

Join Candace's list to keep abreast of new release info, special
giveaways & Reader Crew Extras:
CandaceIrving.com/newsletter

DID YOU KNOW?

**I'm also writing an active-duty
Army CID Detective series.**
Here's a sneak peak for

BLIND EDGE
Book 2 in the Deception Point
Military Thriller Series

Prologue

THE BIBLE WAS WRONG. Vengeance didn't belong to the Lord. It belonged to him.

To them.

To the twelve soldiers who'd stumbled out of that dank, icy cave, each as consumed as he was by the malevolence that had been carved into their souls. A second later, the night breeze shifted—and he caught a whiff of *him*. He couldn't be sure if that rotting piece of camel dung had been left behind as a lookout or if the bastard was part of a squad waiting to ambush his team. When the combined experiences of countless covert missions locked in, allowing him to place the stench wafting down along with stale sweat and pure evil, he no longer cared. Because once again, he smelled blood.

Fresh blood.

It permeated the air outside the cave, as did the need for retribution. As his fellow soldiers faded into the wind-sheared boulders, he knew they felt it too.

By God, they would all taste it.

Soon.

He shot out on point. There was no need to glance behind as he reached the base of the cliff and shouldered his rifle. His team had followed, protecting his back as they'd done every op these past months. The trust freed him to focus on their unspoken mission. On the blood pooling around seven bodies laid out on the floor of that cavern, and then some. He tucked the blade of his knife between his teeth and began to climb. Rock tore at his fingers as he jammed them into crevice after crevice, causing his own blood to mingle with the death still staining his hands. Moments later, he stopped, locking the toes of his boots to a narrow ledge as he scanned the dark.

Nothing.

He resumed his climb. The same moonless night that cloaked his prey protected him and his team. As long as they were mute, they were safe. Unless—

Shit!

He froze as the wind shifted, shooting his own stench heavenward. He caught the answering scuffle of panicked boots.

Too late, bastard.

He was almost there.

His position compromised, he grabbed a scrub pine, using it to whiplash up the remaining three feet of cliff.

Loose rock bit into his soles, causing him to skid to a halt two yards from his prey. The wind shifted once more, whipping a filthy turban from the bastard's face. A second later, he was staring into pure, bearded hatred as an AK47 rifle swung up. He grabbed his knife and lunged forward. Blood gushed over his knuckles as he buried the blade to its hilt. He hauled the bastard in closer, staring deep into that blackened gaze, for the first time in his life embracing the carnal satisfaction that seared in on a close-quarters kill—until suddenly, inexplicably, the gaze wavered...then slowly disintegrated altogether.

To his horror, it coalesced once more, this time into a soft blue hue he knew all too well.

Sweet Jesus—*no!*

It was a lie. A trick. An illusion. This latest flood of adrenaline had simply been too much to absorb. That was all.

Goddamn it, that was *all.*

He'd never know how he managed to hold his heart together as he released the knife and brought his fingers to his eyes. He rubbed them over and over, praying harder than he'd ever prayed as he sank to his knees. But as he blinked through his tears and forced himself to focus on the river of scarlet gushing into the snow, he knew it was true. The body in his arms wasn't that of his enemy. Nor was he in some freezing mountain pass half a world away. He was in his own backyard.

And he'd just murdered the woman he loved.

～

Now I lay me down to sleep,
  I pray the Lord my soul to keep.

If I should kill before I wake,
   I pray the Lord it's my enemy I take.

Chapter 1

Military Police Station
   Fort Campbell, Kentucky
   US Army Special Agent Regan Chase stared at the five-foot fir anchoring the corner of the deserted lounge. A rainbow of ornaments dangled from the tree's artificial limbs along with hundreds of twinkling lights, each doing its damnedest to infect her with an equally artificial promise of home, hearth and simpering happiness. Fifteen months ago, she might've succumbed. Tonight, that phony fir simply underscored the three tenets of truth Regan had crashed into at the tender age of six. One, no one sat around the North Pole stuffing sacks with free toys. Two, reindeer couldn't fly. And three, if there ever had been some jolly old geezer looking out for the boys and girls of the world, he'd been fired for incompetence a long time ago.

The current proof was handcuffed to a stall in the military police station's latrine, attempting to purge what appeared to be an entire fifth of nauseatingly ripe booze. Unfortunately, the majority of the alcohol had long since made it into the man's bloodstream. Even more unfortunate, Regan had no idea whose bloodstream said booze was currently coursing through.

Not only had their drunken John Doe been arrested sans driver's license and military ID, he'd stolen the pickup he'd used in tonight's carnage.

Regan turned her back on the tree and headed for the coffee table at the rear of the lounge, sighing as she sank into one of the vinyl chairs. She reached past a bowl of cellophane-wrapped candy canes to snag the stack of photos she'd queued into the duty sergeant's printer upon her arrival. The close-up of the stolen pickup's silver grill splattered with blood flaunted its own obscene contribution to the night's festivities. The scarlet slush adhering to the tires beneath provided even more proof of yet another Christmas shot to hell.

Make that crushed.

Regan studied the remaining dozen photos. From the angle and depth of the furrows running the length of the snowy street, John Doe hadn't tried to slow down, much less swerve. Instead, he'd plowed into a trio of teenagers making the rounds of Fort Campbell's senior officer housing and belting out carols to the commanding general himself. One of the boys had suffered a broken leg. Another had dislocated his shoulder as he'd tried to wrench his younger brother out of the way of the truck's relentless headlights. Unfortunately, he'd failed.

As far as Regan knew, the kid was still in surgery.

She should phone the hospital. Find out if he'd made it to recovery. She was about to retrieve her cellphone when the door opened. A lanky, red-haired specialist strode in, a ring-sized, gift-wrapped box in his left hand, the naked fingers of a curvaceous blond in his right.

The specialist paused as he spotted Regan. Flushed. "Sorry, Chief. Thought the lounge was vacant."

He held his breath as he waited. Regan knew why. She'd transferred to Fort Campbell's Criminal Investigation Division two weeks earlier. Not quite long enough for the resident military policemen to know if CID's newest investigator had a poker up her ass regarding midnight rendezvous while on duty, even on holidays.

Regan scooped the photos off the table, tucking them into the oversized cargo pocket on the thigh of her camouflaged Army Combat Uniform as she stood. She scanned the name tag on the soldier's matching ACUs as she grabbed her parka and patrol cap. "It's all yours, Specialist Jasik. I was about to leave for the hospital."

Why not?

She wouldn't be getting a decent statement until their drunken Doe sobered up. Given the stunning 0.32 the man had blown on their breathalyzer, that would be a good eight hours, at least. If the man didn't plunge into a coma first.

Jasik relaxed. He led the blond to the couch as Regan passed. "Thanks, Chief. And Merry Christmas."

Regan peeled back the velcroed grosgrain covering of her combat watch and glanced at the digital readout: 0003. So it was —all three minutes of it. Though what was so merry about it, she had no idea. But that was her problem. Or so she'd been told.

Regan returned the salutation anyway, donning her camouflaged parka and cap as she departed the lounge. Nodding to the duty sergeant, she pushed the glass doors open. Icy wind whipped across a freshly salted walk, kicking up snowflakes from the two-foot banks scraped to the sides. The flakes stung her eyes and chapped her cheeks as she passed a pair of recently de-iced police cruisers at the head of the dimly lit lot.

By the time Regan reached her Explorer, she was looking forward to the impromptu hospital visit. It would give her a chance to stop by the ER and commiserate with Gil. Like her, he had a habit of volunteering for Christmas duty.

For an entirely different reason, though.

Regan unlocked her SUV. Exhaust plumed as she started the engine. Grabbing her ice scraper from the door, she cleared the latest layer of snow from her front windshield. She was finishing the rear when an ear-splitting wail rent the air.

Ambulance. On post.

Judging from its Doppler, it was headed away from the hospital.

The police station's door whipped open, confirming her hunch. A trio of ACU-clad military policemen vaulted into the night, their combat boots thundering down the salted walk. The first two MPs peeled off and piled into the closest de-iced cruiser. The third headed straight for her.

Regan recognized the soldier's tall, ebony frame: Staff Sergeant Otis T. Wickham.

They'd met in front of their drunken Doe's blood-splattered pickup, where they'd also reached the conclusion that Doe's intended target did indeed appear to be the trio of caroling kids and not the commanding general. One look at the tension locking the MP's jaw as he reached her side told her that whatever had gone down was bad.

He popped a salute. "Evenin', Chief. There's been a stabbing in Stryker Housing. Victim's a woman. The captain wants you there. No specifics, but it's gotta be bad. The husband called it in. Man's Special Forces—and he was downright frantic."

Regan tossed the ice scraper inside the Explorer. "Get in."

Wickham wedged his bulk into her passenger seat as she hit the emergency lights and peeled out after the shrieking cruiser. They fishtailed onto Forest Road, neither of them speaking. It was for the best. Four-wheel drive or not, it took all her concentration to keep up with the cruiser as they reached the entrance to Fort Campbell's snowbound Stryker Family Housing. The strobes of the now-silent ambulance bathed the neighborhood in an eerily festive red, ushering them to a cookie-cutter brick-and-vinyl duplex at the end of the street.

Regan brought the SUV to a halt within kissing distance of the cruiser and killed her siren.

Doors slammed as she and the MPs bailed out.

She recognized the closest as the gift-bearing soldier from

the lounge. Specialist Jasik had traded the curvaceous blond for a black, thirty-something private. Staff Sergeant Wickham motioned Jasik to his side. The private headed for the end of the drive to round up the pajama-clad rubberneckers. Life-saving gear in hand, a trio of paramedics waited impatiently for the official all-clear from the MPs.

Regan withdrew her 9mm Sig Sauer from its holster at her outer right thigh as Wickham and Jasik retrieved their M9s before killing the volume on their police radios. Save for the crush of snow, silence reigned as they approached the duplex. A life-sized Santa cutout decorated the front door. A cursory glance at the knob revealed no obvious sign of forced entry. The brass plate above the mail slot provided a name and a rank: Sergeant Patrick Blessing.

Regan moved to the right of Santa's corpulent belly as Wickham assumed the left. Jasik was moving into position when the door opened.

Three 9mms whipped up, zeroed in.

A woman froze in the entryway. Roughly five feet tall, Hispanic, mid-twenties. She was dressed in a long-sleeved pink flannel nightgown and fleece-lined moccasins. Given her wide eyes and rigid spine, she was more startled than they. But she wasn't Mrs. Blessing. Though her cuffs were splattered with blood, the woman appeared uninjured. Definitely not stabbed.

She swallowed firmly. "She—uh—Danielle's out back. I live next door. My husband's a medic." Her voice dropped to a whisper. "He's with them now."

Regan lowered her Sig. The MPs followed suit as the woman waved them in.

Regan tipped her head toward Wickham. She might be senior in rank, but right now, she was junior to the staff sergeant's on-post experience. That included knowledge of Stryker's floor plans. Protocol dictated they assume the suspect was on the premises, possibly controlling the actions of the medic's wife—and search accordingly.

Wickham clipped a nod as he and Jasik headed down the hall.

Regan caught the neighbor's gaze. "Stay here."

The relief swirling into her tear-stained face assured Regan she would. The woman had already seen more than she wanted, and it had shaken her to her core. As Regan passed through the kitchen to join Wickham and Jasik at the sliding glass door in the dining room, she realized why the neighbor was so rattled.

They all did.

They'd found Mrs. Blessing. She was twenty feet away, lying in the snow on her back, clad in a sleeveless, floral nightgown bunched beneath her breasts. Like her neighbor, Danielle was delicate, dark-haired and—despite the gray cast to her flesh—almost painfully pretty. But there was nothing pretty about the knife embedded in her belly. Two men knelt along the woman's left. Judging from his sobs, Regan assumed the bare-chested man just past the woman's head, smoothing curls, was her husband. That pegged the man at her torso, leaning over to blow air through her lips, as the medic. Like the husband, the medic had removed his T-shirt. The shirts were packed around the hilt of the knife, immobilizing the blade in a desperate attempt to keep the flow of blood corked. Given the amount of red saturating the cotton, it wasn't working. Danielle Blessing was bleeding out. But that wasn't the worst of it.

She was pregnant.

"*Jesus H. Chri*—" Jasik swallowed the rest.

The MP regained his composure and grabbed his radio to yell for the paramedics as Regan and Wickham shot through the open slider and across the snow. She'd have to trust that Jasik knew enough to secure the interior of the duplex after his call.

Regan dropped to her knees opposite the medic as the man

thumped out a series of chest compressions. Staff Sergeant Wickham was two seconds behind and two inches beside her.

Odds were, they were already too late.

Danielle Blessing's abdomen was extremely distended— even for a third trimester—and rock hard. An oddly sweet odor wafted up from the makeshift packing, mixing with the cloying stench of blood. It was a scent Regan would recognize anywhere: amniotic fluid. Worse, scarlet seeped from between the woman's thighs, pooling amid the snow.

Regan holstered her Sig and ripped off her camouflaged parka. "What have you got?"

The medic looked up. "No breathing, no pulse. Been that way since I got here—six damned minutes ago." The rest was in his eyes. *Hopeless.*

The medic continued thumping regardless. Working around the knife, she and Wickham covered the woman's lower abdomen, thighs and calves with their coats. Danielle's feet were still exposed to the snow and midnight air. Like her face, they were beyond gray.

Regan shook her head as the medic completed his latest round of chest compressions. "I've got it." She sealed her mouth to the woman's lips. They were ice-cold and unresponsive.

Wickham took over the compressions as Regan finished her breaths. But for the husband's raw sobs and Wickham's thumping, silence filled the night.

Two more rounds of breath, and Regan lost her job. So did Wickham. The paramedics had arrived.

Blessing's neighbor dragged the sergeant to his feet as she and Wickham scrambled out of the way. Two of the paramedics dropped their gear and knelt to double-check Danielle's airway and non-existent vitals as a third probed the saturated T-shirts. Ceding to the inevitable, Regan turned toward the duplex. Jasik stood at the kitchen window, his initial search evidently complete.

The MP shook his head. If someone had broken into the Blessings' home, he or she was gone now.

The slider was still open. The medic had reached the snow-covered steps and stood to the left. Sergeant Blessing had turned and slumped down at the top, halfway inside the slider's frame, his naked feet buried in a drift, his dark head bowing over bloodstained hands, and he was shaking.

From grief? Or guilt?

Unfortunately, she knew. As with the icy furrows left by a drunken Doe's stolen pickup, the snow provided the proof.

Footprints.

They covered the yard. But upon their arrival, there'd been but four telling sets. Once Regan eliminated those left by the his-and-her moccasins of the medic and his wife, she was left with a single, composite trail of overlapping, bare footprints. The leading prints were woefully petite; the following, unusually large. Both sets were dug into the snow as if their owners had torn down the slider's steps and across the yard...all the way to where Danielle lay. Finally, there was the blood. Save for the scarlet slush surrounding the body, there was no sign of splatter —at the slider or along the trail.

For some reason, Sergeant Blessing had deliberately chased and *then* stabbed his wife.

Regan turned to Wickham. "I'll take the husband, question him inside. You take the neighbor. Stay out here." She glanced at the paramedics. "They might need to talk to him." Though she doubted it. There was nothing the sergeant could say that would help his wife now.

Danielle Blessing had been placed on a spine board, stripped down to gray, oozing flesh and redressed with several trauma pads. Half a dozen rolls of Kling gauze anchored the pads and the hilt of the knife. As the brawnier of the paramedics finished intubating the woman's throat and began manually pumping oxygen into her lungs via a big valve mask, his female partner attached the leads of a portable electrocardiogram to Danielle's shoulders and left hip.

Silence had long since given way to a calm, steady stream of medical jargon.

"Patient on cardiac monitor."

"IV spiked on blood set. One thousand milliliters NS. Starting second line—LR on a Macro drip, sixteen gauge."

"I still can't get a pulse."

Judging from that last—not to mention the wad of fresh dressing one of the paramedics used to dry off Danielle's chest —the next step involved shocks. In a perfect world, the woman's heart would restart. But the world was far from perfect. Regan had learned that the hard way. Given that this woman's heart had already been subjected to eight-plus minutes of unsuccessful CPR, the odds that she'd recover were all but nonexistent.

Regan shifted her attention to Wickham. "Ready, Staff Sergeant?"

His nod was stoic. But his sigh was resigned. Bitter. "Merry Christmas."

The past crowded in despite Regan's attempts to keep it at bay. She shook it off. "Yeah."

Wickham doffed his camouflaged cap as they headed for the slider. Though his bald scalp was exposed to the winter air, he appeared not to notice. She couldn't seem to feel the cold either. Nor did the medic.

The husband was still staring at his hands, shaking.

Regan exchanged a knowing frown with Wickham as she reached for her handcuffs. Two strides later, the distinctive whine of a cardiac defibrillator charging filled the night.

And then, "*Clear!*"

A dull thud followed.

The shocks had begun. Even if Danielle made it, there was no hope for her baby. If that knife hadn't killed it, the electrical jolts would. Judging by the panic on the husband's face as he shot to his feet, Sergeant Blessing had figured it out.

"Wait!"

The neighbor grabbed Blessing's right arm. Jasik leapt through the open side of the slider and pinned Blessing's left.

"Charging to three hundred."

Blessing thrashed, nearly knocking both his captors to the ground. "Goddamn it! The *baby*—"

"Clear!"

Jasik regained his hold and drove Blessing to his knees, sealing the sergeant's shins to the ground as the paramedics ripped through the final steps of ECG protocol. As they hit three hundred sixty joules—for the third agonizing time—Blessing accepted the inescapable. His wife and child were dead.

He slumped into the snow as Jasik and the neighbor loosened their grips. A soft keening filled the night, laying waste to every one of Regan's meticulously honed defenses.

Her eyes burned. Her heart followed.

She pulled herself together and tossed her handcuffs to Jasik, her unspoken order clear. *Get it over with.*

Jasik caught the cuffs neatly and bent down.

That was as far as he got.

One moment the lanky MP was behind Sergeant Blessing, pushing him to his knees; the next, Blessing had twisted about, bashing his forehead into Jasik's skull.

A sharp grunt filled the air.

Regan caught the flash of blackened metal as Blessing ripped the 9mm from Jasik's holster. She lunged across the remaining three feet of snow, launching herself at Blessing as the weapon's barrel swung up.

She was too late.

The 9mm's retort reverberated through Regan as she and Blessing smashed into the slider.

To continue reading BLIND EDGE
CLICK HERE

MEET THE AUTHOR

CANDACE IRVING is the daughter of a librarian and a retired US Navy chief. Candace grew up in the Philippines, Germany, and all over the United States. Her senior year of high school, she enlisted in the US Army. Following basic training, she transferred to the Navy's ROTC program at the University of Texas-Austin. While at UT, she spent a summer in Washington, DC, as a Congressional Intern. She also worked security for the UT Police.

BA in Political Science in hand, Candace was commissioned as an ensign in the US Navy and sent to Surface Warfare Officer's School to learn to drive warships. From there, she followed her father to sea.

Candace is married to her favorite soldier, a former US Army Combat Engineer. They live in the American Midwest, where the Army/Navy football game is avidly watched and argued over every year.

GO NAVY; BEAT ARMY!

Candace also writes military romantic suspense under the name Candace Irvin—without the "g"!

Email Candace at www.CandaceIrving.com
or connect via:

bookbub.com/profile/candace-irving

facebook.com/CandaceIrvingBooks

twitter.com/candace_irving

goodreads.com/Candace_Irving

ALSO BY CANDACE IRVING

Deception Point Military Detective Thrillers:

AIMPOINT

Has an elite explosives expert turned terrorist? Army Detective Regan Chase is ordered to use her budding relationship with his housemate —John Garrison—to find out. But John is hiding something too. Has the war-weary Special Forces captain been turned as well? As Regan's investigation deepens, lines are crossed—personal and professional. Even if Regan succeeds in thwarting a horrific bombing on German soil, what will the fallout do to her career?

A DECEPTION POINT MILITARY DETECTIVE THRILLER: A REGAN CHASE NOVELLA & BOOK I IN THE SERIES

BLIND EDGE

Army Detective Regan Chase responds to a series of murders and suicides brought on by the violent hallucinations plaguing a Special Forces A-Team—a team led by Regan's ex, John Garrison. Regan quickly clashes with an unforgiving, uncooperative and dangerously secretive John—and an even more secretive US Army. What really happened during that Afghan cave mission? As Regan pushes for answers, the murders and suicides continue to mount. By the time the Army comes clean, it may be too late. Regan's death warrant has already been signed—by John's hands.

A DECEPTION POINT MILITARY DETECTIVE THRILLER: BOOK 2

BACKBLAST

Army Detective Regan Chase just solved the most horrific case of her career. The terrorist responsible refuses to speak to anyone but her. The claim? There's a traitor in the Army. With the stakes critical, Regan heads for the government's newest classified interrogation site: A US Navy warship at sea. There, Regan uncovers a second, deadlier, terror plot that leads all the way to a US embassy—and beyond. Once again, Regan's on the verge of losing her life—and another far more valuable to her than her own...

A DECEPTION POINT MILITARY DETECTIVE THRILLER: BOOK 3

CHOKEPOINT

When a US Navy captain is brutally murdered, NCIS Special Agent Mira Ellis investigates. As Mira follows the killer to a ship hijacked at sea, the ties to her own past multiply. Mira doesn't know who to trust—including her partner. A decorated, former Navy SEAL of Saudi descent, Sam Riyad lied to an Army investigator during a terror case and undermined the mission of a Special Forces major. Whose side is Riyad really on? The fate of the Navy—and the world—depends on the answer.

A DECEPTION POINT MILITARY DETECTIVE THRILLER: BOOK 4

~MORE DECEPTION POINT DETECTIVE THRILLERS COMING SOON~

Hidden Valor Military Veteran Suspense:

THE GARBAGE MAN

Former Army detective Kate Holland spent years hiding from the world—and herself. Now a small-town cop, the past catches up when a fellow vet is left along a backroad...in pieces. Years earlier, Kate spent eleven hours as a POW. Her Silver Star write-up says she killed eleven terrorists to avoid staying longer. But Kate has no memory of the deaths. And now, bizarre clues are cropping up. Is Kate finally losing her grip on reality? As the murders multiply, Kate must confront her demons...even as she finds herself in the killer's crosshairs.

A Hidden Valor Military Veteran Suspense: Book 1

IN THE NAME OF

Kate Holland finally remembers her eleven hours as a POW in Afghanistan. She wishes she didn't. PTSD raging, Kate's ready to turn in her badge with the Braxton PD. But the wife of a Muslim US Army soldier was stabbed and left to burn in a field, and Kate's boss has turned to her. Kate suspects an honor killing...until another soldier's wife is found in the next town, also stabbed and burned. When a third wife is murdered, Kate uncovers a connection to a local doctor. But the doc is not all she appears to be. Worse, Kate's nightmares and her case have begun to clash. The fallout is deadly as Kate's lured back to where it all began.

A Hidden Valor Military Veteran Suspense: Book 2

BENEATH THE BONES

When skeletal remains are unearthed on a sandbar amid the Arkansas River, Deputy Kate Holland's world is rocked again. The bones belong to a soldier once stationed at a nearby National Guard post. The more Kate digs into the murdered soldier's life, the more connections she discovers between the victim, an old family friend...and her own father. Fresh bodies are turning up too. Will the clues her father missed all those years ago lead to the deaths of every officer on the Braxton police force—including Kate's?

A Hidden Valor Military Veteran Suspense: Book 3

~More Hidden Valor Books Coming Soon~

COPYRIGHT